If you want to find yoursᵉ
that will capture your heart, you'll love *Books Afloat!*

— USA TODAY BESTSELLING AUTHOR SUSAN MAY
WARREN

Delores Topliff captures the can-do spirit of WWII and
1940s America in her debut novel, *Books Afloat,* as Anne
Mettles overcomes the odds against her to bring her
beloved books to families living along the Columbia
River. Intriguing characters, a sweet romance, a
suspenseful twist—readers will long remember this story
beyond "The End."

— PATRICIA BRADLEY, WINNER OF A READER CHOICE
AWARD IN SUSPENSE, AND AUTHOR OF THE *LOGAN POINT
SERIES, MEMPHIS COLD CASE NOVELS,* AND THE *NATCHEZ
TRACE PARK RANGER* BOOKS

In her debut novel, Delores Topliff skillfully combines
adventure, history, and romance into an intriguing story
set on the Columbia River during World War II. I
cheered for courageous Anne Mettles and her crewmates
as they traveled in *Books Afloat,* a sailing library, meeting
one-of-kind characters along the way while facing the
threat of possible espionage. Topliff beautifully captures
the power of pursuing one's dreams.

— BETH K. VOGT, CHRISTY AWARD-WINNING AUTHOR
OF THE THATCHER SISTERS SERIES, CHRISTY AWARD &
CAROL AWARD WINNER

To my cherished longsuffering family and friends for the times I zone out before returning to home base. You also provide great story material and the best heart-filling memories

BOOKS AFLOAT

Columbia River Undercurrents ◆ Book One

Delores Topliff

Scrivenings
PRESS
Quench your thirst for story.
www.ScriveningsPress.com

©2021 Delores Topliff

Published by Scrivenings Press LLC
15 Lucky Lane
Morrilton, Arkansas 72110
https://ScriveningsPress.com

Printed in the United States of America

Paperback ISBN 978-1-64917-085-9

eBook ISBN 978-1-64917-084-2

Library of Congress Control Number: 2020949287

Cover by www.bookmarketinggraphics.com.

All scriptures are taken from the KING JAMES VERSION (KJV): KING JAMES VERSION, public domain.

All characters are fictional, and any resemblance to real people, either factional or historical, is purely coincidental.

ACKNOWLEDGMENTS

Years ago, our local librarian nourished my love for books. When I was ten, she told me I read more books than anyone else in our community and asked what I wanted to do when I grew up. I said, "Start a floating library houseboat for folks along the river who don't have books." *Books Afloat* is the result.

As a child, I asked the Lord to never let me be bored. He's kept His end of that bargain. I'm thankful it includes writing! Susan May Warren and Rachel Hauck's writing retreats were life-changing. Besides delivering writing skills, they've provided lifelong friends who pray, laugh, and cheer each other on. I can't imagine life without them. Three of the best are Pat Trainum (writing as Patricia Bradley), Beth K. Vogt, and Alena Tauriainen.

Thanks to former student/always friend, Joseph N. King, for naming *Books Afloat*.

Tuesday, June 16, 1942
Vancouver and Olympia, Washington

"Ted Vincent, I don't need a chaperone to drive me to Olympia." I whip around and glare, the musical background of my beloved Columbia River not soothing me this morning.

Men can be so difficult sometimes. Ted's making me sorry I walked to the A-1 Garage to borrow his car. During his break, he's out front, rag in hand, dusting a gleaming fender.

"If you won't let me drive Henrietta, I'll ride the bus."

"That bus doesn't run today, Annie." He rubs away a water spot. "It's just that she can be cranky, and I've never let anyone else drive her. Tell me again why this is important now? During wartime?"

I let out my breath with a whoosh. What's with Ted? Since I moved from Oklahoma to Vancouver during high school, Ted usually understands what matters. Why doesn't he get this?

"You've heard me a hundred times. Having a library during the terrible Dust Bowl days gave us kids hope. Books taught us there was life worth aiming for in a world beyond our troubles. Books saved my life." I say it so passionately I blink back tears. "Besides, I promised Grandpa."

"Promised him what?"

"It's a long story. I'll tell you some other time."

"Okay, maybe I get it."

Ted moves his cloth my way as if he might dab my eyes but apparently thinks better of it and stuffs it in his pocket.

"And you want to give others the same opportunity now. Even if it's dangerous?"

In the distance, boats sparkle in sunlight, and ocean-going vessels unload at the grain elevators. To the east, Mt. Hood is a glittering triangle shining like a promise. I can't wait to pull up anchor. I won't even consider getting turned down.

"Being alive is dangerous," I answer. "People get hurt climbing out of bed or crossing the street. But if God's in this, He'll keep me safe." I glance at his car. "And even help me drive Henrietta. I promise I won't hurt her—she'll be fine."

Maybe Ted's car means more to him than me. But Henrietta Ford doesn't tease him like I do.

"It's not Henrietta I'm worried about. I want *you* to stay fine." Ted exhales an exasperated sigh. "If I'd known sooner, I could've arranged time off work to take you myself."

"But you don't need to." *Is that the problem? He thinks I'm leaving him out?* "I would never ask you to do that. You're vital to the war effort."

"As a mechanic?" His face forms a question mark.

"A really *good* mechanic. It's time you knew that." I uncross my arms. I'm tired of Ted not seeing his value, but then I don't have a father with super-high expectations like his. "Besides, I only got the call last night that Governor Langlie could meet with me today. I have to get to the capital before he changes his mind. Please understand how much this matters."

My stomach knots. I must find a way. Since moving here and seeing that people along the river have no libraries, I've dreamed of helping them. After all, where would I be without books? Or Grandpa believing in me, even when Mom and Dad didn't?

Ted rubs the back of his neck, catching and holding my gaze until my heart stutters.

"I'd feel awful if you got stranded," he says. His eyes mirror concern

"I won't. I promise."

"Maybe I can still get off work." He jerks his head to flip the sandy-brown hair hanging over his eyes back where it belongs. "You're not going alone."

"Yes, I am. What could go wrong?" My voice rises, and I lift a hand to count fingers. "You taught me to change tires, change oil—even hotwire cars that won't start." I'm scoring points and pleading silently. He must agree. "Besides, you keep her running perfectly."

"Pretty much." The furrow across his forehead eases. "What would your folks say?"

"You know them. They're nearly two thousand miles away, helping Grandma. They have opinions but pretty much leave decisions to me."

I see Ted weakening. He rocks back on his heels and studies the sky. It's perfect weather for river navigation, just what I need to launch *Books Afloat*.

"If your meeting weren't so important, I wouldn't consider it."

"But you will?" I fling my arms around his neck. "Thanks. I promise I'll baby her."

"I know." He holds me close a moment after I let go. "I'm happy I said yes."

"Thanks for trusting me."

His Brylcreem aroma sends pleasant thoughts to my brain.

An odd disappointment stings my heart when he releases me. I almost hug him again but instead blaze a smile into his eyes.

Ted's blush makes the freckles across his nose and cheeks stand out. When he shoves his right hand into his pocket, something rattles.

"What's that?"

"The magnets I carry." He clicks them together, and the noise repeats.

"I bet you even sleep with those," I tease.

"Naw." More red creeps up his neck as he grins. "But they come in handy lots of times. Do you know what the governor wants?"

"I hope he's going to finance my library boat. He'd phone or send a letter to turn me down, wouldn't he?"

"Probably." He opens the hood to check the oil. "She starts like a charm but has a racy engine under there." He cocks his head. "Kind of like you."

"Me?" My hands find my hips. "Ted Vincent, what are you saying?"

"Good things." He laughs.

My eyes widen. Where is mild, reliable Ted today? Right now, he looks like he has a racy engine under his hood, too.

"I wish I could come along." His eyes deepen from gray to green.

"I'll be back before you know it. Besides, you'd get bored in government offices."

"With you there? Not a chance. I hate for any woman to go alone—even if you are over twenty-one now."

"I had to grow up fast, and I'm not *any* woman." I draw myself to full height, which brings me past his chin. "I'll soon be the first one to pilot a boat down the Columbia to the Pacific."

He closes the hood and opens the driver's door with a flourish. "Here's the key. Good luck."

Before he closes my fingers over the key, it glitters in

sunlight like gold. I step on the running board, and he helps me in.

"Thanks again." My voice trembles, and I smile until my cheeks hurt.

"Phone as soon as you're back, and I'll get Henrietta. Then you can tell me all about Olympia, and we'll celebrate."

"I appreciate this more than I can say." My eyes catch his—they're even darker green now than before—but then he looks away.

"I know."

I crank open the window and turn the key in the ignition. The engine catches with a satisfying purr that broadens Ted's smile.

"Don't take her above 50."

"But the speed limit's 60." I press the ahooga horn and lurch past him, scattering gravel.

"Have a great trip." He gives a jaunty wave, his voice carefree.

But my glimpse of him in the rearview mirror doesn't look carefree. Does he think the governor might turn me down?

HEART in my throat and generating confidence I don't yet feel, I turn the brass knob on the frosted glass door leading to the Governor's chambers. One glimpse reveals his inner sanctum is safeguarded behind this outer entryway. This chamber is fancier than I expected with stylish furniture, polished floors, and shelves of leather-bound books from ceiling to floor.

But it's Miss Pruitt I'm eager to meet. The professional behind the ornate mahogany desk is the governor's right hand and devoted guard dog. By letter and phone, she's guided me and *Books Afloat* through every stage of creation to today's final grant approval. We haven't met but recognize each other instantly.

"Miss Pruitt," I cry, like someone just coming home for the holidays.

"Anne!"

She springs up from her desk and extends her hand as I quickly cross the parquet floor. We linger, shaking hands, our smiles cordial. She looks older than her cheerful phone voice suggests. She's sizing me up, too.

"I'm so pleased to meet you. So grateful for everything you've done."

"I hope your long drive was okay."

"Fine." But if it hadn't been, I wouldn't admit it.

Suddenly her lipsticked mouth wilts under her Victory helmet hairstyle. "I'm so sorry," she says, dropping my hand and looking down.

"Sorry? About what?" I flex my fingers as icy shivers travel down my spine.

She glances toward the Governor's office. "This isn't turning out as we hoped. I'm thankful I collected all those culled books for you. I know we promised state funding, but—"

"But Pearl Harbor and its aftermath happened." A man's deep voice booms from the office. His shadow slides across the doorway before he appears.

As soon as I see him, I stand so fast my chair wobbles. Governor Langlie. There is no mistaking him. He matches newspaper photos—stylish gray hair, smart dresser. When he shakes my hand, his spicy aftershave tickles my nose.

"Welcome to Olympia," he says in the deep voice I've often heard on the radio. "Forgive my intrusion, but I asked Miss Pruitt for time alone with you to balance our bad news."

"I'll let you two talk in private." Miss Pruitt rises and scoops books and papers aside as the governor moves to her desk.

My gaze follows this woman, who has been so instrumental in planning and equipping my floating library, as her high heels clack down the hall. Swallowing nervousness, I face the governor.

He pins me with intense brown eyes and waves for me to sit before sitting himself. "Your proposal to take books to people on both sides of the Columbia all the way to the Pacific is stellar —American ingenuity at its finest. The kind of project I love to champion in normal times." He leans forward. "But these are not normal times. Where were you when Roosevelt addressed our nation after Pearl Harbor?"

"About to eat lunch." That memory is stamped forever in my brain. Sunday lunch after church, the announcement interrupted soft piano music on the radio as I sat down with two good friends to a meal we never ate. "It's a day I'll never forget."

"It ruined our dinner, too." Governor Langlie nods. "And drastically shifted state and national budgets. War costs are devastating. Miss Pruitt was about to say that we're terribly sorry, but we can't fund your proposal this year after all."

His words strike my gut like a fist. I quit breathing.

"You can't?" I dumbly echo his words. "B-but each planning letter was approved. I thought that was why I'm here."

He rocks back, sadness lining his face. "You're wondering why I had you come all this way when I could have explained by phone and saved you the trip."

"Frankly, yes." I clasp my hands tighter, so he won't see them shaking. I've worked months to win his support.

A twinkle brightens his eyes. "I admit to using subterfuge so I could talk to you in person. I don't have library funds, but I do need a boat, and the military has money." He studies me a long moment. Apparently satisfied with what he sees, he continues. "Your floating library is a perfect cover."

"Cover? For what?" I try to see where this is going but can only focus on his 'no.'

"It's my business to watch events on the river. Your

neighbor, Smitty, is a good man, a legendary captain, and my friend."

"You know Smitty?" My retired tugboat captain neighbor taught me everything I know about boats—even helped me lease and prepare *Books Afloat*. "What does he have to do with—"

"A lot. Have you been following Japanese activity since Pearl Harbor?"

Pearl Harbor and its aftermath have already claimed several high school friends, maybe even Josh. Ted would be in the Pacific with him now, except for his flat feet.

"The media doesn't tell us much." I flounder. The governor jumps topics faster than a grasshopper in a summer cornfield. "It's hard to get information, but Smitty did mention recent bombings in Alaska."

"One hundred Americans died when Japanese planes dive-bombed Dutch Harbor in the Aleutians." His lips tighten. "The Aleutians are steppingstones to Seattle. That Alaska diversion divided our forces while they attacked Midway."

Midway. That awful word again. I try to stop twisting my hands. We're guessing Josh was near there the last time he wrote. Nothing since.

"Forgive me for being insensitive." The governor's voice gentles. "Smitty mentioned a good friend of yours is missing there."

I press my feet hard against the floor to steady myself. "Josh Vengeance. His last letter hinted he might be near there, but no one is sure. There's no conclusive report."

The governor pulls a map of the Pacific from under the desk blotter and taps the island with his fingernail. "Midway was our greatest victory since the disaster at Pearl Harbor. Each day we get news of more missing sailors being found. Don't give up hope."

I picture Josh's eager face and teasing blue eyes. Navy officers told his folks he was assigned to the sunken *Yorktown* but also helped make supply runs to shore. After torpedoes hit, he was officially listed as Missing in Action. But if there was any way to survive, Josh would find it.

"I'm sure he'll make it back."

"I hope you're right." The governor taps the map again and shifts his gaze as if he's reached a major decision. "We have a network of volunteers tracing sightings of Japanese heading this way."

The hair rises on my neck. "Seriously? How close are they?"

"Close enough. They're moving down the coast and have been sighted near the mouth of the Columbia. We withhold updates until we have confirmation so we don't spook the public." He steeples his fingers. "It's a fine balance."

"I'm sure." I won't think about Japanese military on the U.S. mainland.

The governor stands and paces to the window, his hands clasped behind his back, but then he turns and peers my way. "The Japanese wouldn't suspect a boat full of books as being a threat." His fingers count. "If you would perform visual checks, record data, and maintain occasional radio contact ..."

He stops to scrutinize me. "Sorry to add pressure, but because of a military timetable, you need to complete the first trip in thirty days." His eyelids drop, reading my expression. "Is this too much for you?"

"Not at all." I swallow hard, my pulse racing. I long to help people along the river but didn't bargain for this. It's even better. I didn't dream I could help the war effort, too. My spine tingles as I square my shoulders. This is the kind of thing that would thrill my Grandpa. "I'll be proud to help."

"Good." He leans closer. "What I'm suggesting involves secrecy and risk. I've talked with Oregon's governor. If you do surveillance for both sides of the river, Oregon will also give library support." He peers at me over his glasses. "This is highly confidential.

"As a top advisor, Smitty works closely with me. I'll communicate with you directly sometimes. For your own protection, you'll know the names of some volunteers, but not all of them." He takes a folded paper from his breast pocket and glances at it. "Smitty will accompany your first trip. I swear that man drinks from the Fountain of Youth."

"You're right."

We laugh at our shared joke.

"My pilot exam is Friday, and Smitty says I'm ready. We've worked hard for six months. If I don't pass," I laugh, "the fault's only mine."

The governor gives a salute. "As a matter of fact, you remind me of my wife. She also earned her college degree with honors in three years. You've accomplished a lot for someone barely past twenty-one.

Gratitude swells my heart. "Actually, I just turned twenty-two. Thanks for believing in and supporting me." *Especially since my folks don't.*

He uses a pen from Miss Pruitt's desk to scribble a note. "No thanks needed. I love to find promising individuals and help them become key leaders. We'll call this the Governor's Challenge."

"Yes, sir, that's perfect."

As he stands and rounds the desk to shake my hand once more, his spicy aftershave envelopes me again.

"I see you have a camera." He inclines his head toward the Kodak Brownie I brought to document the contract signing. We hear high heels tap our way "Here comes Miss Pruitt now. May I have her take our picture together?"

"I'd love that."

When Miss Pruitt enters, the governor hands her my Kodak. "Please snap us together."

"Certainly." Miss Pruitt smiles and gestures for us to pose in front of the U.S. and Washington State flags flanking her desk.

"Send me a photo when they're developed," the governor says. "I'll keep one on my desk to remember to pray."

"I appreciate that." I gather my things in a daze.

I leave the capitol building, barely watching where I'm going. I'm so focused on the governor's words I forget to count the forty-two granite steps in front of the structure marking Washington as the forty-second state to enter the Union. Raucous white seagulls call overhead until one swoops low, forcing attention.

"I'll see plenty of you when I reach the Pacific. Then I'll fling handfuls of breadcrumbs to you every direction." I hop in Ted's car and let my mind race the three-hour drive home. He'll be surprised that in grim economic times, I have library funding after all.

If it hadn't been for library books during Oklahoma's Dust Bowl, I would have dried up and blown away like our farm's topsoil. I gulp, remembering Grandpa's words. 'Get all the learning you can, girl.'

Sure enough, books brought me from dry fields and small horizons to broader opportunities. Now I can pass on that gift to others, so circumstances don't imprison them. Plus, guard America's mainland. The stirring beat of marching bands fills my head.

I'll share some of this information with my folks before *Books Afloat* sails but won't tell everything. I miss them since they're in Oklahoma, working to save Grandma's farm, but they considered my library dream nonsense from the start.

'We love you, daughter, but we learned the hard way that flighty ideas don't put food on the table,' Dad had said. 'Only gumption and hard work do that. Besides, education is mostly wasted on girls. Wait and see—when this war ends, women will stop working outside the home. It's always been that way, and it always will.'

I'm glad they aren't here asking questions. Even with Smitty, my ace-in-the-hole captain's support, they don't want me traveling the river. What would they say if they knew I had an active wartime role? I. Will. Not. Tell. Them.

Can I meet Governor Langlie's expectations? Uncertainty sends shivers over my body and raises the hairs on the back of my neck. I'll do my best or die trying. I pray lots driving home. *Lord, give me gumption. And help Josh, wherever he is.*

I drive past my driveway to turn into Smitty's, passing the neatly-trimmed evergreen hedge guarding his apple tree and the circular flower bed of bright-colored perfumy roses surrounding his bird feeder. As soon as I park the car, he opens his front door and stands on the porch smiling, his faded gold-braid captain's hat pushed back.

"Welcome home, Annie. Governor Langlie phoned. I'm proud of you."

I rush into his hug. We have lots to discuss. And I'll phone Ted—but not my folks.

THREE JAM-PACKED DAYS LATER, Smitty calls from the wharf, "You'll do fine, Annie, girl. Stay confident."

Standing at the helm, I smile my thanks. Ted boards and scurries past Smitty, hoisting a heavy trunk of books in his well-muscled arms as if it holds feathers.

"Annie, where shall I put this?"

"Here in the main library room, Hercules. Or shall I call you Popeye? I know that weighs a ton."

"It's not so bad."

I move the woven curtain aside as Ted muscles the trunk into the center of the enclosed room. Smitty helped me maximize space here and even knocked some shelves together. Color-coded children's books line lower spaces. General and popular reading fill our mid-height spaces, and reference books and magazines occupy higher spots.

Nicely displayed favorites are centered on child-sized tables with groupings of polished rocks, seashells, and arrowheads nearby to raise interest. It's the kind of library I loved to explore as a kid.

I think Ted approves, too. His grin reaches his eyes as he dusts off his hands.

When did his shoulders get so broad? He's surprisingly strong for his medium build. He's not movie-star handsome—more like Hollywood's heart-warming Jimmy Stewart with his shy boy-next-door sweetness. And I can count on him. Good old Ted is always ready to help.

"Smitty and I will wait on shore while you pass your pilot exam," he says.

"Fair enough." Smiling so wide my teeth are a target for bugs, I turn the brass key that thrums the boat's engine to life. Its throaty roar belches oily diesel plumes into this morning's electric blue sky. Beyond, the mighty Columbia River rolls west like a blue-green ribbon unspooling in sunlight, its waves sparkling and splashing.

As soon as I ace this exam, I'll lift anchor and chug *Books Afloat* one hundred and six nautical miles to the Pacific to defend my country.

Feet planted, I make my first entries in the ship's log in flowing black ink using my best Palmer Method handwriting: Date: June 19, 1942. Home port: River Mile 106, Vancouver, Washington. Destination: Mouth of the Columbia. Cargo: Library books and materials for towns and people along the river between Vancouver and the Pacific.

I won't record my other duties.

Today, for luck, Ted wears his beloved Fort Vancouver High sweatshirt. My favorite picture ever is of him and Josh standing side by side in those shirts, clowning the day before graduation.

I ache now, seeing Ted alone without Josh here. Where you saw one, you saw the other, Ted's tousled sandy hair next to Josh's almost red. Ted's sober gray-green eyes next to Josh's blue, sparkling with mischief.

Two men trapped in the ship's sinking hull were rescued after they fired machine gun rounds to attract attention. We pray constantly though hope fades. It's especially hard for Ted, whose friendship with Josh made them like brothers.

But today, I must focus. I need my pilot's license to get underway, since only pilots can take boats across the treacherous bar at the Columbia's mouth. Piece of cake. I don't require the advanced license since we won't carry paying passengers. I pace the deck with nervous energy as I look up and down the road for the testing officer to arrive. Lord, let him hurry. I can't wait to get underway.

On shore, Ted lifts his hands in prayer.

Beside him, Smitty shouts, "Looking good. You were born for this," and flashes a V for Victory sign.

That boosts my confidence, and I stand straighter. "Where's Evie?" I call. Smitty's niece will travel with us after the Coast Guard testing officer leaves, so there will be three of us on board—not just Smitty and me, for appearance's sake. I shade my eyes. "What have you heard from her?"

He frowns. "Not much. There's a delay, but she'll make it."

"Sounds good!" I assemble paperwork and maintenance records, adding my thick stack of passed navigation tests. After today's practical exam, we can raise anchor.

I hiccup as a sleek black government car sweeps our way and brakes to a stop. The examiner hops out. His large angular nose divides dark eyes that remind me of olive pits.

He stands at attention in gold-trimmed starched whites, doffing the stiff military hat covering his salt and pepper crew cut to snap off a smart salute. "Request permission to come aboard."

"Permission granted, sir."

He climbs on board without returning my welcoming smile. "Ship's log?"

"Here, sir." Sweat trickles down my back.

He thumbs through my paperwork and grunts. "Just because you've passed written tests doesn't mean you'll qualify today. Many grown men don't, and you're a woman." He looks me over from head to toe. "Young, too."

"I've been trained by the best." I glance at Smitty. "And I'm older than I look."

"I hope so."

This man's attitude curdles my stomach. He doesn't like me. If Josh were here, he'd charm the man before he set foot on deck. Josh has that way about him.

"Take me below to your engine room." He opens his clipboard to remove a checklist and follows me into the boat's belly. "Read me your gauge settings."

I call out oil pressure, gas mixture, engine speed, and depth finder numbers. Ears straining for his commands.

"This is no job for a woman."

I barely catch his muttered words. Did he really say that? Doesn't he know that with so many men gone to war, America's women must fill the gaps? Our world is changing.

Climbing back to the main deck, his fingers drum his clipboard. "Back her out at five knots, take her across to Hayden Island."

"Aye, aye." Hayden is directly across the main channel. I've taken many practice runs there. I wrap my hands around the wheel, so I won't be tempted to swipe that smirk off his face. But five knots isn't enough power. I stare. What is he thinking? "Are you sure, sir?"

"You heard me. Five knots."

I white-knuckle the tiller and fight for control as our slow speed turns *Books Afloat* crosswise in the strong current. She bucks, refusing to head where I steer, drifting off course.

The man squiggles black marks. I've never been seasick, priding myself on good sea legs, but now clammy heat climbs my neck and thickens my throat. I will not be sick.

"Wheel sharp hard to Hayden's west end."

Our depth finder reads fifteen feet and falling. We need twelve. By Geological Survey charts, I'm in trouble. I catch my breath but hold my mouth shut.

"Turn sharper," he snaps. "Add speed or you'll hit."

The boat strikes soft mud and shudders. I grip the tiller but lose balance and stagger as the prow sticks fast in sand and muck.

"What happened, missy?" He gives an icy I-told-you-so glare.

"I did what you said." I swallow acid.

His grin stabs. "Mature pilots use sound judgment." He scribbles something, signs his name with a flourish, and hands me a pink sheet. "Retest in thirty days. Don't feel bad. Most grown men need two or three times to pass. One woman earned her papers, but that was a fluke. When hers expire, they won't be renewed."

I know of her, Smitty's sister-in-law, Charlotte. But defeat sours my mouth, and I swallow more bile. "I don't have thirty days. Governor Langlie wants this trip completed in thirty days."

"Sorry, missy. That's not my concern. I don't care if Roosevelt himself gives you orders. People meet my standards. You've shown again, this job isn't for women." He snaps his clipboard shut and jams his pen back into his pocket. "I'll back your boat out to show you how it's done—if your propeller's okay."

"It better be," I whisper. Teeth clenched, I bite my cheek, so I won't say anything more.

A thin smile curves his lips as he grasps the tiller and expertly backs my boat out.

I hiss out the air I've held, and my stomach lurches like the Titanic hitting the iceberg.

I've never been seasick. Not once. But now I lunge for the rail and lose my morning coffee over the rail.

He watches and smirks.

"That's never happened before," I say, wiping my mouth.

"Sure." He docks with a flourish as smooth as a hand entering a glove and marches across the wharf. He nods at Ted, salutes Smitty, starts his car, and drives away.

I wrap my arms around my stomach and stare after him. I'm glad my folks aren't here,

Even before the examiner's road dust clears, Smitty runs toward me, but Ted is faster, even on flat feet, and reaches me first.

Ted's hands bookmark my shoulders as his concerned eyes stare into mine. "Annie, what happened?"

I slump and can't return his gaze. "I failed."

2

Friday, June 19, 1942
Port of Vancouver, Washington, River Mile 106

"What?" Smitty climbs on board, puffing short breaths, hands fisting his hips.

My heart stutters. "I failed. I knew better than to do what he said, but I didn't use good judgment. You saw what happened."

"Tarnation! He's letting personal issues affect his job."

"What do you mean?"

"His wife left him last month. I've heard he dislikes all women now."

I can't hold back tears. "He tricked me, so I ran aground. I thought I had to follow his instructions."

"It's okay, Annie girl." Smitty slides his arm around my shoulder.

"When can you retest?" Ted jams his hands into his pockets.

"Thirty days."

"That's crazy." His jaw tightens. "Did you tell him about the Governor's Challenge?"

"I did, but he doesn't care." I heave a sigh. "Thank God,

Smitty can navigate. I'll swallow my pride and just stick to library duties so he and Evie—"

"Annie, there's something I have to tell you." Smitty rubs his stubbly chin. "I waited until after your test, but my ticker's been acting up. Doc says I flunked last week's step test. He won't renew my captain papers until that improves, so I'm grounded. I've sent word to my pilot sister-in-law, Charlotte, to come take my place."

I stagger at his words. "Your heart? How bad is it?"

"Not awful. Just bad enough I can't come this time. And Doc says I can't be alone, so Evie has to stay with me.

This arrangement isn't what I planned, but I'll manage somehow. The two of us can run *Books Afloat*. I crane my neck and stare up the road. "When do you think she and Evie can get here?"

"I'm not sure. I expected them before now." He tugs an ear. He only does that when he's worried.

"You don't know?"

"Not exactly. Evie's trying to contact her, but she's on a boat somewhere. So far, she can't reach her."

"I *have* to make this trip. Even if I have to hire a river pilot I can't afford, or *Books Afloat* won't float. I can't fail Governor Langlie." *Or my country.*

Smitty and I lock eyes. The governor shared his river surveillance program with me in strict confidence. The fewer who know, the better. I won't tell Ted.

"I'll let the church know," Ted says, face taut. "We'll start the prayer chain,"

Smitty pulls me into a hug. "Annie, calm down. It's going to be all right."

I stiffen, face burning. "I hate that you're sick, but if I can't meet the Governor's Challenge, it's a disaster. We have to find Charlotte, or I'm sunk. Everything's at stake." I pull away. "I doubt even God can get us a pilot in time."

"You don't know that, Annie," Smitty says. "I've issued an All-Points Bulletin—police and military radios, Coast Guard ship to shore—the works. Plus, we're praying."

I jut my jaw. "Why didn't the testing officer pass me?"

"Who knows?" Ted's brows pinch. "Maybe he hurts so bad from losing his wife, he feels like a dead dog who wants others miserable, too."

"That's not very nice." I take a ragged breath. Sometimes Ted's kind-heartedness frustrates me. Our pastor calls it strength. Today, it makes me mad.

"Here's the plan." Smitty crosses his arms. "Either God's in charge, or He's not. We'll finish getting the boat ready and pray. I believe God wants you to launch today, so we'll see what He does. Like Moses at the Red Sea."

"Or Annie on the Columbia. I like it." Ted laughs and checks his watch. "It's 10:25 a.m. You're determined to leave at noon? That gives God an hour and a half."

"Thanks." I manage a half-grin. God has a way of stretching people beyond their strength before He answers. To build spiritual muscles, our pastor says. "I have some things to complete, Smitty. If we can find any river pilot, we're set."

"There's a ship at the grain elevators. I'll stroll over there to see what they know."

My stomach spasms. "Should you do that? I mean, should Ted drive you?"

His face darkens. "I'm not dying—I just have to slow down. Exercise is smart."

"You're sure?"

"Yes. Trust me." He squints at the sun and tilts his skipper's hat. "We'll meet here for a noon launch."

I snap off a salute. "Aye, aye, Captain."

Ted surprises me with a quick hug.

"I'll tell Josh's parents to get prayers going." He jogs toward the red brick church on Columbia Street and the parsonage next door.

I check the propeller and find one bent shaft but no permanent damage. I sigh relief and unroll the navigation chart I'll need later. And re-read the weather report—fair skies through tomorrow.

"Lord, we have to get underway. Please help. And help me believe."

TED HALF RAN, half walked up the hill, passing Smitty's Dodge coupe holding his duffle bag on the way. He couldn't believe the testing officer failed Anne. If there was a way to help her situation, he'd find it.

He'd never met a girl like Anne before—so much power wrapped in one cute package, with serious brown eyes that bored straight through a guy but made him laugh. And her upturned nose sprinkled with freckles that she tried bleaching one day in chemistry class. Her feistiness was what he and Josh liked most when she entered Vancouver High. She had more Okie accent then—except if she got mad—like today.

When he'd teased her and called her *prickly Anne Nettles*, she'd shoved him down and said, 'I'm Anne Mettles. Two classmates in Oklahoma called me Anne Meddles—and barely lived. Count yourself lucky.'

He laughed at that memory and kicked into high gear, taking the porch steps to the parsonage two at a time. He gave the door two quick raps while twisting the knob and entering. The tantalizing scent of sugar and cinnamon wrapped around him.

"Pastor? Sue?"

"In here." Sue Vengeance poked her head out of the kitchen.

"Anne failed her exam, so she needs a pilot, and Smitty's doctor grounded him because of a heart flareup, and we can't find his sister-in-law." He blurted it in a rush and finally took a breath. "We need the prayer chain fast."

Sue hurried toward him in her flour-dusted apron and greeted him with a one-armed hug. Her free hand held a plate of cookies.

"Slow down." She offered him one. "That is a lot going on, but you might pass out stringing that many words together in one breath. Smitty's sister-in-law has pilot papers, right?"

"Right."

"Then we can pray but don't need the prayer chain."

"Why is that?" He rocked back on his heels.

"Bob's been working on a solution since last night when Smitty told us about his heart and that the testing officer might be tough. Bob's friend in Astoria traced Charlotte to a fish cannery. She mostly works along the coast, but he thinks she'll help out on the river. He left early this morning to find her and bring her and Evie to meet Bob halfway. They should be here soon."

Ted gave a low whistle. "Great, but that's ninety miles. Can they arrive in time? And how did Bob get enough gas rations?"

"We're covered. We had our eight gallons for this week, and Grandma Foley across the alley gives us her four since her car's on wooden blocks."

"Terrific. Anne's been frantic." He brushed away crumbs and reached for a second cookie when she offered the plate again. "These are delicious."

"Take the rest to Anne." She slid the cookies into a bag.

A photo of Josh caught his eye. "Any more news about Midway?"

Her smile fled. "No. And waiting is hard. Thank God only the *Yorktown* sank, and they still don't have a full list of those missing. I guess it's a miracle more men weren't lost."

Ted nodded.

"If Josh is gone, Bob and I think we'd know, that we'd feel it inside, but we don't."

Ted's Adam's apple bobbed. "He's the finest guy I know."

"Thanks. He feels that way about you, too." She set down the bag and empty plate and gave Ted a tight hug.

"I love you guys." He stepped back and opened the door heading for the steps.

"One last question," Sue called. "Will that boat leave without a man on board?"

He grinned over his shoulder. "Not if I can help it."

With Smitty unable to go, it was not a good situation. Even if his sister-in-law Charlotte arrived on time, the two most-capable women in the world shouldn't make this trip alone. Especially on a river where the governor suspected possible Japanese activity. It wasn't clear if Anne knew that part yet or not. He didn't want Annie worried if she didn't. And he sure wouldn't tell her. He was just watching out for her.

When it looked like it would be just Smitty and Anne on the boat, Smitty had invited Evie for appearance's sake. Now with roles changed, there should still be three onboard, not two, whether Annie liked it or not. Ted set his jaw. No matter how much she refused and how hard it was to oppose her, Annie wouldn't get her way this time. He and Smitty had talked. His packed duffle was in the trunk of Smitty's car.

Annie Mettles was in for a surprise.

3

Friday, June 19, 1942
Port of Vancouver, Washington, River Mile 106

"I don't know what to say, Annie." Smitty's shoulders sag. "The men at the grain elevators have a waitlist for river pilots. There's a shortage everywhere."

My slumped shoulders match his. I'd hoped there'd be a pilot at the wharf. What if I can't realize my dream? And I have to meet the governor's request. He believes in me.

"If anything else goes wrong—"

"Don't give up." Smitty grips my hand. "Overcoming hardships is who you are. The people along this river need you."

"But I'm not sure I can pull it off. Maybe God doesn't want me doing this after all. What if my folks are right, and I belong in Oklahoma?"

Smitty clucks his tongue. "You don't believe that. I love your folks, but they birthed an amazing daughter with big dreams capable of making them happen. And God's in it. Don't lose sight of that."

I hear commotion and see Ted lope to the wharf in long strides, waving and shouting.

"Josh's dad has Charlotte and Evie. They're almost here."

"What? Charlotte's coming?"

He skids to a stop. "Pastor Bob's friend found her near Astoria and is driving her and Evie to meet Bob halfway. He left early, so they're almost here."

I squeal. "Soon, you say?"

Smitty claps Ted on the back.

"Any minute." Ted smiles so broadly his ears rise.

"I could dance a jig."

I grab Ted's arm and swing him around until we're breathless.

"It's nice seeing you happy."

He holds me loosely while I steady, then releases me.

"I like being happy." His touch still warms my skin.

We watch a '35 Buick rattle toward us, honking.

"Thank God, that's them." Smitty waves the car over.

When it pulls up, I hug Pastor Bob while the women exit. Charlotte steps out first, then Evie, her slim perky daughter, who doesn't resemble her mother much.

Visibly tired from the ride, the stocky woman in Navy coveralls wears a bright yellow Sou'wester hat smashed down on steel-gray hair. A compass dangles from her pocket loops, along with so many gadgets and tools, she jingles as she walks. My kind of woman—she looks ready for any kind of action.

"You're lifesavers." I welcome them. "I don't know *how* Pastor Bob found you in time, but thank God."

"Yes, He's responsible. And this beats the fish cannery I was on." Charlotte sniffs the air. "Smells better, too."

After carrying her gear on board, Pastor heads to his house to get Sue. Meanwhile, I show Charlotte and Evie around.

"Welcome to *Books Afloat*. She's fifty feet from bow to stern and fifteen feet wide." I sweep my arm around to point out different areas. "Our head and galley are down those stairs along with the engine room and sleeping berths for two. There's another short set of stairs aft. Much of our main deck is dedicated to the enclosed library plus an outer office and chairs on deck where we can relax if there's time to grab a breath."

"That won't happen much," Charlotte says matter-of-factly.

I point up the stairs. "Your berth is up top, near my captain's cabin. What do you think?"

"So far, she looks good." Charlotte runs her hand along the red-trimmed rail above the white hull. "Neat and trim, the way a boat should be. If her engine's as good as her outside, she'll slice through the water fine." She takes off her hat to fan her face. "Excuse my Sou'wester. The days I wear it, it doesn't rain— as simple as that. But if I forget, the skies drop oceans."

"Then wear it all you want." I laugh.

Smitty rolls his eyes.

"I put your bag up top, Mrs. Young." Ted pumps her hand.

Charlotte stiffens. "Forget Mrs. Young—not even Charlotte, please. Call me Char if you value your life. I can't stand long names. I just want to be a crewman like the rest of you doing my part in this war."

I level a sharp look. Does she know our boat serves a second purpose? Does Pastor Bob know? "Did Pastor Bob tell you I'll pay what I can?"

"No need." She waves a dismissive hand. "J.P.'s Navy check comes regular, plus Smitty makes sure we don't lack. We just need air to breathe, bread to chew, something to drink, and clean laundry sometimes. A body doesn't need much in this world to be happy." Her blue eyes gleam, and she shades them to check the horizon. "When can we get underway?"

"As soon as Pastor Bob gets back to send us off with a prayer."

Out of the corner of my eye, I see Ted near Smitty's car. He lifts a bag from the trunk and hoists it over his shoulder.

I block him at the steps. "What are you doing?"

"Coming along. Smitty and I want you to have a man on board."

I don't budge. "Thanks, but you're needed on land."

"You don't want a man?" Char interrupts. "It might be nice having one on board." She glances from Ted to Smitty and back to me. "As headstrong as I am, I listen to Smitty, just like I do J.P. —I respect them both that much." Char drops her eyelids to half-mast and shakes herself like a wet dog flinging water as if even saying her husband's name might make her weep. "If this nice young man can come, I say let him. Extra hands always help."

"But it's wartime, and our best men are gone."

Ted winces.

I catch his look. "Sorry. That came out wrong. I mean, Ted's a great mechanic, the best in town, so the garage where he works can't spare him."

His eyes flash. "Annie. It's worked out—I traded schedules with a friend. We'll switch back when he needs time off. Besides —" He gulps. "I promised Josh."

"Promised him what?"

"A promise Ted and I will both keep." Smitty's voice is low and calm. "Your trip will be safer with a mechanic on board. Accept it."

"That sounds good," Charlotte insists.

"Am I outnumbered here?" My voice rises.

"Thank you, Mrs. Young." Ted nods her direction.

Char's throat makes a strained sound. She glares until Ted literally backs up.

"Oops, what did I do?"

Her hands send semaphore signals and her eyebrows beetle. "Mrs. Young be hanged. Ted, so far, I like you. But whether you come on this trip or not, I'm Char—not Charlotte, not Mrs. Young, or you'll face terrible consequences."

"Yes, ma'am." He touches his cap. "No offense meant. Is J.P. your husband?"

"That he is. Twenty-eight years strong and counting." She softens and sniffs. "Their mother loved fancy names. J.P. is John Paul Jones Young, Smitty's younger brother, gone to war." She jerks a hand in Smitty's direction. "You know his real moniker's not *Smitty*, don't you?"

"It's not?" I'm all ears.

Smitty reddens. "Skip the family history, Char. A man's entitled to a few harmless secrets. And we're leaving today, not tomorrow." He gestures to his niece. "Evie, come stand by me."

"Aye, aye." She snaps a salute.

The way Evie sizes up Ted grates on me like fingernails on chalkboards. Like he's good enough to eat—but he's not on her menu. Maybe Ted *should* come with us instead of staying here with this boy-crazy girl.

But I still sputter, "Ted, I don't think we need—"

"Then, don't think." Smitty scowls. "Seriously, girl, it's hard enough I can't come. Do you want me worried the whole time? Because that's what I'd do. Give my heart ease and take Ted. Char can pilot, but Ted's the best mechanic I know and a good all-around man besides." He winks.

Ted flushes. "Thanks. I'll ask you next time I need a job reference."

"Any time. It's all true."

I don't quit. "Smitty, it's not necessary—"

"Annie, do me a favor." Smitty folds his arms across his chest, looking like Popeye ready to deck Bluto—and win. "Evie will stay and help me, though that's a waste of manpower. My doctor doesn't understand seamen. We thrive on challenges. So, I want you to have help, too."

"It is smart, Annie." Char waggles her eyebrows almost like Smitty. Maybe it's a family trait. "It's a good trade-off. Ted goes with us to give Smitty peace. Evie helps Smitty, so we know he's fine."

The concern on Smitty's face ends my argument.

"Well, when you put it like that ..."

"I'll keep Smitty out of mischief," Evie promises, "and make him eat healthy."

Smitty snorts. "If you mean salt-free flavorless stuff, we have a problem."

"I have brains." Evie smiles.

She is taller and willowier than me. Her short blonde hair curls from the river's humidity.

"I'll come with you another time and help Uncle Horatio now."

"Uncle who?" I gasp.

"Never mind." Smitty turns crimson. "Ted, stow your gear. It's time to lift anchor."

Smitty slips something small and black into Ted's hand as he steps past. It bothers me that I don't see what. I like being the one with secrets. Pastor Bob and Sue return.

"Ah, here you are." Smitty helps Sue cross the gangplank and claps Bob's shoulder. "Pray a blessing on the launch."

Seeing this sweet group, I choke on the lump in my throat.

Bob pulls a worn leather Bible from his pocket, thumbs through its onionskin pages, and squints at the fine print. "These verses from Isaiah 43 fit, "'Fear not: for I have redeemed thee, I have called thee by thy name; thou art mine. When thou passest through the waters, I will be with thee; and through the rivers, they shall not overflow thee ...' May He bring you all the way to the ocean and back safely. Amen." He closes his Bible and slips it back in his pocket.

"Where do you want this box of cookies?" Sue points to the delicious-smelling shoebox at her feet.

"I'll keep it safe." With a teasing grin, Ted grabs it by its strings and disappears down the galley stairs. His voice drifts up, singing, "Anchors Aweigh, my boys, Anchors Aweigh …"

"I love hearing him happy," Sue says, her eyes filling. "He's been heavy-hearted since Josh … Since … Ted needs a little fun."

I quirk an eyebrow. "Fun?"

"Sure. Good times help," she says.

Char's face looks serious.

"Before we get underway, Can I take just a minute to see the engine? Each one's different and I want to do my job well."

"Sure. Hold on folks. Ted's an expert at servicing it so it's in good shape."

We hurry down the backstairs to the engine room.

Her hands do a vital one-two-three engine check.

She knows her stuff.

"Great. Just like ours. No surprises. I hate learning new things under pressure—glad I won't have to."

"Me, too. I'm still reeling from this morning's failure.

She wipes greasy hands on her coveralls.

"Thanks. Now I'm ready."

"Then we both are."

We rush upstairs, smiles on our faces.

"Everything's fine. She says we're good to go."

"Good to hear." Smitty salutes me and then Char. "I'll cast off lines if you're ready, Annie."

My eyebrows knit. "Can you lift that heavy anchor?"

He rears back. "I should say so, and it's not that heavy. The winch does the work, not me. But you should blow the whistle to get underway. You've waited a long time."

I flash my gratitude. "I'm looking forward to that."

"I've asked God to help you every minute." He places a fatherly kiss on my brow. "It's hard on your folks not being here, but they're doing what they must. I'll call them tonight."

"Uh, skip the part about me failing the pilot exam, okay."

"Roger that."

31

"Picture time," Sue calls, waving a Kodak Brownie almost like mine. "Don't lift anchor until we get a parting shot. Gather close, please."

"Wait," Evie says. I'll take it so you can all squeeze in. "Looks good. Ready? One, two, three!" She presses the button several times before we break pose to hug again.

"Thanks so much, everyone." My voice drops to a whisper. "I couldn't do this without you."

"Remember that," Smitty says, his voice gruff as he goes to the winch.

Bob and Sue step to the wharf as I assume my best professional tone. "Ted, please check oil pressure gauges."

"Yes, ma'am." He hustles to the engine room. "Everything's shipshape," he calls from below deck.

"Smitty, lift anchor."

"Aye, aye." The heavy chain rattles as it spools around its windlass. Once the anchor is raised, Smitty salutes again and leaves the boat.

Char stands at the helm, like the figurehead of a ship, feet planted, hands steady, eyes looking confidently ahead.

This moment is branded in my mind forever. Behind us, to the east, Mt. Hood is still a brilliant sentinel above the Columbia. To the west, an inviting blue-green river road unspools all the way to the Pacific. "Leaving port."

Char snaps off a regulation Navy salute as our engine thrums to life.

"Reverse engines!" I call. "*Books Afloat* now leaving for points west." We back from our berth until a widening expanse of blue water separates the boat and wharf. Our gleaming white hull turns like a majestic swan gliding onto a fairly smooth pond, breasting low waves, eager to be underway to the ocean to fulfill the Governor's Challenge.

Smitty cups a hand to his mouth, "Radio me every night."

"You, too." I blink back tears, wishing he could come.

"We'll pray," Bob and Sue call, standing with their arms around each other's waists.

The rippling current beckons. This isn't how I'd hoped our voyage would start, with someone else at the helm, but we're underway. The engine rumbles, sending propeller wash in V-shaped waves to both sides of this mighty river. Several tug boats and barges share the channel, but no heavy traffic. Things could be worse.

"Departure at thirteen hundred hours, steady as she goes." I enter that in our log.

"Thirteen hundred hours, steady as she goes," Char echoes, her mouth curved in a pumpkin smile.

"God speed," Smitty calls.

"God speed," Ted echoes.

Ten minutes later, Char lifts an eyebrow. "Do you have anything to drink? I got thirsty rushing here, and we couldn't take time to stop."

"Of course, what would you like?"

"Anything wet, water, tea—Coke if you have it."

"I have Royal Crown Cola. Will that do?"

"Absolutely."

I swing onto the stairs to get Char's drink.

Ted dashes up the same steps from the galley. "I wonder how Sue bakes with sugar rationing—" He ducks to avoid me.

Except we swerve the same direction, and our mouths collide so hard I see stars.

"Yow!" Ted's hand grazes my shoulder in a near caress before he pulls back to finger his swelling lip.

I jump away, heart thundering. "I did *not* see you."

"Obviously." A sappy smile rules his face.

"But you're okay?"

"Terrific. You got my attention."

He locks his now deep green eyes on mine. And they

suddenly look as mysterious and worth exploring as the craters of the moon.

"I wasn't trying to get your attention." I pass a hand over my lips—they're fine but burn.

"Let's see," he counts the fingers on one hand. "You crashed into me skiing at Mt. Hood on the bunny slope when we were learning. We piled up at the youth roller skating party, and I cushioned you." His eyes dance. "When you want my attention, just ask."

I swat him. "You're keeping track? Don't be silly. Just focus on the boat."

Blood rushes to my head, and I push past him to the far side of the boat, taking a time-out while still feeling the tingles warming my lips. His upper lip actually swells. Today's pressures have gotten to me. Nothing makes sense—least of all, an accidental kiss with a friend.

Thankfully, Ted stays on the other end of the boat, doing maintenance. When I regain composure, I go to the galley to bring Char the Royal Crown.

"This is delicious." She swallows half without stopping.

We stand, side by side, gazing downriver.

"I'm thankful to be underway."

"I'm sorry the testing officer was hard on you. He tested me, too, but was nicer then. He'll come around—just not this time." She drains more of the bottle, moisture beading the glass, and smacks her lips. "Thanks. That wets my whistle fine."

"You're welcome. There's a small icebox below." My words rush out so Char won't discuss the accidental collision kiss that she saw.

Because that's what it was—pure accident. Totally humiliating, Ted's lip actually swelling. What must he think? Even when he stops teasing, his eyes dance. And melt me …

Char lifts the bottle to her mouth a final time and finishes the last swallows greedily. "Every bit as good as Coke. Maybe better, but don't spoil me."

"I will if I can. I want our trip to be pleasant."

"I'd say you're off to a good start." Char glances Ted's way and winks.

He's at the boat's stern, coiling loose ropes around the deck's steel cleats. He again touches his lip and smiles before pushing the winch's movable arm out of the way for safety. Besides being a skilled mechanic, he has boat sense.

I may die before admitting it, but it's good having him onboard, although it would be nice to have Josh, too, all three Musketeers together again like in high school. If only someone knew where Josh is— I remind myself that God does. I stay at the prow. Ted joins me after completing tasks near the stern.

"A penny for your thoughts."

"I've run out." I smile weakly.

"Not true, you're always thinking."

"Then they're worth more than a penny—maybe a dollar each."

"And worth it. I'll pay." He opens his worn wallet and riffles through, removing two one-dollar bills before I push his hand away.

"Don't you dare take me seriously. You know better than that. My thoughts are free, probably more than you'll ever want. But irritate me, and I'll bury you alive in them."

"Promise?" Grinning, he returns his wallet to his pocket.

"I need to focus on the boat."

"Who's stopping you? You ran into me, remember?" He chuckles. "Or is it Leap Year, and I don't know it?"

"Stop!" My elbows drop to my hips. "I appreciate your help but leave me alone." I rush to the top deck. Too much has happened today. And now my comfortable friendship with Ted is changing.

I shake my head, wanting the river breeze to clear my mind.

He almost hugged me. Am I imagining how I felt? Have I read too many romance novels and seen *Gone with the Wind* once too often? I have a boat to run and library stops this very afternoon. And war reports to gather and send without others noticing. I brush water from my eyes with the back of my hand. Why is life *so* complicated?

This morning's crisis took its toll. Even the river's surging current looks calmer than my churning insides. *God, don't let pressure turn me into some crazy girl I hate. Help me do what I have to and do it well.*

4

Friday, June 19, 1942
Port of Vancouver, Washington, River Mile 106, and west

This far down the channel, the river smells like fresh rain. I inhale a deep breath standing on deck, feeling like Scarlett O'Hara fighting for Tara. For that's what I must do—complete this Challenge no matter how much the unfair pilot exam rattled me. The sky overhead is shimmering blue silk. At the helm, Char's eyes sweep back and forth, judging the channel's growing waves.

Ted returns from the stern, face hangdog.

"I didn't mean to upset you," I say, my voice gentler. "Thanks for wanting to come. I just hoped to do this on my own."

He shrugs. "It's okay but unwise these days. You're doing Smitty and me a favor by letting me come so we don't worry."

I quirk an eyebrow.

"I hope you'll eventually be glad I came."

"Probably." My shoe rubs spilled paint marks on the deck. I worked too fast when I spruced things up—like usual.

"Is that still Sauvie Island we've seen for the past hour?" Ted points to the long, low, marshy landmass on the Columbia's southern shore.

"Yes. It stretches forever—biggest island on the river."

He steps near. "Will we stop there?"

"Maybe coming back." I smell Brylcreem. "If the Army Corps of Engineers used flood-control dikes on Hayden like they did on Sauvie, I wouldn't have run aground today." My teeth grind.

"That was rough."

"Nothing I can't handle." I fluff my hair and point to Sauvie's western end. "This part's a wildlife refuge. There are good farms around St. Johns on the southern side. I haven't heard from their library yet."

Ted rolls his shoulders, then eases them back. "Josh and I picked strawberries there summers as kids. Earned three cents a box plus all we could eat. Riding through small towns early mornings, we sang goofy songs through open bus windows."

I laugh. "I'll bet that was appreciated. Feel free to sing on board."

"More 'Anchors Aweigh'?"

"Anything, really. While you guys picked berries, I picked Oklahoma cotton. In summers with enough rain, Dad and Grandpa harvested wheat until our soil dried up. Then we mostly raised dust."

Ted's lips twitch. "Sorry. The way you said that made it funny."

"We can stand some humor."

"Even hardships turned out good since they brought you here." His eyes don't tease now.

His face carries an intensity I'm not ready for.

So, I change the subject. "Dad's mom isn't well—you know that's why my folks went back."

"I'm glad they let you stay."

"I'm legally a grown-up. Grandma needs help, but my folks can handle it. Grandpa understood my need for big horizons.

It's time to make my own way, whether my parents agree or not."

"I think they'll understand in time. I know what parental disapproval feels like."

The kindness in his eyes makes my insides quake. I busy myself with our compass.

"River Mile 99, River Mile 98," Char calls out numbers.

Books Afloat chugs downstream past wooded hills with clearings where small farms have been carved out. Foaming streams rush from heights through widening valleys to join the Columbia. Songbirds increase. Robins, finches, and sparrows warble above our engine noise, like choristers in paradise.

Except paradise also holds serpents. I'll stay watchful.

Ted unbuttons his shirtsleeves and pushes them up as he reads Char's chart. "Is Ridgefield our first stop?"

"There's one before," I answer. "Pioneer Grange at Mile 93, a special request."

"I haven't heard of that. Is it small?"

His hand slides into a pocket, and I hear the familiar click of the magnets he carries as his fingers tumble them.

"Very—a farming area of three families. But a grandma there wrote a letter saying they have no school, few books, and if we could stop where a small dock juts out from the Grange hall, she'll watch for us."

"How can I help at each stop?"

His open smile earns mine. He genuinely wants to help.

"Basically, what you're doing—mechanics plus fixing other things before I know they need it. You're already doing that."

This time when his shining eyes seek mine, I meet his gaze.

"Maybe …" I clear my throat as my voice falters. "Maybe bring boxes from storage to the main library room for people to access easily."

"Yes ma'am, glad to." He waves a hand and is on his way.

Char shades her eyes to gauge the channel depth.

"What's our speed?" I poise my pen above the map.

"Nine knots in straight parts, less where the river bends."

"How long do you estimate until we reach the coast? I'd love to get there sooner than thirty days."

Char stretches a kink out of her back. "From here to the Pacific? Or there and back?"

"The governor says one way is fine with stops only where people really want books. Or are seriously considering a library site."

"If we were just traveling the river, it would be easy—a little over a week with overnight stops, not counting boat maintenance or repairs. It depends on how much time we give each place. Anything's possible if we plan right."

"Then let's make sure we do. I'll show you the calendar I roughed out." I haul out desk blotter sheets stapled together. "Take a look and tell me what you think."

Char lifts her eyebrows and shuffles through. "This is a good start, but why not copy all of it onto one huge sheet to post here that we can all see? That way, we're encouraged as we mark things off."

My cheeks warm. "That wouldn't seem like pressure?"

"Nope. It would help our team. Your chart will be a thermometer showing where we are and where we have to be." She pencils notes in the little black book she carries in her vest pocket, underlining some words and adding exclamation points by others. "The stops you have are fine, but we can't calculate exactly until we know what we'll find in each place. Reaching the Pacific in thirty days with the stops you're listing now should be fine."

"Music to my ears." I sigh my relief.

"And keep good notes," she says. "This trip should be worth writing a book when you're done."

"Doing what?" I laugh, almost bending over.

"You heard me. You're the book lady, and this is quite a

voyage. Think about it. No other woman has done this. You're like Amelia Earhart on a major American river. Her books sell like hotcakes."

"She married a book publisher."

"Sure, but that's not why hers sell. Disappearing in the South Pacific gave her greater fame. But your notes and maps are heroic, too" The shining light in Char's eyes makes her look fanatic—like a visionary glimpsing reality before others do.

"I promised Smitty—"

"Promised what?" She lifts her Sou'wester hat to fan her face.

"That I'd write human interest stories from the trip that don't belong in a ship's log—things to make him laugh on rainy days since he couldn't come."

"We all need good reads on rainy days. I'd love a copy, too." She looks me dead in the eyes. "Just don't put me in there. I know I have idiosyncrasies."

Either she reads minds, or my face has betrayed me. "Bullseye!"

We both explode with laughter.

"I don't mind any idiosyncrasy as long as we complete the trip." A rising wind cools my cheeks. "I'm hoping for mission accomplished with few surprises."

Ted pipes up. "But enough to keep things lively— Show me which book boxes for our first stop, and I'll bring them."

"Follow me." I show him the stack and return to the bow.

Char plops her hat back on and mops her forehead to catch perspiration trickles dripping down her face. "Meanwhile, I'll wear this so we only get good weather."

"If that's a guarantee, wonderful."

She points out three Cascade Mountains that come into view as the river curves. "I've seen calendar photos, but being here is incredible."

My eyes follow where she points. Sunlight sparkling on high

peaks. "We'll be places where they're even closer and more majestic."

"Is that possible?" She folds her hands as if in prayer. "I don't know how much beauty I can stand. I save notes for J.P., so he'll see how I fill my days. He was afraid I'd be a stay-at-home wallflower with him gone, but this wallflower is staying too busy to wilt." She snaps her fingers in emphasis.

As the day warms, she peels off her outer coveralls to reveal the next layer of clothing underneath—a long-sleeved blue cotton work shirt tucked into navy cotton drill pants. Red and yellow striped suspenders hold shirt and pants together.

"All those years working with J.P., we were never apart except the week Evie was born." She hooks her thumbs snapping the suspenders absentmindedly as she talks.

If I start laughing, I won't be able to stop. I bite my cheek until my fit passes.

"Day in, day out, together with him on ships, I learned to pilot and got my papers, too." She dabs her eyes. "I didn't know one person could miss another like I do him—if you know what I mean." She squints my way.

I gulp and think of Josh. And of Ted, too. "I might," I concede.

"I'll hush." Her face falls. "As we drove here, Bob told us about Josh being missing. I don't know how he and Sue serve people so well while their own hearts are breaking."

"Me either." I nod. "But they sure do."

Ted brings the last boxes and dusts his hands.

Char peers forward to spot the next river marker. "Mile 96, so Pioneer Grange must be close. What's there?"

"Not much. Three families without books. The grandmother heard about us and asked me to stop. She says there's a tiny dock out front, and she's desperate for books for the kids."

"So, you're stopping?" Ted jerks his head again to flip his hair out of his eyes.

"What if people hadn't helped me years ago? Where would I be? Stuck in Dust Bowl Oklahoma with no chance of life beyond." I answer my own question as I scan the shore until a rough-hewn dock appears. A small Grange hall stands nearby, a U.S. flag flapping in the breeze, but no other sign of life.

Ted cranes his neck. "Where are the people?"

"Beats me but try these." I hand him binoculars. "Maybe we're early. Please motor closer, Char." I scan the horizon but see no movement except the river's flow.

Char polishes her glasses for a closer look. "You're sure this is the right spot?"

"It has to be. She said Pioneer Grange, and that's what the sign says." I clutch her letter and read again, "3 p.m. on the 19th." I search the empty road stretching past the Grange until my eyes ache. Besides wind kicking up puffs of dust or tree leaves fluttering on oaks and maples, there's no sign of life. "Eerie. Something must have happened."

"Looks that way." Ted waves toward the hall. "There's a robin's nest above the door with the mama in it. It doesn't look like anything has disturbed her for a while."

I spot the nest. "You're right. But I hate to fail anyone."

"You're the boss." Char checks her watch. "But we can't stay long and still be on time for Ridgefield. Any chance the folks came early and left?"

"Anything's possible." But the dusty road looks clean. I don't see foot or traffic marks. My fingers drum the rail. "It is disappointing. I don't know what the mix-up could be. Let's stay five more minutes."

"Five minutes it is, but it's hard to make up the schedule once we fall behind. Maybe you can stop here coming back." Concern pinches Char's brow.

My heart sinks. "I wanted a good start. I don't even see a place to leave a message."

"Will these same boxes work for Ridgefield?" Ted studies the books he's carried to the main library room and wipes his hands on his pants.

"Yes, except we'll also need the next stack in the storage area." I look at my watch. Five minutes have passed.

"Use this." Char tosses him a clean rag. "Can you leave word with Ridgefield's teacher?"

"Maybe." I heave a sigh. "You're right. We have to go." *Lord, our first library stop is a bust.* I look from the silent Grange hall to the churning river. Things have to go right at the next stop, where hopefully a whole school is waiting, or *Books Afloat* might fail on our first day.

Just then, an old blue model car roars to the dock creating a dust storm. The driver parks haphazardly and leaps out wearing a green fedora tipped back on his head and rushes forward, swinging a leather satchel in one hand.

"Ahoy!"

"Ahoy?" I shade my eyes. The tall grinning young man keeps coming fast.

"You're *Books Afloat*? You have to be."

"Yes?" My lips form a tight line. I don't need interruptions. Today is already crazy enough.

"Then I found you in time."

"In time for what?"

"For making history on the Columbia River."

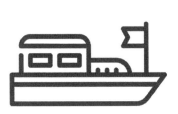

5

Friday, June 19, 1942
Pioneer Grange to Ridgefield, Washington, River Mile 89.5

The young man's grin shows him friendly, though his sudden appearance raises more questions than answers. He's tall with such long legs, he obviously can't find pants long enough. His creased brown dress slacks stop short of well-shined wingtips, now getting dusty. I wait, hands on hips, as he strides forward.

"You're the library boat, *Books Afloat*," he cries in a single breath. "I've raced to find you, and here you are!" He radiates triumph as his piston legs pump.

Ted raises a hand to stop him. "Wait, who are you? What do you want?"

The man's tall and limber with bronze freckles dotting his face. His blazing green eyes measure us and our boat like twin telescopes searching the far corners of the universe. He doesn't stop until he sees Ted's upraised hand and then teeters where the dock joins our gangplank.

"Your reporter."

"Our what?" Ted and I ask in unison.

"The reporter sent to cover you."

My voice carries frustration. "We don't need covering—we have work to do."

"Yes, and I'll help." He lifts his green fedora with a flourish, and the fingers of his right hand crease its pinched crown. "Didn't word reach you? I'm Sparks Corrigan, lead reporter from Kennewick, Washington's *Tri-City Herald*. I read what you're doing in *The Columbian*, and it's red-hot news—except they don't do you justice. I'm here to cover you so our readers can experience this history-making journey."

He sweeps a hand along the river. "After all, the same mighty Columbia flows from our Tri-Cities area to the Pacific. And when we heard the Governor's Challenge, we contacted his office. Your trip is the greatest adventure since Lindbergh crossed the Atlantic, and Earhart attempted the globe. I can't wait to be part of it."

"Be part?" I stare, slack-jawed.

He inches a toe forward, but Ted doesn't budge.

"On your amazing boat, getting the inside scoop for several days, and returning other times when I can arrange days off as you near the coast." His joy dims when it's not returned. "I'll pay my own way and be no trouble. My stories will raise the support you need."

I bristle. "How do you know what support I need? Tell me your name again—and who sent you. What did you say about the governor's office?"

The man sighs, and his shoulders slump. "I thought I was clear. I'm Sparks Corrigan and saw your story two hundred and sixty-three miles east, which is how far I drove all night to find you. This is one news event I won't miss." His eyes survey Char and Ted before returning to me. "You're clearly Captain Anne Mettles, but the picture they ran in *The Columbian* doesn't do you justice."

As his eyes probe, I feel like a deer caught in headlights.

"You're swell," he says appreciatively. "Their photo isn't good at all. I'll run a good one in my full-page spread. Once I heard you were underway, I hopped in my Dodge and raced here. Some ride, I'll say, Captain Mettles. It took two tire patch kits plus a wad of Beech-Nut chewing gum on my radiator hose, but here I am." He attempts to step forward.

But Ted doesn't move aside.

Heat climbs my face. "I'm not Captain yet. There's a formality first."

"Never mind. In readers' hearts, you are. Magazine editors are missing out by not being here, maybe even Pulitzers." He pushes back his hat one more time, where it dangles from a springy curl before dropping into his hand.

He has a myriad of facial expressions, a perpetual motion machine. As he loosens his tie and slides free of his tweed jacket, his crisp white shirt shows perspiration stains at the armpits, but he smells like Lifebuoy soap—nothing unpleasant. No *Columbian* newsman has shown such interest.

"The governor did mention hoping to send a reporter."

"His staff is swamped. Luckily, he accepted me." He plops his hat back on his head.

My anxiety climbs as he shifts his leather satchel to his left hand and reaches around Ted to engulf my hand in his large right paw, pumping my arm up and down like an Oklahoma farmer seeking oil. We three stand at awkward angles, all in danger of falling in the river.

His eyes are intense. "I'm very glad to meet you."

"Thank you." I take a step back, at a loss for words, although Sparks spouts plenty.

"Like I said, I drove all night to catch you before you lifted anchor but was too late. *The Columbian* phoned Bob Vengeance, who knew your route, so I've checked every river bend along the way."

His blue Dodge touring sedan is slung crosswise near the dock, heat waves radiating.

"Say, she's snazzy." Ted's hands flex like he's itching to look under the hood, so now he takes a step forward, which the reporter notices and immediately gains some distance.

"She's old, but gutsy. Sorry to surprise you, but I couldn't miss my chance." Dangling his satchel, he pulls a notepad and pen from his tweed sports jacket pocket. "I'm ready to go."

Ted has lowered his hand but crosses his arms. "You're serious about coming?"

"It's settled. I *am* coming."

"That's for Miss Mettles to say. She decides who's on board."

"But the governor's signed note is in this briefcase." He had swooped his hat back on his head, but now it tilts back again where only hair oil or some freak of nature holds it on.

"I'll be indispensable. You'll wonder how you managed without me. I'll be no trouble and eat like a bird ... well, a big bird." He guffaws until his shoulders shake. "I'm an extra set of hands to polish your brass, swab your decks, anything ..." He smiles wider, so sure of acceptance. His eyes shrink to slits. "What do you say now?"

"What can I say? Show me the note. Do you expect me to say it's my lucky day, and my ship has come in?"

"Ha, ha, good one." His chuckle broadens. "I'll quote you."

I leave the gangplank and step back on deck, clutching the rail, dizzy from his flood of words.

"I'll start with the Governor's Challenge, rebuilding courage in the hearts of Americans at war, especially since you're a woman." He scans me again, one thumb jerking approval. "An attractive one."

"Thanks, I guess." I cross my arms, feeling like a slab of meat on display in a butcher shop. "No one said you were coming. This trip is a trial run to prove the usefulness of library service on the river. It's premature to report much until we succeed, plus Governor Langlie has to approve each person on board for insurance reasons."

The man snaps his fingers. "The governor has approved it."

Ted backs up slightly, and the reporter inches forward until he's on the gangplank.

"I don't need insurance because I'm not a paying passenger— just recording your amazing journey. I'll scoot home in a few days to meet our paper's deadline, hit the presses, put this week's issue to bed, but come back before you can say, 'Jiminy Cricket.' Your story is absolute crackers. Here's my lead." He closes his eyes and tilts his chin. "'Washington girl meets challenge worthy of war heroes.' What do you think?"

I choke, nearly spitting out my Juicy Fruit gum. "It's blatantly untrue. I've lived longer in Oklahoma than Washington, although Washington is home now. I'm just a young woman eager to carry books to people needing them because books change lives—they changed mine."

"Great. I love personal angles but need details." He taps his pen against his teeth. "Still, my lead might be true—you never know in wartime." His green eyes flash as if he craves danger.

Char clears her throat loud enough to be heard over our boat's idling engine. "Do we stay here talking? Or can we cast off and get underway?"

"Thanks, Char. As you heard, this is Sparks Corrigan, a reporter from eastern Washington. I guess he's along for a few days to cover the Governor's Challenge."

Her lips blow a raspberry sound. "In due respect, there won't *be* a Challenge if we don't get going." Her face reminds me of the mythical Greek goddess Medusa whose frown turned people to stone.

"Uh, right. Sparks, what about your car? You can't leave it there."

"Yes, I can. I keep a key tucked in a place the governor's office knows about. If I radio them, they'll have someone drive it to Kelso-Longview, which is where I have to leave you this time."

Char taps her watch. "I have questions but guess they can be settled later."

"I still need the governor's note," I remind him.

"Sure thing. It's in my satchel. I'll put my stuff down and grab it." He takes one final long step and is on *Books Afloat.* "Ahhhh, it's good to be on board."

"Char, head us out."

"Aye, aye." She steers into the main channel at full power, leaning over the bow, eyes straight ahead, like the inspiring figurehead on the prow of a ship. White foam churn in our wake.

Maybe this reporter can do us good, but he's also one more person to avoid while I gather information and send reports to the governor.

6

Friday, June 19, 1942
Pioneer Grange, Washington, River Mile 91.5

"Show me the note," I repeat once the reporter is firmly on board.

"Here you go." He fishes it from his satchel's side pocket.

I recognize the governor's stationery and handwriting.

Dear Anne,

We follow your progress with interest. Sparks Corrigan comes highly recommended and has won journalism awards. Humor him, and he'll do us good.

Cordially, Arthur B. Langlie, Governor

Having Sparks on board complicates things, but I'll cooperate.

Books Afloat breasts the river current as the thousand

butterflies that lodged in my stomach this morning still flit around. Except now a thousand buzzing wasps join them. Sparks wants to help. *Lord, give me grace.*

He's on good behavior, observing and jotting copious notes. He hides a grin watching Char. I wonder what he's writing. His notepad is an extension of his hand, and he mutters some words aloud about our boat's size, crew, and the river's waves as he works capturing everything resembling news.

Three aspirin do not touch my headache. I doubt four can tame the pounding behind my eyes. Nervous before this morning's exam, I skipped breakfast to write hopes and fears in my diary named *For Anne's Eyes Only* instead. Though my stomach begs for food, I doubt I could keep it down.

"Are you feeling okay?" Char asks.

I must look bad. "Not the best. My stomach's rocky."

"Let me get you something to drink," she says. "Tea or lemonade before Ridgefield?"

"I'd love mint tea."

Char scurries after it with our boat's course set chugging west. I step to our large trip calendar showing *Ridgefield* written inside a two-inch square with today's date and slash it through with a bright red X—the color of Christmas and happiness. Or of blood and disaster. My two-dimensional plans must become a successful three-dimensional reality. Or fail. No-show people at Pioneer Grange except for Sparks is not a good start. Readers *must* see us at Ridgefield.

What if we're a bust here, too? Especially with Sparks reporting. My stomach spasms. It would have been easier to go with Mom and Dad to Oklahoma, where I'd be a noble heroine abandoning personal dreams to help my widowed grandmother. People might praise me for returning to save the farm.

With Mom and Dad's help, she should be encouraged enough to return to growing prize-winning sunflowers again and happily scatter grain from her apron to her flock of chickens. I rub my eyes. I can't think about her, or I'll blubber ... After all, I owe her a huge personal debt for not keeping Grandpa awake.

The scene replays where I failed her and failed Grandpa. I wouldn't blame her if she can't forgive me since I can't forgive myself. The memory mocks me. I'm nine-years-old again and riding with Grandpa in his truck during harvest.

'Keep me awake, Annie. Grandpa's tired tonight.' His words still ring in my ears. But when I fell asleep, he didn't wake me. He must have nodded off, too, missing the only curve on our straight Oklahoma farm road and crashing into a large irrigation culvert. I felt his hand push me down to safety. I wish I could feel that loving hand again. But after the crash, when I called Grandpa's name, he didn't answer.

I'm not good at keeping promises. Not then—not now.

"Approaching Ridgefield," Char calls, our engine screaming high RPMs with choppy waves spreading in Vees from our bow. "What's there?"

"Potato-growing country carved from wooded hills near Battle Ground, named for an Indian uprising." I can recite the information in my sleep. "Some warned Ridgefield was too small for us to bother with, but no place is too small.

"I remember the joy of learning to read for the first time from a *Fun with Dick and Jane* book, 'A red ball, a blue ball, a yellow ball (drumroll) for Sister Sally.' That was the best day in my life until Grandpa took me to a library filled with books."

Char's eyes rivet. "So, that's where your inspiration comes from."

"That's right. Books and the people bringing them helped me break through as many limits as the Wright brothers learning to fly. Later, when I asked my first librarian how I could thank her, she said, 'Share books and learning wherever you go.'"

"And that's what you're doing!" Char's smile broadens to a dentist's full-page ad.

I nod. "The best I can."

"I'll use that." Sparks scribbles more.

"And she'll succeed." Ted's voice gushes confidence. "Nothing stops Annie."

"Thanks." I smile at both him and Char. They get it. They're here for me.

"Tell me your general trip plan," Sparks says. "What will library stops look like?"

"There's no set routine. Each place will be different. Since Ridgefield is small, I contacted the elementary school teacher two miles inland. They're new with few books, so even though it's summer and classes haven't begun, she said if we'd come at four o'clock, she'd have a crowd."

"A library Pied Piper." Sparks writes faster.

Char steers toward shore. "I see lots of people."

"Thank God." I forget to breathe.

Sparks lifts an impressive camera from his bag. "Great photos sell stories." He attaches lenses and filters.

"Mine's ready, too." Ted aims a poor man's camera.

I hand my Kodak to him. "Can you snap some for me, too, while I help patrons?"

He doesn't take it.

"If you don't mind—"

"Mind?" A grin curves his lips, but his hands stay at his sides.

"Please?"

"My pleasure." He grins and accepts my camera. "A captain with manners." Now his eyes are gray-green tide pools with interesting sea life I'd like to explore.

My cheeks burn. "I need photos to show folks we're successful."

"I'll gladly help. And you're right, Sparks. Action shots will show people that *Books Afloat* matters."

"That's why I'm here." He pumps a fist. "In fact, let's win a Pulitzer!"

I stare. "You have grandiose ideas."

"Somebody has to win. I think you're the story of the year."

Char also hands Ted her camera. "If you can, please take some for me while I help Anne with books. I can't send J.P. pictures yet because of censoring, but he'll love them later."

"Sure." He loops her camera strap over his head along with his and mine. "Smile." He snaps Char and me. "Great candid shot. Give me another." He clicks again. "Here's a protocol question. Do Sparks and I salute you two each time we see you? Or treat you like regular folks?"

"What do you think?" My eyes flash. "Even when I'm captain, I won't put on airs."

"Not many, at least." His eyes tease again.

"Try saluting me, Buster," Char's fists form, "and I'll toss you to the fishies. I hate formality."

Sparks waves, "Ted, stand by them for a team picture."

Ted reddens but joins. As we near shore, he leans against the rail.

"Arriving Port of Ridgefield," Char calls.

Sparks snaps pictures while I focus on shore.

Ted joins me, shielding his eyes. "Beautiful and peaceful," he says.

"Yes." *But not my insides.* Is anything on shore that shouldn't be? *I doubt it.* But neither did we guess Japan would bomb Pearl Harbor or invade Alaska's Aleutians. This river entering America's interior makes us a prime target.

Ted steps close. "I'm glad to be here."

I count library registration cards. "I'm glad you are, too."

Ted tugs his ear. "Excuse me, did you say you were glad I came?"

"I may have. There! Satisfied?"

Ted clasps his hands overhead like a winning prizefighter.

"I can't wait until you're glad I came, too," Sparks quips.

"Some things take a while, but I may get there."

"She's worth the wait," Ted says, smoothing his hands over his jeans, and though he seldom blushes, he does now.

Or is it hot sunlight? I've only seen him embarrassed when Josh trapped him in funny pranks. All three of us are comfortable old shoe friends who do lots of teasing. Why does Ted turn red now?

"Right now, I'm thanking God for that gorgeous wharf full of people."

"Request permission to anchor in Port of Ridgefield," Char calls.

A man on shore answers, "Permission granted."

Ted readies our anchor and gives a jaunty salute. "Steady as she goes."

I salute back. "Char, may I dock her?"

"Yes, Ma'am." She steps aside as I pull two blasts on our whistle and line up *Books Afloat* with the pier. I also grab the daffodil yellow and shimmering blue library flag Mother stitched in spite of her misgivings—an open book on a field of blue. I didn't use it at Pioneer Grange because nobody came.

'Don't forget,' Mom's words echo in my mind, 'you can always come home if your plans don't work.'

As I hoist the flag, it unfurls smartly in a breeze directly below America's red and white with forty-eight stars. In the half-second I look away, we sideswipe the pier, making people jump and shout. The sturdy pier isn't damaged, but a thin strip of painted wood peels from our boat—and a broader stripe from my pride. What's wrong with me? I only looked away an instant.

"It's okay, Annie. No real harm done." Ted tosses a line to a man on shore before cranking the winch to unwind our rattling anchor chain.

"A dab of paint can fix it," Char says. "Look at that crowd."

"My heart swells, and I open my arms. *"Books Afloat* floating library is open for business. Welcome aboard."

Sparks' camera clicks steadily, and the stampede begins.

Friday, June 19, 1942
Ridgefield, Washington, River Mile 93

I adjust my captain's hat and hold out my hand to Sparks. I need the negative of me scraping the pier."

"Later. Great crowd!" He clicks more pictures.

A tall man hops on board and presses a stiff folded paper into my hand.

"Smitty said to give you this."

"Wha-at?"

"Shhhh." Tall and lanky like a leather-fringed Daniel Boone, he slides a hand aside his mouth. "Don't say nuthin'. You'll understand once you read." He looks around to make sure all on board are busy, "I'm Wayne Sanders."

And that's how I meet the first undercover member of our volunteer river network. I resume breathing. "I'm Anne Mettles."

Ted approaches. "And I'm Ted Vincent. Thanks for tying us up."

"Pleasure." Sanders shakes Ted's hand. "It's a good thing

you're doing, bringing books. We need them. That's our schoolmarm, Miss Clark."

He points to a young woman barely out of State Normal School—medium height, modest dress, nice smile, leading a flock of children. I start to count but lose track as the moving sea of faces bobs up and down.

"Most youngsters can't visit the river much and don't attend school regular with all we have to do clearing land and planting crops, but today's special." Wayne returns to the pier helping children board as the swarm pushes forward, nearly overflowing the gangplank.

An older woman wedged in the middle of the flock grabs shirttails and sleeves to slow some children as the group presses on, dragging her along. "They're so excited." She gives a weary smile and sweeps past. "We all are."

"Welcome," I tell everyone, directing traffic and guiding them toward our large library room at the main deck's center. "If you don't know which books you want, I've placed wonderful classics here."

I wave toward attractive book displays on tables and the loaded shelves behind. "Here are *The Box Car Children*, *Black Beauty* and *Lassie* books, plus the *Hardy Boys* and *Nancy Drew*. We have non-fiction, biographies of presidents and other famous people, plus stacks of magazines."

The children crowd in, taking spots around varnished tables and filling child-sized chairs.

Ted moves quietly, taking photos from different angles. He's great with children.

"This is my dream come true," I whisper.

"I can tell." He squeezes my shoulder.

One little girl in front of me looks like she might be the weary woman's daughter. "Did you say we can keep books until you come back?"

"Yes. Three weeks—maybe four. I'll send word once I know

our schedule. For now, write your name and River Mile address. One book per person, but after your parent or teacher signs your membership card, you can borrow three books each time."

"The girl squeals and grabs two books as her mother signs, hugging them tight against her chest.

I blink away tears.

Char clears her throat as if she's swallowed a frog. "I don't have this library bug as bad as you," she says, "but I love seeing kids happy. I'm glad you needed me."

"You're a treasure, Char Young."

"Shucks." She turns red

The teacher arrives. "We're excited you're here. Families have talked of nothing else all week. We hope to start our own library, but it's involved. We're more talk than action. I'm Miss Clark." She extends her hand to shake mine.

"I'm Anne Mettles. Believe me, I know it's complicated."

"After I help this child," she says, "I need to mention something."

"Wait," Sparks insists. "Repeat that handshake." He snaps two photos and turns for his next shot.

Miss Clark helps the shy lad pulling her arm. A taller overall-clad boy pushes shaggy bowl-cut hair out of his eyes to read book titles. He chooses *George Washington, the Making of a President,* and *Tall Tales of the American West* as if he has found treasure.

Char nudges me. "He might be a future president."

I beam. "Abe Lincoln loved books."

"What in tarnation do you mean defying my civil liberties, Miss Clark?" A cloud shadows the sun as an older man pushes through the crowd and stomps on board. His Old Testament prophet voice and angry steps shake the deck. "You ignored my wishes, bringing Charlie here. I wrote he didn't have permission to come."

"Not come?" Miss Clark's face is whiter than the paper she holds. "I didn't understand that from your note, Mr. Gibson. Charles was at my house, chopping kindling. He saw I needed help escorting the younger children and volunteered. I thought you meant he couldn't get a library card until you signed it. What's the problem?"

"Problem? Be sure what people want, or you're a poor excuse of an educator. With real men gone, the rest of us work extra hard." He grabs one of Charlie's books. *Tall Tales of the American West.* Kids shouldn't read craziness."

Before I can speak, the man shoves Sparks to stop him from taking pictures and grabs Charlie's collar.

"Drop that thing before I break it. Charlie. We're going home where there's real *work* to do—that new field to root pick and pasture to plant. Better than readin' fool stuff that don't put food on the table."

"Yessir, Grandpa. I meant no harm." The boy's shoulders slump.

Miss Clark touches the man's arm. "Mr. Gibson, I wouldn't ignore your wishes. Charlie's a valuable worker, but also has a bright mind. I didn't think you'd deprive him of this wonderful—"

"I'll decide what's wonderful. I wrote he couldn't come. What more does a man have to say?" He shrugs her off and faces me.

"With Charlie's dad's flying bombers in Europe and his mom dead in childbirth, Ma, Charlie, and me work our place 'til we drop, or the grave claims us. Why are we fightin' wars over there? We need to fix things on this side of the water. I told our neighbors not to come to Pioneer Grange. Sorry my wife was dumb enough to ask."

I shudder at his vehemence. *Your neighbors fear you.*

He shoves Charlie forward, almost knocking me down.

Ted blocks him. "Sorry you feel that way, sir, but you owe

these ladies an apology."

"Apology? For the truth?" Mr. Gibson snorts. "What kind of sissy man floats on a river when real men fight overseas. C'mon, Charlie. Hard work makes true heroes." He moves Ted aside with one well-placed hand.

Sparks still snaps pictures.

The man swells like he may have a stroke. "Quit, or I'll break that picture box."

Yet as he shoves Sparks, I almost think Sparks hands him a black film cartridge. Sure I'm seeing things, I shake my head to clear it. Ted's hand balls to a fist until I capture it in mine.

"Ted, it doesn't matter. I know what you're made of."

The man stomps to the gangplank.

"He's the problem I wanted to mention," Miss Clark says. "I didn't dream Mr. Gibson would do that. His wife is the lovely woman who wrote asking you to visit Pioneer Grange."

"We did stop. There was no one."

"He threatened them. I'm sure Mrs. Gibson feels terrible."

I don't envy her. "If you see her, tell her if he ever changes his mind—"

Char makes a strangling sound. "That might be a cold day in a hot place."

"I'd be willing to stop again. Could she come here?"

Miss Clark rolls her eyes. "If Charlie's allowed to attend school once crops are in."

Char snarls, "If J.P. were around, he'd dunk that man in the river to cool him off. There's no accounting for how some people think—or don't." She taps her Sou'wester. "Not much upstairs, if you know what I mean."

The main library room is full of happy, chirping children. Ted turns to help, but I feel his ache. I keep Char busy collecting signed library cards and issuing books.

As the crowd calms, a sunny brown-haired girl age seven or eight approaches pushing a wicker doll buggy. One of the last children to board, she waits until Mr. Gibson finishes his rant and leaves before she crosses the broad plank Ted laid between shore and boat. As she pushes by, I glimpse a stuffed animal in her buggy wrapped in a blanket.

"A bunny doll. How cute," I say.

"Thanks," she lisps, pushing her buggy past as Sparks takes her picture.

"Great imagination," I tell Ted.

"No imagination, I saw an ear wiggle." He strides after her as the live bunny works free from its blanket.

In slow motion, it hops across the deck, looking every direction, nose and whiskers twitching.

"It's alive," children cry, rising from their little chairs.

Their actions scare the bunny, so it hops to the open space at the river side of the boat and goes overboard in a flying jump.

"My bunny," screams the girl, running to the rail.

"I'll get it!" Ted holds her back, kicks off his shoes, and dives, splashing blindly as his right hand comes up empty. He grabs a breath and submerges again, this time popping up, clutching the bunny.

"Got it!" Char extends a dip net and rescues it. "Safe." She hauls up the bedraggled rabbit and shrugs off her seaman's jacket to warm it. "It'll be fine."

"Did this child come with you?" I ask Miss Clark.

She shakes her head. "I don't know where she's from."

"Not mine." The weary mother lifts a hand to point north. "She came from that direction."

"Alone? How on earth? Let's get her back on land, but let her choose a book first."

"That's nice. I'll make sure you get the book back."

Miss Clark guides the girl to the shelves where she selects an illustrated Peter Rabbit book she holds to her chest. I check it out, and Miss Clark looks at her watch.

"Time's up now. Our visit has to end. Thank you, everyone. Our children are happy, and we'll look forward to next time."

Wayne, our Daniel Boone lookalike, missed the excitement while exploring the boat but reappears now. "I'll see the little girl home. I think I know where she lives."

"Where's Ted?" I turn to check. "Oh, no!"

Eyes wild, he struggles in the river, unable to reach the boat as the current pulls against him. Each time he sinks, he pops up farther away.

Sparks leans over the rail, snapping pictures.

"Help him!" I scream, rushing to help Ted myself.

"I have a gaff hook." Char sweeps past me and misses Ted the first time but snags his shirt the second. She guides him to where he grips our boat's rungs and climbs onboard shaken.

"Another great action shot," Sparks says.

"Enough!" Ted pushes the camera away before sprawling on deck, gasping for breath. Water sloshes from him.

I kneel, hands on his chest, ready to do compressions. He's so pale it scares me.

"I'm okay, Annie."

"No, you're not. Why did you dive? What were you thinking?' I want to shake him—or hug him. He looks as miserable as I feel.

"I wasn't thinking. Saw the bunny, saw the girl—had to stop her."

Departing children stare.

"Well, you did." Char tosses a blanket over him. "Good thing it was you instead of Mr. Gibson. He might have let the bunny drown. As for you, Sparks—" she turns his way "—the Good Book says there's a time for everything under the sun. This was a time to help a fine young man, not take pictures."

"You had things under control," Sparks counters. "Action shots sell news."

Her eyes flash. "I might show you some action."

Sparks withers.

"I thought we'd prepared for everything," I say. "But with children on board, we can't lower our guard a minute."

"You were super." Ted is back in dry clothes. "It ended fine. We made library history."

I roll my eyes. "Including some I'd rather forget."

"Brave, Vincent," Sparks comments as he photographs the last children leaving.

"You don't even look worse for wear," I fuss at Ted, "but I wish you'd skipped the scary part."

He laughs while sliding library chairs back under the tables where they belong, like everything's normal.

I stretch to ease kinks out of my neck and shoulders. "Okay, team. We have a choice. We can stay here tonight and get an early start tomorrow or chug across to St. Helens and be there in the morning. Either suits our schedule."

"I don't care." Char drums the fingers of one hand into the palm of the other. "Do what suits you."

Ted snaps his fingers. "I'll wrangle dinner. In that last box Sue brought, she also packed a dinner fit for kings."

In minutes he has spread a feast—fried chicken, green beans, and fried potatoes. We eat without talking

"Great folks," he says when it's time to clean up. "I wish Josh were here. I sure miss that guy. He's got to be alive out there somewhere."

"Alive, where?" Sparks asks, pencil poised.

"A friend of theirs—I'll tell you later." Char drinks another Royal Crown Cola. "Don't you ever quit? Or take time out? There are men being found every day."

"A few," Sparks admits.

We stand at the prow, watching the sun slant low, painting river bends and hills the evening shades of rose, lavender, and blue found in Monet's Impressionist paintings.

I yawn. "Ted, can you find space for both you and Sparks to sleep near the engine room?"

"Sure, I'll find a spot. I'm nearest the engine room to watch things."

"Char? You're okay up top in that curtained area?"

"Great. With luck, you won't hear my buzz saw snores. Evie complains, but J.P. doesn't dare because he's a snoring machine himself. I just hope the Japanese don't hear him coming."

"Where is he?" Sparks asks, notebook out.

"In the Asiatic Pacific."

She climbs the stairs, and I'm ready to follow.

As Ted pivots on his heels, he lays a finger against his swollen lip with a slight smile. I blush again, remembering our collision. I finger my own lip, and my heart tingles. Was today's collision an accidental kiss? Or more?

Or is it the kiss itself that confuses me and heats my cheeks? I push those thoughts away. I have a river Challenge to complete and a promise to keep to Grandpa and Governor Langlie. I'll prove I can help people without harming anyone else on my watch ever again. No matter what.

After quiet descends, I open the black briefcase in my quarters and examine the radio. I think of Smitty. I should have guessed that was a nickname, since other initials are on his mailbox. When I see him next, I'll worm details out of him.

My head aches from too much thinking. Time to carefully read the note "Daniel Boone" handed me. Later, I'll send a radio report and update my personal diary.

My heart churns with unanswered questions or swarming emotions. *God, thanks for today. Please help us and Books Afloat.*

8

Saturday, June 20, 1942
St. Helens, Oregon, River Mile 86

The boat tugged at its anchor as the river's roll and splash caused it to bob on low waves. Ted loved waking here instead of in his small room above the mechanic shop.

Except ... He sat up fast. Where was he? Not in his bunk near the engine room. Had he checked boat safety in the night and sprawled across this hard chair on the main deck? Surely he didn't sleepwalk like when he was a boy. Annie faced enough challenges without him failing. She hadn't wanted anyone on board besides Char after Smitty couldn't come. She could order him off if he caused problems.

What would he do if he found Japanese in the river? For sure, he wouldn't tell Annie it could happen, although she probably suspected. *God, help me keep her safe.*

His thoughts of yesterday's surprise kiss made his heart explode again like Fourth of July fireworks. He fingered his lip —slightly swollen, but bringing the sweet memory of an amazing girl crashing into him—the best way in the world to bruise a lip.

What did Anne think of yesterday's kiss that turned her crimson? The memory of her lips made his tingle again. Did she notice he'd nearly hugged her? Pure red-blooded American male instinct, and who could blame him? She was more tempting than a cherry malt on a hot day. He couldn't hide his feelings much longer.

It was rough with Josh missing and unaccounted for. The memory surfaced as if it happened just yesterday. They'd stayed honest with each other and flipped a coin to decide who'd take Annie to prom. It was fine that Josh won. Ted didn't dance.

Transitioning their Three Musketeers friendships—no girlfriend, boyfriend stuff—was awkward, although Josh agreed one of them might end up with her.

'She's not right for you,' Josh had insisted. 'She's a spitfire, where you're cool and collected. It takes a joker like me to handle a pistol like her.'

'You think so?'

Josh was right about most things, but not this. Annie's spunk was what Ted loved most.

Dodging a diving seagull brought him back to the present.

"Crazy wonderful if I do get her," Ted said softly, "though my chances are better for being struck by lightning." If he told Annie what she meant to him now, she'd shut him down, saying the timing was wrong with a goal to accomplish.

And she'd be right. The Governor's Challenge mattered more than personal longings. Especially with the invasion risks increasing as the governor told Ted when he gave him his instructions. And he must protect Annie.

He headed down the stairs. Sparks was still sleeping. The reporter's arrival complicated Ted's plans. He'd have to be extra sneaky to do river patrol duties without detection. No one could know those details.

Ted entered the galley and started a pot of coffee. Despite rationing, he'd splurged on real beans, adding generous spoonfuls of dark grind to make the brew strong. He inhaled its rich aroma. It would taste great going down.

Back on deck, sunlight drew white mist from the river in rising curls like fluttering angels' wings. Like the impressionist paintings Mom loved. He spotted Anne at the helm, eyes straight ahead.

"Beautiful," he breathed.

"What?" She didn't turn.

"The river is beautiful." *You* are beautiful, he wanted to shout.

"I love early mornings." Now she turned, sweet and vulnerable. "You scared me yesterday when you dove in the river. What made you do that?" Tears glimmered in her lashes. "I can't lose you."

"You'd rather lose the bunny?"

"Don't tease." Her eyes lowered to his mouth. "How's your lip?"

"Fine," he lied. *Kiss it and make it better.*

"No scar?"

"I'd wear it proudly." He chuckled.

She swatted his arm. "I hate scars. I'd rather cause blessings."

He groaned. *Oh, Annie, you do!* This girl who barely reached his chin could tear his heart out. He wanted to say, *You're always a blessing, the finest girl I've ever known,* pull her into his arms and press his lips against hers, tasting their sweetness.

Instead, he rattled the anchor chain. "You're always a blessing. Ready for coffee?"

"I'm not dreaming? I do smell it?"

"Yes—the real thing." *Like you.*

"Wonderful. Where did you get it?"

"Splurged. But some treats are worth it." *You're worth it.*

"Want a cup?"

"Please." She lifted something red. "By the way, is this your sweatshirt I found draped across a library table? I thought I saw you on deck early, but when I called, you didn't answer. Were you sleepwalking?" She peered intently.

He felt himself flame as hot and bright as his sweatshirt. "Dunno. I did years back. I hope not now because I could walk off the boat."

"Right. Your swim in the river was shock enough. Maybe you left the shirt behind after dinner and didn't notice." She moved closer, reading his face. "All the same, maybe you should sleep in a harness tied to the mast—in case." Amber lights danced in her eyes.

"I don't—"

"Good morning." Char clattered down the stairs. "I'll pull a simple breakfast together."

I smile my thanks. "Wonderful, Char."

She scanned the deck. "Where's that reporter?"

"Asleep." Ted pointed downstairs.

"Nobody should miss these views."

"I can call him." But Ted didn't stir.

Char peeled off her Sou'wester and hung it above her oilskins on a peg. "I don't cook in my hat. J.P. and Smitty's mom taught me. She was great and raised four kids with take-charge names and personalities."

"Smitty's real name is Horatio?" Ted asked.

"That's right."

Char laughed so broadly her dental fillings showed.

"Smith is common, so she begged her husband to give them inspiring monikers. She taught literature and chose names from famous books. Horatio is from *Captain Horatio Hornblower*. School kids razzed him. Going by Smitty helped him avoid fights."

Ted winced. "I'll bet. And your husband is John Paul Young?"

"John Paul Jones Young after that great patriot who said, 'I have not yet begun to fight.' And that's what J.P. is like. I hope his name helps him now." She teared up.

"I pray for him and Josh every day," Ted said.

"Me, too," Annie brushed her eyes.

"I'm going crazy waiting for letters." Char sniffed the air. "Do I smell coffee?"

"Coming right up. What do you take in yours, Char?"

"Black, thanks."

Annie looked up. "Do you remember how I like mine?"

"Wouldn't forget. Scant sugar with a little cream."

"Bingo. I'm impressed."

Her smile pierced his heart.

Sparks climbed the steps sliding his arms into his jacket while trying to tame his springy curls. "I slept like a baby rocked in its mother's arms."

"The river does that." Char grinned. "Fresh air helps." She set out oatmeal with apple chunks, toast, and jam. "Ted, ask the blessing, and we'll dig in."

After finishing and clearing the table, Anne spread out her river chart. "Next stop, St. Helens, straight across at River Mile 86."

"Show me." Sparks looked over her shoulder. "What's special there?"

Did Sparks have to lean so close his chin grazed Anne's blouse?

When Ted cleared his throat, Sparks raised his head.

Anne kept reading, unaware. "On perfect days, five major Cascade peaks are visible from there."

"I see three." Char swiveled. "Can we see more from the other side, Anne?"

"Sometimes. This stretch has lots of traffic—cargo ships, tugs, barges. By crossing early, we'll miss most of them."

Char took the helm. "Ready to start the engine, Ted?"

"After my visual check." Ted loved this routine—checking

the engine, doing record maintenance, morning prayer, casting off moorings, and getting underway with good crew interaction. He completed his checks and raced back two steps at a time. "Everything's shipshape. She's a great engine."

"Smitty likes it," Char said. "But you know engines better than him."

Ted's chest swelled.

They left Ridgefield, chugging across the main channel. Sparks sorted camera filters.

Anne read more details on St. Helens and Columbia City and then looked up. "I love history, and it's worlds better watching this river unroll like a blue-green road than speeding past in cars. I doubt it's changed much since pioneer days."

"You're right." Sparks stepped to her side. "It's easy picturing early times here. But there's also a fresh sense of discovery—new history in the making. If all citizens worked as hard as you on this library boat, wars would end fast."

"You think so?" Anne offered a cautious smile. "I want to make a difference."

"You do." Sparks tapped his forehead. "I wonder what project a girl like you will pursue next. You chase big goals. I admire that."

Ted couldn't believe the line Sparks was spinning. Or that Anne was buying.

"Some special young man will ask you to settle down." Sparks kept going. "Or has one already?"

Annie blazed red and sputtered. "Why would you ask that?"

Ted dropped his grease gun with a clatter.

"I'm a newsman. It's obvious."

Sparks' eyes danced, making Ted grab his grease gun too tight when he picked it up. A stream of thick grease shot out and hit the deck. As Ted began wiping up the mess, grease spread wider and soaked into the wood.

"I'm glad that thing isn't a handgun." Sparks crooked his

trigger finger like an armed weapon. "You'd be dangerous."

Ted glared. "Maybe so."

Anne stepped between them. "Sparks, are you trying to be obnoxious? Or does it come naturally?"

Sparks shrugged.

Ted's Adam's apple bobbed. He jammed his hands into his pockets, and his magnets rattled. He didn't need Annie fighting his battles.

"What about you, Sparks?" Anne persisted. "Are you a family man?"

"Not yet." He fingered his hat absentmindedly while facing east toward his home. "I haven't found the girl who deserves me, but I'm about ready."

Ted's mind flipped back to the schoolyard when he'd dropped the bully pummeling his younger brother. He hadn't pulverized him as badly as Dad wanted.

'Hit him harder next time,' Dad had ordered. 'Finish him off. Your principal agrees. He has it coming.'

Mom begged Ted to forgive Dad's anger. 'His father's life was hard, so he raised your dad rough. He thinks it's how to make boys into men.'

'It drives us away,' Ted muttered.

Mom touched his cheek. 'Try to understand, for my sake. He drives his players hard to man-up. He thinks softness weakens them.' She leaned her forehead against Ted's. 'He wins record games and trophies.'

'At what cost?'

Memories of Dad's cruelty still twisted Ted's gut. Dad was wrong,

Violence was never the right choice, was it? He clenched his teeth. If it were, Sparks would be dead.

For now, they were packed together on one small boat. A possible Japanese submarine was the enemy Ted had to stalk. He bent to clean up the grease, but it wasn't easy to do.

9

Saturday, June 20, 1942
St. Helens, Oregon, River Mile 86

Char helps Ted mop up grease when I join them. It's hard to concentrate while I'm trying to make sense of the note Wayne gave me. I don't understand it all. There are too many code words, or someone skipped vital information. Fingers crossed that tonight's radio transmission went through since the governor must know the code. I give myself a shake and pay attention to my friends.

"That's the most personal conversation Sparks has shared since joining us," I say.

Ted looks up. "Naw, he talked lots when he first came, but what he said is true. If this wasn't wartime, and there was time for romance, you are quite a catch." He risks a glance.

"Thanks—I guess. I don't know what got into Sparks." I twist my hands.

"I do." Char looks at me like I need a dunce cap. "You're a college grad—figure it out."

"You didn't answer his question," Ted's repeats evenly. "What *do* you want next?"

I stand, and my elbows drop to my hips. Char's watching, listening.

"Seriously, Ted? You know me as well as anyone."

"Do I?" A frown crinkles his forehead. "It's a simple question. What *do* you want?"

I toss my head and stare at the sky—anywhere but at their faces. "To be the first woman to climb Mt. Everest and maybe fly a spaceship to the moon to see if it's green cheese." I huff out a breath. "Your questions make me *crazy*. I don't want anything except to finish this Challenge and help river people like others helped me. And see my folks save Grandma's farm." My breath releases on a sob.

Ted touches my shoulder. "It's all right, Annie. I didn't mean to upset you."

"You didn't," I say too loud. "I just want this war to end, so our friends come home, and life can be the way it was!" Suddenly my fist slams the rail hard. "But it won't be, will it?" I turn and flee into my library office and past the dividing curtain.

"No, not ever," Ted says after me.

Five minutes later, Char knocks on the doorframe by my curtain. "Better?"

"You can come in. I didn't feel bad."

"Oh?" She opens the curtain and stands, shifting her feet. "We're approaching St. Helens. Are you ready?"

"Sure. Just rinsing my face." I'm splotchy in my mirror. I rinse again and hang the washcloth over its rod as if this is a routine freshening up.

Her eyes flicker. "What's the plan for St. Helens? Where shall I dock?"

"Let's look." We go to the rail nearest Oregon.

Ted swabs the deck to a polish. No spilled grease is visible now. Sparks is nowhere in sight. Everything looks shipshape.

I point to fishing boats at the wharf. "Let's tie up by them."

"Will do." Char fans herself with her hat. Her eyes regain their twinkle.

An inviting backdrop of white-painted homes and larger brick and stone buildings rises from a grassy plain.

Ted inhales. "I love the smell of evergreens. Never tire of it. Is St. Helens named for the volcano?"

"Let me check." I bury my nose in a brochure. "The mountain is thirty-nine miles north, and this town has the best view of anywhere along the river."

"Nice." Sparks saunters up as if nothing has happened. "Any special history here?" he asks.

I won't look at him. "The short version is it was founded in 1840. A steamship company wanted exclusive rights to dock here, but Portland won." My finger travels the page. "St. Helens has shrunk to four thousand people now. They want a library but can't finance it."

"That seems true everywhere," Char says.

"News stories help." Sparks opens his notebook.

I close the brochure. "Once the war ends, Governor Langlie says he'll float bond issues or find local benefactors, like Andrew Carnegie."

Char snorts. "Don't hold your breath. There are few of them in these parts. Local folks earn their living logging, fishing, or farming."

"There are occasional successes like James Hill's Northern Pacific Railway and Weyerhaeuser Timber," Sparks says. "We just have to interest them."

"That's two out of how many?" Char says. "Convince me."

Ted points downstream. "Is that Columbia City?"

"Yes, but it's the western part of St. Helens now. My town hall contact has quite a few families excited to see our boat."

Char slows our engine to a rumble and chugs into an empty slip between two fishing boats.

"Ted, please drop anchor." I smile.

He lifts fingers to his forehead. "Yes, Captain."

I ignore him. "That three-story building on the town square must be the courthouse. My contact has saved us a room with shelves for five boxes of books readers can use and exchange while we're downriver."

"How long are we here for?" Sparks asks, poised over his notebook.

"Most of today. I'm checking book lists."

Char braces as *Books Afloat* snugs against the wharf with a soft thump. "Is that your town contact coming now?"

"Probably. But who on earth is getting out of that delivery van behind her?"

"Where?" Ted drops anchor and looks. As the running youth windmills downhill, he passes the woman, and his rooster red hair bounces. "Who does that look like?" Ted asks me.

"No one else runs like that."

"Harlan Boyd," we both say at once.

"He pestered me to come, but I'd said no. I told him he was in the middle of mechanic school and should finish. But the truth is, he's too immature to take seriously—especially when Smitty was coming."

"What are you doing here?" I ask.

Harlan leaps aboard. "Joining you."

Grinning ear to ear, he gives me a tight hug, though I push free. He ignores Ted.

"Hey," he sulks. "Is that any way to greet surprise guests?"

"What are you up to?"

"It's thirty miles from Vancouver to here. I met a guy who brings groceries here twice a week and hauls fish back. I caught a ride with him, so I can go with you to Kalama for Pastor Bob's service tomorrow and drive back with him and Sue after. Isn't that great?" He levels a sharp look. "Or maybe I can stay longer."

"You need to check with me." Exasperation roughens my voice.

"You knew I wanted to come, but you said you would only take Smitty. How come Char and Ted are on board?"

"Harlan, I don't have to explain. Char's my pilot. She and I could have handled *Books Afloat* alone, but when Smitty couldn't come, he and Ted wanted us to have a man on board. I'm humoring them."

"Humor me. I want to be that man. I can still come." He puffs his chest. "Who's this guy?" His finger targets Sparks.

"A reporter Governor Langlie sent."

"A reporter?" Harlan looks Sparks up and down. "I guess that makes sense."

Ted hooks his thumbs in his waistband. "What about your classes? The semester isn't done."

"Close enough. I passed basics and worked ahead. I can take time off and still catch up because I do good work." He assumes a proud stance. "Annie, I want to help for Josh's sake—after all he's done for me—and represent him here since he ... he can't." His eyes glisten.

Ted steps forward. "Josh doesn't need you to repre—"

But Char cuts Ted off. "Wait. Another mechanic? How many do we need?"

"Harlan is studying to become a mechanic," Ted answers. "He's not yet. He's a hard-working young man from Eastern Oregon."

"Eastern Washington," Harlan corrects.

"Sorry, Washington. When Harlan came to Clark College and didn't have a place to stay, Josh met him and invited him home."

"It turned out great." Harlan brightens. "Let me tell it. Josh is

like a brother, and Bob and Sue act like parents. Best place ev—"
His eyes narrow. "I'm not *that much* younger than you, Ted."

"Didn't say you were. What, four years?" Ted studies Harlan's
face. "Are we in a contest?"

"No," I answer. "You're not." My hands jam into my pockets.
"Harlan, explain about wanting to go to Kalama. We can't carry
passengers."

"I'm not a passenger. I'll work for you. I asked Smitty where
you'd be, and he said St. Helens, so I finished class and caught
the ride." His eyes shine. "If I missed you, I'd have gone back
with the grocery man, but here I am." His chest puffs again. "I
took a chance, and it worked out."

"I appreciate your willingness, but you didn't ask. Where do
you plan to sleep?"

"Sleep? Anywhere." He looks around the boat. "There must
be lots of room."

"Open deck space is bad when it rains," Char says, pointing
to gathering clouds. "It rains lots on the river, even when I wear
my hat."

"Welcome." The plump woman huffing and puffing down
the hill arrives and spreads her arms wide. "I'm Elaine Hodges,
town clerk. We're thrilled you're here."

Ted secures the gangplank.

"Come aboard." I offer a hand.

The woman steps back as if horrified. "Thanks, I can't
possibly." Pear-shaped, she resembles the colorful humming top
I owned as a girl. I wonder how she'd look spinning.

"Call me superstitious, but I don't walk narrow planks. Since
I can't come to you, please come to me."

I walk the plank and join her on the dock.

"We're so pleased with your floating library—what a *novel*
idea. My counterpart in Columbia City and I team up. She's
here twice a week."

"I need photos," Sparks says, hopping on shore.

"Gracious, I'm not ready." The woman waves for Sparks to wait while she rearranges her skirt. "My side view is my best—please use that. My husband, Al, our town maintenance man, will bring his truck to carry boxes, but I couldn't wait." She waves an acknowledging hand, ignoring Harlan's sour look. "I was so excited to meet you, I hurried down. Our reception starts at noon."

Mrs. Hodges grips my hand as Sparks snaps again.

"Your courthouse is lovely. Perhaps you'll give us a tour. I've read your Chamber of Commerce brochure."

"I wrote that." Mrs. Hodges glows. "In 1845, Captain Knighton sailed here around Cape Horn from New England to found our town. He named it Plymouth for his birthplace, but townspeople changed it to St. Helens for our amazing view." She points to the glittering cone. "Do you know how the mountain was named?"

She rattles off more facts as a man arrives in a green Ford truck, and she introduces him as her husband. Ted and Harlan bend their backs loading boxes. Sparks takes photos from every angle. Mrs. Hodges has Char and I ride uphill in the truck with her, still relating facts while the men unload boxes in a side room of the town hall's main hall.

"That's our story in a nutshell," she says. "Do you want to hear about Columbia City?"

I catch a breath. "Maybe later. Could we look around here first?"

"I'll welcome guests." She moves briskly, her skirt swirling.

Ted and Char sigh relief.

Visitors swarm, glad for books to borrow. Mrs. Hodges reserves some for library references. Appreciating such high interest, I ask her husband and Ted to drive back to our boat to bring three more boxes.

"Where's your red jacket?" Mrs. Hodges asks her husband when they return.

"Jacket? Dunno. I got hot unloading books and took it off. It's probably on the boat. I'll get it when I drive them back."

Our reception includes a cold lunch, good visiting, and lively book discussion.

"These people are interested," Char says.

"I need to know their political angles," Sparks adds.

"They're various and conflicting, wonderful but loyal Americans," I say and spin in happiness.

Mrs. Hodges clasps her hands once the flow of people slows. "Will you hear about Columbia City now?"

"Yes, please."

As she begins, Harlan surveys the room, looking at wall displays, and then disappears.

"Columbia City was founded in 1867 by the Caples brothers who came overland on a wagon pulled by oxen. They sold firewood to riverboats and built that fabulous home on the bluff. When you come next time, I'll arrange a tour. But now I must photograph your boat and crew for our archives. Please stand on our courthouse steps."

As we oblige, Harlan reappears.

"Join us," Mrs. Hodges insists.

We make our way downhill.

"Next, I'll photograph *Books Afloat*," Mrs. Hodges says. "Al, please position me at the dock, so it looks like I'm on board. Though, of course, I can't be. Such exciting times for our town."

Ted's forehead puckers. "Exciting *and* difficult."

"But good books inspire courage, don't you think?" She places a hand on her heart as if pledging allegiance. "This war is birthing heroism. Great books will result. You say you'll be back in three weeks?"

"That's our plan."

I think again of my childhood spinning top as Mrs. Hodges slows down. Her sentences are shorter now.

"We have stops scheduled all the way to the coast," I explain. "Once we know a return date, I'll contact you."

"Splendid. God bless you." She poses by *Books Afloat* with one foot near, but not on, the gangplank.

Several townspeople gather to see us depart. At four o'clock, they shout goodbye as Ted starts our engine, and we chug west.

"Thanks, everyone. That went great," I tell my crew. Gratitude fills my heart.

Char catches my eye. "At each stop, I see more how this library boat got hold of you. I'm convinced."

I grin until my cheeks hurt.

Harlan jerks his head toward the Washington side. "Do we go to Kalama now?"

"First, we'll pass Columbia City for a closeup view and check the island next to it."

Char stands at the helm, matching her nautical chart to the riverbank slipping by. "What speed do you want?"

"Your setting is fine." I jot down numbers.

Ted studies me. What was he really doing on deck last night? Checking security? Sleepwalking? Or something else?

TED NARROWED his gaze as Sparks scurried everywhere, trying to reach the top of his profession. He was certainly motivated for juicy stories. Was it his reporter role to be invasive and push limits until people cracked and spilled how they really felt? Or was Sparks genuinely nosy? If so, it didn't bode well for his time on the boat.

Anne was updating her log. What did her detailed notes mean? Was it all library business? Was she *that* interested in river history? Or was she adding the careful observations of someone doing naval surveillance and reconnaissance? Smitty would have told him if she was in the river defense network—wouldn't he?

Last night's radio message held good news. Smitty had done better on last week's cardiac step test. If that continued, he might be able to meet them later somewhere on the river.

For now, Ted would keep that quiet and only talk to God. But how could he keep Annie safe if he didn't know what she was up to? He had plenty of questions for Smitty the next time they connected. God grant them clear radio signal again soon. They had bad static last night. More than solar flares should account for. Almost like an enemy was jamming radio signals.

Lord, keeping Annie safe isn't easy. Help us both. Make her see I'm the man she needs. Inside, something rankled. *How can I convince her if I can't convince myself? Help me be the man she needs ...*

10

Saturday, June 20, 1942
St. Helens, Oregon, River Mile 84

With the enthusiasm of a tour guide, I wave toward Columbia City, rising from the river with dark green evergreens climbing the hill and a sparkling stream tumbling down.

"This brochure says," I tell my crew, "'Here, the Columbia is a mile wide. Fir-clad slopes form the town's backdrop. In good weather, from north to south, the five highest Cascade peaks are visible—Mt. Rainier, St. Helens, Adams, Hood, and Jefferson.'"

I lower the brochure. "Now that I know the mountains are named for real people, I'll research more."

"That's the most amazing view ever." Char's camera snaps. "Wait until J.P. sees these. He'll be impressed."

Sparks clicks from all angles. His film bag weighs a ton. "I have trophy shots from the crow's nest—all prizewinners," he boasts. "Once they're printed, I'll share copies."

Harlan fidgets with his jackknife, flicking its blades open and shut, open and shut, his eyes clouded. What is his problem?

I keep reading. "We're near Deer Island, named by Lewis and Clark for good hunts in 1805 and 1806. It's uninhabited now except for the small town with that name on Oregon's side. Past that are Goat Island and Coon Island."

"Let me guess." Ted grins. "All named for animals."

"Bingo," I say. "Give that man a box of Cracker Jacks."

"I wish I'd brought one," Harlan drips sarcasm. "Then we'd see what he'd do with the prize ring inside." He smirks and snaps his jackknife shut before stomping away.

"What's that about?" Sparks asks.

I shrug. "Who knows. I think he wants to be a hero, but I don't need heroes—just a reliable crew."

Harlan worries me. He's not doing well with Josh gone. He's hurting, but I don't know how to help. Pastor Bob reaches him well most days. I'm glad we'll meet Bob and Sue in Kalama.

Moments later, I have the eerie sensation we're being watched by someone or something on the island we're passing. The shore appears empty, yet I spot what looks like thin smoke curls rising. Maybe the island is occasionally used by hunters or fishermen. I strain my eyes to look again. The screened evergreen branches look undisturbed. No boat skid marks or footprints disturb the narrow sandy beach, the only possible place a boat can pull ashore.

Even so, the back of my neck prickles. Something moves, and I peer more closely to confirm what I see. A square white cloth attached to a pole flutters as it's waved by a man who looks like a blend of Rumpelstiltskin and Ichabod Crane.

"Ahoy, come ashore," the wizened gnome calls once he has my attention. A curly white beard covers his lower face below intense black button eyes. "C'mon in. It's safe to land." He gestures. "I'll extend my gangplank so you can put ashore."

I can't risk running aground. "What do you need? Can you come to us?" I check my watch. I have a schedule to keep and a goal to accomplish.

He doesn't appear hurt. He can leave this island by whatever means he came. Or swim the shallow channel to Oregon.

Char glances at me for instruction.

I hesitate, but curiosity gets the best of me. "Take us in."

She steers toward the man, who pushes aside what looked like a mossy log blocking entry to the beach. We now see that thin veneer covers the log as the top slice slides along a groove. He withdraws a lightweight ladder hidden inside and extends that, attached to the log's massive butt end, to cross the water and overlatch our prow.

"What on earth?" Ted's nostrils flare.

"When did you do all this?" I ask. "Are you shipwrecked? Left by fishermen?" But as I ask, I realize his preparations show invested time and ingenuity. This is no short-term event.

"I'm here a purpose for years. Sometimes here, sometimes there, you never know where, like the wind blows where it wants. I saw you go to St. Helens. Saw you come back, decided to know you."

"Is it our library you're interested in?"

"So that *is* what you are—like your book flag. All the better." He rubs his hands together.

His patched shirt is crisscrossed pieces of sewn leather under forest green suspenders. The garment has been mended so many times, it's hard to name its original colors—as if he's sorted through piles of cast-off clothes at a thrift store and blended the best into camouflage.

"I'm John."

"John who?"

"Hofer, if it matters. Don't know your name but like your frame and the cut of your jib." He cackles. "Good seaman's talk — *like your frame, the cut of your jib.* I read Stevenson's *Treasure Island,* one of the finest books a boy can read." He squints. "Do you carry that?"

"Of course."

"Good." He smiles and strokes his beard. "Nice boat. Who's in charge?" He glances at Char, Ted, Sparks, Harlan, and returns to me. He stabs the air. "What's your name, since you're Captain?"

I gulp. "Mettles, Anne Mettles. But how do you know?"

"I just do." He reels back. "Mettles. That's a strong handle. I need library smarts, plus a ride to Washington's side. I'm out of ammunition and tired of eating fish. Deer and rabbit taste better, though I hate killing, so often set snares to be merciful. Plus, I need war news—do you have any?"

He thrusts his face so close I smell wild garlic. His eyes probe with a wild light as bright as the new foot X-ray machine in our Buster Brown shoe store.

"I think you do. Come ashore and see my home."

I hesitate.

He waves us forward. "C'mon. I don't bite. I ate already. A man gets lonesome for his own kind. Not much to see or do here except sleep, dream, and watch the river. Come ashore. It's safe." His extended hand appears clean though callused, and his nails are broken.

I accept his hand and cross the plank to the beach, while behind me, Ted makes warning sounds in his throat.

"I'm coming, too," he says.

The small man sighs. "Suit yourself. There's not room for many. You can take turns. I need books to remind me of the right combinations for bullets. If you'll bring sulfur and saltpeter, I'll pay you well to save me going to town—my least favorite place on earth."

Ted blinks. "You have money for that?"

"Sure do, salted away, or I wouldn't waste my breath asking. I won't say where, just that I have plenty." His smile shows neatly capped teeth. He's been to civilization somewhere long enough for dental care. He laughs and jingles coins in his pocket, removing a handful. As he lifts one, framing it in his fingers, we see shiny silver dollars. Also, that his right hand has a thumb but only three fingers. His index trigger finger is missing.

Ted nods, staring at the man's hand.

John follows our gaze. "It's a sad story how I lost that. Took a rifle into the woods on Ma's home place the year our country entered Europe's Great War—came back minus a trigger finger, an unfortunate accident that keeps me from being drafted. Strange how things happen if you have relatives in the Old Country." He grins.

And I place his strong accent. His *Ws* are closer to *Vs*, saying, 'Vent into de voods and Europe's Great Var.'

"Are you American?" I ask.

He draws himself to full height, which barely tops me. "I surely am, as much as anyone in these parts. As American as baseball and apple pie. Delivered by a doctor in Eastern Washington, though Ma and her kin hailed from Germany. We got stirred into America's Melting Pot and added good flavor."

"When did they immigrate?"

"When the Kaiser's Republic collapsed, and things went nuts. His Weimar money made cheap wallpaper but couldn't buy food." He lays a finger aside his nose and winks. "I read history and know history repeats itself. But a man can't enter war and risk fighting his own cousins or uncles by birth, can he?"

I shudder. "Probably not. That *would* be awful." Like America's Civil War that sometimes pitted brother against brother, this war in Europe also at times assigns men to opposite sides by accidents of birth or land boundaries— delivering death across invisible lines.

"Now that you mention it, my Grandma's sister, Aunt Pearl, mentioned their folks joining the Melting Pot in the 1880s," I tell him. "I've seen spidery handwriting in our family's old German Bible. None of us speak German, but we have relatives overseas."

"Ja, it's that way for many. But let me be hospitable." He prances three steps left, showing remarkable agility for a man of uncertain age. He lifts the lid of what looks like a giant cedar stump, except it's hollow. From inside, he hauls up a long rope, hand over hand, and hoists out a pitcher of cool water. He pours its clear contents into blue enamel cups. "Come, drink water as sweet and fresh as heaven itself."

"As sweet as heaven?" Char looks doubtful.

"Yes, ma'am. *Taste and see*, like the Good Book says. Heaven's where it comes from—fresh rainwater He provides."

I sip and tilt my head to drink deeper. "This *is* delicious."

Ted drains his cup, too, smacking his lips.

Sparks leans over the rail, eager to see what's happening, but hesitates. The little man sees him and laughs.

Meanwhile, I take in everything. There's so much more than I noticed at first. When I stand near the little man, instead of him smelling unwashed or rancid, he smells like cool, clean pine needles. I inhale fresh evergreen forests on sunny days.

"What's that marvelous aroma?" I ask.

"Me." He grins. "I chew spruce gum and pine needles for mouth freshener." He offers a handful from his pocket. "Take some."

I accept several and chew. "These are good. You live on this island?"

"Sometimes—not always. I don't announce my whereabouts, but think I trust you. A man gets lonely for folks, if ya know what I mean. I have reasons to be here. Are you hungry?" He scrambles sidewise like a crab scuttling across a beach. "I have good food, better than most."

"You do?" I step back. "Thanks, but we ate a big lunch in St. Helens."

He peers intently. "Town food's not as good as mine. Don't be shy. You'll be hungry once you taste this." He takes another step and from behind the next tree produces a cunningly fashioned wooden box. He lifts its tight-fitting lid, and the aroma of smoked salmon tantalizes our nostrils.

"Take, eat, enjoy. I smoked it myself and know what I'm doing."

I break off a morsel. The first flake on my tongue proves this is the best I've ever tried—better than feasts at the Indian reservation on this river.

"You know what you're doing, John."

"Johnny to you, Captain. Take more. There's plenty." He breaks off a generous portion and wraps it in green ferns.

"Thanks. This is wonderful. But if you live here, where do you get supplies—salt, sugar, matches—things like that?"

His eyes narrow. "That can be a problem. I won't tell you everything, but I usually have ways. Now about your books on war and ammo."

"I have them." I look around. "Do you have a place to keep books safe and dry?"

His shoulders stiffen. "Of course. My home is dry and snug, I guarantee. I don't look soggy and dingy, do I?" He whirls in a circle.

"N-no." I choke on my last bite of fish. "No offense. I found a bone."

"You didn't." He stretches taller. "I pulled them all out. You're just embarrassed and don't know what to think of me, but you'll find I'm a friend. Come inside, but step where I show you, nowhere else, or you'll set off my man traps for the uninvited."

Ted freezes—then follows, carefully stepping exactly where Johnny leads around ferns and rocks, dodging low branches, and finally stops beside the biggest cedar tree. Char joins us. From the boat, Harlan appears to be deciding whether to come ashore or not. Sparks is taking long-distance photos.

"*Books Afloat* is safe," Char says. "Thought I'd see what you're up to."

The little man's fingers reach inside a narrow groove in the tree's fissured bark to swing open a door. "Here's my berth. Don't need more. Snug as a bug." Four small steps descend into the tree's heart. Four more lead upward to a cozy sitting and cooking area with a sleeping loft higher still.

Ted gapes. "You made this? I'd like to learn your skills."

The man rears back. "That might happen, young man. But then again, it might not—depends on why you want to know."

Shifting from foot to foot, he says, "Sit yourselves down and give me news. Has that mad German dug a hole deep enough to pull the lid in on himself and his Socialist party yet? He'll pull his nation and the whole world through a knothole backwards and make us spout German if we let him." Johnny bares his teeth like a dog guarding a bone.

"Last winter, Hitler suffered terrible losses at Stalingrad," Ted's voice deepens. "That huge setback slowed but hasn't completely stopped him."

"Not much does." John pops more pine needles into his mouth. "The durn fool won't listen to reason. What's the world coming to?"

I bite my lip, glancing at Char and then Ted. Does this man fit the category my dad calls 'nutty as a fruitcake and twice as crummy'? Or brilliant and eccentric?

"Hitler made impressive gains." Ted isn't through. "But our Allied forces are ahead of him now. He's digging a deep hole for himself, so you're right to be concerned for any family you have there. The worst part is how he punishes Germans who aren't Nazis."

"I know, including my relatives, if he catches them." He grinds his teeth. "I fear that. Yes, I do. He needs a dose of his own medicine. Terrible days ahead. But our troops are a match for him, aren't they?" His eyes beg for agreement.

"We believe so, sir." Char stands at attention. "My hubby's in the Asiatic Pacific doing all he can, just like we are here."

"Good." The man squints again. "Of course, you are.

Sometimes I wonder how far this war will advance—maybe even to our shores. But if that happens, I'm ready." He shakes a fist. "They'd better watch out, or I'll forget I'm German. I'm not afraid of them or those empire-building Japs. I've heard horror stories. They don't act human."

His gaze pierces me. "Captain? In case those monsters show up, pay attention. I'll teach you tricks, so keep your eyes peeled." He taps the side of his nose and winks knowingly. "And camouflage your boat."

"Camouflage?" I wince. "But we're a public library. People need to recognize us."

"All the same, for days ahead, you'd best listen."

I shudder. "We'll discuss security later. Meanwhile, here's what I can offer. Besides ammunition data, I have recent newspapers and magazines covering the war."

"Ja, I want those." He prances several steps, showing amazing agility.

I'm impressed with his exquisitely stitched leather boots. I've never seen a leprechaun, but he might qualify. "Your boots are beautiful." I finger the soft leather. "But books are my reason for being here."

He stops. "Books are why I flagged you down. Take me to your boat, so I can read." He rubs his hands together again and fastens his door shut tight, so it again looks like a huge untouched cedar tree.

"If you need books I don't have," I say, "I'll request them. Olympia's doing all they can to help us."

"That's good." He strokes his chin. "Since you're few people, I wasn't afeared."

"What if we're armed?" Ted asks.

"You're not." He whips around. "I'd know, and I don't see bulges. Anyway, I would disarm you with special gadgets."

"Special?" My stomach tumbles.

"That's right." His eyes glitter. "Where's your homeport?"

"Vancouver. That's painted on our bow."

"Just checking. Your destination?"

I count off on my fingers: "Astoria, Ilwaco, the Pacific, and most spots in between." I explain the Governor's Challenge.

"That's good, but means you're in a hurry. When you come other times, approach when daylight's fading with just enough light left to barely see. Drop anchor, and I'll come to you in my canvas dinghy." His face shifts from mysterious to begging. "I'm desperate. My usual contact can't come this month."

I wonder if that could possibly be Smitty.

"No problem, Johnny." Ted claps his shoulder. "I didn't know what to think of you at first, but I like the cut of your jib, too."

"You'll be gladder than you know." He laughs at some riddle only he knows. "You don't read me clear because of the flawed human race—that's why. But it's necessary. When you come again, I'll flash my square white cloth if I'm ready. If you don't see it, keep going."

I study his shore again as we board *Books Afloat*. Seeing Johnny, Sparks looks like a starving man spotting food, except Harlan blocks his way. Sparks starts to climb around a metal scaffold to pass Harlan but gives up, then stands and watches.

"Johnny, you're amazing," I say as we leave his world.

His face brightens. "I have survival skills for everything. I'll teach ya. Even catch bugs on the fly." A mosquito darts near. "I catch 'em by knowing where they'll be before they get there. Like so." He swoops and traps one and also captures a dragonfly in midflight. "It's like flying airplanes using earth's telemetry."

"Earth's what?" My voice hikes. "Are you a pilot?"

"Not officially." He hiccups. "Might as well be. Let's say I haven't always lived here and have had fascinating experiences many places." He taps his forehead. "I'm here for a reason I can't explain. Now, find me the proportions of sulfur and saltpeter. And don't forget, I'll pay well for what you bring when my flag's flying."

His hands slide along our ship's rail. "'Cause I can't go to town in broad daylight, can I? That's my least favorite place anywhere except when I absolutely have to go, like today."

"Why today?" I check the current.

Ted starts our engine. Char's at the wheel, and Sparks tucks himself behind the galley stairs, watching and writing. Harlan stares.

"Who's that?" Johnny startles, seeing him.

"A friend riding to Kalama."

"That's where I'm heading," Johnny says. "Best town for river folk. Besides needing supplies, I had a disturbing dream. Pastor's coming, so I need to see him. Later, if you take me downstream a ways and drop me by my other home, I'll pay for that, too." He jingles the silver in his pocket again.

"Pastor Bob Vengeance?

"That's right."

"He's holding church in Kalama tomorrow. Do you know him?"

"Sure do. Best pastor on the Columbia."

My eyes widen. "How do you know he's coming?"

He taps his forehead again. "Told you, I just know. Maybe birds tell me— Just get me there. Here's money."

"You don't need to pay. We can't officially take passengers."

"Then take me unofficially but keep this. Running boats costs money. Call it a donation, since it's wonderful you're floating a library. Besides, I have plenty." He tumbles coins into my hand. "Now, let's go."

11

Saturday, June 20, 1942
Deer Island, Oregon, River Mile 83, and west

As we cast off from Johnny's beach, I tell Char, "Let's sail around Deer Island and look around before we cross, but not close enough to run aground."

"Like Hayden," she says matter-of-factly.

I wince.

"Glad to see her from the water myself," Johnny says, standing on tiptoe. "Don't get that chance to when I come by night. You can't see my place from the water, can you, Captain?"

"Nope, no trace."

He slaps his thigh. "I'll show you the only shallow spot, so you'll be fine."

After I'm sure there are no surprises between here and Washington's side, I relax. "Okay, Char. Please, take her across."

"Kalama?"

"Woodland first, since we didn't stop there after Ridgefield yesterday. It made sense to cross to St. Helens after to avoid backtracking. Woodland's small. Not many people, but I promised we'd come."

"Of course, you did." Char flashes a grin. "Mile 82, Port of Woodland, coming up." She turns the helm, and the blue river unfurls behind us.

As we leave his island, Johnny tours our boat, his pixie face shining. Sparks watches Johnny write his name in elegant script on a library card. He lists *Columbia River* as his address and pushes his feet under a low child's library table where he fits fine.

Johnny inhales a deep breath. "I love books and their good smell. Forget I'm here. I'll stay put until Woodland."

My eyes meet Ted's. "We won't forget," I say.

The next time I check on Johnny, he's thumbed through many books and stuck slips of paper between pages.

"Thankee. I found what I need." He scoots his chair back. "This is wonderful. It fills up my people and idea tank." He winks but regards Sparks as if he's a fly that needs a flyswatter.

This is how I want my library to serve river residents, although I didn't picture a client this colorful.

Char whispers, "J.P. met him once. Says he's brilliant and harmless."

"And eccentric and fascinating." My brain cells ping.

"It's dangerous to trust people you don't know and take them on board," Harlan mutters.

"I think we're fine, and Woodland isn't far." I start a shopping list. What does Johnny want besides sulfur and saltpeter? Maybe a few inexpensive treats for this wizened man? Maple sugar, dried apples, sulfur matches? What does he use to start fires? Does he have plastic sheets for rainproofing? Or weave cedar foliage together to shed water?

He belongs in a book. I chew my pencil, less tasty than Johnny's pine needles. Maybe I'll write the book—*Robinson Crusoe of the Columbia*.

Inhaling river scent, I lift my face. Today is good. We're on track. Maybe I'll write more than one book.

"If I had talent," I fling out an arm, "I'd paint this."

"You should try," Ted encourages.

"Ee-oouu, give it up, Ted." Harlan's face twists. "You're fattening her for the kill."

"What does that mean?" Ted goes slack-jawed.

"Quit chasing her. We all see what you're up to. I think about Josh and hurt for him, since you don't."

Ted's hands double. "Are you nuts? We all hurt for him and miss him like crazy."

"Then act like it!" Harlan's voice shrills.

I step between them. "Harlan, stop."

"It's the truth." He hunches into a fighting stance.

Sparks looks amused.

"Calm down." Char slips her arm through Harlan's. "We're a team with important jobs."

"I'm not part of your team," Harlan whimpers. "That's the problem."

"Dry up right now." Char surveys us all, even Johnny. "We can't waste time on foolishness."

Harlan sulks.

"I like women with grit." Johnny beams. "Maybe you should be in the White House."

"Those two women have it in spades." Ted salutes Char and me.

Char laughs. "That won't happen, but we'll soon reach Woodland. Annie, what's there?"

"Like Ridgefield, farmers were offered land, hoping they'd clear it and stay—not log off hillsides and leave."

"That's America's pioneering way," Johnny says. "Europe's not that way."

I want to know Johnny's story. I've updated my official log and jotted notes about him in my unofficial record. The first has nautical reports for river and Coast Guard authorities. The second has stories I'll share with Smitty and maybe Governor Langlie.

"And next Kalama. How big is it?" Sparks grips his note pad.

"Only a thousand, but an important port. It's an Indian name. The first people were the Cowlitz tribe with the same name as its river, except it's named for John Kalama, a Hawaiian who came on a Hudson's Bay ship a century ago. He was a king back home, avoiding a local war. That's when American ships sailed around Cape Horn and stopped in Hawaii for fresh fruit and water. Many Hawaiians came here."

"Really? And shaped history." Sparks' eyes brighten.

"After 1870, Kalama was the end of the line for Northern Pacific. They built this town with the motto, 'Where Rail Meets Sail.'"

"Catchy," Sparks says.

Harlan makes a rude sound. "Why is Sparks here?"

"To help with fundraising so I can do this. Anyway, they brought Chinese laborers from San Francisco and built a ferry to Goble, where we go next. That was the only way trains could cross the Columbia until the bridge got built that we'll see downstream."

Johnny cackles. "Once railroad headquarters moved to Tacoma, the town shrank as fast as a wool sweater hitting boiling water. I like it small. I know most oldtimers."

"I'll bet." I have a thousand questions I'd like answered.

"Which books do you need here?" Ted asks.

"Like at St. Helens, except more on logging and farming instead of fishing. It's close to Mt. St. Helens, so readers want to know about volcanoes and earthquakes."

"Fine." He pushes up his khaki shirt sleeves.

I'm surprised again by his well-muscled arms.

"Show me which boxes, and I'm your man."

"Sure, you are," Harlan interrupts. "Anne, you know I want to help, too."

I sigh. "Really? I appreciate your willingness, but there's no need for a simple task to get complicated. It would take longer to explain than to have Ted do the job. He knows my system."

"I'll bet." Harlan pouts.

Char asks, "Are there Chinese residents in Kalama?"

"I'm not sure. Do you crave Chinese food?"

"No. Just wonder if Japanese folks live there, too. We didn't have many back home, but native-born Japanese got rounded up and shipped to camps." Her eyes cloud. "Don't get me wrong. I know it's risky in wartime to have foreigners with sympathies. The government can't watch everyone."

"That happened to our high school friend, Fred Ono," I tell Char. "His folks were from Japan, but he was born here. You never met nicer people."

"His parents truck gardened," Ted adds. "They worked so hard, their fields produced like a dream, but they got sent away after Roosevelt's executive order." He slumps. "No one works their fields now. I don't know what will happen."

"Maybe I'll write about internment," Sparks says. "Except, I'm not sure papers will publish it."

"Our government is in a hard place," Ted says. "If only solving things were as simple as splicing rope." He's fixing a broken place by braiding new strong cord into the separated fibers. "After Japan killed thousands at Pearl Harbor, plus attacked Alaska's Aleutians, the administration must take steps to protect our mainland."

"What could happen?" Sparks shrugs. "America is safe. Building big camps is overkill."

I shake my head. "I wouldn't want the president's job, Constant headaches."

We're approaching Woodland. It's quiet as Ted finishes his rope and coils it.

"What's your friend's name?" Sparks asks.

"Fred Ono."

"How do you spell it?"

"Just O-N-O."

"I'll try to look him up if I write an article."

"Please do. I'd like him to know we're thinking about him."

Ted adds a grateful look.

Sparks turns to Char. "They sent Japanese folks away from your area?"

"We didn't have many, but they went to Idaho." She swallows hard. "I don't think they would have betrayed us, but it's hard to know who to trust these days with men like Josh and J.P. faraway risking their lives every minute."

Harlan stares. "It's good to know someone remembers."

"Remembers?" I stare. "It hurts every minute, and we pray every day."

"You and Ted are softies," Harlan grumbles. "Feeling sorry for slanty-eyed Japs when locking them up is the smart thing."

I huff a breath. "Harlan Boyd, quit."

"I won't. Trains haul them past my grandma's place to camps, and I say good riddance. Roosevelt is a strong leader. They're enemies. Do you want another Pearl Harbor? Do you want Japan to win? You know Josh isn't coming back, don't you?"

"I know no such thing. How dare you!" I slap his face so hard it leaves an imprint.

He cups his cheek. "Ow. Why did you do that?"

"Figure it out. If you don't know my values by now, you don't belong on this boat."

"I thought I did, but maybe not. Josh said you were a spitfire."

"Well, he's right. And patriotic, but all-American citizens deserve dignity and respect."

He raises a hand. "Get off your soapbox."

"Nope. Smarten up, or you're leaving us in Woodland."

"There's nothing there. Or you'd throw me in the river? That's choice." His cheek is still red from my slap. "I ride back with Bob and Sue tomorrow, remember?"

"Do you two need a referee?" Char calls.

"No." I prop my chin on my fist. "It's wartime. We should pull together."

"Don't bother. We'll never agree." Harlan's voice drips disgust. "I'm going below to find something to eat." And he stomps to the galley.

"What's happened to him? Sure, he had a sad childhood, but he shouldn't act this bad. He does well with Bob and Sue."

"Besides missing Josh, I think I know," Ted says.

"What?"

"Not worth discussing." Ted shakes his head. "Just pray for him."

Char calls, "Do we follow the main channel? Or the smaller one on the right?"

I whip to attention. "The smaller channel, please. The teacher described a long dock."

Compared to other stops, this small settlement on wooded hills along Washington's shore looks easy. We pass the town to follow the smaller channel to open farmland. We see more work-worn older folks line up than children. *Books Afloat* rests perfectly against a long dock, and Ted ties off, getting splashed by low waves in the process

"It's a fine thing you're doing," a grizzled gray-haired man in overalls says as he steps on board. His face is tanned leather. "I can't get to big towns these days, and few of us have books besides Bibles. Even those get worn getting passed around so much. We're glad you're here. Rainy nights are long."

I turn to introduce Johnny Hofer, but he's nowhere in sight.

Ted steps forward and gives the man his hand. "I'm Ted Vincent. Welcome to *Books Afloat*. Are you from around here?"

"I'm Joe Worth, logging close by to carve a farm out of the woods." He points west and spits sunflower seed hulls over the boat rail before wiping his mouth clean. "Don't have much of a farm to show yet. I'm grubbing out stumps and roots, but it's good soil. It grew these strawberries for ya." He opens a brown bag and displays large ripe red strawberries that smell so sweet they attract a buzzing bee.

I chase it away. "They're beautiful. Thank you."

"It's the least I can do. A few more years and I'll have a showplace. It's good for a man to own land. It helps avoid wars."

"Maybe that's what this war's mostly about." Ted rubs his chin. "Wanting more land."

"Yep." The man shifts his feet, favoring one leg.

"I hope to own land when I have a family," Ted says.

I give a questioning look. I've never heard Ted mention owning land—or having a family. Something's shifting.

I eat a strawberry. "Delicious! Char? Ted? Try these." I hold them out.

"Yum." Ted makes short work of his. "This is better than the ones Josh and I picked as kids, and those were Birdseye's best."

"Thanks." Joe ducks his head and enters the library. After choosing two books on farm production, he signs a membership card, a smile creasing his face. "Do you have anything on the Indian attack here last century?"

I tilt my head. "I'm not sure. Tell me more."

"Warriors from the Yakima tribe came to burn our settlers out. But a Cowlitz native told residents to skedaddle across to Oregon until the Yakimas went home. There's a monument in our town park thanking Indian Zack."

"I hadn't heard that, but that's what I love about libraries. I learn so much getting books for other people. I'll find something and bring it next time."

"Fire!" a voice bellows. Harlan shoots up from the engine room, eyes wild in a soot-streaked face, holding two red flaming rags. "Quick. Water. I'm burning." He throws one rag over the rail as smoldering tongues of fire consume the cloth he still holds. "Help! I found this just in time."

"Drop it," Ted yells. "For goodness sake, Harlan, toss it."

Char lunges, but Harlan is faster, tossing the disintegrating fiery cloth into the river and stuffing his blistered fingertips into his mouth.

"Ow, it hurts! I smelled smoke and found this. A few minutes more, and I hate to think. But I saved you." He shakes his head, sorrow on his face. "You could have lost everything."

Ted stammers. "I was just down there, and everything was fine." He races to the engine room with Char close behind. When they return, Ted's as white as a sheet. "I don't know what happened. We found burnt rag bits—but no visible cause."

"It's suspicious." Char looks angry. "I'd checked, too, and I'm impressed with how Ted keeps things. He's not careless."

Harlan's eyes narrow. "He was this time. Leaving oily rags near the engine? Stupid."

"I didn't have oily rags. We left Vancouver so fast I didn't have any rags. I planned to get some in Kalama. Where did these come from? Things were shipshape in St. Helens."

"You *thought* they were shipshape. You were wrong." Harlan stuffs his fingers back in his mouth.

My voice breaks. "Harlan, no matter how this happened, thank you. I can't imagine the result if you hadn't found this when you did."

"It's a good thing," he thumps his chest, "or your trip would have ended. I should have been your man on board from the beginning."

Ted opens his mouth but shuts it, looking like a fish jerked from water and gasping for air.

This is another time I wish Sparks wouldn't take photos, but I'll get the negatives. "Harlan, whatever the cause, you were here when it mattered, and I'm grateful. I'm sorry your fingers are burned. We have first-aid cream somewhere."

Char grabs it and hands it to me. I spread ointment on Harlan's fingertips while he resembles the Cheshire cat illustration in *Alice in Wonderland*. Ted and Char exchange glances.

"Harlan," she says, "it's odd you found the problem so fast."

He shrugs. "Lucky, I guess."

Ted sniffs. "What are these splashes on your clothes? Smells like gasoline."

"Water." Harlan rubs the spots. "I got splashed fighting the blaze."

"How? There's no water down there. I planned to fill a barrel tonight. If that's gasoline on your shirt, you're lucky you didn't become a human torch. And how did your fingers blister?"

Harlan jerks his hand back. "I got too close—had to move fast. I know how much this trip matters to Annie, so I took a risk." He stares meaningfully at me. "It could have ended *Books Afloat*."

Ted doesn't stop. "I still want to know—"

"What? I put out the fire."

I touch Ted's arm. "Leave it—but I do wonder ..." My forehead scrunches. "Is there any chance the burned rags are from your red sweatshirt?"

"My?" Ted lurches. "I don't see how. I took it to my room. It should be there." He rushes down and comes back, looking sick. "I don't know what to say. I can't find my sweatshirt. It was under my pillow, but now it's not."

"Even if we can't find where the rags came from, Harlan's a hero," I insist.

Ted droops. "You're right. Sailors say, 'If you're in a boat, you're more afraid of fire than water.'"

"True." I lift my hands in surrender. "With things like this happening, who knows what could be next? As soon as we finish at Woodland, I want to head to Kalama. I have friends there. This close call shows we need support—and the sooner, the better." I fight tears.

As the last stragglers leave, Ted pulls up anchor

Char opens up the engine. "Next stop Kalama."

12

Saturday, June 20, 1942
Kalama, Washington, River Mile 73

R ose and blue sunset colors deepen, reflecting from water
to clouds as the sun sinks behind western bluffs and
fades to night. Wind ruffles the dark water making it tricky to
approach Kalama.

I peer into the failing light. "What do you think, Char?"

"I wish I'd bought those newfangled bifocals my eye doctor
prescribed." Her jaw clenches. "But I'll manage."

I chuckle. "I radioed ahead to Jeb and Janey Jarvis, the people
I leased *Books Afloat* from. They'll try to meet us." I lean forward,
shading my eyes as two figures approach the wharf carrying
bobbing lights. "That may be them now."

"Welcome," Jeb calls over the water. "We're happy to see you,
Annie, and we brought lanterns to help you land."

"Thank you."

We tie up and scramble ashore, where Janey and I fall into
each other's arms. Pastor Bob introduced us because of their
need to lease their boat and leave the river. We connected well.

I squeeze her again. "I'm glad to see you, too, Janey!"

"We couldn't wait." She peers at the boat. "Do you still have my red geraniums in window boxes?"

"Yes. In the morning, come and see. Church ladies added white geraniums and blue lobelia, so now we're patriotic—red, white, and blue."

"Good." She clasps her hands.

"*Books Afloat* is a great name," Jeb adds, voice heavy. "She needed a new name after our troubles."

"How are you," I rest my hand on his arm. "I've been concerned."

"Doing well. We don't miss the boat." He hugs Janey. "It helps to be off the water, so we don't relive Davey's death. But life goes on, like that powerful river flowing by." He points to the Columbia. "If your library gets approved, maybe the boat can work for you permanently."

"I'm willing. We'll wait and see."

"How do any parents survive losing a child?" Janey swipes at her eyes.

I shake my head. "I can't imagine. I know it helps when Bob and Sue come."

Janey nods. "They keep us sane." She pulls a hankie from her dress. "They're wonderful, although they have so much heartache themselves."

"There's still no word about Josh," I say, and then I notice Ted, Char, Harlan, and Johnny hanging back. "Please meet my crew. You may know Char Young, J.P. Young's wife?"

Jeb shakes hands. "We met him at the bridge opening, but Char wasn't with him."

"Our Evie was sick, so I couldn't go." She gives Janey a hug. "It's a privilege. I hope J.P.'s with me next time."

"So do we."

"This is Ted, best mechanic on the river."

"That's high praise," Jeb says, "because we have good ones."

Ted flushes.

"I'll ask for tips, since I pull wrenches here." Jeb throws an arm around Johnny's thin shoulders. "Of course, we know Johnny."

Johnny flames lobster red. *How do you know him?* I'm burning to ask Jeb. Harlan hangs back, sulking. I don't see Sparks. The rest of us exchange greetings.

"Let's head to the house before the mosquitoes see there's fresh meat." Jeb swats bugs and leads the way. "We have room for all of you since Uncle Ed's in Tacoma on business, plus the apartment above the store is empty—lots of room."

I pause. "Thanks, but for security, I'll sleep on the boat tonight."

"Me, too," Char says.

"I prefer boats," Johnny says. "Might spend more time in that library."

"I'll be on board," Ted adds, "but give Harlan and Sparks real beds. We're short of space."

Sparks arrives smiling, camera bag in hand. "Did I hear my name? Pleased to meet you."

Harlan emerges from the shadows, "I'd rather stay—"

"No problem," Jeb grips his hand. "We have spots for both of you—make you right at home. Johnny, we don't see you enough. Sleep on the boat if you must—with strange events along the coast, we understand the need for security—but save us visiting time.

Ted quirks an eyebrow. "Strange events?"

"We'll talk later. Come in for dessert. Janey made blackberry cobbler."

Char peels off her Sou'wester. "Are you kidding? I'm drooling already. Blackberries do poorly at the coast."

As we near the house, the porchlight shines on yellow shingles with white trim. The front door swings open, and two more beloved people jump out.

"Surprise!" Bob and Sue's voices soar like happy birds as they rush forward to pull us into hugs.

"We couldn't wait until tomorrow to hear how you're doing. Get over here," Bob commands Ted. "We missed you so much, I'm going to wrap you up." And he does.

Sue folds Char in a hug. "You're such a blessing. We didn't get time with you in Vancouver. Thanks for helping Annie."

"I'm loving it." Char beams. "And keeps me busy with J.P. gone."

"Harlan, don't hang back." Sue and Bob surround him with a three-way hug. "It's only been a day, but we miss you, too." They step back. "You look rough. What's going on?"

"Just tired." He stomps away.

"How many do you expect for church tomorrow?" I ask, once we're inside.

"A full house," Jeb answers. "There are small churches along the river, but there's high interest in something new. Hard times make people want to dig deep and get together."

Bob flexes an arm. "Jeb and I rearranged the store and set up plenty of benches."

"I love your meetings," Janey says. "Having good people around eases our pain." She and Jeb lock eyes as she begins spooning up cobbler.

"I'll help, Janey." Sue jumps up. "Tomorrow after church, we'll have potluck and a river folk gathering—visiting, singing, maybe a skit. There's no group like river folk."

"That's true. I want to bring that atmosphere to our church in Vancouver," Bob says.

Johnny receives his cobbler and dips and smacks until his bowl is clean. Soon, he stands and stretches. "Time for bed. I need beauty sleep." He sticks out his hand. "Harlan? Sparks? Sleep well."

Harlan ignores Johnny and pushes past him to the stairs.

Sparks yawns. "I'll enjoy a good mattress."

Johnny pulls me aside on his way to the door, eyebrows beetled. "Keep a close watch on that young boy—something's cockeyed. Check everyone these days—even me."

"It's a shame." I bite my lip. "Harlan's been fine at Bob and Sue's. But today, I don't know if he was the hero or the cause of our fire."

"Me neither. Take care."

THE NEXT MORNING, Pastor Bob greets each arrival at church. "Good to see you, Wayne. It's been a while, Joe. How's the highway?"

"Tolerable, Pastor. Faster than the river. A few of us rode together to save gas."

"Smart." Bob taps his forehead. "And good fellowship."

I recognize Miss Clark and several students and parents from Ridgefield but not the girl with the bunny. I also spot new people that pique my interest. If I can sign them as library members, maybe I can learn where their loyalties lie.

Bob stands behind a varnished table and props up his Bible. "Did you know last Sunday, June 14th, was National Flag Day? President Wilson signed that into law, but people are just now seriously observing it."

"I fly mine high every day," Joe Worth says.

"These are important days for our Stars and Stripes to fly. Who knows what today is?"

A child reads the wall calendar. "June 21st."

Laughter ripples. "Father's Day," a boy squeaks.

"Right. How many men here are fathers?" Many hands rise. "Good. Quite a number. Next to marriage, being a dad is my best way to learn about God. He loves us perfectly."

Bob presents the Prodigal Son story, bringing the passage to life, making me miss my dad and Granddad even more. His loss makes my gut ache. I hate how I failed when he asked me to keep him awake.

Failure tastes bitter. I can't be counted on when it matters and can't ever repay that debt. *Lord. Don't let me ever fail anyone again. I'll stay distant from people before I let anyone get hurt because of me again.*

Head down, Harlan sits behind Sue, mumbling.

"Not everyone has a good father," Pastor Bob says. "Some don't even know their dad. If you're not a parent yet, you'll learn most do the best they can."

Harlan scowls.

"Dads that don't know God's love can't give it the way they want."

Ted shifts in his seat.

"Because the father never quit watching for his prodigal son, both the younger and older sons changed."

Bob adds closing points and has us pray for President Roosevelt and the load he carries. Also, for men like Char's J.P. and all on front lines. Then His voice breaks. "Jesus knows where our son Josh is and every other missing man. May victory come soon, and all loved ones come home." He gets nods and amens.

The potluck is amazing. Skookum Jim, a well-built Indian, brings melt-in-your-mouth smoked salmon as good as Johnny's.

"How do you catch so much?" a tall, lean white man with two hungry-looking boys asks. "I can't catch enough with a rod and reel to feed my family."

The native studies him. "No use rod and reel. Indian nets better. Where you live?"

"River Mile 72. We homestead a few acres in the woods."

"Come visit Cowlitz Reserve—not far. I teach you."

"Really? Thank you, sir; I will." He smiles.

At the meal's end, Pastor pushes back his chair. "Thank you

again to the best cooks along this river. Before we close, let me update you on recent events."

People listen, and silverware quits clinking.

"We talked last time about Japan attacking Alaska's coast. On June 7th, the *USS Coast Trader* was torpedoed and sunk by a Japanese sub off Cape Flattery on the Olympic Peninsula."

"That close?" someone exclaims. "I have a cousin there."

"Too close for comfort," the lean man with two young sons says.

"Thanks to a U.S. fishing boat and Canadian Navy ship working together, only one crewman was lost, but the *Coast Trader* was the first American ship lost near our coast in this war. Civil defense volunteers in Port Angeles are using binoculars and aircraft recognition photos from rooftops."

Jeb waves a hand. "We're selling binoculars at cost in our store this week."

"Thanks, Jeb. We're thankful the rumor of a Japanese landing near the Neah Bay Reservation was false."

"Great news." Joe Worth slaps his knee.

"National Guard troops are manning northern beaches and adding anti-aircraft emplacements. They think enemy subs are prowling our waters and may try to enter rivers. May God keep us vigilant."

"They'd better watch *their* rivers," a jowled stranger growls.

Wayne Sanders sits with two men I haven't met. One frowns at Pastor Bob's words.

"We must do everything needed to prepare. Did you know that four Nazis invaded our East Coast last week?"

"Nooo." Many gasp.

"They were naturalized Americans living in Germany sent back here as saboteurs. A U-boat dropped them on Long Island, but one surrendered to the FBI because he feared being hung if caught."

"Good thing." Joe Worth says.

"The FBI didn't believe him until he turned in $84,000 in cash, explosives, and a list of targets."

People murmur.

"Targets here are military installations, bridges, and Bonneville Dam. We can't let the enemy get that far."

"We won't." Another stranger slams a table.

Benches squeak as people lean forward.

"Rumors say four more Germans were dropped on Florida's Panhandle, but the FBI caught them." He removes his glasses. "We pray that every attack fails."

"Amen." Heads nod vigorously.

Bob's voice deepens. "Last night on Vancouver Island, a Japanese sub fired at the radio station. They missed, but their goal is clear." His hands trace a map in the air. "First the Aleutians, then Vancouver Island—they're heading here!" He singles out faces. "Both U.S. coasts are under attack, but we're facing this together. Keep contact lists up to date. Have survival supplies on hand for yourselves and others. Every home needs a weapon."

"Seriously?" An old man asks.

Nearby, Johnny nods.

I shudder, unable to absorb information fast enough. How does Pastor Bob get privileged information? How do scattered river residents seem so well-connected? Are these people some I send voice and radio messages to? I'll mingle and try to match voices with faces.

I thought I knew Ted's friends. How does he greet so many people I've never seen? And for someone who acts like a mysterious recluse, Johnny knows everyone. If the Japanese enter the Columbia, every bridge, town, railroad track, dam, military site, and road system could be targeted. I must do my job well. Like it or not, lives do depend on me. A shiver travels my spine.

"In closing, these verses from Psalm 107 promise help, 'They that go down to the sea in ships, that do business in great waters … He maketh the storm a calm, so that the waves are still … so he bringeth them unto their desired haven." Bob closes his Bible. "God bless you all."

Ted leans over. "Good sermon, huh?"

"Yes. But I'm shocked the Japanese are getting that close." My gaze pins Ted. "How do you know so much of what's going on?"

"Not *that* much. I mostly read or listen to the radio. Or sometimes talk with military guys home on leave."

"Not when I'm with you."

He grins. "Then you should be with me more."

"I mean hush-hush stuff."

"I guess I'm at the right place at the right time." He rubs his jaw. "Pastor's comments about Father's Day hit me. I left Vancouver so fast, Dad doesn't know I'm gone. There wasn't time to tell him, and today's Father's Day."

"He won't like that."

"No, he won't. I feel bad about Dad. You've met him. I wish I understood him better. He has strong leadership skills but not with family."

"I've met him but don't know him. I see his picture often in the paper. He's probably too busy to be much of a family man."

"That's the truth. He even, heaven forbid, talks about running for mayor."

Ted's expression makes me ache.

"Dad has that megawatt smile strangers love, but less time for family. I try to show him love but am weak in that department myself." He grips his left elbow tight as if it holds the answers to questions.

"You're not weak in that department. You're great." I glance at his arm. "Does your elbow hurt?"

"A little." His eyes follow mine. "I rammed it running to the engine room to check the fire. The thing is, I don't want to be like Dad. Family matters. I hate that I couldn't encourage

Mom to fight harder to live." His voice breaks, and he can't speak.

I cover his hand with mine. "You're not like your dad. You never will be. Your heart shines solid gold clear through."

Ted's voice becomes a whisper. "How do you know?"

"I just do, and I'm the world's best judge of character." I clown to lighten his mood. "Don't judge yourself so hard. You're maybe a little forgetful if you sleepwalk and leave red sweatshirts around." I wink when I really want to reach out and shake him. Or reach out and hug him.

He looks at my hand on his. "Thanks for your support."

"I'm right. I'm sure it complicates things to be on different wavelengths from your dad and brother."

"Definitely." He gusts a sigh. "And I can't phone dad today because the store phone is out."

"It is?"

"That's what Jeb says."

I finger the silver chain around my neck with the delicate scrolled cross hanging below that Dad gave me. "Pastor Bob's calling my dad for me when he gets home. Maybe he'll do that for you."

"Really? That could be a lifesaver." His eyes brighten. "Dad sent a note asking me to attend his birthday dinner, but we left so fast, I missed it. Didn't even get to tell him I'd be gone." He drags a hand through his gorgeous hair. "I want Dad to see enough of God in me that one day he'll believe." He swallows hard. "At least, that's my prayer."

"You can't make him. He has to choose himself. Like Saul of Tarsus. Maybe he has to get knocked off his horse."

Ted sighs but stands straighter. "How are your folks? How's the harvest coming?"

"Maybe enough to save Grandma's place."

"Good. I'm also praying God helps us with ways we've failed so we can go forward strong."

A lightning bolt strikes. Ted has my attention. I've never told him my part in Grandpa's death. Has God shown him? Is he talking generalities but hitting a bullseye? He's into magnets. Do I transmit guilt waves he picks up? I won't display weakness.

I squeeze his hand like everything's fine. But it's not. "You're a good friend."

"You're better. Will you open the library?" He looks like he wants to say more.

"After lunch. Char will help."

"Good. If you need anything, let me know."

He slides off the bench and saunters off, his shirt fabric stretching tight over his powerful shoulders. There's more confidence in his step. Ted is changing before my eyes.

13

Sunday P.M., June 21, 1942
Kalama, Washington, River Mile 73

"When a reporter's too busy to see news happening because he's writing up old news, he's too busy," I tell Sparks when he says he's finishing an article for his home paper before attending church.

"It can't be helped," he says. "I'll get to church when I can."

"Try hard. Bob Vengeance is a great preacher."

"That's what I hear. I'll sneak in the back door when I finish. May I borrow your notes for what I miss?"

"I take good ones, but it's not the same as being there."

Sparks' article must take longer than he expects, because I don't see him again until he's loading a plate at the end of the lunch line. Once he's through, I bring him to where our team sits with Bob and Sue.

"Great service, Pastor Bob," I say as we sit. "Sparks is along reporting part of our trip. I didn't ask you last night, but he mentioned a celebration Governor Langlie might have in Longview. Do you know anything about that?"

Bob's eyes flicker. "Maybe."

"Okay," I say. "Spill the beans."

"The governor hopes this isn't added pressure, but he sees your trip as a great morale booster. He's asked Oregon to join a two-state celebration of *Books Afloat* being halfway."

"Wouldn't it be better to wait until we succeed?"

"He thinks this builds momentum and gives people positive things to think about during frightening times."

"Hmmm. According to Sparks, sounds like plans have gone pretty far. When would this be?"

"In Kelso-Longview, this Friday."

"Five days!" I wipe my forehead. "There's so much to do beyond literally floating a library downriver. It demands public relations, press releases, and who knows what." A headache worms its way into my brain. I slide a small bottle from my pocket and shake two white tablets into my hand, then gulp them down dry.

Char points to a nearby pitcher of water.

"Thanks. I'm fine.

"Is this celebration surprise too much?" Sparks stops forking lasagna into his mouth and gapes.

"It depends on how big it gets. It's just one more thing I hadn't counted on."

"But added coverage guarantees generous funding—"

I toss my head. "So, you've said. I need time to regroup." I move to the next table to calm down and list priorities. Does the governor view book deliveries as important as surveillance? It provides our cover. How do his plans mesh with that?

Bob leans toward Sparks. "We didn't get to chat last night, so I'm glad to visit now. I believe you've met our young friend, Harlan."

"I'm not so young," Harlan mutters.

"He was on the boat, but we're not acquainted yet," Sparks spares a glance. "I'll catch him soon about his heroics yesterday but need to interview you two first. I've heard great things about you, including your son being missing near Midway. Sorry about that." Sparks shines his megawatt smile.

Bob spreads his hands. "We're only one of many families enduring that."

"But it's all the more reason for encouraging articles. Can you help Anne see the value of my reporting?"

"I think she does. She's just facing many pressures at once."

Bob earns my appreciative glance.

"So, your name is spelled like it sounds, V-E-N-G-?" Sparks raises his pen.

"Don't focus on us. We're ordinary."

"Not true."

"Yes, it is. Check your sources. You're from eastern Washington? How's the war effort there?"

"Unexciting, That's why I'm here from Kennewick, lead reporter for the *Tri-City Herald*. I heard about *Books Afloat* and recognized a prizewinning story. I asked the governor if I could get involved. He agreed."

Bob nods, but I'm confused. What does the governor want? Can I juggle book deliveries, river surveillance, and a public celebration? Doesn't more exposure about us threaten our mission? Why didn't he contact me directly?

"Kennewick is near your grandma's place, isn't it?" Bob turns to Harlan.

Harlan moves his chewing gum wad to one side. "Closer to Richland, but she shops in Kennewick."

"Sparks, do you know Harlan's family?"

"What's the last name?" His pen stops.

"Boyd. Harlan Boyd."

"I know some Boyds."

Sparks writes again. I wonder how much ink he uses per week.

"Wait." Harlan lifts a hand. "Don't write unless I give permission. Is *everything* news to you?"

"Pretty much. Especially if it connects my part of the state to this floating library."

Sparks slaps Harlan's back so hard, he loses his gum.

Face aflame, Harlan reclaims his wad but hides it in his hand. He makes no effort to mask his anger.

"Practically neighbors," Sparks gushes. "I know two Boyds—maybe your uncles?" He scrutinizes Harlan. "There's resemblance—something about Benton County boys."

"I hardly know them."

Harlan's eyes hood, but Sparks doesn't notice.

"Don't be shy. They're good guys. I'll run your picture."

"Only if I say." Harlan stands and steps away.

Bob turns to Ted. "You're on the boat. How's Annie coping with a reporter on board?"

"About like you'd imagine. She dislikes attention, but figures she needs support."

"Char?"

"It's awkward but helpful. She'll find the balance."

"So the Governor's moving ahead with his celebration?" Bob asks.

"That's what I hear," Sparks replies.

I've reached my limit and march back to their table. "Do you know what it's like to hear people discussing you as if you're not there? Why didn't the governor talk to me directly? He said he would sometimes."

"He's super busy," Sparks says. "He's letting me cover the celebration as a go-between. News excites people."

"*Good News* excites me." Pastor Bob brushes Sparks' shoulder, "though mine may differ from yours. I'll bet you add enthusiasm to the trip."

"That's an understatement."

Sparks earns my annoyed look.

"Full coverage means the public won't miss a beat. They'll beg for more like people reading about Lindbergh's flight. Anne's library will benefit everyone. Now, someone show me a phone, so I can call in this morning's article. I phone daily to keep the home fires burning and presses turning."

"There's a payphone at the front of the store." I gesture that direction. "But it's out of order."

"Out of order? That can't be. What's the backup?"

"A repairman tomorrow," I smugly say.

"Another boat or neighbor might have a phone," Ted suggests. "Or maybe Pastor Bob would call it in for you from Vancouver."

"Thanks. But I have to do it myself." He jumps to his feet, looking stressed for the first time.

Bob and Sue also stand. "We hate to say goodbye, but we're heading back for meetings tomorrow."

"Already?" I realize more than ever what they mean to me, especially when the Challenge feels like I'm riding an elevator, falling out of control. "I loved seeing you."

"Same here, but people tend to need their pastor most when he's gone."

"Keep in touch," Sue says. "We'll try to make it to Longview."

"I'd love that. If you talk to the governor," I appeal to Bob, "have him downplay the celebration."

"If that's what you want." He conveys full conversations with his eyebrows. "But you know him. He thinks this builds patriotism. Once his wheels are turning—"

"I know." I linger in their goodbye hugs.

Harlan will leave with them, so comes for a hug, too.

I shake his hand instead. "Have a great week."

"I'd rather stay with you," Harlan says. "Let me board in Longview and travel with you to the ocean."

I sigh. "Harlan, there's too much going on."

"That's why you need me. Let me help—and look after you."

"I'm fine. What makes you think I need looking after?"

"Doesn't everyone?" His face hollows, like he's nursing a bad tooth.

I don't have time for needy emotions. Not even mine. "Just pray for us, Harlan. That will help."

"If you say so." He walks me to the Jarvis's front door. When we're almost there, he says, "In Longview, I'll replace Ted. After all, I found the engine fire that saved you."

"What fire?" Jeb asks, opening the door.

"A problem Harlan took care of. I appreciate that, Harlan. Haven't I thanked you enough?"

"I guess. But if you change your mind—"

His eyes plead as I enter the house and close the door.

"Wow, you're rich with people wanting to help," Jeb says.

"Too rich."

And then Janey mentions the Vacation Bible classes she hopes to hold this week for Kalama children for the first time— except she's not ready. Excitement shines on her face. If I had more time, I'd stay and help, but I must put the Challenge first.

14

Sunday, June 21, 1942
Kalama, Washington, River Mile 73

Ted's stomach turned to lead as he saw Annie hurry to the Jarvis home with Harlan hounding her.

"What's happening with Harlan?" he asked Bob and Sue.

"I'm not sure." Pastor Bob snugged his jacket tight. "Harlan's not the same with Josh gone. He's desperate to prove himself."

Ted flipped back his hair. "Maybe that's it. What do you think of Corrigan? He's a very intense reporter."

"Agreed—an eastern Washington windstorm that needs to blow itself out." Bob turned to Sue. "What do you say, babe?"

"That sums it up." Her gaze warmed Ted. "You know, you're like a son to us."

He nodded, a knot thickening his throat. "I love you both."

"As we pray for your team, I feel you'll complete the Challenge but face serious tests."

"Please keep praying. Char and I do our best, but Annie puts us to shame. Josh and I thought we knew her in high school, but she's a whole new gal on *Books Afloat*."

Sue brushed his arm. "That bad?"

"Besides visiting every spot between here and the coast, she wants to win this war single-handedly and brainstorm ways to save the world."

Sue snorted. "That sounds high-geared. Are you saying she should run for president?"

"If women could, I'd vote for her—maybe run her campaign." Ted flushed.

Bob threw back his head and laughed. "Hard times build strong women."

"Traveling with them makes strong men, too." Ted quirked an eyebrow.

"I'm sure." Bob cleaned his glasses and put his handkerchief away. "I'll give her parents the mild version when I phone. They still worry but will be glad to hear she's doing well. They know she has backbone." He turned to Sue. "What do you mean, you think she'll face tests?"

She shrugged. "Not sure. Just something I sense." She pulled a list from her pocket. "While you talk to the last people you need to, I'll have Harlan load the fresh lettuce and vegetables Janey's sending with us. Plus, Skookum Jim gave us ten pounds of smoked salmon wrapped in newspapers. You get to enjoy that aroma all the way home."

"Just the aroma?" Bob groaned. "You're killing me. How can I drive and not taste?"

Sue patted his cheek. "Love, you know you'll get some."

"That's my girl. Twenty-four years married, and I love you more every day."

The look they exchanged made Ted ache with longing.

Once Sue left, Bob gripped Ted's sleeve. "I need to see you. Meet me on the riverbank past the Jarvis's house in five minutes. There are details you need, and the governor sent you a present."

"He did?"

"Yes. One you'll like."

Five minutes later, Ted strolled to where Bob stood but stopped short when he saw Harlan with him, scowling and pitching rocks into the river. Neither Bob nor Harlan noticed Ted approach. Not wanting to embarrass Harlan, Ted stepped behind the house where weeping willow branches hid him.

"That's just it. I'm not your son. No matter how hard I try, I mess up and don't fit. I work hard for things to go right, but they don't." Harlan threw more rocks.

Ted didn't intend to eavesdrop, but Harlan's voice carried.

"Don't get me wrong. I love you and Sue—you're wonderful. But if I really belonged, things would turn around for me."

"I don't see it that way. Sue and I truly welcome you. You are part of us."

"Not like Josh is." Harlan closed his eyes. "I never knew who Dad was. Mom's gone on some save-the-world government assignment—at least that's what she says. If Grandma knows more, she's not saying. I'm just the boy she took in."

"That's not how we or your grandma feel. You have good things going on. You're doing well in school." He gripped Harlan's shoulder. "When your grandma calls each week, she's excited and proud of you. I hear that just answering the phone. In fact, maybe have her come visit?"

"Seriously?

"Sure."

"Thanks, but it's hard for her to travel. When I earn my mechanic's papers, I'd like to build a career and take care of her. Maybe join the military, like Josh—go places."

"Hold on, Harlan. Just now, things don't look great for him."

"But he's a hero. I want people to look up to me, too."

Ted glimpsed them at times through waving branches.

"In time. But there's more to life than impressing people." Bob raised his collar against the wind. "Your grandma raised you because she loves you—not to be paid back."

As Bob poured in love and faith, Harlan rubbed a place over his breastbone like it ached.

"My Grandma deserves more. I want to give her more. I want to be like you—" His head dropped. "I'm awfully far away."

"Not that far." Bob slipped an arm around him. "God has great plans for you."

"I'd like to believe that. Sometimes I mess up and do bad things." He tossed a larger rock that fractured soft shale. The fragments rattled and scattered. "I can't stop."

"God can fix anything."

Harlan rubbed the same spot over his breastbone. "I won't talk in front of Sue, but can we share later tonight? Back home?"

"Sure. But let's pray now." Bob grabbed Harlan's hand. "Lord, You hear this son's heart and feel his pain. Show him how real You are and how much You care …"

Bob finished and hugged Harlan. "Expect great things, because they're coming. Now, please help Sue load our car while I catch the last person I need to see."

Though the willow branches screened Ted, Whis-purr, the Jarvis's tortoiseshell cat, rubbed against his legs. As Ted picked up Whis-purr, her hair tickled his nose. He fought for control, but his sneeze exploded.

Harlan whirled. A dozen willow trees couldn't hide his hatred "Vincent! How long have you been spying? You're always against me." Harlan fled.

Ted joined Pastor Bob. "What a mess."

"I didn't know he was coming. When he stepped up, I hoped you two wouldn't run into each other. It's *not* your fault."

"I didn't know what to do. I figured you wouldn't be long, so I waited—but that pesky cat."

Bob grimaced. "We do our best but can't win them all. Because of Harlan's needs, I didn't feel right brushing him off. I'll tell him later that I asked to see you. That should help."

"I'm not sure anything will. I'm his least favorite person."

Bob nodded. "I noticed. Can you give a short version of what's going on? And I'll tell you more events on the river. Let's step behind this garage before someone else comes."

Ted stopped. "We're near the house? Can people inside hear?

"I doubt it. But we'll whisper just in case."

"Maybe I'm paranoid."

"No wonder." Bob turned every direction. "It looks safe. The governor sends his regards. You heard me mention increased Japanese activity on the coast. So far, they haven't accomplished much, but there's more happening than I shared. Here's the scoop." They bent their heads together.

"Wow," Ted said. "I didn't know all that was going on. I'm glad you and Smitty stay on top of things."

"After Pearl Harbor, we take threats seriously." He dropped his voice. "How's Annie—really?"

Ted sighed. "She has fears but hides them behind a brave face. Harlan's been hitting all of our pressure points. I clearly trigger his."

"Josh was his anchor, so Harlan's adrift. He goes home with us tonight. We'll get some good talks in. He mentioned wanting to visit your team on *Books Afloat*, but I didn't dream he'd actually do it."

Ted spread his hands. "He's motivated. I'll give him that. Probably no lasting harm done, although that engine fire could have ruined us. Plus, he burned his hands." Ted shook his head. "I don't know what he was thinking?"

"Maybe he wasn't. Are you sure he started it?"

"I don't see any other explanation. It didn't start itself."

"Right. I'll pray harder—for him and you. Meanwhile, Smitty's people report more activity around the river's mouth. I don't want Anne to know yet, but you should be aware. Plus, remember when we talked about you having a handgun?"

Ted's eyes snapped wide. "I don't like weapons, but the closer we get to the Pacific, I know we need something."

"The governor agrees. He and Smitty got you a great one." He looked around. "It's dark enough now. It's under the driver's seat in our car. I didn't want Harlan finding it when he loaded the trunk."

They crossed the yard.

Bob retrieved a rectangular package wrapped in dark cloth and placed it in Ted's hands. "It's a Smith & Wesson's preferred military-issue sidearm. Everything's legal. Is there a place on the boat to hide it?"

"It's harder with Sparks on board, but I'll find one."

"Good. We need to leave before it's too dark to drive. I will call your dad, and you have our prayers for the rest of the trip."

They hugged.

"You're a fine man, Ted Vincent. Don't listen to any other opinions."

Ted ducked his head. "Mostly mine."

"Then quit." Bob waved a hand. "Your dad will wake up and recognize the fine qualities in you. Meanwhile, only listen to what God and your friends say. We're right, and you're wrong.

Ted sputtered a laugh. "Well, when you put it like that. And tell Dad I'm sorry I missed his birthday. *Books Afloat* left so fast, I couldn't let him know, but I'm sure he was offended."

"He understands wartime emergencies. I'll use layman's terms but tell him what a great job you're doing."

"Lots of luck. He only values sports records."

"Have faith." Bob smiled. "I've seen God crack harder nuts than him. Keep transmitting messages. I'll answer when I can."

Ted relaxed. "I log on morning and night, but it's hard keeping Annie from seeing. She glimpsed me on deck two nights ago checking signal strength and thought I was sleepwalking."

Bob laughed. "Did she buy it?"

"Maybe. I told her Dad claims I did as a kid.

"You're probably tired enough to sleepwalk." Bob's voice thickened. Stay safe all the way to the Pacific and back."

"Will do."

They hugged again and parted.

AFTER STASHING the dark-wrapped package behind a loose cement block in the Jarvis's garage, Ted entered the house to see if Sparks had found a phone. On his way, he passed Johnny Hofer carrying a bedroll.

"What's up, Johnny?"

"Rigging a hammock on board. I like it better than the deck, even though I'm at home on boats. Annie's leaving early, and I'm glad that reporter fella's staying in the house.

"He's coming with us, isn't he?"

"If it's his choice, yes. But not if he oversleeps and misses our departure like I think Annie hopes he will." His eyes scrunched. "By the way, Annie's quite a gal. I see how you look at her. I'm rooting for you."

"What?" Ted froze.

"You heard me. I'm rooting for you. Don't act dumb. You love that girl, and she's worth it. She likes you, too, or she wouldn't give you so much lip."

Ted forgot to breathe. "You're kidding."

"I don't kid about important things." Johnny's gaze held steady.

"Bob's son, Josh, is the one she cares for, and I don't blame her." He rubbed his jaw. "He's great in every way."

Johnny wagged his head. "Fine, but listen up, don't sell yourself short. I like the young man standing in front of me just fine. I'm saying, Annie does, too."

Ted's jaw hung.

"I'm no romance expert. Missed some fine chances in my

day. Don't want you blind like I was, but I learned. Now, I can see when a girl cares for a guy. And Annie does." He tapped a finger by his eye. "Pay attention. Figure it out. Or buy glasses." He slapped Ted's back and sauntered to the boat.

Was Johnny serious? Was there truth to it? Ted's heart hammered. In the house, he found Sparks enjoying a second slab of apple pie.

"We saved you some," Janey said.

"Great people here," the reporter said, loosening a vest button.

Ted accepted half a piece of pie and sat next to Sparks. "Did you get your transmission sent?"

"The store's phone was out, but a radioman on another boat helped me." He forked two last bites of pie into his mouth.

"How do you stay thin?" Ted asked. "You're a serious eater."

"I burn energy constantly." Sparks finished chewing and brushed crumbs from his vest.

Ted glanced at Sparks' shoes. "By the way, did you buy better footwear at the store for our boat? You'll slip in those when the decks get wet."

"My wingtips?" Sparks studied his feet. "They're fine for most situations. I might have boots in my duffle. Thanks for the reminder. Do folks get seasick on board much?" He crossed his legs.

"Only in bad storms."

"Then here's hoping we don't have any."

Ted pictured Annie sick on *Books Afloat* after failing her pilot's exam. He'd pitied her. "It gets worse near open ocean. Most folks have trouble then."

"I'll bet I have good sea legs."

Did he plan to be with them the whole voyage? "I guess we'll find out. See you in the morning."

Sunset's last colors faded to black velvet. With Johnny, Anne, and Char on board *Books Afloat*, it took extra care to send and receive messages. Nights were best. Ted would have to improve his spycraft with codes and drop spots to avoid being seen. He wondered how Sparks transmitted his article. Many boats were anchored for church services today. Some probably had better transmission systems than *Books Afloat*.

Ted stood by the river and waited for Anne and Char to board and settle. When all was quiet except Johnny's snores, he retrieved Bob's package from the garage base, carried it on board under his jacket, and tiptoed to his quarters. Inside the brown case, he found a streamlined Smith & Wesson .38 with the operator's manual wrapped around the barrel.

He opened the manual and smoothed out its pages. Besides attending a gun show with Dad once years ago and shooting a .22 on someone's ranch, Ted hadn't used weapons. He had to find ways to manage serious practice. Hopefully, he wasn't too old to master it now.

Hand shaking slightly, he lifted the revolver and lined up its sights. He admired its brown walnut grips, polished blue finish, and six-shot barrel. Smith & Wesson had made guns for Britain before America entered the war. Now they manufactured *Victory* models for U.S. troops with *V* for victory stamped before serial numbers.

Yes, here was the mark—a large supply of bullets, too. After reading how to clean, oil, and load the weapon, he rewrapped it and pushed it to the farthest corner under his bed. *Lord, I'm no murderer. Don't let me have to kill anyone.*

He'd rest until midnight when his network people preferred handling messages. It was hard to sleep light and stay alert.

Ted remembered nothing more until the small alarm in his shirt pocket vibrated against his chest. He rose and climbed the boat stairs.

Books Afloat was almost halfway to the Pacific. The Governor's Challenge allowed thirty days. Nearly a week had passed with one major catastrophe avoided.

Keep me alert and strong. Don't let us face anything we can't handle.

The moon raced behind clouds, and shadows increased. Ted fought the growing sensation that mounting dangers lurked in the dark.

15

Monday, June 22, 1942
Kalama, Washington, River Mile 73

In the middle of the night, I hear thumping noises on deck. Sparks hauls his paraphernalia on board.

I pull my robe tight and meet him. "What's up?"

"I was lying awake, afraid I'd sleep through your departure. I missed most of Pastor Bob's sermon but heard enough that I want to do my part to guard the boat."

"Thanks. We're covered. You'd do better to enjoy that nice room on shore."

He sets down his stuff. "Thanks, but I'm here."

"So, I see." I step aside. "In the morning, show me the stories you've written about the Challenge before they go to the governor."

"I can't do that!"

"Why?"

"I sent one from St. Helens and wired another when we first got here. They're published and getting great reviews."

"What?" My heart thuds. I taste acid. "You promised I'd see them to approve even before the governor."

"Did I? Things change. News is time-sensitive. After reading several of my award-winning articles, the governor sent word that I don't need his approval. He trusts me. You will, too, once you read them. Remember? I offered to show you one, but you were too busy." His eyes accuse.

I do vaguely remember. At that instant, a Stone-Age savage sneaks up to cleave my skull with a flint ax. Thankfully, I only suffer a giant headache, not decapitation. *How could I be stupid enough to let Sparks' news stories slip by?*

"You certainly need my approval. You promised me that I'd have the full right to approve pictures, quotes—the works." I thump my finger against his chest. "I expect you to keep your word!"

"Calm down, Cutie, it's not so bad. We'll work it out, cross my heart."

He reaches out as if he might slip an arm around me to pull me close, but when I stiffen, he thinks better of it and steps back.

Wise decision. "It's plenty bad, Sparks. I don't know what kind of misunderstanding we've had, but we'll settle it with the governor soon."

"Fine. We'll see him in Longview in two days."

"Two days?" Where is Sparks getting information? "He'll be there for sure? It's definite?"

"That's right. He's inviting citizens in Washington and Oregon to celebrate *Books Afloat* reaching the halfway point and values good reporting."

"I'll bet." The Stone-Age savage swings his ax again.

Char reaches deck, hat on and ready for action. "I hear raised voices. What's wrong?"

"Nothing much," Sparks says.

"Something I hope we survive," I say, grateful to see her.

"Between Ted possibly sleepwalking and Sparks publishing stories without my approval, there's lots going on. I haven't seen his stories, but he tells me two are published and getting good reviews."

"How can that be?"

"That's my question."

Sparks wears an innocent face. "You heard me offer to show Annie, but she was too busy."

"Once." Char gapes. "Even if she was busy, you should have asked again before sending anything."

"But time makes all the difference in good reporting."

"Because I didn't have time the one time asked, you're making this my fault?" I thump his chest again.

"Not fully." His complexion pales.

I like seeing the fingers on his right hand flutter. Maybe he's less confident than he acts. "I assumed the governor was our final clearinghouse," I say. "If not, I reserve all rights for final approval myself."

"I'll help her." Char plants her feet.

He steps back. "That's unnecessary, ladies. We'll solve this with the governor in person."

"When?" Char asks, running the risk of getting Sparks in full smooth-talking mode again.

"He'll meet us in Longview at the celebration," Sparks says in triumph. "There's a parade and air show—"

"Wait!" I interrupt. "That's a full publicity firestorm."

"Goodness!" Char gulps. "That sounds wonderful and terrible, depending on how you slice it. Still, the governor's a wise man. Just because we haven't seen Sparks' stories doesn't mean they're bad."

"That's right." Sparks perks up, like he may avoid execution.

Char fans herself with her hat. "This might be when my J.P. would say we hope for the best and prepare for the worst."

"Wise man, your J.P.," Sparks says.

"The best!" Her face calms.

Even my cleaved skull feels slightly better. Is Sparks an answer to prayer? He tracked us down in an impossible place and offered credentials. While I don't like juggling surveillance, publicity, and library duties, it may be necessary. All I want is to deliver books to people while performing clandestine duties for Uncle Sam that help end this war.

I glance at Sparks again—intelligent forehead, aquiline nose, eager eyes—actually, good looking. And sometimes amusing. But right now, he's 100-percent annoying as he blathers on.

"When you see interest grow from stories and donations pour in, you'll thank me. The public craves good news in tough times, and you're it." His head bobs like a metronome, beating time.

The throb in my head keeps rhythm.

"After Pearl Harbor, our nation needs—"

"Stop!" I plug my ears. "You exhaust me."

Ted appears from downstairs, yawning and tucking in his shirt, yet looking alert. How can Johnny snore in his hammock?

"Is everything okay?" Ted asks. "I heard some discussion."

"Is that what you call it?" Even my eyebrows hurt.

"I have to hand it to you, Sparks," Ted says. "You're a great salesman."

Sparks laughs. "Good reporters are. I also handle advertising."

"Figures." Ted gives a thumb's up. "You've made me a believer."

"Ted Vincent!" I swat his arm, seeing too late it's his sore one. "Don't you dare agree with him."

"He's right, Annie," Sparks says. "It's your boat, and you're in charge. But Ted understands there are times in history when nations need inspiration. This is one of them." *The Columbian* should be here. Hordes of reporters should stand in line." He gestures wildly.

"There isn't room on deck," Char quips.

"*The Columbian* is understaffed." I hang my head. "I told them I'd send travel notes and photos, but I've been busy—"

"That's the point!" He springs in the air and lands in the same spot like a basketball star. "Each day matters. Why aren't major papers here? Newsboys should shout your name on America's main streets. Radio stations should announce each time you lift anchor. Our nation needs this heart-warming journey.

"Thank goodness I picked up the ball when *The Columbian* dropped it. *Time* and *Life* should be here. *Look* magazine might miss a Pulitzer since they claim they present ordinary people doing extraordinary things, and that's you in spades, Annie Mettles."

"Sparks, do you have a screw loose?" I hold my pounding head with both hands. "You make my head hurt."

"Sorry," he clucks his tongue. "But I meant what I said. I'll find a way to stay on board to the Pacific. I don't want to miss a minute of your journey."

The Stone-Age savage strikes a final blow. "Don't try too hard," I say softly. "Maybe I can write stories."

"You don't mean that. Not with everything else you have to do. The governor's office and I are a tag-team. I share the scoop and byline with his staff on the top half of the front page— prime newspaper location." He claps his sliding hat firmly back on his head, where it immediately slips again. It dips more with each word spoken, until it teeters dangerously.

Char and I watch. She seems as fascinated as I am.

"Like I said, we'll finalize arrangements with the governor at the big celebration in Longview—"

"Big celebration?" Char repeats. "Please define big."

My skull is finished. I may be ready for embalming.

Sparks stretches his hands wide. "This big, Char. How is it possible none of you know?" His mouth forms an *O*, like a wolf ready to howl. "Don't messages reach you? What's wrong with your communication system?"

"I'm wondering, too," I say, defeated.

"I know the governor sent you a telegram about it because he copied me on it. He calls it a shot in the arm honoring civilian efforts during wartime, when a daring unstoppable young—" He glances my way, "extremely attractive, courageous young woman faces insurmountable ..."

"Sparks, quit."

"He actually said *almost* insurmountable. Why, you may outshine Annie Oakley or Amelia Earhart!"

"Do you have an off switch?"

Sparks grins, reminding me of the wolf waiting for Little Red Riding Hood.

Ted elbows me. "I said you remind me of Annie Oakley, and that's your name, too!"

"Don't remind me." I cock my index finger like a gun. "They called her 'little miss sure shot.' Watch out, or I'll shoot."

"My kind of woman." Char glows. "She said women should be as comfortable handling guns as caring for babies. That's what we need. I might have a little surprise for anyone giving us trouble."

"Great crew!" Sparks vibrates. "Look, I'm on board until Longview to meet the governor. I'll write up the celebration and phone that scoop to my assistant, who'll arrange national spread while I race home and put our paper to press. Then the governor joins you on board for several days as public interest builds. His office writes that part of the story in another above-the-fold byline until I'm back—professional journalism at its finest."

"I get it."

"Then your story crosses the ocean by Trans-Atlantic cable like Boston's shot heard round the world, and other countries read of your accomplishment. I'll be here to cover your glorious completion of the Challenge. So, what do you say now?"

He reaches for my hand, but both of mine grip my head. He grabs Char's instead with supreme confidence. Sparks mistakes my silence for approval.

Until I shake my head no. "Nothing's decided until Longview."

His wattage dims. "You're giving me hoops to jump through. Governor Langlie said you'd be glad to have me, that you'd be easy to work with." His tone rankles.

My hands find my hips. "I guess he was wrong. I know you want to help *and* further your career. I'm weighing the pros and cons."

"Most boats would be glad—"

Ted lifts a hand. "Sparks? Shut it down. Nothing gets solved tonight, and we have a big day tomorrow. It will get solved at Longview—or not."

"J.P. would agree," Char says.

Sparks clamps his mouth shut like a mousetrap snapping too soon and missing its prey—until he finds more words. "When you see the job I do, you'll change your tune. You think too much about delivering books and not enough about your nation." He whirls and clatters downstairs.

16

Monday, June 22, 1942
Kalama, Washington, River Mile 73

Throaty foghorns blast me awake before first light. I doubt I've slept, yet my watch shows several hours have passed. Thankfully, my savage headache is now hunting other victims. A full moon and clear skies dropped the temperature, filling the river's banks and hollows with a gauzy white blanket. Foghorns blast at intervals from buoys dividing the main channel's shipping lanes to warn ships of dangers.

I consider more sleep, but then my eyes snap open. This is day four of the Governor's Challenge. He's given us thirty days. I'd love to finish sooner to prove the value of my idea and support the war effort—with or without river pilot papers, thank you very much. Someday I'll make that Coast Guard testing officer eat his braided hat.

Because who am I kidding? I'll complete this trip in style or die trying to make up for being the useless kid standing at Grandpa's grave, tears sliding down my cheeks, while adults discussed Grandma's hardships and failed finances in hushed tones. How tragic he died before harvesting his pitiful crop and getting the farm mortgage paid. Family and neighbors did what they could, but times were hard.

The mourners didn't blame me outright, but I overheard hushed comments and accusing thoughts come every day. 'If only the granddaughter had stayed awake. Or a responsible grown-up had been along.'

My eyes scan the shelf near my bed, where book volumes shine like jewels. I'm thankful for the beauty they capture. Biographies prove that people can succeed and inspire others. Histories show that nations can solve tough problems and improve lives. Fiction brings experiences from other places and times so we can gain that wisdom without repeating mistakes from the past.

My heart swells. They've taught me so much. Reading has changed my life. I'm privileged to share riches with people I've never met. And, during wartime, help my nation, too.

When I open my divider curtain and look out, I'm startled at first to see Johnny in his hammock stretched between the center deck support and overhead wires on our outside wall. Snug in his blanket, he swings back and forth with our gentle rocking. I've never met anyone as colorful and fascinating.

I inhale the river's raw smell mingled with odors of crumbling earth, green ferns, and roots. That fragrance energizes me like tonic.

Ted is asleep, or I'd start *Books Afloat*. Rumbling snores rise from his space. He must be exhausted to sleep that hard and make such racket. But then I remember, Sparks is there, too, adding his own gasps and whistles.

The deck chills my feet as I tiptoe to the galley. I'll start coffee to surprise my crew, careful not to disturb sleepers beyond this partition.

As I return to the main deck, Char's feet hit the boards above me, kerplunk. God bless her. She does great, holding our course.

Next, I hear quieter thumps as she dons rubber-soled deck shoes and clomps downstairs, her yellow Sou'wester askew from wearing it all night or putting it on too hastily to keep us from storms.

"Morning," she calls, her voice husky with sleep. She glances Johnny's way before studying the river. "Pea soup weather." She points her nose like a coyote sniffing scent. "It smells fresh with no salt, so the wind's east from Mt. Hood, not west from the Pacific. Strong winds burn off fog fast. We'd be wise to wait an hour or two."

"I'll take your word for it. I'd rather not travel in murk." I shiver. "Running aground once was enough for me."

"Smart girl. Nature tells her story plain if we read her signs."

All of me smiles. "Teach me. I want to learn what you know."

She turns the color of boiled lobsters. "I don't know much compared to J.P., but I learn easily. God gave me that."

"He sure did."

"You do fine yourself."

She slants a look. "Bossy for your age, but we'll survive."

"Whoa, am I that bad?"

Her honest face grins. "Not *bad* since you don't mean anything by it. You've just got a job to do, so you don't let anything stop you." She slices her hand through solid fog. "This is thick enough to cut and sell for building supplies. No one should lift anchor in this."

The foghorn blasts continue.

"Thanks for putting up with me," I say in my quiet voice. "What do you suggest?" My hands grip the rail.

She leans forward. "Let's face it, folks put up with me. I like you enough to treat you like my daughter. Evie's feisty, too— most leaders are, and you are one. You just haven't lived long enough to learn the best ways to lead."

"So, that's my problem?" Relief surges through me.

An emotion I hope Char will overlook as the foghorns distract her.

"Listen to those bellow. They're saying if we wait an hour or two, things will be fine." She adjusts her hat. "Did you see Janey give me sourdough starter for flapjacks plus the fixins for breakfast?"

"I saw her hand you something but didn't know what."

"I'll whip those up. By the time we're through, the fog will be gone." She stares into the distance. "May I ask a question?"

"Sure."

"What's the story behind Janey and Jeb coming to Kalama? I feel such sorrow around them."

My eyes widen. "I was hoping it wouldn't come up again."

"If you'd rather not, it's okay. I caught enough bits and pieces to guess I shouldn't ask them."

"Their son's drowning was in the papers six months back, but maybe you didn't connect the name." I point to a library table chair. "Sit down, and I'll tell you while I prepare a few library cards."

"Give me some, and I'll help." She carefully lowers herself onto a small strong chair that supports her. "They lost a son?"

"Yes, their only child. Months back, when spring snows melted and flooded rivers, four-year-old, Davey, fell off the boat."

"How awful!" Her face contorts. "How do people survive things like that?"

"Not all do. Jeb and Janey almost didn't. Davey was taking a plate of cookies from the galley to his dad. He slipped at the only place on the lower level where a small, hinged door opens outside for loading. His hands were full. Perhaps he bumped the door's bolt as he passed. Somehow, it opened, and he fell into the river. The current pushed him under the boat before anyone knew he was gone. Neither parent heard a thing. Davey didn't stand a chance."

Tears track Char's cheeks. "I'd go crazy."

"Janey kind of did." I bite my lip to stifle my tears. "They each thought the other had him. It broke their hearts when Jeb searched and found him too late. Janey had a breakdown. She kept going to that side of the boat and jumping in, looking. Jeb couldn't guard her and work, too. For months, he faced losing them both."

"Did you know them then?"

"Not until after. I'd heard their names from Pastor Bob when he and Sue came downriver for meetings. Later, when I needed a boat, and they needed to lease theirs, he introduced us. Jeb's work had been catching runaway logs from booms with a pike or floating cove to cove harvesting trees on public land near water. He made a living but couldn't keep going with Janey so bad. They left the river for her sanity."

"I guess so." Char finished her stack of cards. "How can she be this good so soon after?"

"We call it a miracle. Outwardly, she's fine, but she struggles inwardly. She may for years but is so much better than before. At first, our doctor in Vancouver worked with her, but nothing helped. Then, Jeb heard of a psychiatrist at the state hospital who used electric shock, something from Europe, to dull the brain's worst memories so she'd quit seeing Davey's body."

Char shudders. "That hurts my heart. J.P. and I have Evie. I can't imagine—"

"At first, Jeb feared electric shock in case it made things worse. But he got desperate. After four weeks, he glimpsed the real Janey waking up—like the fog lifting out there." I point beyond the boat. "Janey cries often—a person never forgets—but she knows Davey's with God, and they'll be reunited one day."

Char dabs her handkerchief. "I'm so sorry."

"Bob's helping them not blame each other or themselves. Especially Janey. She'd called to Jeb that Davey was coming but didn't make sure he'd heard, and he didn't over the engine noise. Helping them is the other reason Bob and Sue come here often. Depression and heartache are terrible enemies, but Jeb is getting his Janey back."

"They're amazing."

"They chose Kalama so they could run Jeb's uncle's store while he helps a daughter in Tacoma. Janey also volunteers with local school and church projects, which helps—even with the river close."

Char stacks her cards in a neat pile. "I wouldn't have guessed they'd faced such problems. Thanks for telling me."

"I'm thankful God connected us in a short time. For now, leasing the boat meets their needs. Did you hear her mention Vacation Bible School last night?"

"No."

"She's pulling lessons together for next week but hasn't taught it before. I helped Bob and Sue do theirs for two summers. I guess I'm a hoarder, because I even have most of those materials on board but haven't had time to find them. You never know when the craziest things come in handy. I wish I could drop everything and spend a day helping her. It's just that—"

"I know, the Challenge. You're under the gun for the biggest deadline of your life."

"I'm praying for her, but that may not be enough. I'd stay if I were sure it would make a difference."

She slides back her chair. "Ask God for a sign. Could this fog be it?"

"Maybe. I need to be sure."

She speaks in a rush. "I understand pain. I had a miscarriage and a stillborn son before Evie. It's long ago and doesn't compare to their loss, but it broke our hearts."

"Char, I had no idea." I take her hand. "Yes, it compares. I'd like to know your story, too. When will I learn we don't know anyone else's situation until we spend time with them?"

"True. Most people have fascinating stories below the surface. That's how great books get written."

I wave toward my bookcases. "Even how Smitty and your husband got their names."

"When I came to their family as a youngster, their smarts impressed me." Her face eases into a smile. "I believed everything Mother Young said. When J.P. asked me to marry him, and we had a daughter, I bought the fancy name idea, too." She laughs. "Evie still threatens to kill me for that."

"Her name isn't Evelyn?"

"Nope. Don't ask her full name if you want to live, but her legal moniker is Evangeline Christian Rose Young—Rose after her grandmother."

"Wow. And Evangeline for Longfellow's poem."

"Yes. Evie vows she'll never give any child of hers a complicated name. I hope she marries. I'd like to be a grandma."

"You'll be a great one." But then I squint. "What do you mean when you came to the Youngs? Weren't you always part of their family?"

"I couldn't have been and married J.P. I was an orphaned fourteen-year-old distant cousin, who came a year before he went to the First World War. When he returned, I'd grown up. He eventually convinced me he loved me and wanted to marry me." Her eyes shine. "Best thing I ever did. We're best friends, and I can't imagine a better husband."

I pat her callused hand. "I want to meet him someday. And hear all your stories."

"And I'd like to hear all of yours." Char pursed her lips.

"Mine are boring."

Char made a rude sound. "Liars go to a very warm place. I don't believe that for a minute, and I've only known you a week." She points east. "Look, the fog's lifting. I'll whip up those flapjacks."

"Char, you're worth your weight in gold."

She drops her hands to her hips and snorts. "I like helping. Besides, this fresh river smells much better than fish canneries." Her blue eyes twinkle. "As for being worth my weight in gold—that would be a tidy sum."

As her snort becomes a guffaw, Johnny opens his eyes.

She claps a hand over her mouth. "Sorry, Johnny."

"No problem. I like hearing folks happy."

He rolls out of his hammock and drops to the deck on leather-clad feet, reminding me of leprechauns in Blackmore's *Lorna Doone*.

"What marvelous boots." I bend and touch the soft leather. "Where did you get them?"

"Made 'em myself." He draws to full height, his dark eyes almost level to mine. "I tanned the deer hide, and my friends on the Cowlitz Reserve taught me the rest. When you go there, tell 'em Johnny sent you. They'll teach you skills they don't show most visitors."

"You're fascinating, Johnny Hofer."

His laugh rumbles, and he slaps his thigh. "You don't know the half."

"But I'd like to. Where do we drop you today?"

"This side of Sandy Island. I'll show you once we're there. Like my other place, you won't see anything 'til we're near, but you don't need to land. There's a flat rock close enough in deep water. A good-sized log fell just right for a bridge. I'll hop on and scoot home in a jiffy. You won't see me again until I choose, but here are the silver dollars I promised." He drops clinking coins into my hand.

Which I try to give back, but he closes my hands around them.

"I don't want these. You're no trouble."

"Running a boat costs money. I like what you're doing. Call this a donation."

Sighing, I drop the coins into my pocket. "I'll bring sulfur and saltpeter."

"I'll watch for you." He tips an imaginary hat and pats down his haystack of gray hair.

By the time we drink coffee, eat Char's flapjacks, and clear dishes, the foghorns stop. Silence reigns under clearing skies like a benediction. Soon, the main channel clears all the way downriver.

Char points to the sparkling horizon, "Like I said, when the fog burns off, it's a brand-new world."

I check my watch. "Let's take our stations. Coordinate time —8:37 a.m. Western Standard, course south by southwest. Goble, here we come."

"Ready to start the engine?" Char asks.

As soon as I nod, Ted scampers down the stairs. When the powerful engine roars, Jeb and Janey rush outside, waving. We cast off, and open water spreads between us and shore.

"Thank you. Come back after you finish the Challenge."

Arms limp at my side, I'm frozen. "Char, I can't leave when staying a day could help Janey."

I'm fine either way. Give me instructions."

"Head back in, please. Ted, cut the engine."

Sparks pulls at his ears. "What are you doing? Why aren't we leaving?

"I can't. Not when I have materials to help Janey get her first-ever Vacation Bible School going here."

"Tarnation." Sparks checks his notebook. "I thought we were racing the clock."

"Barring breakdowns, I think we can make it," Char says.

Janey's still waving goodbye as I cup my hands and call, "If it helps, we'll stay today."

"You'll what?" Her hand freezes. "But your Challenge?"

"Will still be there. You matter."

She throws her apron over her face to smother sobs as Char steers in. Ted tosses the hawser to Jeb, who catches it and ties us back up.

"Explain," Sparks demands. "What's going on?"

"The best thing in the world, young fella," Johnny answers. "Anne and Char were jawing when they thought I was asleep, but I have ears like a fox—kind of pointy, too." He laughs. "Listen more, young fellow, and ask fewer questions. That way, you'll learn what you need to."

I fill in today's square on the Governor's Challenge calendar with a bold black *X* and write *Kalama*. "Now, where did I store those materials?"

God, I meant it when I asked You to take charge. Please make today perfect for Janey. Guide every minute.

17

Monday, June 22, 1942
Kalama, Washington, River Mile 73

"Thanks for cooperating, even when you don't understand —especially you, Sparks." I offer a half-smile that he doesn't return.

"I had no choice."

I sigh. "Some of you know Jeb and Janey's story. If you don't, it's not mine to tell. This stays off record, Sparks."

He mutters and lowers his notebook.

"Janey's arranging the first-ever Vacation Bible School for children here. She led Girl Scouts years back and did 4-H projects as a girl but hasn't taught Bible. She asked for Pastor Bob and Sue's help, so besides church yesterday, they planned. They got a good start but couldn't finish. She needs materials that I have."

Sparks studies his wingtips.

Char leans against the rail, her fingers flashing A-OK. "When Janey taught little kids yesterday, something wonderful happened."

"Always. She and Jeb are miracles for surviving what they did."

"Which is?" Sparks' ears perk up.

"It's their story, printed months ago. Don't ask unless they volunteer."

"Sounds mysterious," he persists. "Are you saying tragedy is the recipe for success?"

"No." I roll my eyes. "Don't put words in my mouth, or I'll help you find some tragedy. Janey doesn't have enough materials. By staying today, I can dig out lessons plus arts and craft supplies. She didn't ask me to stay—she wouldn't. But I want to." I study their faces. "Are we okay?"

Ted checks the big calendar. "Don't get me wrong, but do we have time?"

Char counts the squares. "If we plan carefully, the actual distance left isn't bad, barring unforeseen delays."

I place a hand over my heart. "I'm praying there aren't any. One of my goals for *Books Afloat* is to strengthen people's learning skills. Staying today helps Janey succeed. Vacation Bible School in Oklahoma is where I first heard that Jesus loved me. My granddad got me there. What I learned is the other major event that changed my life."

"Taking Evie to VBS is how she learned about God," Char adds. "Near as I can tell, most folks who go receive the Lord."

"Then it's decided." Ted crosses his arms, which makes him look bigger, stronger.

"Good call, Annie." Johnny pulls green pine needles from his jacket pocket and chews them like they're a savory steak dinner. "Vacation Bible School taught me lots when I was a little shaver. What about you, Sparky?" Johnny's eyes sharpen. "Did you go?"

"Doesn't everyone?" Sparks rubs his jaw.

"Not everyone. But if you didn't, you should." Johnny's eyes stay on him. "Just wonderin'."

"Staying isn't all bad." The hint of a grin lights Sparks' face. "I'll find stories on shore."

"I'll bet you will." I relax. "Every person on this river is amazing. The more I hear, the more I want to learn their stories —like mining gold. Char, will you invite Janey on board?"

Her eyes register concern. "Here?"

I palm my forehead. "No, not here. What am I thinking? Ted, if I point out two boxes, will you carry them to Janey's?"

"You can count on me." He steps forward.

My face softens. "Thanks. Tell Janey we'll bring what we need to her house. If you folks come at mealtime, we'll try to serve something, but Janey's my priority."

Johnny pulls coveralls from his backpack and slips them over his patchwork clothes. "Bread and peanut butter work fine. And I whip up decent mac and cheese in a pinch." He eases his shoulders. "I'll help Jeb rebuild engines or serve store customers —don't matter which. Coming, Sparky?"

"Yeah. Guess I can help, too. But I'll bring my camera bag, in case." He hoists it over one shoulder and, with long strides, follows Johnny uphill.

HOURS LATER, after gleaning great materials from cartons of books, seven of us surround the Jarvis's table enjoying leftovers that taste better the second time around. Jeb's arm rests across the back of Janey's chair.

She glows. "Anne, I can't thank you enough."

"It was nothing." My face heats. "I'm thrilled to help."

Johnny elbows Sparks.

"Uh, yeah. Glad it worked out."

"Annie, it was too something," Johnny chides. "You gave Janey a gift. Let her say a proper thank you."

My heart stalls. This conversation is a can opener for

emotions I'd rather hide. If mine get ripped open, I fear what might tumble out. "You're so welcome. I believe in what you're doing." My eyes meet Janey's and fill.

Sparks finds a fresh page in his notebook and pushes his chair back, scanning our faces. "Can I ask questions? I can't waste opportunities. Anne, what idea birthed *Books Afloat?*"

Good grief, has he no sensitivity to Jeb and Janey? "Like most good stories, this begins, 'Once upon a time …'" I dodge. "I was a little girl in the Dust Bowl when Andrew Carnegie started libraries. We had one ten miles away. Grandpa took me there when he had time and money for gas, so I read all I could.

"Books changed my life and made me want to learn, especially answers to life's big questions. When disaster struck Oklahoma, our family came here. People living in remote spots on both sides of this river need books. I'd like to correct that. It's as simple as that. A few key people supported me. The war nearly stopped us, but we're on our way. I'm happy and thankful."

"Excellent." His pen scratches. "What a great opener. Keep talking. I'll write fast to keep up." His voice rises. "Name your favorite authors. Do you want to write books yourself? Tell me everything."

But then he stops. "Say! Why didn't the war stop you? How did you get money when most projects were shut down? Most civilian funding is frozen. Only military projects get approved now."

I command my breath to calm. "Thankfully, there are exceptions."

"Talk about them."

"Every once in a while, a deserving project sneaks through. You know Governor Langlie." I wave a dismissive hand. "He's a master at pulling rabbits out of hats when he finds projects he believes in. He approved this before the shut-down. But we have to complete the Challenge in thirty days and prove that the need for books on the river is enough to earn continuing support—even during wartime."

"I see." He taps his pen against his strong white teeth. "I guess that makes sense. I need to explain that part convincingly in my article since people with solid proposals are being turned down left and right." He scribbles more words, firing questions.

Until I wave him off. "Sparks, let me catch a breath. You have enough material for days."

"Maybe." He turns Char's way. "How did you join this crew? What's the common denominator?"

She raises her fork and points. If I were Sparks, I'd look out.

"None," she says. "It just worked out. We live on the coast near Long Beach. My husband took me with him seafaring our whole married life, and I learned what he knows. Now I'm a river pilot, and Annie needed one. So here I am."

"It's unusual for a woman to fill that role. Congratulations."

"When I worked ships with J.P., we didn't dream I'd use that skill while he served the Navy in the Asiatic Pacific."

"Ah, the Asiatic Pacific? I'm sure he gives great service. Just so I'm clear, can you show me on this map where he is?" Sparks pulls a map from his camera bag and spreads it out.

"Not exactly." She peers down, adjusting her glasses. "Nothing looks familiar. And he can't write much in letters—just the far-western Pacific, past Hawaii. Somewhere past the Philippines." She stands. "Janey, I'll help clear plates."

Sparks pushes his plate away. "Your turn, Ted. What's your relationship with Anne?"

"Relationship?" Ted looks at me, and something he's eating catches in his throat. He coughs and sputters. "Friends since tenth grade. I hardly remember when she wasn't around. She's a smart gal with guts. I'm glad to help."

"Very smart, or she wouldn't head up *Books Afloat*." Sparks turns to me. "Anne, what do you say about Ted?"

I study Ted. His lip looks almost normal, no more puffiness

from our collision. "He's a good friend, totally reliable and helpful, and a great mechanic. I planned to make this voyage with my retired captain neighbor and his niece, but the captain couldn't come. I hate taking any good man from his work these days, but Ted arranged things."

Ted drops his eyes, looking disappointed. What did he hope I'd say?

Sparks clears his throat. "Totally reliable and helpful? That's odd. Harlan mentioned a careless fire on board."

"No." My voice sharpens. "A small problem got solved."

"All the same, it sounds good Harlan was on board. So, you and Ted are just friends?"

"He's like a brother." I tap Ted's arm. "I'm the pesky little sister he never had, even if he still doesn't know he does." I laugh.

But Ted's eyes close as if he's in pain.

Char points her fork at Sparks again. "Seems to me you ask pesky questions past news stories. Don't wear out your welcome."

"She's right," I remind him. "Your writing needs to focus on *Books Afloat*."

"But it's my job to add human interest. The public eats it up."

"And gets indigestion." Ted wads his napkin. "Char's right. You're going beyond library boat news. Stick to basics."

Sparks lifts his hands in surrender. As he smiles, I picture the barracuda with pointed teeth in the Seaside Aquarium.

"Besides, Anne's the prettiest captain on the river, so it would be easy for more to happen." Sparks continues. "After all, it's summertime. Romance is in the air."

"Stow it." Ted's lips thin. "We're concentrating on making this trip work."

"But reporters find stories behind the obvious."

"Don't push," I say, "and don't invent things. You're on board two more days. Save a few questions for later."

"Only two days? You'll change your mind." His eyes turn to Johnny. "You're on board for a while, too, aren't you, Mr., uh?"

"Hofer."

"I'm not sure how you connect to this crew."

"I don't. Just hitchhiking home." He rises on soundless leather boots. "Right now, my hammock's calling. If you're smart, you'll follow my example. Goodnight, all."

Sparks looks after him.

"We leave at dawn." I stand and stretch. "It was good to stay today, Janey. We'll pray God blesses you and the children all week."

"I can't thank you enough." A light I haven't seen before shines in her eyes.

I AWAKE the next morning as dawn spills soft pink light along low hills and splashes the river molten gold. I drink it in as Jeb calls, "Good morning, *Books Afloat*. Janey has a hot breakfast ready. Come and get it so you can leave early."

"Are you kidding?" I lean over the rail. "Perfect."

She serves platters of fried potatoes and onions, eggs with home-cured bacon, and feather-light biscuits.

"How early did you get up to do this?" I ask.

"It was fun."

"Oo-ee, I've died and gone to heaven *again*," Johnny cries, patting his flat stomach. "Another biscuit, please and thank you. They're so light, I have to hold them down or they fly off."

Janey laughs out loud for the first time since I've known her.

Jeb stares. "I love your laugh, sweetheart." He pulls her close as tears wet his cheeks. "It's been too long."

"Pass the salt and pepper," Sparks says, missing the moment.

Whis-purr purrs like a machine and curls around Char's ankles until she picks her up and smuggles bacon to her.

The cat purrs louder and moves to Ted and then on to me.

"Whis-purr, you are purr-fect. You can stay here all day." I lift her to my lap and draw my hand along her orange-gold fur. Her motor increases. "I wish I could bring you along."

Ted watches me pet her, looking like he wishes he were the cat.

When I put her down, Whis-purr moves past Spark's wingtips but slips and claws the gap between the reporter's trousers and socks.

"What the devil!" he shrieks. "Someone take her."

"Strange." Jeb cocks his head while putting Whis-purr outside the door. "She likes most people."

"It's my aftershave, but most animals love me. Thanks for another amazing meal, Janey." He pushes to his feet. "Well, I'll go to the boat to write."

"And miss doing dishes?" I ask his retreating form. "Smart."

Char pushes up her sleeves and goes to the sink.

"No," Janey says, her eyes clear and shining. "You're our guests, and you have to get on your way."

"Pray for us," I say as we hug.

Janey and Jeb wave goodbye as we walk to the river. Ted starts the engine. I pull the whistle. Char casts off. Sparks snaps pictures. And Johnny waves.

"Come back when you can," Jeb says.

"I won't forget," Janey calls.

We enter the channel and chug forward. "Slightly overcast, but not pea soup weather." Char wets a finger to lift in the wind. "This breeze from the west will cool things off and maybe bring a weather change."

"It perfect now," I say, facing east for one last glimpse of Mt. Hood. "The prettiest dawn I've seen in ages."

"It's gorgeous everywhere here," Char says, waving her hand, "though the weather can change fast."

"This morning's sky showed a touch of red," Johnny says.

"Do you know that saying 'Red sky in morning, sailors take warning'? It's truth, or they wouldn't say it."

"Red sky at night, sailors delight," Ted adds. "I prefer that."

"We seldom get what we wish, son. We trust God to give what's best, and search for the good in what we get."

Ted can't hide his smile. "Are you a philosopher, too?"

"It comes from livin' alone. You see God's patterns around you, and wisdom climbs inside."

We move west through growing waves as Sparks looks around. "Is that Goble over there? It looks small. What do you know about it?"

"Not a lot." I grab a brochure. The town's named for a man who homesteaded here in 1853. Within thirty years, a 360-foot ferry ran between Goble and Kalama carrying twelve passenger and twenty-seven freight cars. That's the only way trains could cross until they built the bridge in Vancouver."

"The bridge at Vancouver opened when?"

"1917."

His pen scratches. "That was another wartime."

"Right. At Longview, you'll see the biggest bridge of all, the Lewis and Clark, linking Washington with Oregon, at Rainier, River Mile 66. It has a 1200-foot-high center span with supports on both ends large enough for ships to pass under. The man who designed it also designed the Golden Gate Bridge."

"No kidding. I visited there and bought postcards. I'm surprised to find something similar here."

"It's a big river that does a lot of shipping. When they finished in 1930, the Lewis and Clark was the longest cantilever bridge in the U.S., and only the second to cross the Columbia."

Sparks rubs his nose. "There's talk of building a bridge at Astoria instead of a ferry, but I don't see how they could. That's four full miles of open water."

"They'll probably manage it someday," Johnny says.

"I want to stay on board to the end of this journey just to report your triumph," Sparks says.

"No guarantees," I say, "and we'll be too busy for interviews."

"I'll know your routine so well by then, it won't matter. I'll just describe what I see and add some bridge stories. Boy, the Golden Gate or these would be prime targets if the Japanese seriously wanted to enter."

Ted's eyes flash. "Don't mention that in anything you write."

"Why? It's true." Sparks cocks his head. "It's easy enough to guess what Japan would like to do. Any thinking man reads past the brief reports the government gives. Japan has won major battles, so targeting bridges would be obvious. Isn't that why Roosevelt moved Japanese nationals inland? So, they don't betray coastal areas and help our enemies?"

Ted's voice deepens. So does his scowl. "I repeat, no writing about the bridges. Don't give the enemy ideas."

"Hah! They've already got them. They read newspapers and scan our radios for information, just like we do theirs." Sparks' face darkens. "Frankly, I'll bet they find lots."

"There's a difference between reporting news and helping enemies," Johnny growls louder than Grandpa's neighbor's pit bull.

"I follow censorship guidelines but add interesting news." Sparks loosen his collar. "You can depend on me."

"That reminds me," I say. "I still want to see those stories."

"So, you said." He lowers his pen. "Frankly, I'm surprised you're asking since the governor is happy with me. I'm also surprised he's planning a celebration in Longview. That might draw too much attention to *Books Afloat*."

"Weren't you saying how good attention is for this trip? Make up your mind. Which is it?" Ted's hands clench.

"The governor usually has good reasons but maybe not always. I guess we'll find out when we get to Longview." Sparks tears out his last page of notes, folds it, and slides it into his shirt pocket.

TED WATCHED Anne climb to the top deck to check river maps with Char.

Sparks yawned. "That thin pad on the engine room floor hurts my back. Let me stretch out on your bed for forty winks 'til we reach the next place."

Ted's heart hammered. "Suit yourself, but we'll dock in Goble soon. It hardly seems worth it."

"Even a few minutes stretching will help work out the kinks." He knocked a fist against his spine as he headed downstairs.

Ted willed Sparks to overlook the handgun under his bed. *Do not go there.* He whipped around as Johnny appeared, his eyes bright and beady.

"Young fella, have you thought more on what I said about Annie?"

"I sure have." Ted unbuttoned the second button on his shirt. "I didn't hear you coming. You sneak up quietly."

"From practice. But you should listen to me." He shook his head. "You've got it bad, young fella. No use saying otherwise, and I don't blame ya." He kneaded his bicep. "She's worth liking. She stands out in any crowd, like a pearl in a mud bank."

"A pearl in a—? We're just good friends."

Johnny made a choking sound. "I don't believe that, and you don't either."

Ted checked to see who else might be listening. The coast was clear. "It's Josh she talks about when she's not thinking about this boat. And that's only right, since he's missing."

"Hard times, yes, but are you blind? I see how she looks at

you. If you can't see, you need these glasses more than I do." He snatched his off his face and waved them toward Ted.

"No, thank you." Ted pushed Johnny's glasses away. "You said that before, but I don't see it. When she's ready, she'll set her cap for somebody lots better than me."

Johnny gave a strangled cough. "That's where you're wrong. For a bright young man, you're poor at reading women. And at reading yourself."

"And you've got a wild imagination."

"Nope. And you hope I'm right." Johnny's eyes riveted him like a hawk tracking a mouse.

"Who wouldn't? I'm a red-blooded American male. And she's, she's—everything a guy could want." Ted licked his dry lips, suddenly needing water.

"We're discussing you."

"I'd be a fool not to hope, but she's totally focused on the Governor's Challenge. Plus, we need to consider Josh." As red heat climbed his neck, he fanned his face.

"But he's not here, and I see her affection for you. Don't let anything stop you. You've got lots going for you. Wake up and don't miss her by not trying."

"But what can I do? How can I show her I care?" Ted sputtered.

"*Butt* is what Billy goats do. Just tell her nice and easy like, and a little romance."

"I'd like to." He tugged his hair. "I can hardly think straight and work, too. I'm going below to check gauges." *And make sure the Smith and Wesson is safe.*

But Johnny called after him. "Just so you know, you're still the man I'm rooting for."

Ted didn't acknowledge he'd heard, but a bounce entered his step.

AFTER JOHNNY'S TALK, Ted felt more confident concerning Annie. On deck, he warned her to be careful crossing the welded ridged metal plate joining two sections.

"Don't warn me," she fumed. 'If you think I'm fool enough to fall on that, you've got another thing com—"

At that exact moment, she tripped on the ridge plate edging the top step and fell into his arms. He caught her but lost his balance and fell, too, both crashing in a heap with him cradling her. This day had just gotten better. He sat up, saving her from harm, but that metal plate might be his new favorite spot on the boat.

Anne's arms flailed, and her cheeks flamed. "Of all the clumsy— I'm sorry. I can't believe I did that. Thanks for catching me."

"Any time. But I'm not sorry." He couldn't stop grinning. "I'm glad to help."

"I did catch my heel on the plate." She quit struggling and raised an eyebrow. "You didn't push me, did you?"

"No, but it's a good idea." His smile widened. "Maybe that will help you take suggestions and not be so independent."

"I'm not—all the time." Her dark eyes held something new he hadn't seen before—like maybe she liked being in his arms.

He returned her gaze, their faces close. Another second and he would combust.

"You're calling me Anne, not Annie. Why?"

"Right now, you're Anne—a little mad because you needed help, which makes you cuter. You're more grown up, less scrappy."

"Scrappy?" She struggled. "Is that what you think?"

"In the nicest possible way."

"That doesn't sound nice." She frowned.

He wanted to kiss her frown away.

"I'd rather give help than receive it."

"Who wouldn't?" Bending closer still, he tucked a strand of

her hair behind her ear. As her breath warmed his cheek, he swallowed. "We all need help sometimes. Forget scrappy. You're plain cute." He loved the freckles sprinkled across her nose, each one an angel's kiss, and longed to add his own.

She pounded his chest. "Okay, you've proven you're a hero. Let me go."

"Are you sure you're steady on your feet? I don't want you falling again."

"Yes. As steady as a rock."

"Convince me." But he didn't release her.

She twisted. "Char? Why didn't you tell me men are infuriating?"

"Not all of them are. Most are quite nice." Char's grinned like a Cheshire cat.

"Not this one." Anne squirmed. "At least not now. Make him let me go."

"He will, in time," Char chuckled.

"Whose side are you on?" Anne reared back. "Ted, *please* let me go."

"That's better." He gave one last squeeze and tipped her to her feet.

"Don't get in the habit of rescuing me." She smoothed her shirt. "I manage fine on my own."

"Do you?" He hiked his eyebrows. "Those days might be over." She reminded him of a day of mixed sunshine and rain.

"What do you mean?"

"We all need help sometimes. When Char hauled me out of the drink, it was humiliating but made me a better man."

"How?" She searched his eyes.

"Humble. Grateful." Was Anne even listening? She looked confused, like maybe part of her liked being held. Did he dare hope? "I'm here anytime you need me. Always."

Her eyes gentled. "I know." She whispered so softly, he wasn't sure he'd heard.

"But how can I help you?"

"You do all the time. You did today."

"I've done nothing this whole trip but make you miserable. When did I help today?"

"When you let me hug you."

"I *did not* let you hug me," she sputtered, then pulled free and dashed through the dividing curtain to her quarters. *"Men are insufferable!"* Her words floated back.

He chuckled. "I'm not a man. I'm your long-term friend," he told the swaying curtain.

Strange sounds emanated, like a face muffled in a pillow while a fist pounded a mattress.

Char's gaze met his. "Give her time. She'll be okay."

Thank God Sparks was below and missed this.

If Ted kept a diary, this would be a red-letter day. Anne protested as he'd held her, but she fit in his arms just right and didn't fight the whole time.

Their relationship was changing. She must know it, too.

18

Monday, June 22, 1942
Goble, Oregon, River Mile 74

"Goble in five minutes." Char points to Oregon's shore. "Where shall I dock?"

I shade my eyes. "That long brick building must be the train station. Any berth near there is fine."

"Any action in Goble these days?" Sparks asks, notebook back in hand.

"Not much I know of. It began as a logging boomtown when wood-burning steamboats stopped to refuel. Later, six trains stopped daily between Portland and Seattle until the rail bridge got built at Portland."

"Impressive." Sparks' pen flies.

"Today, the major activities are fishing, railroad exhibits, and the Goble Tavern."

"That's been here forever," Johnny adds. "Their food's better than their brew."

"We won't have time to go there. This book says Goble has interesting caves."

Ted readies the anchor. "Big enough to explore?"

"Naw." Johnny wiggles a loose front tooth. "Small and on private land—hard to get access and not much to see. I toured them years ago. The best thing about them is their naturally occurring zeolites."

"Naturally occurring what?" Sparks' forehead wrinkles, and his fedora tilts.

"Zeolites."

"Define?" His pen is poised.

"Geological formations found few places in the world. Two rare ones here are tschernichite and boggsite. The latter is named for the man who found it."

"Interesting. Spell those, please. Are they worth much? Will they help the war effort?"

Johnny spells both words. "Sparks, in school, didn't they teach you to ask one question at a time? Scientists study both crystals. They're microporous aluminosilicates used as commercial absorbents and catalysts."

"Whoa!" Sparks slants Johnny a sideways glance. "I've underestimated you. Where'd you get educated? You have lots of knowledge. What's your life story?"

"Not much, but that has to wait, because here's where I get off." With an infectious grin, Johnny swings his pack on his shoulder and steps to the rail. "Pull along that flat rock past the island, Char, and I'm set."

She slows to the last bit of land before Goble, and before I can blink, Johnny waves, hops on the flat rock, and scampers ashore over the giant cedar log like a squirrel swinging through tree branches. In seconds, he enters a thick screen of evergreens and is gone.

"Who is that man?" Sparks asks, sounding like someone meeting the Lone Ranger.

"You saw us pick him up before Kalama. We don't know

more than you, except he's eccentric, charming, and I hope we see him again."

"Me, too," Ted echoes.

"Unusual, for sure." Sparks stares. "I didn't get his picture."

"Goble straight ahead," Char calls. "Pretty small. This map shows Rainier farther west and a place called Hunters on old charts but not the new."

"That's right," I say. "Hunters is so small they lost their post office. Their last census added them to Goble."

"Will we do both towns together?" she asks.

"Our contact combined Goble with Prescott instead. That's a nearby sawmill town crowded on forty acres with quite a few interested families."

"Forty acres? I like that about you, Anne. J.P. will, too." Char fans her face with her Sou'wester and plops it back on her head. "There's no place too small for you to help people. What's the plan here?"

"Like St. Helens, the Prescott folks will join here since Goble's bigger. We'll meet in the train station, which may soon become a museum."

"My camera's ready," Ted says. "Do you need boxes carried?"

"Always. There are three labeled behind my library curtain."

"At your service." He bows from the waist.

"Sir Galahad, alive and well," Char says to the air.

"Did you save me boxes?" Sparks asks.

"Ted's got them. Did you want to help?"

"Yes." He stretches.

I notice again how tall and thin Sparks is.

"I said I'd be useful." He reaches in his news bag for a new notebook but comes up empty. "I've run out," he squawks. "I thought I had more, but they're all full!" His hat wobbles, and he smashes it down with one hand. "Is there somewhere here to buy paper? I can't miss stories."

"That would be a shame," I smirk. "With your great memory, you won't miss much. Folks used to write letters using every bit of paper writing crisscrossed both directions. You could try that."

"No, thanks." His nose twitches like a rabbit chewing carrots. "Don't you have any extra paper on board?

"I can't promise."

The gleam in Char's eye matches mine.

As we step from *Books Afloat* to shore, the barrel-shaped stationmaster rushes out, briskly pumping our hands up and down in welcome like a Texas wildcatter drilling for oil. He's dressed like a museum diorama of the past century with stiff black pants and matching vest, starched white shirt with long sleeves, and black garters gripping his elbows. Silver-rimmed eyeglasses glinting in the sun remind me of *Pinocchio's* Jiminy Cricket.

"Excuse our small but warm welcome. I'm Biggs, Alfred Biggs. Been watching for you." He points west to rising smoke. "Unfortunately, there's a local forest fire with high winds spreading flames this way, so most folks have to stay home, guarding property. They told me which book titles they hope you'll have next time."

"Fine," I say.

"The radio forecasts rain. People may come later if enough falls to dampen the fire."

"I knew I felt rain. Smell it, too." Char removes her yellow Sou'wester and folds it, putting it in her pocket. "My bones tell me when the weather's changing. Sometimes the earth plain needs a drink, so I won't fuss."

"We do. It's been terribly dry." He pushes the building's solid oak door open and waves us in. "Dad and his dad were stationmasters here before me. They'd be thrilled to see you here. They always said this river had a future, that one day it would develop from its Canadian headwaters to the Pacific."

"They were right. It just took a while." Sparks compares a

map on the wall to a smaller one in his hand. "I like your outlook. The Columbia is one of our world's mightiest rivers. When this war ends, you'll see a huge boom." He snaps his fingers in emphasis and takes Biggs by the elbow, leading him several steps away while I set up library books.

"Tell me your dad's and granddad's stories," Sparks says, "so I can write them up. Plus, their vision for this area. America needs to know more of our greatness to have pride in our past. Is that Biggs with two Gs?"

"Yessir, like Biggs Junction, opposite Maryhill, east on the Columbia at Mile 208. My forefathers settled there until they understood rail and river would unite in this direction in big ways—no pun intended. So, they pulled up stakes and floated here to build their dream. Goble named the town, but Dad and Granddad shaped it. Plus, I have historical records, diaries, photos, and future plans, if you have time."

"I'll make time." Sparks' eyebrows waggle as he removes his hat and sets it on the counter. Next, he opens his filled notebook on the counter. "Biggs. I have a dilemma. Could you give me a few sheets of paper to tide me over? I've run out."

"My pleasure!" With a happy smile, Biggs reaches under the counter and pulls out good bond stationary. "This has *Historic Goble Depot* printed on it. It'll make it easier to remember us."

"I won't need a reminder. You're interesting. Now, how'd they get here from Biggs Junction? Which year? Floated, you say? Fascinating."

"Yes. Cows and people on the same barges. Children, other livestock, and household goods piled high, floating on the strong current, long before powerful dams were built. Of course, they had to portage around Celilo Falls. That was tricky, still can be."

"True. I'm from eastern Washington, so I know how people traveled in the early days."

"You don't say." Biggs glows with excitement. "Lots of goods lost and some lives. Rail improved things and helped connect vital links across America."

"I couldn't agree more." Sparks grasps his hand. "It's nice meeting a progressive thinker like me. We're birds of a feather."

Biggs fills the counter with maps, rail charts, and more.

"I see you're in good hands, Sparks," I say.

"The best. There's enough information here to write stories for ages. Thank you, Biggs." A pleased smile lights Sparks' face as he grabs his camera and clicks shots. "To your right, please, Mr. Biggs. I need you in this one. Yes, closer. Hold that chart, please. Perfect!"

"Will you send copies once they're printed? I might write my own history someday."

"You should, and I will. Show me your work once you start. Maybe I can help you get published."

"Seriously?"

"History matters. No guarantees, but it's important, and I have contacts."

"Splendid." Biggs' face shines like he's in church. And now he turns to me. "That reminds me, Captain Mettles. Besides book requests from folks who couldn't come today, I'd like specialty volumes on the transcontinental railway and its tunnels, plus true stories behind ballads like 'John Henry' and 'Casey Jones.'"

"Don't forget the 'Wabash Cannonball,'" Char said.

"I have good sources." My voice flows like honey.

"You just named three of my favorite songs," Ted says, throws back his head, and sings 'Casey Jones' until Sparks points a camera his way. Then Ted's mouth snaps shut.

Library users come but then dwindle.

Biggs walks us to the wharf. "I nearly forgot," he suddenly cries. "Our postmistress had to guard her building today. She's lived here forever and wants books on basket-making from spruce roots or pine needles, like coastal Indian people do. Do you have those?"

My brows knit. "I'll search."

Char's eyes brighten. "I'll help, Anne. I've seen them but never figured out how early people made baskets and boxes watertight from cedar bark. I want to try that, too."

"Lewis and Clark have drawings in their journals. Those can help."

"I have a friend who makes porcupine quill jewelry and decorates baskets with quills—beautiful." Char bubbles. "I'm not sure what your postmistress wants, but picture a gift shop here as part of the train museum offering crafts like that."

"Wonderful!" Biggs claps his hands. "That would enhance our history nicely."

"I'd shop and buy." I jingle Johnny's silver dollars in my pocket.

"Me, too," Sparks agrees. "When your museum opens, I'll do a full-page spread with photos plus mention your family history —if you approve, Biggs."

"Of course!" The stationmaster's smile is as bright as pictures of the North Head Lighthouse where the Columbia joins the Pacific.

Finally, Ted, Char, and I return to our boat and prepare to leave. Wearing a look I can't read, Char calls me to her.

"The way I see it," she says as Ted casts off, "steering a boat is like driving a car. You do that fine. That Coast Guard officer tricked you and dented your confidence. Take the helm. I'll stand so close, you'll be an extension of me, and my license will cover you. If that pesky guy shows up, even he can't make a fuss. And if he tried, I hate to think what I might do."

Char's face combines love and fierceness, like a mama lion licking her cubs into shape but ready to destroy all adversaries.

"Char." My eyes widen. "Thank you. You're an angel."

"I doubt that," she stammers, face red. "Maybe in disguise."

"A perfect disguise!" I stand straighter and enter our new notations in my log. "We're making progress. The town of

Rainier is next, River Mile 68, opposite Kelso-Longview. In the last election, voters changed its name to Port of Longview."

"Longview's growing fast," Sparks says. "So, here's what I want. You at the helm, Anne, as we arrive for the governor's celebration. That's where you belong anyway, and Char made it possible."

Have I misjudged him? Sparks is wishing me well. "What do you say, Char."

"He's right." Her face flushes crimson. "And don't embarrass me by being grateful. Just take your place and shine."

"Yes, ma'am." I smile and snap off a salute. As the blue-green river slips by, my happiness thermometer soars, and I break into singing, "Somewhere over the Rainbow."

"Nice." Ted's smile rivals mine. "You've seen *The Wizard of Oz* often enough to learn the lyrics?"

"But not often enough." Holding the helm with both hands, I feel it surge beneath my fingers. "Now that it won an Academy Award, I want to see it again."

"I'll take you." His eyes hold steady. "And Char has you where you belong, like a bowsprit at the front of a sailing ship."

My forehead scrunches.

"You know—those classy figureheads of women at the front of ships."

"Are you waxing poetic?" Sparks had approached silently. "That sounds like Homer's *Iliad* when Helen of Troy's lovely face launched a thousand ships."

"Anne could. She launched this one, but this is a private conversation," Ted barks.

"Jealous?"

"No, but you get involved in things beyond your business."

"Newsmen do," Sparks admits. "Anne, you at the helm is great, but my camera's below. Ted, will you take one and give me a copy?"

"Nope. Take your own."

"What?" Sparks scrambles below as Goble grows smaller behind us and Rainier grows larger.

"Full steam ahead," I call from the helm.

"Full steam ahead," Char echoes, charting our progress as blue-green waves curl from our bow.

We smell salt brine and spot white seagulls circling and crying overhead.

We're almost halfway and moving forward. Lord, help me see what I need to. Guide us through the other half.

19

Tuesday, June 23, 1942
Kalama, Washington, River Mile 73 and west

Ted laughed as Sparks scrambled for his camera. *Books Afloat* did need a figurehead at the bow, and Anne would be perfect. He'd carve a gorgeous one if he knew how, although Anne wouldn't approve. Besides, such distinction might make them stand out to America's enemies. It was better to look like a simple houseboat delivering books.

Could Japan's red rising sun flag rule these waves? From what he'd heard on privileged radio and telegraph transmissions, that was their intention. His fists clenched. *God keep me alert.*

But it wasn't only *Books Afloat* he cared about. The library was Anne's passion, and she had his full support. Every beat of his heart pounded out her name, Ann-ie, Ann-ie.

Who was he kidding? He'd fooled himself. No wonder Johnny guessed he'd fallen for this wonderful headstrong girl. The sound of a wounded animal rose in his throat. He wasn't good enough for her, never could be. But he wouldn't forgive himself if he didn't try. He clamped his teeth so tight his jaw ached. He'd let Anne know he loved her before they reached the Pacific if it was the last thing he did.

He clattered down the steel stairs to the engine room for the wrench he needed to tighten bolts but stopped mid-stride. Sparks knelt on a sleeping bag next to Ted's bunk, wadding up papers. He thrust them behind his back when Ted appeared. But not fast enough.

"What are those?" Ted's eyes bored. "What are you doing?"

"Nothing. Getting rid of junk." Sparks wadded more papers. "Anne said I could spread a bedroll here next to your bed since rain's coming. Said I'd get drenched on deck, and you wouldn't mind."

"She didn't say anything to me, and we both need privacy to rest decently. I'll find you a better spot since it's too crowded in these small quarters for two grown guys. Especially since you're so tall." He sized up Sparks. "Show me what you're hiding?"

"Nothing. Just getting rid of old notes."

"Give me some. I'll help you." Ted stepped close and held out his hand. "I need extra paper to wipe up oil drips and keep things tidy. We don't waste anything."

When Sparks didn't move fast enough, Ted grabbed his arm and pried his fingers open.

"Ow, what are you doing?"

"Enforcing security."

"Don't you trust me? If you want to fight, I'll take you." Sparks shook his shoulders and huffed like an animal.

"I doubt that, but there's not space here to find out." Ted released him.

Sparks rubbed his wrist. "You hurt me. Don't take liberties."

Ted widened his stance. "What are you doing really?"

"I told you. Nothing." Sparks' chin jutted, and his nose pointed. "Biggs ran some reports for me from my Associated Press privileges, but I also have a message for Anne's eyes only."

"From now on, show those to me, too."

"Who says? Last I heard, she's captain, and you're the mechanic."

Ted flipped his forelock back where it belonged. "I thought reporters knew how to relate to people. Get up on deck. We'll show your notes to Anne when we dock. I'll get her and *Books Afloat* to the coast safely. Or know the reason why."

Sparks shrugged. "Calm down, Vincent. We're on the same side."

"It doesn't much feel like it." But Ted's posture eased. "Look, if I'm wrong, I'll eat your paper and apologize. We can't be too careful these days."

"You're right about that but wrong about me." Sparks rubbed his wrist again. "Are you sure you want to make a big deal out of this? I'm as loyal as they come. I organize Civil Defense back home, but after things Harlan said, I wonder about you."

Ted's lips tightened. "What things?"

"Just concerns, but stay calm." Sparks lifted a hand. "Like you said, we can't be too careful these days."

"Get this straight," Ted planted his feet. "You, Anne, and I will meet soon. It's not an option."

"Will you be there because you're afraid for me to be alone with her?"

"Afraid? Why, you!" Ted formed a fist.

"I hit a nerve. She's attractive." Sparks grinned like the timber wolf Ted once spotted ghosting through trees when Dad took him hunting.

That wolf got away. This one wouldn't. He itched to punch Sparks but didn't. "Get on deck, but stay calm. This is Anne's chance to steer *Books Afloat* like she deserves. Nothing can stop that."

"You're pretty invested, Vincent." Sparks' grin broadened. "You still say there's nothing between you?"

"Are all newsmen this nosy? Write your story but stick to facts—not imagination. Get going."

On deck, Anne was talking with Char. "Since Rainier is small, we won't be there long. Kelso-Longview is opposite."

"Is that named for Mt. Rainier?"

"Yes." Anne waved the pamphlet. "And the mountain was named by Captain Vancouver for the Rear-Admiral of England's Royal Navy."

Sparks shaded his eyes to glimpse the mountain, mostly hidden behind clouds. "I lived in Washington my whole life and didn't know that."

"I had to dig but love learning." Anne looked from Sparks to Ted. 'Is everything all right?"

"We need to settle something," Ted said, "but it can wait."

Char shrugged on a yellow rain slicker and fastened its snaps. "I doubt we'll see Rainier today with those clouds closing in. The wind's rising. It looks like a storm's brewing."

"How can that be?" Anne grinned. "You're wearing your hat."

"A girl has to remove it sometimes to wash her hair."

"The wind's fierce." Ted pulled on a green turtleneck. "It's colder, too."

"We've had good weather until now," Anne said, "so can't complain. We're due some wet stuff, or folks can't tease about Northwesterners having webbed duck feet."

"No doubt about it," Char said. "Rain's coming."

Sparks studied the sky. "If that's so, I'll snap more river shots now." He opened his kit bag and grabbed his camera. "Is it me, or are the waves higher."

Char nodded. "As Anne knows, tides affect the river more the closer we get to the ocean. Twice a day now, we'll see increased tide variations." She inhaled. "Taste that salt air. It smells like home. Those seagulls overhead are cheering us on."

"They're circling because I'm tossing breadcrumbs." Ted flung another handful overhead just as one gull spattered him.

Anne giggled. "Feeding them looks fun. Give me some bread."

Sparks swung his camera toward Ted after he got spattered, but Ted blocked the shot. "Don't do that unless you want to go swimming."

"Uh, not really."

"Smart." Ted turned from Sparks, grabbed a rag to clean up, then tossed the next breadcrumbs farther away.

"What's the tension between you two?" Anne asked. "Can't you get along?"

Sparks shrugged.

"We're fine, just two guys in confined quarters," Ted answered.

She cast a narrow glance. "Make sure."

AT THE HELM, I steer *Books Afloat* close, but not too near Oregon's shore, when a fast-moving tugboat blasts its horn. Pulling no barges to slow it down, the tug surges past, sending giant waves to both sides of the river and pushing us dangerously near the bank.

"Wheel hard right," Char barks, leaving me in control. "Wait. I know that man." She shields her eyes. "Captain Albright. And he knows better." She waves. "He'll be embarrassed it's me. Turn sharper still."

"He rounded that bend so fast, he forced me to the bank. I'm not sure he saw us."

"He should have, or he's getting too old to navigate the river. I'll remind him good next time we meet."

I wrestle the wheel so hard the boat shudders and turn my head to measure the bank, working to stay clear. "Wait. Is that a homestead? That must be Earle Reynolds' place."

"Who?" Ted's eyes follow to where I point.

"The tall man in Kalama with two sons who look like him. The one who raved about Skookum Jim's salmon."

"We all did." Ted smacks his lips.

"His family took over an abandoned homestead around here. That might be it." I wave toward a partial clearing, where a small stream tumbles down a hill. "I would have missed it if that tug hadn't pushed us close to shore." A weather-beaten house perches on the hill's edge. "But the wharf looks rickety. Is it safe, Char?"

"Let me study." She shields her eyes. "I think so. And close enough that from the house, we can watch *Books Afloat* to see she doesn't pull loose. We should get off the river before this storm breaks."

"Yes, ma'am. Is the water deep enough to anchor?"

"I'll sound it." She drops a lead weight on a line over the rail and pulls it back. "Yup, deep enough here."

A gingham-clad woman hurries to the wharf, choosing safe boards to step on while avoiding loose ones. Two cute little girls in matching dresses follow.

"Halloo. Can I help you?"

"Mrs. Reynolds?"

"Yes?"

"We're the library boat. We met your husband Sunday. He mentioned there's no school here, and you needing teaching materials. Said we should stop if we could."

"Oh, my. Yes, he told me. Come ahead. Earle and the boys aren't home yet, but they should be soon." She examines the sky. "Our weather's turning."

"We noticed. This is Char, my pilot, Ted, my mechanic, and Sparks is a reporter, covering our trip plus the celebration Governor Langlie will host Friday in Longview when we reach our halfway mark."

"Goodness. You're celebrities. We haven't heard of the celebration, but there's little news here." She glances uphill at their ramshackle home with wobbly steps. "Please overlook our circumstances. This homestead was abandoned. We love it, but there's so much to do to prove it up."

"No problem. We understand. I saved out several books in case we found you."

"You did?" Her blue eyes blink.

"Yes. I had great teachers and books as a kid, so I sometimes put aside items without always knowing who they're for. When I met your husband, I chose a few in case we met. And just now, a tugboat pushed us so close to shore, we found you."

She clasps her hands. "How wonderful."

Her girls inch closer.

As Char cuts the engine and coasts to the wharf, Ted grabs a rope. "Mrs. Reynolds? Will you catch the other end and help us tie up?"

"Gladly."

As he spins the golden coils through the air, she reaches up and catches it easily on her first try.

"Perfect. Now, please wrap the extra length around your piling several times, and we're set."

"Sure thing. I help Earle with his boat all the time." She ties us quickly, the muscles in her thin arm rising like knots in firewood. "Call me Ella. Our girls are Sally and Lilly." She drops a hand on each of their shoulders. "Earle and our boys are at Skookum Jim's learning to make salmon nets."

"Good. We met Jim at Kalama, too."

She scans the sky and frowns. "They should be here by now."

I raise my jacket collar. "It's turning nasty. Ted, would you mind getting the box marked *Family* inside my library curtain."

"Will do." He returns almost immediately.

The girls stare at the box and then at us, like wise owls.

"Momma, may we open it?" the oldest one says.

Ella ruffles her hair. "Let's go to the house first. Keep Lilly close, so she doesn't fall in." She turns to Anne. "Please come to our home for refreshments. Afterward, we'll see what you have."

We leave *Books Afloat* and step over loose boards to climb the hill. "I have materials for boys and girls, plus special items. You're also welcome to board our boat to borrow what we have." We climb the last rickety steps to enter the cabin. It's clean and smells of good cooking, although there are gaps and narrow cracks where walls and floorboards don't meet.

"I apologize. We make our own furniture and do repairs ourselves, but it's slow. Make yourselves as comfortable as you can." She gestures toward log benches covered with red and white checked cushions. "Girls, bring the chairs."

They scoot to side rooms to bring two chairs, resembling cleverly woven baskets.

Ted plunks himself on the floor. "I prefer this," he says convincingly.

"Me, too." Sparks drops beside him.

"You're kind," Ella says. "So, you've met Earle. Our son Junior is ten, and Lester's eight. Sally here is nine, and Lilly's five."

"I read fast," Lilly lisps.

"Yes, you do." Ella pats her youngest daughter's brown curls and lifts her bangs.

"What a lovely family. We're happy to meet you," I say.

"Not as happy as we are." Ella boils the kettle and brews mint tea. "The mint grows wild, and our girls pick it. We also harvest raspberry leaves, rose hips, and many fruits and herbs—nature's abundance."

Sally serves our tea in blue enamel cups.

I gaze in the cup, studying its depths. "Delicious! Do you record what you collect? The proper amounts and how to process them?"

"It's fairly easy, but the girls do make drawings and list consumables."

"There's little literature available on edible wilds. What you're doing is interesting, and many people would like to read how to use what grows around us."

Ella's cheeks bloom. "If you're serious, we could try. Maybe make carbon copies or mimeograph papers."

"I am serious. Now, I'll show you what I have." I remove the box's lid. "First, basic materials: arithmetic, handwriting, spelling, social studies, general readers, and art—*Dick and Jane* books, things like that."

"And Spot and Puff." Lilly claps her hands.

"Yes. But I'm most excited about two new books that just won awards. Especially one that combines several subjects." I hold two children's books in my hands. "First is *Make Way for Ducklings*, by Robert McCloskey, this year's Caldecott Award winner."

"I've heard of this one but hadn't seen it." Ella's fingers brush the colorful cover reverentially.

"Momma, can I hold the book? And see the pictures?" Sally wipes her hands on her print dress, making sure they are clean.

"If Miss Mettles says so."

When Ella looks my way, I nod.

"Show Lilly, too."

"The second is *Paddle-to-the-Sea* by Holling C. Holling, also a Caldecott Honor Book. This is a total learning experience."

Ella gasps. "I've heard about it, too, but never imagined we'd see one here."

"I'm glad we found you." I smile. "This one's setting is a lake in Ontario, Canada. A native boy carves and paints a toy wooden canoe with a figure inside he names Paddle-to-the-Sea. He lets his canoe follow the stream from his woodland lake through the Great Lakes, to the St. Lawrence Seaway, and to the Atlantic Ocean. It describes fascinating geography and has interesting pictures."

Ella glows. "That sounds like how Earle describes your

library boat. You started inland to journey to the sea but stop at places in between to help people."

"Goodness." My mouth drops open. "That's interesting." I turn pages. "Maybe that's why I love this book so much."

"Nice," Sparks adds. "I may make that parallel in my article."

"Each chapter is a complete story, weaving into the overall tale. Besides black-and-white drawings, many watercolor prints show trees cut into logs, floating to sawmills to be cut into boards—lots of accurate information." I hand the book to Ella.

"I'm glad we live here in the Pacific Northwest where people help each other—like you're helping us." Ella's smile lights her eyes.

"Mrs. Reynolds," Sparks stutters, "sorry to bother you, but I'm out of notebook paper. Do you have any to spare?"

"I'm sure we do." She opens a home-built wooden cabinet and hands him a lined tablet. "You may have this."

"Thank you very much." He opens his billfold and pulls out a crinkled dollar bill. "I'll pay you."

She waves his money away. "No. We share anything we have."

"But you hardly have—" he quiets and flips to the first page, rubbing the clean, lined paper with his thumb. "Ah … well-armed again."

"These are yours," I insist, closing Ella's hands around the books.

Her daughters stand close, gazing at the pictures and the other items in my box without touching them.

"Ella, how do you know about recent books living clear out here?"

She pulls a hand-made rocking chair close and settles. "My mother's amazing. We discuss books when we correspond. I told you I taught before. Earle farmed, trying to earn funds to buy a place. No matter how hard we worked, we couldn't get ahead. And then, tuberculosis damaged his lungs."

Char made a sympathetic sound. "Awful stuff."

"But we didn't give up. When the military reactivated the draft, Earle got called up. He'd recovered by then, but doctors found new scars on his lungs, so they wouldn't take him. Then, we heard how everything here flourishes like the Garden of Eden, and some homestead land was available, so we came west. Two more years, and this place will be ours. A dream come true," her voice trills. "We'll own land our kids will always have and enjoy the future we've longed for."

"Every parent's dream," Char says.

"I hope you succeed," I say. "If there are ways we can help, let us know."

"You already have by coming and bringing these." She hugs the books to herself.

A hullaballoo rises from the river with loud thrashings and screams. For an instant, we freeze, and then all leap up to dash down the rough steps to the river. Ted and I lead, but somehow Ella reaches the scene first.

"Earle!" she screams.

20

Wednesday, June 24, 1942
Reynolds Landing, Oregon, River Mile 69

S wirling water and bodies. It takes a moment to realize
Earle had nearly reached home when disaster struck.
Struggling to haul the salmon-filled net onto their dock, he
toppled out of their small boat and is trapped under the net's
weight. His older son hangs, half-in and half-out of the boat,
reaching for Earle, while the younger fights to upright their
filling craft as spools of netting and cork float by.

"Stay safe." Ella shoves her girls back and darts toward the
river.

But as she runs, Ted surges past.

"I have a boat oar." He thrashes through waist-deep water,
tipping their boat upright, and snatches both endangered sons
to safety before plunging under the net himself to free Earle.

Earle lifts his head above water once and grabs a breath
while Ted slashes the net with an emergency knife. But Ted's in
trouble, too, fighting to fill his lungs as the net pulls at him like
he's another fish to trap.

A small figure dives in from the seemingly uninhabited wooded shore across this narrow part of the river and cuts through the channel with sure strokes. Ted boosts Earle up once more and saws at the net before both sink under the surface and send up bubbles. The swimming figure strokes on, closing the distance, and attacks the net.

Johnny Hofer blows water and spouts like a porpoise as he gives the mighty heaves that free Earle and push him forward. Ella stretches across the water and pulls Earle in.

Rising and sinking, Johnny cuts Ted loose and shoves him our way on the oar before going under himself. Both men have been in the river too long and have taken in too much water. Johnny bobs up, fighting to untangle himself, but disappears.

"Quick!" Char leaps from the wharf onto *Books Afloat* to free our lifeboat. "Ted, hold on."

Char hands me a gaff hook. As I extend it, Ted grabs hold and pulls himself near, hand over hand. Next, I snag Johnny's patched leather vest by one edge and reel him in.

Dear God, his wonderful vest. It only suffers a small tear. When he bobs close, Char manages a strong grip that hauls him over the bow and rolls him on board.

Ted pulls himself into the lifeboat, gasping. His eyes ask about Johnny.

"Not good," I say. "We're doing all we can."

Shaken, we kneel to work on all three, making them release enough water to resume ragged breathing.

Earle responds first.

Ella rubs his hands with her own. "Thank God," she says.

Their boys race home for blankets. I spread my coat over Ted.

"Bring towels. I'll force out the water he swallowed." Char drops to her knees to roll Johnny over. She gives chest compressions.

Johnny gags and spews out small rivers. His chest hardly moves. His eyes stay shut.

Somehow, Ted staggers up. "Why isn't he responding?" he asks. "How bad is it?"

"Bad," I say. "Maybe first-aid isn't enough. Can we radio Doc Brower in Vancouver and ask what more to do?"

"On my way." Ted now tucks my coat around Johnny.

"Take care of yourself," I plead, reaching a hand as he hurries past. "We can't lose you, too."

"Don't worry—I'm indestructible."

On hands and knees, we stay with Earle and Johnny, praying and singing.

The Reynolds boys return with quilts.

Ella asks, "Who is this man who saved Earle?"

Earle clutches his quilt. "He risked his life. Will he be okay?"

"We hope so. He's amazing. We'll tell you about him later."

Dark storm clouds churn overhead almost like Noah's flood. When there's no change in Johnny, Earle clutches Ella's hand and adds his wobbly baritone.

Ella lifts her head. "This singing is beautiful, but it's more than us here. How can so few of us sound like a thousand angels?"

"I hear it, too." My voice breaks. I hear Josh's strong tenor and turn to look, but he's not here. *Dear Lord, don't let Josh be with the angels.* I hear more rich harmonies as heaven itself seems to join in. I still kneel, gripping Johnny's hand, as Char continues chest compressions.

Lord, I lost Grandpa. Please save Johnny. My tears drip on his forehead. Does he blink?

"God, he saved our daddy." Earle's oldest girl howls. "Don't let him die."

"Ella," Earle says, "please take our girls home. Get them settled. After all this man's done, I'll stay and help."

"You're weak. You almost drowned. I'll stay." Her face shows the grief of someone who's nearly lost a loved one.

"Our children need you."

Their eyes lock. Great love passes between them.

"I'll cook something hot and nourishing for you all. Nothing's too good for this man."

Yet Ella lingers, unable to leave the scene.

"He's not out of the woods yet," I caution. "That was an amazing feat for someone his age."

"Not-so-old ..."

I hear a whisper.

One of Johnny's watery eyes opens. "Where am I?"

"On *Books Afloat*. You saved Earle," I answer.

"I'm glad. Good family man. They need him." His words slur, and his eyes shut.

"Johnny, stay with us."

"Tired. It hurts. Let me go." His voice rasps like a dull saw.

"No," I say in his ear. "Don't you dare give up."

Earle leans close, a sob in his voice. "Thanks for saving me when you don't know me."

Johnny's chest rises slightly. "Kinda know you. Been watchin'"

Char's chest compressions force out the last trickles of water.

"Aarrgh. Relentless." His thin smile flickers.

"Stay with us, Johnny. We're your friends."

"Don't have many."

"We are, too," little Sally insists. She clasps his hands and lays her blonde head across his chest. "Daddy, he's cold. Make him warm."

Ted returns as Earle takes the quilt from his shoulders and adds it to Johnny's cocoon. We carefully move him into the library that's more protected.

I point toward my day bed there for Ted to bring more blankets. "What did Dr. Brower say?"

"We're doing the right things. Just keep doing more of the same." Johnny's breath rattles.

My words choke. "We need you, Johnny. I need you."

"Heart's bad. The Lord'll decide."

"If your heart's bad, why did you do it?" My tears drip.

Johnny pants. "Old codger, almost done."

And then, though I've heard no sound above the raging storm. I feel new eyes on me and turn to see Captain Smitty.

"Thank God, how did you—?"

"Sorry to startle you, but I have business here." He grips Char's shoulder as he passes to kneel by Johnny, speaking softly until the half-drowned man's eyes flutter open. "John Hofer. You did a brave thing, and God helped you. I order you to fight with everything and live. I need you. This whole river needs you. It takes us all to win this war."

Johnny's right hand flexes. His dull gray skin flushes slightly pink. We hear him faintly say, "Aye, aye, Captain."

"Stow it, John. Just get strong." Smitty leans close and speaks more quiet words before he turns to me. "Sorry, I can't stay. I'll be back as soon as I can."

"When? And why now?"

"Because you needed me." He crosses our boat's rail and hops to shore.

"Did the doctor release you?" I call.

"Better yet, he brought me." He points downriver and keeps walking.

"In this storm? Can't you both stay here tonight?"

"Not this time." He doesn't turn again.

"Can we help?"

"You're needed here. Take care of Johnny." Even from a distance, there's joy in his voice. "You were made for this, Annie.

You'll do fine." He passes through evergreen growth where there is no trail.

I stare. And then turn to Johnny, who seems to rouse.

"Obey Smitty's orders!" I say.

"If you care … so much … I'll try ..."

"We do care, Johnny. We love you." I'm crying now and can't hide it. Johnny's gray skin tinges pink. He takes a stronger breath. And another.

"A man knows when he's licked." His voice trembles, and his eyes trickle. "If I'm gonna live, I need my beauty sleep." His grin widens, revealing two gold teeth. "Not afraid to die. Just needs to be the right reason." His eyes flutter closed again, and wrinkles and age flee, leaving him more youthful, almost handsome, as he sinks into a refreshing sleep.

We sigh with relief.

Sparks appears, camera in hand. "What did I miss? I finished my notes and labeled film."

"Don't even think about it." I snap. "Real life matters more than news."

"It doesn't hurt to ask."

"You asked. I'm saying 'no.'"

As the storm continues, Char peers outside. "We'd best decide how to spend tonight. We dasn't go anywhere. 'T'would be plain foolish."

"We shouldn't move Johnny," I say.

"I'm not sure about your space on board," Ella says, "but we have room at our place. We'll crowd up and share."

"Sparks needs a place," Ted says. "I can only give him floor room below deck."

"Fine. Come eat with us in the morning. I'll send Earle Jr. to tell you when the food's ready."

"No need. My nose will guide me." Ted grins.

"In fact," Earle Sr. adds, "please spend tomorrow here. After what we've been through, you need rest, and we're connected. We want to know you more."

I look at Char, and then Ted. They nod. "That might work. We don't have to reach Kelso-Longview until tomorrow evening. Our last stop before that is Rainier."

"It's small, not much happening," Earle says. "Having few towns and families along this river stretch is one reason we love it."

"We could use rest," I admit, "and check Johnny. I know first-aid, so I'll stay with him the rest of tonight. You others should sleep."

"I'm not leaving," Earle says. "Not after what that man did. Kids, go with your mom." He kisses his fingertips and lays them across his wife's lips. "G'night, sweetheart."

Ella turns to Sparks. Are you coming?"

"Yes, ma'am."

"Wait." Ted blocks Sparks' way. "We're forgetting something. You and I need a few minutes with Anne first."

I start to protest until I see Ted's face.

"With all that's happened," Sparks says, "can't this wait?"

"Nope."

Sparks heaves a sigh and checks his watch. "Two minutes."

"We'll use what it takes." Ted crosses his arms.

I frown. "If it's that important, should Char join us?"

"Yes, she's a core member." Ted beckons her near. "Sparks needs to show us something."

Icy rain still streams down, and thunder rumbles as Sparks pulls wadded papers from his pocket and smooths them against his slacks.

"What are those?" I ask.

"Nothing. Like I told Ted—just newspaperman stuff." He begins wadding it up again.

"Not so fast. Explain the details." Ted grasps part of one page. "This looks like gibberish."

"These are Associated Press messages, for Pete's sake. I'm allowed news feeds. Some come in code. Biggs printed these telegraph updates for me." His finger highlights several. "You may find this interesting. On June 15, Nazis in Poland arrested Jews on broad charges."

"That's strange." My brow furrows. "Hitler's part Jewish."

"His real name's Schicklgruber." Sparks points to the next line. "'On June 20, Japanese planes bombed Singapore but didn't capture it.'"

"I hope they don't." I shudder. "That's near Midway, isn't it?"

"Close. 'On the twenty-second, a Soviet sub in the Baltic sank a neutral Swedish ship carrying iron ore to Germany. They killed fourteen people and wounded eight.'"

"That's ridiculous." I turn to Char. "Why would they do that if the ship was helping Germany?"

"Who knows?" She shrugs. "War doesn't make sense. J.P. usually writes once a week, but not lately. Do you have news of the Asiatic Pacific?"

"I wish I did." Sparks looks away. "Maybe no news is good news. See, Ted?" He pulls out the linings of both empty pockets. "These papers were harmless. You owe me an apology."

Ted shuffles. "If I do, I'll man up."

"Something about eating paper, wasn't it? I can't show the public most of what I get. Usually, the more people know, the more scared they get. So, I'm told to destroy my notes. Except you wouldn't let me." He crumples the wad again. "Are you ready to eat this, Ted?"

"With salad dressing and salt and pepper?" With thumbs hooked on his belt and swaying with tiredness, Ted manages a sheepish grin. "Sorry if I accused you falsely, but high security is important. All boats, including Anne and *Books Afloat*, could be targets. We must take precautions and stand constant guard."

"Anne and *Books Afloat* could be a target?" Sparks laughs. "That seems preposterous, but I guess anything's possible. I'll spare you eating paper this time." He sticks out his hand for Ted to shake.

Their hands connect awkwardly.

"Apology accepted, Ted. You don't need precautions with me, but don't try that again. And yes, Char. I'll follow up story leads, especially the Asiatic Pacific. I hope there's good news soon."

"We're counting on it," I say, glad for a truce. "They're half a world away, but we're all connected."

He nods. "Thanks for arranging a good bed for me again, Ted—thoughtful."

Ted returns a wry smile.

"Wait." Char puts a hand on Sparks' arm. "You're sure there's no news from J.P.'s area?"

"I wish there were." His eyes warm. "Maybe if you gave more details of his location."

"I don't have them. Navy censoring doesn't allow much. When he left Hawaii, he hinted they might be between the Philippines and Okinawa. When you mentioned Singapore, I got hopeful."

"I understand." He scans his notes one last time. "Nothing, but I'll keep looking."

She knuckles her cheek.

I tug Sparks' sleeve. "What about our coast?"

"Nothing." He shrugs and disappears into the darkness.

Ted braves the dying storm to check that *Books Afloat* is secure, and then he settles in a corner to watch Johnny, Char, Earle, and me. The fussbudget should take care of himself.

"Ted, you're beat up. Please rest. Earle's awake. He'll keep me company."

"Nope." He fixes unblinking eyes on me. "Earle needs rest more than me. I'm not going anywhere, Anne. Accept it."

My lips curve. This man is taking care of me. I don't want to admit it, but it feels good. "You're still saying Anne? Not Annie?"

"Things have been serious, and you're doing great. You're Anne."

"Thanks, I think." I turn to Char. "Please sleep, so you're fresh tomorrow."

"Sounds smart." She yawns and heads upstairs. "Sleep tight, and God bless."

"You, too. Thanks for everything."

"I don't want to be anywhere else. God helped us."

"Yes, and prayers from Bob and Sue and church." I gaze west toward Vancouver. "We needed every one of them …"

Coaches say athletes build new muscle by stretching beyond pain. I wonder how many more muscles we'll need to complete this Challenge.

21

Wednesday, June 24, 1942
Reynolds Landing, Oregon, River Mile 69

Grownups lied to me. While Mom and Dad made Grandpa's burial arrangements, I wandered upstairs to the side room where grownups said he was "resting." He wasn't. The cold unsmiling thing lying on the mortuary slab looked like Grandpa but wasn't him. Grandpa was funny and warm, in constant motion, with laugh wrinkles in the right places. He wouldn't lie there, eyes closed, with his face like stone.

When I touched him, this pretend man felt stiff, cold, hard—not real Grandpa. Where had they put him? I flung open the door so hard it bounced against the wall, and I ran helter-skelter downstairs and hid in the back of the big closet by the front door. I cried my eyes out behind dusty lost-and-found coats until my parents finally found me and coaxed me out.

That didn't change the fact that real Grandpa was gone. Stone Grandpa lay in the mortuary. And it was my fault.

No matter how many years pass, it still hurts. The pain feels like whirling sharp knives, cutting away bits of my heart like people peel apple skins in long strips before throwing them away.

Tonight, I sit cross-legged with Johnny, remembering, watching, and praying. *God, don't let him become stone. Don't let him leave.* I tuck another blanket around him and pat him when he cries out or thrashes.

Good or bad, everyone has family somewhere. I know little of Johnny's, except he said his mother came from Germany. He is fascinating and eccentric but risked his life tonight to save someone he didn't know. My breath catches again at the memory of him trapped and entangled under the net while he pushed Earle free.

He sleeps in that deep place God and prayers reach. Sometimes his eyelids flutter. Gradually when I squeeze his hand, he squeezes weakly. Can that be?

Johnny must be the age Grandpa was when he passed. Sometimes I wonder if Grandpa bears any blame for the accident. Working day and night, sometimes all night, to save his meager crop to pay the mortgage without taking the breaks that mortals need. When I asked my folks, they said, 'We don't discuss things like that.'

My questions seem unloving even to me, when Grandpa worked so hard to help Dad and Mom save their drought-ridden farm, too. The one they lost anyway, sending Dad anywhere and everywhere to find work until it finally brought us here to Washington, where Dad worked in wartime shipyards.

Even if any fault for Grandpa's accident was his, how can I blame the finest man I've ever known? He never tired of my questions. He saved hard-earned pennies and bought me books each birthday. When he didn't have money, he wrote stories with drawings I thought should be published. I still think so.

He drove me to Vacation Bible School each day that week, brought me early and picked me up after harvesting distant hot fields, which made his long days longer still. He attended my VBS graduation—up long before daylight and drove home late. Grandma was sick, so Mom and Dad had stayed with her.

'Help keep me awake till we get home, Annie.'

I tried hard, and he helped by tickling me and singing "Froggy Went A-Courting," but I'd been up since dawn. My words slowed, and my eyelids blinked. Once. Twice. And then closed. My head sank against him, and I felt him pat my head. After that, nothing until screaming metal and choking smoke and fumes from burning gasoline and tires.

How did I survive when he didn't? The first man there reached through fire to pull me from where I huddled under the truck's dash as if I'd been pushed there, sheltered by Grandpa's hand.

"Lord, I'm sorry." I sob now, quietly. "Terribly sorry. I failed him, and I failed You."

Because if Grandpa wasn't to blame for the accident, I was.

"God, can You forgive me? Can you help me never fail anyone again?" I carve that cry deep in my heart with the knife of regret until, like stone Grandpa, I'm also cold and unmoving on a slab.

Finally, I stir and find myself sprawled on a low cot close to Johnny. Did I sleep? Wedged in a wooden folding chair near the door, Earle sprawls in unconscious exhaustion. Char's snores drift down from the upper deck.

Sitting across the room, if Ted notices, he stays mercifully silent. Everyone else sleeps. He studies me through kind but bloodshot eyes.

"His breathing is weak," I say. "Can you tell if he's asleep, or—?"

"It's shallow, but okay. Exhaustion can do that. He'll make it."

A weight lifts, but anger makes me sit ramrod straight, mashing my hair in place with stiff fingers. Why do the men in my life let me sleep when I need to be strong and do my part?

"Why did you let me sleep when you need sleep? I told you I would stand watch."

"You did for a long time. And then, I decided to give you a break."

"Did you put me on the cot and cover me up?"

"Yes. Why do you think you have to do it all? You don't always have to get your way, you know."

His words sting, but I can't resist his smile. "What do you mean?"

"You do more than your share, too. When will you learn, none of us is meant to do everything alone? God wants people to help each other, not carry the world." Exhaustion lines Ted's face, but his voice is gentle. "Besides," his smile broadens, "I like watching you sleep."

My face heats. "You're dead-tired, and I let you down."

"Stop. Why can't I talk sense into your pretty little head?"

Pretty? He finds me pretty? I sit straighter.

"We're doing this voyage as a team. We all want to help. By sleeping now, you'll have energy later. Besides, Johnny's looking better. I asked God to help him, and He is."

My head nods, and I slide into sleep again.

By dawn, the storm abates. *Books Afloat* rocks gently. When I open my eyes, sunrise pokes gold through black boiling clouds and shreds the darkness. *Lord, please end all darkness.*

Ted still watches, his face peaceful. "You look better," he says.

Some of the deep lines in his face show character. He looks distinguished. And more handsome. Why haven't I noticed before?

"Soldiers who sleep on duty get shot," I say.

"Not if they're released from duty. We're a team. Can't you accept help from close friends who care?"

"Yes, but ... Maybe not." And then something breaks inside, and I say the words I've been thinking inside a hundred times this week, that I should have said long before now.

"Ted, I know now Char and I couldn't have sailed *Books Afloat* alone. I shouldn't have wanted to. I don't know what I was thinking, except that's how I'm used to handling things. Thanks for coming. Thanks for caring."

A smile lights his face brighter than the rising sun. "You're welcome. You make things fun. I wouldn't have missed this trip for the world. Besides, you're cute when you sleep. And sometimes you talk in your sleep."

"What?" I stand, hands clenched at my sides. "What did I say?" A boulder hits my stomach.

"Nothing bad. Don't worry. You mentioned your grandfather. That you miss him. That his death hurt terribly. You never told me how he died."

"I don't talk about that to anyone. I messed up so badly. I can't … You'd never …" But then I blurt it all out. "Don't you see? I killed Grandpa by failing him. It's hard to trust others when I'm the one that—I can't let anyone in close and risk failing like that again. I work hard to make things up, but it's never enough—" I'm breathing, but no air reaches my lungs.

"Anne. Do you even hear yourself?"

He comes and puts his arm around me. I try to shrug it off, except he won't let me.

"You were a little girl. No one's holding you responsible. What if things had ended differently here? What if Earle needed someone to catch his boat's rope when he was in trouble, but Ella dropped it, and no one else could catch it? Should his girls blame themselves?"

"No, but—"

"Look at me."

His eyes melt me.

"Please believe me. Do you know how much God loves you? Do you see how much I care?" What would your grandfather want you to know? He'd want you to be at peace." Ted trembles.

I tremble, too.

His face glows with all the love and comfort I can ever long for. I do see how much he cares, but I can't let him. I don't deserve him.

"I'm sorry ..." I whirl and flee.

TED GROANED. Everything in him wanted to care for Annie. To reach out and hold her. But she couldn't let herself trust anyone. Why couldn't she see the qualities many saw in her—her quick mind, endless energy, her loving heart. She always accomplished anything she put her mind to.

Why had he hoped she'd accept him with all she had going for her? His head ached. His heart hurt.

As much as I love her, I don't deserve her.

TEN MINUTES LATER, I return scrubbed and in clean clothes. I wish changing my personality were that easy.

Ted's still here, watching Johnny. "Feeling better?"

"Yes, thanks." I study the floor. "I'm sorry about the waterworks."

"It's been a rough night. Think nothing of it." He flutters a hand. "My girl cousins taught me well." I see sadness behind his smile.

"You do think Johnny's okay?"

"Yes. He's sleeping more deeply now."

"Thank God. When we left Vancouver, I figured the biggest dangers would be the river and sandbars or hidden shoals—or maybe runaway logs from booms. Not world war gearing up, or Japanese subs sneaking up and down our coast."

"Hopefully, that's unlikely."

"I'm not sure."

He levels a long look. "I guess crazy things happen anywhere."

A man's voice squeaks. "You. Don't. Know. The. Half—"

Our heads jerk.

"Johnny?" I ask.

We share a grin, because Johnny's eyes open, and he sits up, fingers reaching in his pocket.

"Thunderation, it's hard when a man can't find what he wants."

"What do you need, Johnny?" I lean close.

"A pencil, consarned it! Dreamed I was home under attack. I want to sign a paper in case that happens. Get me paper and a pen or pencil—if Sparks hasn't made off with them all." He ghosts a smile.

"Yes, sir, coming up." I move quickly.

"I've got money. If I kick the bucket, I want you to know where it is and how to use it."

"Don't talk like that." I shake my head. "You're not dying. We won't let you."

"You don't have much say in the matter during wartime. We none of us are promised more breath than we hold right now." He takes a deep one and holds it until he turns purple.

"Johnny!"

"How long was that? A minute? Maybe two? Earle and his family are good folk, the way families should be. I've got gold and silver coins in hidey holes. I'll draw a map and sign my name. If anything happens, give Earle enough for Junior and Lester to go to college or trade school—whichever they want for good lives on the river. I also want *Books Afloat* to keep doing what you are. With Smitty to advise."

I tear up. "Johnny, you don't have to—. Wait. Do you remember Smitty coming last night?"

"I sure do. There aren't two Smittys, are there? One is enough. He won't let me give up." His eyes shine.

"But we met you near Kalama. How do you and Smitty know each other?"

"Some things are meant to be." He draws a rattling breath and scratches his nose. "That long sleep helped me."

Ted and I exchange looks. Johnny's sleep was almost too long.

"I study this river. Smitty does, too, but he's better at it. We share ideas, and he asked me to look after you, which I'd a mind to do anyway, once I met you and knew what you were up to. Now, bring pen and paper, please."

"Yes, sir."

I bring materials, and he writes instructions in beautiful cursive. "That sums it up. Now you two sign as witnesses."

We do.

I bring him hot tea. "You're amazing, Johnny. Who are you, really?"

"That's for me to know, and you to find out—which you may. Now I'll add my name." He signs with a beautiful flourish.

"Wow," I lean close. "How did you learn to write like that? That's better than my Parker Penmanship teacher, and she was a state finalist."

"Where do you think I learned? My teacher stayed on me until I mastered it. This was easy to write, since I knew what I wanted to say." He closes my fingers on the paper. "Put this somewhere safe."

"I have a place—" And then I palm my forehead. "I don't know what to believe. First, you wave a white flag on an uninhabited island."

"Wasn't uninhabited. I showed you my home. You'll never see another like it."

"You're right. You show up and save Earle. Are we going to keep seeing you all the way to the Pacific?"

"If I have my way, and the Lord preserves me, you will." He coughs, but his grin broadens. "Chances are, if you need me, I'll be there. As often as it takes. 'Til you reach where you're going —and back. If I stay healthy."

"You will."

He lies back down, balling up one blanket under his head. "Is the storm still raging?"

"No. It's through. The sun's trying to shine."

"That was a dilly. Don't wake me 'til later. Need. More. Rest."

His face slackens into sleep. As the lines in his face smooth, he looks as innocent as a newborn babe. Soon, he's snoring like an Oregon buzzsaw spitting sawdust, as if he hasn't been awake and talking at all.

"Have mercy," I say. "What other mysteries live along this river?"

"Plenty, I'll bet," Ted answers."

"I thought the Challenge meant delivering books to people along this river in wartime. That shows I didn't know much about what's really happening. Do you think we'll survive the days ahead?"

"We have every chance, with the Lord on our side." Ted's chin drops to his chest, and he sleeps, too.

"FIT AS A FIDDLE," Johnny crows the next time he sits up. "A brisk night swim does a fella good." His laugh brings a breezy cough as he stretches his scrawny arms. "Yup, almost ready for full action." His movements shift his blankets to reveal a Teddy bear tucked in beside him. "What's this?" He looks closer and swallows, his words breathy. "Which young'un did this?"

"Earle's youngest. She had Sparks bring her Teddy bear here so you'd feel better."

"If that don't beat all." He swipes his eyes, pulls a red-patterned neckerchief from somewhere, and honks loudly. "Those kids make anyone recover by pouring in love."

"Yes. Love's the best medicine, and we're pouring ours in, too," I say.

He blinks. "I know, but please don't say more now, or I'll go mushy on you." His ears flame, and the rest of his face follows. "How does a cranky old man get so blessed? It makes those Carnegies and Rockefeller fellows look like paupers."

Char appears, looking younger, now that she's rested. "Good morning, Johnny. Tell it like it is. I'm glad to see you lively. It took me thirty years to learn about love, but I finally did."

"Smitty's told me stories," Johnny says and winks.

Char turns red. "Keep 'em to yourself."

Earle's eyes snap open, and he looks around. "I slept hard!" He sits up. "Is everyone all right?"

"Better than all right," I answer. "Johnny thinks the people on this river are rich."

Earle catches on. "That's right. Rich enough to save people and give them their lives back." A smile blooms from deep in his heart. He swipes his eyes with his sleeve.

I fold a quilt. "I guess none of us are much worse for wear."

"Looks that way." Johnny waggles his eyebrows. "If I felt any finer, I'd howl at the moon."

"Spare us." Char chortles. "J.P. told me you're full of surprises."

"Did he now? He's a good man." Johnny removes a boot and scratches his toes before sliding it back on.

Earle looks toward his house. "What time is it? Why haven't my kids called us?"

"They did," Ted says. "But when Earle Jr. came to check on us, I said we needed more time. We're having early lunch instead. We can go up any time."

"Good." I check my watch. "We do need to get our library farther."

"Remember, I asked you to spend today with my family?"

Earle tucks in his shirt and pulls on his boots. "We'd love for you to do that if you can."

"If we cut our Rainier visit short and reach Kelso-Longview in time to hear the governor's plans—and ask him to keep them simple."

"I want to visit." Johnny attempts to stand, but he wobbles. He steadies himself, smoothing his garments until they resemble a living green-brown skin.

Char looks him up and down and frowns at her own clothes. "I swear, Johnny, you're as handsome as a grasshopper. I'm pitiful by comparison, but my clothes are more seaworthy."

"Maybe. Maybe not. I'm tempted to sign on with *Books Afloat* for the full trip," he says.

"Our boat is small, but we'd find a spot," I say.

Earle raises a hand. "Here are my kids now."

Four neatly dressed Reynolds children spill down the hills, taking a few shortcuts through evergreen bushes on the way before stopping at the wharf.

"Good morning. How are you, Daddy? Mr. Hofer? Captain Mettles? Ted? Mrs. Pilot?" Earle Jr. was their polite spokesman.

"Please, call me Char."

"Yes, ma'am." The girls say in unison as they curtsy.

"Momma wants to feed you, so please come eat," the oldest one says. "If you're not strong enough, we'll carry food down."

Earle Jr.'s eyes sparkle. "Daddy, there's still salmon tangled in our net. If we're careful, I think we can still get them all."

Earle moves to the wharf and looks. "That's great news. We'll simply find a safer way to haul them in."

"I know ways," Johnny says. "I also need to return this Teddy bear that helped me feel better."

The girls giggle.

He searches their faces. "Which one brought it?

"It's mine," Sally says, "but Lilly helped."

Lilly squeaks as she takes it and hugs Johnny's leg.

"Thanks, little darlins'." Johnny rubs his eyes. "Fool wind's blowing dust in my eyes again." He brushes away a tear.

"Find a better excuse." Char beams. "I love hard times connecting us closer together."

"Hard times can be good times. That sounds like a headline Sparks would use," Ted says.

"Now, if you don't mind," Johnny adds, "my backbone just met my stomach, and I've a mind to eat. Lead the way, children." He puffs out his chest like a bird preening feathers.

"Not much to see here yet, folks, but we've made a start. You're as welcome as sunshine, and we hope you'll come often," Earle says.

We climb the hill in bright sunlight that helps us forget last night's destruction. The rain-fresh air soothes my insides. If everything goes well from here on, we can afford a few hours with Earle's family.

Especially since I'm learning that the experience means more than the journey. If we survive it.

22

Thursday, June 25, 1942
Reynolds Landing, Oregon, River Mile 69

I *hope to have a husband and happy children like these.* My thoughts shock me as I'm with the loving Reynolds family around their table.

My friends call me bright, adventure-loving, ready to conquer life, and too goal-oriented to accept less. I studied enough psychology to know that high achievers can be lonely misfits. I expect lots from life and not to be alone. The Reynolds family tugs my heartstrings.

After chicken barley soup and fresh bread and butter for lunch, Ella shows us their homestead. "So far, besides our garden, we raise rabbits and chickens. We're considering getting goats for milk, but without a road here, getting them across the river could be hard."

I wince. I won't volunteer.

Ella displays her sewing and weaving projects in the craft room at the back of the house.

After Earle shows us his woodshop, we gather in the living

room, and he reaches for his well-used fiddle. "While Ella dishes up rhubarb cobbler, I'll play for you."

Its wood glows under many coats of varnish, although it's scratched under the bridge where he plucks. He plays lively tunes until the cobbler is served, and we dig in. He nods to Ella, and she and Sally lift beautiful wooden instruments down from the cabin wall, tuning them perfectly. With dimples flashing, all three swing into harmonized runs and rills.

"Beautiful," I say, "but I don't recognize those two instruments."

"Earle made them," Ella says. "Sally's is a dulcimer. Mine's a mandolin."

"*Made* them?" I gape. "He's a master craftsman."

He ducks his head like a shy boy. "The tone's good from quality wood here, but I used plans from traditional craftsmen back home." He swings into "Turkey in the Straw."

"Earle, your music is wonderful, and your workmanship is poetry in wood. I wish the world could hear you. Why hide your gifts out here?"

He lowers his bow and stares. "Hiding my gifts? I'm surprised to hear you say that. We're not hiding. This is where we choose to live." He tightens a fiddle peg. "I could ask you the same thing. Why are you bringing books to a few people up and down this river when you could lead a state program and make a big name for yourself?"

My mouth drops open. "That wouldn't appeal to me. I'd rather help people like you, training children to be our next leaders."

Sparks is rested from lounging in the house. "Touché," he says, and jots several lines in his notebook.

"No offense," Earle adds. "Your floating library is appreciated." He nods to Junior. "Ready?"

"Yes, Pa." Junior takes a flute from its resting place on the fireplace mantle, puts his mouth to the mouthpiece, and fingers its openings. He blows notes while his brother holds a hand near, capturing escaping air with glee.

The walls echo. When the song ends, joyful notes hang in the air.

"Thanks for playing." Char drums her fingers on the table. "I wish I could bottle this for my husband and daughter to enjoy."

"Bring them anytime," he says. "You're welcome here."

I lean forward, arms hugging my knees. "Earle, you and your family are treasures—and your instruments are amazing!"

Sparks' camera clicks.

"Do you do that everywhere you go?" Earle asks.

"Pretty much. Until I run out of film—unless you object."

"Actually, I do," Earle says, face stern.

Sparks lowers his camera.

"I'm thankful you're passing on your gifts to your children," I say, "but I also wish a wider audience could see and hear you. This mustn't be lost."

"You're kind." Earle ducks his head again. "That might be possible, but doing much publicly doesn't fit our lifestyle."

"Annie, don't back down," Sparks chimes in. "Cities and towns should hear your talent. And they'd pay. Maybe I can help."

Earle shakes his head. "Thanks, but no."

"Earle, we're privileged to hear this," I say, caught in the beauty of the moment. "Would you please play one more song?"

"Yes. And I'm glad you like our instruments." He cocks an ear. "But what's that jingling sound I hear?"

Ted jerks his hand from his pocket like he's touched a hot stove. "I'm afraid that's me. I've loved magnets since I was a boy and carry them in my pocket. Without realizing it, I reach in and clink them together every once in a while.

"If you do it in rhythm, they're instruments." Earle grins. "We love magnets. Show us later."

But Ted has pulled his hand out of his pocket and now beats rhythm on his knees.

"You may know this next one." Earle lifts his fiddle. "It's 'Barbara Allen.' But while courting Ella, I changed it to 'Ella Darlin'' with a happy ending."

Ella flushes to the roots of her hair. "Sing the original, Earle —not ours."

"Nope. Here we go, one, two, three." His chin clamps down on his fiddle, and his arm works the bow.

His family harmonizes while he carries the melody.

In Scarlet town where I was born, there was a fair maid dwelling
And every youth cried well away, for her name was Ella Darlin'
'Twas in the merry month of May, the green buds were a swelling
Earle nearly on his deathbed lay, for the love of Ella Darlin' ...

Years flee from Ella's face, and her cheeks bloom.

I tent my fingers. "Wonderful! How did you learn to play like that, especially making your own instruments?"

"From my Granddaddy in Kentucky, where we're from." Earle eases back in his rocker. "He was quite a man. You'd have loved him. He and his cronies made our hillsides ring."

My hand traces the curve of the hand-crafted solid maple of the chair I'm in. "You do beautiful work in everything you touch. If I come again, will you let me record a few songs? For my enjoyment?"

"We're counting on you returning. Of course, we will."

"You could teach music and give radio concerts." Sparks won't stop. "Seriously, most performers aren't half as good as you."

Earle laughs. "Thanks. Probably not in these times. And we

live where we want to. It didn't work for us to buy a farm back home, but then we heard there were a few abandoned homesteads here where land produces like the Garden of Eden, so we came and found ours."

"Our kids are happy and healthy here," Ella says. "That makes us rich."

"If I have a family someday, I hope it's like yours, and that they know you." Ted studies their faces as if committing them to memory.

I stare. He says exactly what I'm thinking.

Late afternoon sunlight slants through the windows at a lower angle, reminding me we have to go. "I'm afraid we have to leave, but we want to see you often. Will you consider coming to Longview for the governor's halfway celebration Friday? There will be a picnic, a parade with brass bands, fireworks, and more."

"We hadn't heard of it." Ella looks at Earle. "Do you think it's possible?"

"Maybe. Tell us more."

"Even boat tours," Ted adds, "including ours."

"Really?" Char swallows. "I hadn't heard that. Can we handle it? The governor's plans grow faster than Jack's beanstalk."

The children laugh.

"Yes," Johnny says. "Reynolds family, please come."

"Can we, Daddy? Please?" Sally says.

Four sets of eyes plead.

"We've had a close call, and our boat is small."

"What if we tow you?" I suggest. "Some of you could ride on *Books Afloat* and maybe catch another boat back."

The children cheer.

"We haven't said yes," Earle cautions.

"Please show me your library first," Ella asks, "in case we can't come."

"Yes, and I'll stop whenever we're near. Would you sell me

herbal teas, fresh eggs, jams, and jellies? I'll bet others would buy them, too."

Her face lights. "We would ask the Kalama store to sell for us if we could get things there."

"I can help with that," I say.

She startles. "Really? That could help turn things around for us. This is answered prayer—the most excitement since we left Kentucky." She laughs, and air swooshes out of her lungs until she has to stop for breath.

Earle slips an arm around her. "We'll make it happen—and get to the celebration."

Four children leap and shout.

JOHNNY PULLS Ted and me aside. "I need to talk to you."

I take his hand. "What's wrong, Johnny?"

"Not wrong." His head droops. "Smitty needs me to handle things, but last night left me tuckered. When we leave, please drop me opposite the narrowest shore. I need my own berth tonight."

"On Washington's side?" Scanning that bank, I only see unbroken trees. "You have another place there?"

"Yup. Near where I dove in."

"Are you sure you should be on your own?"

"I'll manage."

I give a long look. "How will you get to Longview?"

He points up. "Wait and see."

Ted cocks an ear and places a hand on Johnny's chest. "Why do I hear wheezing and feel rumbling?"

"I'm old but been worse. Smitty needs me."

"How do you know?" Ted massages his jaw.

"I just do."

"Can't we help?" I ask.

"Nope. He won't let you."

I narrow my eyes. "And there's no point arguing?"

"Nope. If we need help, we'll ask, and vicey versa." He turns to the others and waves Earle near. "I have a good-sized boat hidden that your family can use."

"You do?"

"Yup. It's better for it to be used than to sit and rot. I'm not here much."

"I'm thankful you were this time," Earle says. "There's no way to thank you enough. You'd really let me use your boat?"

"That's what I said. I'm glad to know you."

They shake hands. "My whole family wants you around, Johnny. Come often and stay with us."

"I will, and you're worth saving. I know'd that the first time I watched you. But you're safer not knowing me much."

They share a back-pounding hug.

"Aargh," Johnny sputters. "That loosened things up. Annie, can you spare time for me to show Earle and his boys how to use her?"

"Yes."

"We'll dock in my hidden cove, but you won't spot my home. I might invite you there one day, though."

Char steers where Johnny points. Another overhanging network of lacy hemlocks and cedars forms a natural screen that he guides us through to dock.

"Drop anchor and extend the gangplank to shore. Now walk fifteen yards around this point, and there she be."

We find the *Vengeance*.

"That's Pastor Bob's last name," I exclaim.

"No coincidence," Johnny answers. "He's a fine man, who does the Lord's work—like my boat."

He puts a key in Earle's hands. "You'll need this to take her downriver. When you're back from Longview, dock her in that wide stream behind your place. That way, I can get her when I need her, but you can use her, too—train your boys."

"And girls?" Sally asks.

Johnny laughs. "I don't see why not."

All four kids give ear-splitting whistles.

"If I live to be a hundred," I tell Char, "I'll never understand things on this river, but wouldn't miss them for the world."

Johnny explains the engine's quirks and then straightens and turns. "I need to go, but I'll be seeing you."

As he nears the rail to climb his braided ropes network to shore, I pull him into a hug and kiss his weathered cheek. At first, he's frozen, but then thaws and returns my hug.

"Thanks, Annie."

"Thanks, yourself."

Char hugs him, too.

"I won't forget your kindness," he says. He pounds a hand against his bent back to push stiffness out. "You're making me rethink *family*. I might not be too old to get married someday."

"It's never too late," I raise my eyebrows. "And we're your family, too."

"Much obliged." He tips his cap. "I'll be watching for you, Earle. But next time, I want better circumstances."

"Agreed."

"Family," Johnny looks around and whispers. "You're family. Consarned it, my eyes are leakin' again." He gives a feeble swipe, and his lips twitch. "I ain't used to people caring." A hint of smile curves his mouth.

"It's time you let people," I say.

"Listen to yourself, gal." A smile crinkles his cheeks. "Who'd figure folks could love an old coot like me?" He coughs. "I've got another frog in my throat—from swimmin' that river, no doubt."

"No doubt," Char echoes. "Make sure we see you soon, Johnny."

"Yup, in Longview." He swipes his eyes again.

"You're an American hero," Ted declares. "The kind that deserves newspaper writeups."

"Exactly," Sparks says. "I have plans."

"Hold off," Johnny fusses. "It'll interfere with my work. Besides, the best stories are lived, not read."

"What work?" Sparks asks.

But Johnny's already gone.

23

Thursday, June 25, 1942
Rainier and Port of Longview, River Mile 66

Ted readied the anchor. "Rainier is small. I don't see activity."

Char cut the engine. They drifted past a ramshackle fish-processing plant on shore that might mark the town.

Anne peered over the boat's rail. "It looks like there are homes and businesses past that fringe of trees, but I didn't get a response from here. Maybe I'll ask in Longview, and we'll stop another time."

"That would help our schedule," Char said.

"Look," Ted pointed. "That sign on the processing plant door says, 'Gone Fishing.' That explains it all."

Near sunset, Ted dropped anchor in Longview as Char reversed the engine and berthed. They all needed to talk to the governor. A fit young man strode confidently toward *Books Afloat*.

"Welcome," he called in a pleasant voice. "I'm Miles Bronson, aide to Governor Langlie. He's sorry he can't be here, but he's in top-level meetings, putting out fires."

He shook Anne and Char's hands at the wharf while Ted secured ropes.

"Understood," Anne answered.

"We've booked suites for you in Longview's finest hotel, meals included. He'll join you first thing in the morning. After your hard work this far, he wants you to have some luxury. But rest assured, the cost is his treat—not taxpayer dollars."

"My kind of man," Char quipped. "Remind me to vote for him every time." She adjusted her hat and slung her seaman's bag over her shoulder.

The young man took it. "He appreciates every vote."

"I like beds that don't move," Ted said.

IN THE MORNING, Ted awoke in nice surroundings in a twin bed across the room from Sparks, whose snores rumbled like Sherman tanks rolling across France.

As he shaved, he heard Char belt out "My Blue Heaven" through the thin bathroom wall and realized he'd been humming it first but had now progressed to "Cuddle Up A Little Closer, Lovey Mine!" He slapped his mouth to shut off words like people twist off leaky faucets. *Did I sing the words out loud?* Worse—he heard strangled laughter on the other side. Was that Char? Or Anne?

He prayed Anne was asleep, except pipes rattled in that bathroom as someone showered. *If that's her, let her ears be full of water, so she didn't hear.*

When he joined the ladies in the lobby, laughter sparkled in their eyes. They oohed and aahed about enjoying comfy mattresses.

"Sleep well, Ted?" Anne asked.

As Char chuckled, he feared the worst, but mercifully, hotel staff rolled in a cart offering a fabulous breakfast buffet, and they began eating. They hadn't quite finished when Bronson arrived.

"Good morning. I hope you found everything to your liking."

"Totally," Anne said. "Thanks for looking after us."

"Our pleasure. The governor is here and eager to see you, if you're ready." He beckoned them down a maroon-carpeted hallway to the executive suite.

The governor rose to his feet and quickly crossed the room.

"Anne, Char, Ted, so good to see you." He hugged them and shook Ted's hand. "You're doing great. We're so proud. I wanted to greet you last night but had to deal with wartime politics."

"I can imagine," Ted said. "I'm sure they're enough to give you headaches."

"You're so right." The governor's distinguished face sagged with exhaustion, but his voice held joy. He waved them to comfortable chairs placed around the room. "Please, sit—plenty of room for all of us. I hope you'll forgive me for skipping niceties. We need to get down to business."

"Of course, sir." Anne sat.

Ted did a double-take. She looked like a little girl again, as timid and shy as when she'd first arrived at Vancouver High, though on the outside, even then, she sometimes acted pistol tough.

She twisted her hands. "Thanks for taking time, sir, when you're so busy."

"Ah, but you're at the heart of some important morale-building. You matter to me and our whole state. But I have been worried. That's why I sent an urgent message." His eyes darkened. "What did you think when you heard the Japanese had shelled Astoria?"

"Shelled Astoria?" Anne shot upright. "Sir, we've heard nothing."

Char slapped her chair's arm. "When? That's nineteen miles from my home. How did they get past our mine network? Did they actually enter the river?"

Furrows crisscrossed in the governor's forehead. "It's a miracle it wasn't worse. What do you mean, you've *heard nothing?*"

"Exactly that. No message came. How did you send it?"

Anne looked so miserable, Ted ached for her.

The governor reared back. "Impossible. I sent a top-priority level telegram telling you to take extra precautions through the reporter assigned to you since he has special means for conveying messages. I almost pulled you off the river. What's his name?" He turned to his aide. "Callahan? Corrisson? I knew he wasn't on board yet, but he could get messages to you."

"Do you mean Sparks Corrigan, sir?" Ted asked

The governor snapped his fingers. "Yes, that's the man. An accomplished older fellow. He would have been with you now if your boat were adapted for his wheelchair. We'll correct that today."

"Older man? Wheelchair?' Ted's brain boiled. "Sparks has been with us since Kalama. But he's a young guy. No wheelchair. He said you sent him and showed us a note to prove it, but he's delivered no telegram from you."

"Preposterous." The governor snatched off his glasses and folded their earpieces as if that would clear his thinking. He frowned deeper until his eyebrows almost met. "Surely, we're not discussing the same man."

Anne puzzled. "Could there be two of them?"

"I doubt it, but we'll find out. Where is the man you're discussing?"

"Asleep in our room," Ted answered. "He was worn out and asked me to bring him details from this meeting."

"How interesting," Anne said. "He's usually Johnny on the spot to collect all possible news himself."

"Bring him here." Governor Langlie looked like thunder. "We'll settle this now."

Five minutes later, Sparks entered the room, following Ted, sleep lines still marking his cheek.

He stopped cold. "Governor Langlie?" He held his green fedora in one hand while extending the other. "It's a pleasure to meet you, Sir."

Instead of accepting Sparks' hand, the governor stood back, considering. "You're Sparks Corrigan? Strange. We've exchanged messages through my Public Relations office. They describe you as an older man in a wheelchair. My information appears faulty, but I assure you, we'll get to the bottom of this."

Perspiration beaded Sparks' lip. "I can explain. The older Sparks Corrigan is my uncle—my inspiration. Childhood polio put him in a wheelchair, so I cover the stories he can't physically handle."

"Why wasn't I told?" the governor barked. "You two work together then?"

"Always. He owns the paper, but I'm his editor and lead reporter—literally his feet on the ground."

"So, a working partnership?" The governor gazed through a window. "I'll check with a few top advisors. My main concern involves national security. After the Japanese attacked Fort Stevens, I sent an emergency telegram for immediate delivery to Anne in your name. Why hasn't she received it?"

Sparks' eyes bulged, and a damp spot spread where he gripped his hat. "The Japanese attacked Fort Stevens? When?"

"The twenty-first, as my message said."

"You've caught me short, sir. I got no such message. I received word about today's celebration, but nothing more. The twenty-first, you say? Was that the night of the terrible storm? Could that have blocked our reception?"

The governor's eyes blazed. "No. The bad storm was two nights ago. On Sunday, when you were still in Kalama, the weather was fine. I telegraphed through privileged channels so that no matter where you were, it would reach you for immediate delivery to Anne."

Sparks' Adam's apple bobbed. "Wait. In Goble, I received an AP news update regarding Singapore, Poland, and a Swedish ore ship in the Baltic, but no mention of a West Coast attack. There was a forest fire raging locally. Could that have interfered?"

"No. This carried top-rated priority. I made that clear to my staff. Anyone seeing it knew its importance. Communication failure *is* unforgivable."

"Of course." Sparks mopped his brow. "Goble's stationmaster didn't mention an attack either. He must be unaware. Was there much damage?"

"Thankfully, no. And you're right—I doubt the stationmaster would know. We keep most reports of Japanese activity quiet to minimize public concern. In fact, this matter is classified, and I hold you each accountable." He looked around the room as each nodded. "Security breaches constitute treason."

Ted felt goosebumps, like today's temperature had just plummeted thirty degrees.

"That's why I sent Anne's vital message through you, Corrigan. Even if you were in a wheelchair with physical limitations, I knew anyone receiving it would recognize its urgency and arrange immediate delivery." He pulled a paper from his suit's breast pocket and jotted notes. "As I said, I'll investigate further."

"So will I," Sparks' voice wobbled. "I'll talk with my uncle as soon as he arrives later today. I'll do my best."

"See that you do. I expect nothing less. Since he arrives today, we'll meet later. Besides the celebration, this is my second highest priority today—understood?"

"Absolutely." Sparks shifted from foot to foot. "You didn't know of our working relationship? We were confident you did."

"I told you I did not, and I insist on knowing team players well. Top-level communication demands peak performance. This makes me wonder what *other* critical messages have failed.

"Hopefully, none, sir." Sparks stared at the floor.

Ted, Anne, and Char looked at each other during the long uncomfortable silence.

"The other reason I'm hosting this celebration is to give our people happiness during a distressing time." He stepped forward and squeezed Anne's hand, "Thank you for your amazing service. I'm thrilled you're halfway to the coast. When you arrive and drop anchor, you'll find me there, cheering."

"Thank you, sir."

"It enrages me that an enemy sub invaded our Columbia. If it had entered farther, it could have compromised military installations, endangered civilians, and more." He tossed his head like an angry bull. "Winning wars demands perfect teamwork."

"Governor, I'm sorry. But please tell me more about the Fort Stevens attack," Anne said. "What were the results? Were people hurt?"

"Did they catch the sub?" Sparks asked.

"I want to know how it entered the river with anti-torpedo mines in place," Char said. "J.P. said it was impenetrable."

Ted slammed a fist into his hand. "I wish I'd been there."

The governor laughed. "It looks like it's good for them that you weren't." He leaned forward. "Here are the facts. It was a long-range I-25 like one used in the attack on Pearl Harbor. They avoided our mines by submerging and following under the intentional zigzag path of our salmon fishing boats. They surfaced opposite Fort Stevens at midnight and made a full attack."

Ted groaned. "I have a friend there. How much damage?"

"They used 5.5-inch deck guns and fired seventeen shells. Miraculously, the only injury was when one of our soldiers hit his head on a doorjamb, running to a battle station."

"Someone was watching over us," Anne declared. "It could have been terrible."

"Absolutely." When the governor coughed, his aide immediately brought him water to drink. "Our commander ordered his men not to return fire, so the Japanese could not pinpoint our locations. We may never know the full story. One shell nicked an electric line. Another hit a baseball backstop. The rest fell harmlessly on a baseball field, seventy yards from big guns and our huge ammo depot."

Ted shuddered. "Did we pursue?"

"The sub traveled northwest after firing where our scouting plane spotted it and called in an A-29 Hudson bomber. The sub dodged our bombs and submerged. We're on high alert to avoid repeats."

Ted gritted his teeth. "On *Books Afloat*, we're taking precautions to stay safe."

"I'm sure you are." His eyes warmed.

"I didn't expect the enemy to be so bold," Anne said.

"Pearl Harbor was a surprise attack, too." The governor's eyes burned. "Thank God, there's been no harm, and you're safe. But you can't act on messages you don't receive. Invading Alaska was bad enough. It's clear Japan intends to attack our interior. Stay on high alert."

"What kind of news coverage has been written up?" Sparks asked.

"We're downplaying it, so we don't alarm the public." He gave Sparks a stern look. "Don't let any of this slip. I'll have your hide."

"Yes, sir. I mean, no, sir. At least we have victory at Midway. Otherwise, we might already be under enemy rule, learning to speak Japanese."

"That could be true." The governor's eyes X-rayed Sparks. "I won't say more, but for now, our coast is clear, and we're strengthening defenses."

"There must be some of this I can report." Sparks uncapped his pen.

"No. Off limits. But you can report on our celebration."

Anne leaned close and spoke softly to the governor. "Do you have advice for our travel from here?"

His face became fatherly. "Let me consider. I must finalize details for some of today's events, but we'll meet later tonight. You're heading into danger with precious cargo—your books and your lives. I'm keeping my promise to pray for you and *Books Afloat* daily."

Anne's eyes dampened. "Thank you. That helps already."

"One last question, please." Ted led the governor into a corner. "Anne let Sparks on board believing it was your instruction. She recognized your signature on a note he carried. What should we have done differently?"

"I'm not sure. It's unusual that two reporters would have the same name. My staff described a seasoned older man, so there's considerable confusion. We'll tighten our controls."

Sparks apparently overheard and stepped close. "Excuse me, but for the record, sir, I am seasoned and have excellent credentials. I offered to show Miss Mettles my articles when I first arrived, but she didn't have time to read them."

"You mentioned your articles once but haven't given me an opportunity since, although I've asked for them." Anne snapped. "You said the governor had seen and approved your work."

Sparks was all innocence. "Did I? I think I meant his advisory staff. I can get my stories now."

The governor waved a hand. "I need to be on my way. Corrigan, how about we straighten out our confusion in our meeting later today when your uncle gets here. And make sure you bring your articles for Anne."

"Yes, sir."

Governor Langlie's aide opened the suite's door. "Sir? We have a car ready to drive you to Sacajawea Park."

The governor hesitated. "Thank you, Bronson, but that won't be necessary. I'd like these folks to walk those few blocks with me so I can bring them up to date."

He began firing off lists of games and scheduled events the minute they left the hotel and approached the park with its towering evergreens, rolling green lawns, and manicured flowerbeds.

"Beautiful," Char breathed.

He waved overhead. "Perfect picnic weather. You'll love the menu. Rationing be hanged today." We'll have live music in that gazebo, plus volunteers serving lemonade. Others will hand out bookmarks listing *Books Afloat*'s stops and services. We hope to inspire our citizens to request more libraries."

Sparks still wore his wingtips, but the governor's shoes were dressier yet. Both brushed off bits of mown grass as they walked.

The governor pointed. "Main Street is decorated in red, white, and blue bunting, and the Kelso-Longview High School marching band will lead our parade. After my speech, an A-29 Hudson bomber like the one that chased the sub will fly over the highest point of the Longview Bridge." He squared his shoulders. "We can't take everybody, but our closing event will be to offer short rides on *Books Afloat* for the people drawing winning tickets, if you'll agree, Char."

"Sure." She bit her bottom lip. "Excuse me while I do some emergency housekeeping."

"Not by yourself," Anne said, turning to go with her.

"Wait!" The governor laughed. "Don't worry, we'll keep visitors on deck—no inspection allowed. I've also reserved a small Navy support vessel so you can both offer short rides. And Corrigan, that's where you come in." He gave Sparks a kinder look. "We need more human-interest stories. Today offers good possibilities. I have read several published under the name Sparks Corrigan. Are those yours? Or your uncle's?"

"If they're this week, they're mine, sir."

"My favorite is about Char being the first female pilot on this river and how well she's done. That's classic. Wears her Sou'wester to avoid rain? Give me more like that."

Char choked. "What? What did he say?" She snatched off her hat and swatted Sparks with it.

He lifted a hand to block her. "Just the great job you're doing on *Books Afloat*, and that this trip couldn't have happened without you. It was all good—I didn't say anything wrong."

"I'm going to be sick." Anne made a gurgling sound. "Did you write I failed my pilot test?"

"Are you kidding?" He perspired again. "I value my life. I just said Char is piloting until a technical requirement is met."

Char's voice dropped to a bulldog growl. "Pictures? Don't look so innocent. Is that why you snapped Anne and me together? Is that published, too?"

"Actually, it's a great shot," the governor said. "He has my support for that one."

"You'd best be on good behavior, Sparks, or you're a marked man." Now Char *looked* like a growling bulldog. "To think I made sure you got enough to eat, found you places to sleep. Looked after you like a mother ..."

"I appreciate everything. Nothing was wasted." He backed up. "You'll love the articles."

"Wait!" Anne waved a finger in his face. "How many articles? You said I'd see them before they went to the governor. That two were out, and you'd hold more until we met today. Did you break that promise, too?"

He shifted uncomfortably. "I had a time crunch and wanted to surprise you with growing public acclaim."

"You surprised me, all right." Anne's face clenched.

But the governor's curved in a smile. "Ladies, he should have asked, but I understand his point. Your story needs telling, and this builds morale. He hit the right tone—but Sparks, do always check with Anne from now on if you're writing about her. Understood?"

"Definitely. I confess that last article is my favorite, too."

Both he and the governor chuckled.

"Show us the articles and photos soon." Char thumped Sparks' chest. "Or you won't be laughing."

He sobered. "Yes, ma'am."

Ted and drew the governor aside, along with Anne, whose glance gave permission.

"We have more to report when you have time," Ted said. We've met incredible people and experienced strange—almost unbelievable—happenings."

Anne nodded.

"I've heard some." He smiled. "Including meeting a few of my favorite people. I do want to hear from you, too, Anne. But come along now. I'll show you more plans and booths before the festivities start. I even have school kids wearing sandwich posterboards for a parade of famous books and authors. You'll love it."

Anne smiled. "Great idea. I already do."

A gleam rekindled in Sparks' eye. "Great story material." He opened his camera bag.

"And fabulous food." The governor gestured. "We have picnic tables over there."

"What time does this start?" Char asked.

"At 2 p.m. sharp. I need to give my team last-minute instructions. Meet me then at the platform."

"I'll see if my uncle's here yet." Sparks headed the other direction.

"I'll check housekeeping on *Books Afloat*," Char said.

"I'm coming," Anne said.

Ted followed them. *Thank you, Lord, that we're safe. Please keep it that way. And keep me alert.*

24

Friday, June 26, 1942
Port of Longview, River Mile 66

Char dusts her hands as we finish tidying *Books Afloat*, but concern pinches her face. "Am I tempting fate if I don't wear my Sou'wester today?"

I laugh. "Celebrations are exceptions. Besides, the weatherman says no rain."

"But he can't guarantee it," Ted says.

Leaving *Books Afloat* sparkling, we return to the park and spot Bob and Sue setting up the head table. As Ted and I run to hug them, Harlan pops out from behind a tree.

"Surprise!" A grin plasters his freckled face. "I said I'd come, and here I am."

His antics make my heart pound. "Must you always surprise people? Try approaching slowly and saying hello like ordinary folks."

"Hel-lo," he repeats, stepping closer. "Ordinary is boring when *Books Afloat's* crew are heroes, and I'm proud to join you." He spreads his arms. "Where's my hug?"

Char complies, but I give a one-armed greeting. Ted offers his hand, which Harlan ignores.

"We worked hours doing this," Harlan says, waving toward attractively set picnic tables. "Nice, huh? Reward me by putting me on your team, Anne.

"Everything's covered," I say.

"Drat." Harlan snaps his fingers. "When the governor boards, at least let me ride then—for saving your boat. There's no harm in that."

My forehead puckers. "It's a short run to the bridge and back. I suppose that's okay."

"That's more like it." He pats my arm in a familiar gesture.

I rush to Bob and Sue. "How did you manage all this?"

"By planning and using elbow grease to show you what's in our hearts. Governor Langlie provided the food." She indicates nine tables grouped on the perfect lawn below the stage. "These four connected tables will hold mountains of food, so people can pass on both sides to heap their plates. No one will leave hungry. He and your crew are guests of honor at this center table."

"If we can walk after, we'll do well," I say. "Look at this. Napkins folded like fans and white linen on the head table. Who's coming? The King of England?"

"Nothing's too good for you."

"Is that your wedding china and crystal?"

Sue puts a finger to her lips. "You're not supposed to notice. Let people think the governor's team did it all. We're honoring you because we love you." She pulls me into a warm hug.

I almost blubber. "I've missed you and don't know how to repay how good you are to me."

"Anne, don't be silly. There's no repay. We love freely."

Char joins us. "Hello, you two."

"Hi, there." Sue gives her a hug.

Char looks at the tables and then at her clothes. "What's all this fanciness? I'll hide behind the stage since my outfit is nothing special."

"You'll do no such thing." Sue gets close enough to Char's face to make her listen. "People aren't dressing up. This is a celebration honoring you hardworking team members to thank you for all you're doing on the Challenge. We don't know anyone else brave enough to try, and you're already half-way there!"

Char stands straighter. "Well, when you put it like that ..."

"I thought you'd see the light." Sue turns to me. "How are you, Annie?"

"Thrilled, but feeling pressure." Amazingly, the pressure decreases as soon as I see my friends.

"I imagine." Sue hands me ice-cold lemonade. "Try this. It's my family recipe."

I take a deep swallow. "Delicious! But where's Sparks?" I crane my neck. "This is one time he should snap pictures."

"He'll show up," Sue says. "He and his uncle are with the governor."

"Maybe a visit to the woodshed." I try to hide the glee in my voice.

"Here's my camera," Harlan crows. "I'll get good shots. Lean in for closeups. You first, Anne."

After he clicks the first one, I wave the others in to join me.

"How is the trip since we saw you?" Bob asks. "Sometimes, we feel an urgency to pray. Other times, it feels like things are going fine."

"Both situations are true, thanks. We bank on your prayers." I shade my eyes watching people gather. "We'll give the crowd a general report but tell you the scary parts later."

"So far, they end well," Char says. "By the time this trip's over, our tales may curl your hair."

Sue's dimples flash, and she fluffs her straight locks. "I could use that."

"Don't get us wrong, we've had great times too." Ted helps rearrange a table. "Especially meeting the Reynolds family. They'll be here later today. Have you heard anything more about Josh?"

Sue's face dims like a dying lightbulb. "Just a general government letter saying missing men should now be considered lost. But we won't quit believing."

I grip a table to stay steady. Josh's life can't end that way.

"We won't quit either." Ted pats the New Testament he carries in a shirt pocket. "Official reports can be wrong. We hear stories of people being found after being missing for weeks."

"Or hiding in jungles or caves." Char slips an arm around Sue. "Last night, I dreamed J.P. found Josh and brought him home. That was so good, I didn't want to wake up."

Sue gasps. Tears spring to her eyes. "Lord, let that be true."

"We'd throw a celebration no one would forget." I steady my voice. "How are you and Bob?"

"It helps to stay busy. But sometimes, standing in faith feels like getting teeth pulled out."

"I'm sure." I touch my jaw. "I had two pulled when I was fourteen. They stuffed in so much cotton wadding, I resembled a jack-o'-lantern."

"That's how it feels—like a hollow ache no dentist can fix." She dabs her eyes and puts a smile back on her face. "As Governor Langlie says, staying strong is another reason we're celebrating you today, giving people positive things to think about and declaring victory in advance. Bob and I know you'll reach the Pacific. We're so proud, and Josh would—" She takes a breath. "He will be, too."

She pulls a second Kleenex from her pocket. "I hoped I wouldn't need this." She forces a laugh. "Maybe people will think it's allergies."

Wearing a long frock coat, top hat, and waving a cane, the governor climbs the stage with a bullhorn in hand. "Ladies and

Gentlemen, your attention, please. First of all, thank you for coming. Welcome to this great event honoring our nation and its fine citizens serving here and abroad. Let us salute our flag and sing our national anthem."

A man in uniform plays his trumpet beautifully as every voice rises and sings with hands over hearts. I have never heard "The Star-Spangled Banner" sung more beautifully.

"Now, Pastor Bob Vengeance, who serves his church in Vancouver and all of us up and down this river, please come lead us in giving thanks today for our food and our loved ones, here and abroad, who bravely protect our nation.

Bob climbs the platform and bends his head. All the fervor and thanks in his heart pour out.

Governor Langlie claps a hand on Bob's shoulder. "Thank you, Pastor. Our prayers are with you for the safe return of your son, too." He turns to the crowd. the Governor's Challenge Halfway Celebration is officially open. We'll have three-legged and gunnysack races plus a horseshoe throwing contest and scavenger hunts, with prizes for every event." He beckons people forward.

"But first, come gather around. It's time to eat. Don't be shy. Let the feasting begin!"

Crowds surround the tables for treats they haven't seen in years.

"There's sugar in the lemonade," one boy hollers, licking his lips.

"And this is real ice cream!" A cute little girl licks her cone, smearing some on her chin.

The governor waves again. "Eat your fill—have seconds, thirds—we don't want leftovers!"

The Reynolds family finds us. "To save fuel, we hitched the *Vengeance* behind a tug boat pulling logs to Weyerhaeuser," Earle says. "Slow, but we're here."

"I'll introduce you to the governor," I say and turn to do that.

But Johnny Hofer arrives. He wasn't here, and suddenly he is, dapper and debonair in a woodsman sort of way, with the Reynolds children engulfing him. He reaches in his pocket and gives each child a silver dollar.

"Shiny!" Lilly says.

"Go with your brothers and sister. Buy what you want." He pats her blonde curls.

"No. Too much!" Sally gives hers to her mother, but Ella hands it back.

"Johnny, really!"

"Sally, that one's yours," Johnny corrects. "Here's some for your mom and dad." He lays five silver dollars in Earle's hand.

"Johnny, I won't—"

"You will. You said we're family."

"Yes, but—"

"Either we are, or we're not. Which is it?" Johnny fixes a beady eye.

Earle opens and closes his mouth, but no sound comes. He finally shakes his head and drops the coins into his pocket.

"Come board *Books Afloat* later," I say.

"We won't miss it." Ella smooths her flowered print skirt. "Thanks for inviting us. Our children will always remember."

Earle points to the parade forming. "Look, they're almost ready to start. We'd better eat fast."

The crowd stomps and whistles as Kelso-Longview's combined marching band sweeps by, with majorettes stepping high in bright costumes and batons twirling. Trumpets blare, and trombones slide, hitting every note up and down the scale while bass drums pound out the heartbeat of this town.

"Listen," Governor Langlie says, his face all smiles, one hand on Ted's shoulder, the other on mine. "When I hear brass bands, it makes me want to be a Boy Scout again and stay in office doing the best I can for our state and nation."

Ted's eyes shine. "I loved scouts. I'm just sorry my flat feet kept me out of the Navy." He shakes his head.

Char steps close. "Hush, Ted. What you're doing is just as important. In my bones, I feel you're exactly where you should be. And when I feel things in my bones—"

"They happen." Ted smiles wide.

Governor Langlie's jovial face shows no trace of concern. "Come closer, folks, so I don't need the bullhorn. Are you enjoying yourselves?"

"Yes," voices shout.

"Good. Have you met our guests of honor?" He waves us forward. Harlan approaches, too, but Pastor Bob holds him back.

The governor continues, "Ladies and gentlemen, I'm proud to introduce Captain Anne Mettles and *Books Afloat's* crew. Brave people doing difficult things. Especially Anne, who birthed this floating library. First, she had to convince me, which wasn't easy in wartime, since nothing like this had been done before."

People laugh, and he strikes a heroic pose.

"Yes, men and women, boys and girls, find people who dare to dream and make things happen and follow them. All of us should set our hopes high until they become reality." He lowers the bullhorn and angles a standing microphone toward the crowd. "Do you know what I learned as a boy? In 1900, when I was this lad's size," he points to Lester Reynolds, "my folks took me to a Fourth of July parade and picnic almost as good as this."

"Nooo!" someone shouts.

"Almost, but not quite." He flashes a smile. "That governor, John Rankin Rogers, announced Weyerhaeuser was making one of the biggest land purchases in history to make our state a world lumber and pulp mill leader. We're part of that!"

He lifts his hat, and people cheer.

"Our capitol building has the tallest dome in the nation. When I heard Governor Rogers speak, I thought it must be the most amazing thing in the world to lead a state, so I decided to try. I started by loving books—the same kind *Books Afloat* brings to people who don't have them."

I wave.

"After high school, I worked my way through college to become a teacher, and later a lawyer, to enter politics and help our state. Thank you for electing me. I'm proud to serve." He takes a bow.

People clap, and someone yells, "We'll do it again."

He tips his hat. "I plan to give you that chance. Our tomorrows are decided by today's choices. Abraham Lincoln was a great role model for setting big goals and reaching them. He had few books as a boy but memorized them. He wrote lessons writing with charcoal and burnt sticks. How many of you do that?"

No hands rise.

"Me either. As an adult, he even read books while riding his horse. I'm putting a statue of him doing that in this park. Nothing stopped him from reaching his destiny. Courage and hard work helped him succeed, just like it built this great nation."

Below the stage, Lester Reynolds pokes his brother and says, "That's like you, Junior. You love books and learning. Maybe you'll be governor someday."

Earle Jr. scuffs a shoe. "I dunno. I like inventing. The governor's job is hard. And maybe boring."

"Naw, not boring. You could do it. And hold picnics."

The governor surveys the crowd but gazes at individuals. "In a few years, our nation needs younger ones to replace us to lead our state and land. Who will respond? Who will work hard to lead us forward? There's no reason someone here can't become president of Weyerhaeuser Timber. Or of these United States."

Johnny elbows Lester. "Junior isn't the only one. Your brain's good, too."

Lester ducks his head with a pleased smile.

"One major accomplishment we're celebrating today is our existing statewide library system—already achieved, plus future expansion and bold new steps." The governor continues. "How many of you will visit *Books Afloat* today?"

Many hands wave.

"Be sure you do. I even get a ride later, which you may see in tomorrow's paper." He winks at Sparks and his uncle, nearby in a wheelchair. "How many of you like what *Books Afloat* stands for?"

"Yes!" the audience shouts."

"Three cheers to Anne Mettles and her team. Ready? Hip, hip, hooray! Hip, hip, hooray! Hip, hip, hooray!"

Joy ambushes me as shouts roll along the river and through surrounding wooded hills. At nearby cooking fires, ladies in ruffled pinafores roast more delicious hot dogs and walk around serving lemonade. I want to remember this day forever.

"Visit our posterboard exhibit of Washington's library history. When this war ends, I'll build a state library to be proud of, with enough books to supply small towns, too." He scans the audience like a proud father hosting a family reunion. "I'll end by quoting Abraham Lincoln, who said, 'Whatever you are, be a good one.'" Langlie pumps a hand in the air. "God bless everyone here, and God bless America."

As he is drowned out by applause, Governor Langlie shades his eyes. "It's time for our airshow. Do you see the plane?"

Children jump and scream as they hear engines rev up at the airstrip beyond the park and then spot a rising dot in the sky.

"First a Beechcraft C-45 Expeditor utility trainer, our newest model. Ladies and gentlemen, watch and be amazed!" He flings one arm high and points to the plane.

Johnny stands at rapt attention near the Reynolds family, hand over heart as the roaring beauty flies overhead and then under the Longview Bridge's high center span.

"Ohhh," people exclaim, shouting as the pilot pulls up and dips his wings, circling before returning to Portland Air Base.

"We are proud of our United States Army Air Forces," the governor says, "a formidable strength against all enemies. Next is Lockheed's reconnaissance bomber built to defend our coasts. Prepare to be impressed!"

The A-29 roars to life and soars over us.

"This was the first aircraft England's Royal Air Force used to down an enemy plane. It will do that here, if needed." He surveys the crowd. "How many of you boys would like to fly planes? Girls, too, for that matter. There's even talk of officer training opening soon for military women."

Sally Reynolds turns to her mother, but Ella shakes her head. "We'll talk when you're old enough. I hope by then there won't be wars."

"When this war ends, we'll train men and women to fly mail planes, passenger planes, make medical trips, even do crop dusting for farms." Governor Langlie continues. "Why, someday some of you may become Flash Gordons in rocket ships."

"Not yet," Earle says as he rests a hand on each of his sons. "I want family near me."

"Planes will become safer," Johnny says. "In fact, Junior or Lester could be the bright minds inventing better contraptions."

Both boys beam and stretch taller.

Governor Langlie salutes the Hudson bomber making wide loops overhead. "The A-29's usual crew is pilot, navigator, bombardier, radio operator, and gunner, but today they'll drop wrapped candies, so get ready, get set—here they come!" He swoops his hat upside down to catch a few as children and adults everywhere scramble.

As the plane drops its load, bells from the nearby Catholic Church play the Angelus.

Governor Langlie checks a gold watch from his coat pocket.

"Six o'clock already? While there's still sunshine on the river, we'll have ticket drawings for boat rides to wrap things up."

He nods to the band conductor, who blows a shrill whistle for players to come to attention with instruments ready.

A handsome drum major leads the band, the white plume on his tall maroon hat waving proudly as high-stepping majorettes behind him twirl batons in the air. All members march in step until they stand below the stage and play John Philip Sousa's "Washington Post March." The audience again holds hands over hearts while drums thunder, and the band escorts the governor and us to our boat. A small Navy support vessel bobs alongside.

We hurry on board, and Ted scampers below to start the engine. Char records our location and compass reading, even for short runs, but gives me the wheel. As the governor stands at our rail and lifts his hat, *Books Afloat* backs from the dock. She breasts low blue-green waves glinting gold in the sun, ready for a victory lap under this world-famous bridge.

A terrible grinding clang sounds as *Books Afloat* hits something none of us see. Some giant object hits us so hard below the surface we shudder, making everyone on board stagger, and some fall down like pick-up sticks. Ted and Char recover and run to the stern.

"Something submerged," Ted calls. "Whatever it was, is big."

"Maybe a runaway log from a boom," Char says. "We call them widow makers that sink boats before they see what hit 'em. Happens often. How's it look, Ted?"

"Awful. It gouged a jagged hole with enough water pouring in to ruin our engine."

We list to the side like the *Titanic*. The marching band stops playing. At the rail, the governor staggers again and topples slowly overboard, thrashing as he falls. I reach out but miss him.

Char snatches me back. "Steer for shore—I'll get him." She peels off her coat like a caterpillar splitting its cocoon and dives.

Ted also goes in. Bubbles rise in the boiling current as Char comes up empty. Ted doesn't surface.

Not both of them! I steer *Books Afloat* closer without an engine. The Navy vessel moves near to assist. When Char resurfaces, she shoves a floundering Ted ahead of her, guiding his hands to our ladder. He looks fine.

"The governor?" I yell.

People on shore scream, and Char dives again, rising empty-handed a third time, her face taut.

Harlan stands frozen until he sees the governor's hat pop to the surface and goes into action, plunging to that spot with strong strokes. After going under for what seems an eternity, he comes up clutching the governor's weighty frock coat with our friend buttoned inside. Harlan pulls him toward the boat while holding him as tightly as a dog with a meaty bone.

"Thank God!" Char guides the governor to the ladder.

Ted and I lean down to help him reach the deck. The crowd cheers.

"I couldn't breathe," he says, spewing water, and his knees buckle as he sinks to the deck. "I figured I was gone."

"Too close for comfort," I say, helping him peel out of his frock coat.

"Your time isn't up." Char leans him against the boat's side and tucks a blanket around him.

Sparks appears, camera ready.

"Not now," the governor roars.

"But sir, it's story material. Nothing's more important."

"Pleasing your governor is more important."

"Get rid of that camera, and give us a hand, Sparks." Char commands. She points to the listing starboard deck where water pours in. "Grab a bucket and bail—unless you want to swim. Ted, how is it below?"

He reappears, face drawn. "Filling fast. We can't stay on board." His tortured eyes find mine. "Anne, I'm sorry. We have to abandon ship."

25

Saturday, June 27, 1942
Port of Longview, River Mile 66

Ted groaned. He was on *Books Afloat* to help Annie. Not see her fail. Once more, his best efforts weren't enough to avoid a nightmare. He hadn't been able to give his mom the strength she'd needed to live, and somehow he'd failed Annie now.

He placed his hands on her shoulders, "I'm so sorry. We have to leave *Books Afloat*, but we'll find another way to do the Challenge."

Eyes wild, she reared back. "Don't. Say. That. I won't listen." Her face tightened into a mask as she tossed her head like a crazy person. "Go look again. Find a way, because I won't quit."

"I wish I had different news. There's a gaping hole with water flooding in. Barring a miracle, it's over."

"Then find one!" She spasmed as if a torpedo hit her chest and stopped her heart.

Char returned from the engine room, ghostly pale. "The hull is filling. Grab your ship's log. We have to go." Char reached for the bright yellow life raft lashed to the rail. Arms crossed and jaw set, she stood before Anne. "Don't be ridiculous. We don't have a choice. Ted, get Governor Langlie ashore and come back for us."

The Naval vessel nosed near, an officer shouting, "Governor, we're ready to take you."

"No," he roared. "I won't leave without the others."

"You must. You lead our state."

Anne bent over, her arms wrapped around her middle, and groaned. "*Books Afloat* is finished."

"Not yet," Governor Langlie insisted as Ted supported him to the rail. "You've come so far. We'll find a way."

"We'll try again," Char promised, fumbling with a life raft. "Ted, help me release this. The mechanism's stuck." They wrestled until something loosed, and the raft lowered.

"Wait." Sparks hurried forward. "I need to go with the governor to tell his story." He slid down the rope and dropped into the raft, sitting next to the governor.

"In your opinion." Char's lips curled.

"Why aren't I in charge?" Harlan thumped his chest.

"Because we know how to run the boat. Go with the governor."

Harlan hesitated. "I rescued him, so guess I should stick with him. Anyone can see that."

"I see rats leaving the ship," Char muttered. "Ted, you're in charge. Make Anne leave now and get me later. I'm taking another look."

"There's room for us all," Governor Langlie shouted. He turned to the Naval vessel. "Accompany us, but don't make us board your boat. This raft is still officially part of *Books Afloat*."

"Governor, we have an emergency."

"And I'm giving executive orders. Protocol be hanged. These are my friends."

Sparks turned pasty as the blood drained from his face. "If

Books Afloat sinks, it could suck us under. The others are good swimmers ..."

"And you're not?" Anne dripped sarcasm. "Ted's not either, but he's brave."

Sparks clutched the raft's side like it was the rock of Gibraltar.

"Hey," Ted called. "That's inflatable. Hold too tight, and it'll rupture."

Sparks let go like it was fire.

"We'll go together, Anne." Governor Langlie bellowed. "Come."

"I'm sorry, I can't." Her voice shook. "Not without my library files." She rushed in and swept the card boxes into her arms.

Char grabbed a seaman's bag and stuffed the boxes inside. After Anne added the ship's log, a compass, and sextant, Char snugged the bag closed. Together they dragged the bag to the rail, snapped it to a rope pulley, and dropped it to Ted.

Anne sagged with relief. "Char, Ted, I appreciate you both."

Harlan's head jerked. "But not me? Didn't you see what I did back there? How I saved things again?"

"I appreciate you, too, Harlan." Anne sighed. "Let that be enough."

"Anne," the governor said, "I know you hate abandoning ship, but you and Char must come. That's an order."

"But my books, my precious books." She spread her arms, tears washing her cheeks.

"Anne, look at me. They're replaceable. You are not."

Seeing so much kindness in the Governor's gaze, Ted swallowed hard.

"Yes, sir." All fight left her.

Anne bowed her head as Char clipped her into the bosun's chair to slide to Ted's open arms. Ted guided her to a corner of the raft, where she quietly shed more tears. Numb, Ted still managed to start the small portable outboard motor that would power the raft to shore, but a horn blast startled them. An aged tugboat rounded *Books Afloat's* stern, coming fast.

Its captain bellowed, *"Books Afloat, we're here to help."*

"Captain Albright and the *Steadfast?*" Char shrieked relief, her words singing. "I've never been so glad to see you in all my born days."

"That's saying a lot, since we've been friends forever. I owe you for running you aground the other day. Didn't see ya 'til too late, but I'm sure you noticed me." He shook with laughter.

She grinned back. "You're right. I did."

"Well, now you're in trouble, but I think I can help. A flotation bladder should work."

"You have one? Bless your heart," Char called. "You're a knight in shining armor."

"Ha, ha. Armor?" He pointed to his grease-stained seaman coveralls. "Great disguise," and he laughed again. He and his crew wrestled an inflatable orange rubber device under *Books Afloat's* tilting hull and pumped in air. "If this doesn't work, I'll try ship patches. Sometimes water rushing in fills holes tight enough, but flotation bladders are best."

He tipped his hat to Anne. "We haven't met, but we've all heard about the Challenge, Captain Anne. You have my respect. I want to give you a fighting chance."

Anne wiped her eyes. "Thank you. I'm so grateful."

"Now go ashore and stay safe. We'll do all we can and send word."

"You're a godsend." Ted saluted Albright and then followed the small Naval vessel to shore.

Lord, thank You for rescuing us. Please fix Books Afloat.

CHAR and I share a room in the luxury hotel where Governor Langlie extends our stay. Tossing and turning through a long night, I look at my watch and am shocked to see only ten minutes have passed since I last checked. Char's awake, too.

We get dressed and go to the hotel salon to catnap in comfortable chairs while awaiting word on *Books Afloat*. All is silent, except for the tall grandfather clock loudly bonging hours and quarter hours and ticking off minutes. Finally, the hotel's ornate oak front door swings open, and Ted slouches in, shoulders hunched.

I release my hold on my chair's arms and rush to him. "Is there hope?"

"Good morning." His face is drawn and weary.

"Is the damage fixable?"

"Please give me a minute." He half-smiles and sinks into a chair. "Let me catch a breath."

"I'll bet you're starved." Char crosses the room and brings him two bran muffins in a napkin from the sideboard. "I'll see if I can find coffee."

He sighs so deeply, I'm surprised his lungs have any air left.

"That would equal a blood transfusion. Whatever the next rank is above pilot, Char, you're there."

She's back in no time with a pot and cups, making me wish I'd offered instead.

"Please, tell us when you can," I say, "and then we'll find you a full breakfast."

He sheds his seaman's jacket. "This isn't the news I wanted to bring. From the jagged hole and wood splinters jammed into our hull, it had to be a giant runaway log—maybe a monster cedar from a Weyerhaeuser boom that hit like a Japanese torpedo—but we don't have proof. My guess is, it got waterlogged, sank, and the strong current added force. After it hit, it rushed on."

My hands white knuckle. "It should have been a torpedo. We might be insured for enemy attack, but I doubt we are for a deadhead. It's a rough day when I'd prefer a torpedo."

"I know. By the way *Books Afloat* shuddered, I'm glad we survived." He inhales the first muffin and is half-way through the second. "That's a good recipe."

"I'll make you plenty when life calms down," Char says. "Can Albright seal off the damaged part so we can keep going?"

"That's what he's trying to figure out. When you see the hole, you'll understand." A muffin crumb clings to his lip. Ted slightly weaves back and forth, fighting sleep. "Governor Langlie's talking to Olympia. He asked me not to say more until he comes."

Char breezes out and returns with a tray of toast, raspberry jam, and fresh coffee. She pours steaming brew in green-swirled pottery mugs for each of us before adding cream to her own.

"Thanks so much, Char." I flutter a hand. I hold my mug to my cheek, glad for its warmth, and blow on the contents to cool it. "So, it was another runaway log?"

"I'm not surprised," Char says. "There are plenty of sunken boats at the bottom of lakes and rivers because of them, and lots of boatmen who never come home."

I shiver. "Isn't snagging deadheads what Jeb Jarvis did for income?"

"Yes. He was good at it." I see Ted's partly empty mug and am on my feet to fill it.

"I wish he'd snagged this one before it found us." Ted lifts his cup. "He'd get good money for one that size."

Ted's exhaustion tugs at my heart. "Still, I realize if our accident had happened almost anywhere else on the river, we would have sunk before help came."

"That's right," Governor Langlie says, entering the room. "If it had to happen, at least help was here. That part is good news." He hugs Char and me.

"Thanks for staying to help us," Char says. "And for getting us rooms again, especially when you have so many statewide responsibilities."

He inclines his head. "You're high on my list. I won't leave until we have answers. Ted, what's Albright's verdict? Is it repairable? Is there a cost estimate?"

Somehow, Ted instantly shakes some of his weariness.

"Albright says it might be fixable but doesn't have numbers yet. We'd have sunk if he hadn't wedged that floatation device under us so we could limp to dock."

"Thank God." The governor claps Ted's back. "You're impressive, Vincent. I saw you out there as calm and steady as a rock. We need more men like you."

Ted nearly chokes.

"That's who he is—in charge and capable." Char beams.

The governor nods. "Do you ladies know he and Albright worked all night? I couldn't get either one to take a break."

Now I realize the governor looks nearly as tired as Ted. "Sir, were you up all night, too?"

"Almost, but I can sleep riding back to Olympia soon. Ted's our expert. Please share the findings."

He rubs his red-rimmed eyes and pulls a sheaf of papers from his pocket.

I rotate my head and shoulders, working out stiffness, bracing myself to absorb the coming blows. "Tell me straight. How bad is it? Are we finished?"

Ted hesitates and then reads. "Besides the two-by-two-foot gash in the hull, the worst news is your propeller shaft snapped."

I jolt.

"Our gas line tore loose but didn't rupture."

"That's a mercy," Char says.

I cradle my head in my hands, barely managing a whisper. "It's nearly my worst nightmare." I force back tears that squeeze through my closed eyelids anyway. "I don't have repair money. It would kill me to admit defeat, but I doubt we can survive this."

"Hold on, young lady." The governor's jarring voice is a balm.

He and Ted exchange looks.

"It isn't like you to give up easily. Let Ted finish."

"I'm friends with Sid Longmont, head marine mechanic here. We studied mechanics at Clark College together, and now he runs Longview Marina, the biggest repair shop here. He owes me a favor and wants to help, so we both checked *Books Afloat* from stem to stern."

"And? Even if she can be fixed, I can't afford expensive repairs. Besides, where could we find a replacement propeller shaft during wartime?"

"Wait. Don't accept the worst." The governor grips my shoulder. "You're facing big challenges with limited funds, but people at the celebration saw the whole thing and want to help. Many dug deep in their pockets, and though most families are facing hard times, they raised one thousand dollars. My team and I will match that from personal funds. It might be enough. It's at least enough to start."

My hands fly to my mouth. "Seriously?"

"Yes, Anne. We all believe in you."

"How wonderful." I choke out my words. "Ted? What do you think? Can that cover the costs?"

"Normally, no. Except Sid is my good friend."

Ted's eyes begin to clear. More weariness leaves his face. "Like I said, he owes me a favor. He has used parts lying around, and would you believe, he found the exact size propeller shaft? That's clearly God's hand."

I burst into tears again—happy tears.

"His marina is closed weekends, but Sid's given us full run of the place, and part of his staff is volunteering at no cost."

I grip my chair arms tight to stop my arms from trembling. "And the hull?"

"Captain Albright and his crew have started work, and,

believe it or not, it looks like his ship patches will fill the hole and hold. At least until this voyage is complete. Listen. You might hear their hammers pounding from here."

I cock an ear. "Yes, I do." Hope refills my drained emotions.

Ted rubs his stubbly jaw and flips his unruly hair out of his eyes. He needs a trim. I wonder if he'd let me try.

"We hope to finish Monday or Tuesday for sure. *Books Afloat* should be nearly as good as new."

"It seems fitting that in wartime, even our equipment has battle scars," Governor Langlie says.

Now, not even trying to hide my tears, I spring across the room and fling my arms around Ted. "You did find a miracle."

Ted blushes but stands and hugs me back. "You told me to, so I gave it my best shot." His hug returns such strength and caring. I don't want it to end.

"A miracle you deserve." The governor steps close and slips a fatherly arm around both of us. "I'm leaving but have assigned good people to help you." He winks. "I agree, Ted is the best."

"How can I thank you all? Especially you, Ted, for all you've done?"

His tired eyes sparkle. "Hugs work fine."

"I heard that." Harlan walks in, scowling. "I'm glad you're here, Governor. I'm sure you agree that since I've saved *Books Afloat* twice, including pulling you from the Columbia when Ted couldn't, I'm the man to escort Anne and *Books Afloat* the rest of the way."

"What?" Our voices blend.

"I've arranged a leave of absence from my mechanics program. I know you're dropping Sparks near his car so he can head home. Maybe Ted can ride with you to Olympia, too and hitchhike from there, because I'll cover everything here."

Harlan's arms cross his chest, ready to fight all opponents, but our response is silence.

26

Saturday, June 27, 1942
Port of Longview, River Mile 66

It wasn't fresh coffee that scalded Ted's throat. Harlan's scathing, bitter words made him clamp his mouth shut. He, Anne, and Char stared at Harlan as the governor cleared his throat.

"You've been Johnny-on-the-spot twice," the governor said. "I'll give you that. I'm grateful you pulled me from the river and will write a great recommendation. But as for replacing Ted on *Books Afloat*, like President Roosevelt said, I don't change horses in mid-stream."

Harlan's eyes hooded. "What do you mean?"

"You will make a good mechanic. I hear you have strong skills, and we need well-trained men, so don't let anything stop you. Get licensed and move forward, through the military or any job you choose. But finish one thing at a time. *Books Afloat's* crew stays the same." He rested a hand on Ted's shoulder. "Ted's doing fine. The team that started my Challenge will finish it."

"That's unfair," Harlan sputtered and glared. "Ted's not doing his job right, or so many *accidents* wouldn't happen."

"I disagree." The governor's eyes narrowed. "I answered you nicely this time, Harlan. Don't make me use stronger terms. My decision stands."

"But it's wrong." Face mottled red, Harlan stood, breathing hard.

"Are you challenging me?" Governor Langlie's voice dropped.

"Maybe I'm not saying it right, but I'm not wrong. Replace him." Harlan jammed his hands in his pockets.

"I have no cause, Harlan. Like I said, I'm grateful for your actions and will recommend you for a good position after graduation."

Harlan stepped back. "I don't understand but would like your letter of recommendation."

"You'll get the best I can write."

"Thanks." Harlan glanced at Anne and Char. "I'll say goodbye then. I hope Pastor Bob and Sue didn't leave without me."

"They haven't," the governor said. "I asked them to wait."

Harlan's breath rasped. "If you change your mind, I'll drop everything to help Anne." He turned her way.

"Thank you, Harlan. Just pray for us." When she extended her hand to shake, he flung his arms around her.

"You know I will." His voice broke.

She shifted to a sideswipe hug. "We'll see you later then."

He stomped past Ted and through the door without comment.

"What's his intensity?" Anne asked once the door closed.

Ted and the governor exchanged glances.

"Probably overactive male hormones," the older man answered.

Ted pinched the bridge of his nose. "Governor, you've increased my appreciation for skilled politicians."

The governor's smile widened as he lifted his briefcase. "We serve a purpose. I must go, but these are days I won't forget. I'm thrilled you can continue the Challenge. Stay safe and finish strong."

"Thank you, Governor. God bless you." Anne stood on tiptoe and kissed his cheek. "Thanks for everything."

"No more than I'd do for my own daughter." He beamed. And that's how I see you. God bless us all—we may still need it."

In the next minutes, Ted finished breakfast and washed it down with orange juice. As he left the hotel for the marina, concentrating on repairs, a big fist slugged him hard.

"What the?"

Harlan jumped Ted. "I've seen how you look at Anne. I know what you're up to."

Ted twisted. "What are you talking about? I'm helping her win the Challenge."

"Liar. You're here for yourself. You're moon-sick when she's around. I can't stand it." He struck again and grabbed Ted's seaman's jacket.

It ripped as Ted jerked. "Turn me loose. I have a job to do."

"But I don't have the right job yet." Harlan kept slugging.

Ted shoved him away. Harlan tried to recover his footing but slipped and fell, cracking his head on the building's sharp corner, so it bled profusely.

Anne and Char arrived as Harlan fell to his knees. In the next instant, he tackled Ted and dropped him to the alley, and they rolled.

"Stop," Anne screamed. "You'll kill each other. Are you nuts?"

"He started it," Ted hollered. "He's out of control." He straddled Harlan, pinning his flailing arms and legs, while his head bled. Ted released his arms.

Harlan clutched his head and moaned. "He attacked me for no reason. Look." He showed his bleeding scalp. "He hurt me bad. Real men don't do that."

Anne knelt by Harlan. "Let me see. But you left the hotel before him. How did you—?"

"I forgot something, and when I came back to get it, he attacked me." Harlan slanted a glance. "He's not the man you think he is."

"Why, you pesky—" Ted's arms shot out and pinned Harlan tighter.

"Quit, both of you," Anne screamed. "We have a boat to fix and no time for—"

"Stupidity." Ted finished her sentence as he let Harlan up and dusted his hands. "He jumped me as I passed the alley and ripped my jacket. When I pulled loose, he lost balance and cracked his head."

"Liar," Harlan said, dripping blood. "You pushed me."

"You were both fighting, and he's bleeding bad." Horror masked Anne's face. "Ted, what were you thinking? A torn jacket isn't worth splitting a head."

"That isn't—"

"It hurts so bad," Harlan moaned and fell to the ground again. "Get a doctor."

Anne took another look. "It seems superficial, but with this much blood ... Char, what do you think?"

Char frowned at the small puddle. "Head wounds bleed a lot. It's probably good to be safe."

Ted pressed his torn jacket sleeve against Harlan's head to staunch the bleeding. "It's decreasing. But for the record, I didn't hit him. He fell and struck his head on the building corner."

"Says you. He's savage when you're not around." Harlan made no move to rise.

Char sighed, but Anne threw her hands in the air and gave a wild animal cry.

"Arrgh. Quit, both of you. I. Can't. Take. This. It's bad enough *Books Afloat* is damaged, but you make it worse by fighting. I Can't Stand More Trouble!" She held her head in both hands. "And I won't! Neither of you is welcome back on Book's Afloat."

Ted stared in disbelief. What had happened in Anne's pretty head after the recent good things between them? His hands fell to his sides. "You don't mean it. You need me to fix her."

"I do. But once you finish, leave." Her face blazed. "I trusted you but can't trust anyone—except Char. Fix *Books Afloat* and go home."

Ted rocked on his heels. Exhaustion and Harlan's blows had drained him, but this was worse. He waited for Anne to come to her senses, to erase her words, but she didn't.

"If you mean that, after repairs are done, you won't see me again until you're back in Vancouver."

Char's eyes bugged. "Anne, rethink this."

"I can't have conflict." She shook her head wildly again. "If trusting people doesn't work, I'll manage on my own—if you'll still help me."

"Yes, but—"

Pastor Bob and Sue came for Harlan. They hurried close.

"What's happened?" Bob boomed.

Harlan sat up, cradling his head. "He fought me over Anne."

"Over Anne? I doubt that." Bob's raised eyebrows asked Ted for an explanation.

"That's not what happened, but the whole thing's ridiculous." Ted spread empty hands. "Take him home."

Pastor Bob eased Harlan to his feet with a supportive arm. "Come on, Harlan. You may need your head checked."

"I do. Ted nearly killed me." Harlan faced Anne. "You should know what Ted's really like."

"Just stop." She glared.

Pastor Bob wiped his brow. "Harlan. I don't know the whole story, but Ted's given everything he has and is to help Anne and

Books Afloat. Take that into consideration. There may be a time to discuss this, but it's not now. Let's get you treated."

"At least someone cares." Harlan kept a hand to his head, leaning hard on Pastor Bob.

Ted, Anne, and Char silently stared after them.

27

Monday, June 29, 1942
Port of Longview, River Mile 66

As soon as the sun rose the next morning, Ted trudged to the marina to pay Sid and get the key to *Books Afloat's* engine.

Sid stood and hurried forward when Ted entered his office. "For a man who just accomplished major repairs in record time, you look more like you took a bullet."

Ted sighed, shoulders slumped and bruises purpling his jaw. "Sorry, that's how I feel. But we can't thank you enough for all you've done."

He forced a smile. He *had* taken a bullet—but not one people could see. Or that he would discuss.

"Well, come on." Sid grabbed his jacket. "Let's check her out on a test run before I turn her over to you."

Ted's smile became genuine. "Sounds great."

Going the short distance from the marina to the main river wharf, the engine purred smoother than before.

"Wow, Sid, you've worked magic."

"Nothing you wouldn't have done yourself. Just tuned her up good, like Professor Spencer trained us. But she's a good engine."

"She is. Her hull has battle scars, but she looks distinguished like a veteran soldier coming home from the wars."

"That she does." Sid paused and looked Ted up and down. "But that's how you look, too. What's going on?"

"A few situations not worth talking about."

"Okay." Sid slapped the rail and handed Ted the key. "She's all yours. Good to go."

Ted pumped his hand. "Like I said, we appreciate your help more than I can say. You're sure these funds covered it?"

"Absolutely. Happy to help."

Sid nudged Ted's shoulder, and Ted staggered.

"Whoa, I'm not trying to cave you in. You're worn out. Did you say you're not taking the rest of the trip?"

Ted shook his head. "Not right away. There's something I have to do first."

"I'm sorry to hear that, but keep me posted. Stop anytime you're near. You're a friend I want to see often."

"I will. Same here."

One hour later, Ted finished helping Anne and Char load supplies. He released the ropes tying *Books Afloat* to shore, wrapping them in figure eights around the iron cleats on deck.

"I don't know what to say, Ted," Anne stood chin firm, face tight. "Thanks isn't enough for all you've done. I just can't stand more conflict." She shook his hand but gave no hug.

Choking on the lump in his throat, he waved goodbye. Maybe Harlan was right. Despite knowing he wasn't good enough for Anne, Ted still had hopes and let his emotions get out of control. He had this setback coming. If only he could win her—feistiness and all.

There was no understanding some women's choices. They'd

been friends for years. Friendship often deepened into love. Why couldn't theirs? He'd given her his best and more. But it wasn't enough.

As soon as Char started the engine, Anne headed below deck. Char turned the wheel west and waved as they grew smaller in the distance. Ted swallowed hard and turned away.

"WHERE ARE WE HEADING, CHAR?" I return to the deck with cool drinks. "You've never asked to head a run without telling me where, but I guess once is allowed."

"It's a surprise you'll like—eight miles downstream to the ghost town of Stella to meet someone. I heard about this place while we were in Longview. Did you know that when lumberman Robert Long founded it, Stella was the second-largest planned city in the U.S?"

"No." I lean over the bow to let the breeze cool my cheeks. When I crane my neck, Longview is already small, like a toy city. I can't see Ted. I acted crazy. It hurts like I tore away part of my own flesh.

"So, all of Longview has been built since then?"

"Yes. It doubled in size in twenty years. We'll anchor at Stella, which isn't on most maps now because they just count it the western edge of Longview. The first postmaster, Paul Packard, named the town for his daughter, but fire wiped out lots of the town several years back."

"That's a shame, and you're sounding more like me."

She grins. "I suppose we're rubbing off on each other."

I take a breath and look around. "It *is* beautiful."

Wooded hills frame the river, and its shorelines rise in steep cliffs. The river itself holds wooded islands and backwater sloughs, while its deep main channel allows commercial traffic.

"There's more shipping now than ever, especially with things geared up for war."

I shade my eyes as several barges and heavy freighters slip past. "Are you sure there's deep enough moorage?"

"Yup. Checked it out before our damage, while you were busy with the governor. Stella's founder's grandson, Wade Packard, visited on board and insisted we stop. It's on our way. You'll love his story."

I study her carefully. "As long as it doesn't take too much time. You know the schedule we have to keep."

"I do. Trust me." She holds the tiller steady. Eight miles downstream, we approach a small dock. When Char sounds our whistle, a well-built young man dashes forward and secures our lines.

"Welcome," he says, smiling. "You made good time. I'm Wade Packard. Call me Wade." He helps us ashore.

"I'm Anne." I take his hand and look him up and down. I like men with a firm grip and confident air, plus he's easy on the eyes. He's well-muscled and ruggedly handsome, although his face isn't as open as Ted's.

Why did I ever consider Ted homely? The good-hearted smile that lights his face makes him truly something special. What's he doing now? Recalling his expression as I ordered him away makes me sick. After all he's done, kicking him off the boat doesn't make sense. Stress made my emotions crazy. Seeing all that blood made me lose my mind—like Grandpa's accident all over again.

"Our town was named for my Mom," Wade says, "but little survived the fire. At least our family's home did. Come, I'll show you."

We follow a trail, lined with fragrant ferns and evergreens, to climb a bluff a hundred feet above the river. Blue Camas lilies and delicate white Trilliums are so abundant, it's impossible not to trample some underfoot.

Their scent is heavenly, and the view spectacular. "There's beauty everywhere. What a haven."

Wade quirks an eyebrow. "We add an *e* to call it *heaven*."

Char laughs. "I see why."

We reach a stately two-story home, and Wade sweeps his arms around the 360-degree view. "As you see, Grandpa found the best building spot."

"It's everything you said and more," Char answers.

Wade ushers us through the entry into a spacious living room, leading to two walls filled with beautifully arranged books. "Anne, this is what I wanted you to see."

Char glows.

I gasp. "What a remarkable treasure."

"This is Grandfather's legacy. He was a dedicated bibliophile."

"A what?" Char's eyebrows knot.

"A book lover, like me." I smile.

"That's right. Besides being postmaster, he sold cordwood to steamboats and floated log-rafts to California mills. He always invested part of his profits in quality reading materials."

"He certainly did. I examine several volumes. "These are great choices. He must have been well-educated."

"On the contrary. Because he had limited schooling and was mostly self-taught, books became his motivation. He cherished every author he read. Sadly, his library has seen little use these last years. I want to change that, which is why I invited you."

"What do you mean?"

Wade's brown eyes have gold flecks. Ted's are blue and green, depending on the light and the color shirt he wears. They usually sparkle with humor. I clear my head. *Don't think about Ted. Focus on now.*

I lean forward. "You were saying?"

"I'm proud to be his grandson. I'm in the Merchant Marines but took leave to settle Mom's estate. I need a home for

Grandpa's library to honor his desire for the volumes instead of seeing them ruined by time and disuse."

"That would be so wrong." I study his eyes. The gold flecks are fascinating.

"I keep the house locked but can't afford a full-time caretaker. Since the final decision is up to me, I'm considering the best fit for their intended purpose. I need to finalize things soon. It seemed providential when Char, Ted, and I talked at Longview."

"You were busy with the governor," Char says, "but I thought you'd be interested." She grins.

"I need to hear more, but definitely, yes. Wade, what are your thoughts?"

"This location is out-of-the-way. It's costly to hire someone. Few towns between here and the coast have libraries, and town leaders might or might not use these books well. I can't risk a poor outcome. Neither do I want them absorbed into Longview's general library system—they're meant to stay a unit. Seeing *Books Afloat* sparked my thinking. Grandpa would have loved what you're doing."

"That thrills me."

"I wondered if his collection could be part of your floating library yet keep our family name. Ted thought you'd consider it." He looks around. "Where is Ted?"

"Uh, detained in Longview and worn out by boat repairs." My face heats with a twinge of guilt. "Yes, I'm interested—if you're serious."

"Very." His eyes convey as much as his words.

Char pats my hand. "Anne, you look like a kid on Christmas morning. We need Sparks with his camera."

"No. I'm glad he's not along, but I feel like it's Christmas morning. This is fabulous, Wade." I caress gold-lettered leather volumes of Robert Louis Stevenson, Dickens, Jane Austen, Mark

Twain, and so many others. "Wonderful choices!" As I inhale the scent of old paper and rich leather, the heartache of recent days lessens. "Tell me I'm not dreaming."

"You're not. These are real." Wade waves a hand. "Here are the children's books. Grandfather bought those too and gave us kids the run of the place. It's strange how loving them built the foundation that helped me excel in my profession."

"Not strange at all," I say. "That's exactly how it should be, and that's my experience, too." I bend to read titles on the lower shelves. "Some look fairly new. Did your grandfather pass away recently?"

"No. Twelve years ago. Because of his influence, I've made purchases since then. I caught his passion and can't stop." Wade chuckles, and a dimple flashes in his chin.

Ted's chin has a dimple, too.

"There are actually more books than you see. Some are in storage."

"More?" I lift a hand to my forehead. "This is almost overwhelming. You toured our library on *Books Afloat?*"

"Definitely. Talking with Ted and Char got me thinking. When I described Grandpa's collection, Ted got excited. He can't say enough about what you're doing. He really sees your vision for *Books Afloat!*"

My heart spasms. "He didn't mention—"

"He got distracted," Char says.

"And wanted this to be a surprise." Wade extends his hand. "So, what do you say?"

"It sounds wonderful. Let's pursue it." I accept his hand.

He holds mine in both of his. "Grandfather would be so happy."

"I wish I could have met him."

Wade points up. "I think he knows."

"Tell me more about how you'd like these used." As I take

more volumes from the shelf and riffle gold-edged pages, their beauty intoxicates me again. "These look too good to circulate in most river home conditions."

He nods. "But in spite of your recent disaster, I know you care for books well. Maybe you'd save our best volumes as a reference collection that stays intact on board. Otherwise, I don't mind the general books visiting river community homes. After all, I grew up on the river, too." He leans forward. "I would like to print bookplates to paste inside each book telling Grandpa's story."

"That would be wonderful. Of course, you should."

"It will take a while to finalize arrangements, but if you agree, I'll begin transfer steps through our estate. There will be some funds for transfer and ongoing maintenance. I'm thrilled this can work."

"Not as thrilled as I am." My hands itch to hold the books again. How can my emotions hit extreme opposites in a day's time?

He extends papers. "Here's the book inventory. Char said you'd need it to design shelving—"

"She's right again." I flash a grateful look.

"We can't complete this now," he says, "but by your return trip, I'll have the books ready if you'll be prepared."

"I'll make sure we are. We'd like to keep most books in circulation, so as our onboard numbers run low, it will be wonderful to replenish." My eyes fill. "I can't tell you what this means."

"I think I can tell. Believe me, I'm as happy as you are."

We shake hands again, but I throw my arms around him in a spontaneous hug. "Sorry, I don't mean to be forward—I'm just so *grateful*."

"I knew you would be." Char is radiant.

Wade's smile matches hers. "Grandfather would be so

pleased with what you're doing. He'd be one of your strongest supporters."

I scan the room and long hallway. "Do you have a picture of him?"

"Yes, this painting above the fireplace." He points to the oil portrait in a dark wood frame of a distinguished man standing in formal pose before these same bookshelves. He holds a dress hat in one hand and points to the books with the other as if inviting all to enjoy their riches.

The painting seems so alive, I shiver. "I feel like I know him. We have the same life vision. This is so encouraging after our boat damage."

"Yes, the timing seems perfect. This won't be our last meeting. Will you be back before I return to the Merchant Marines in a month?

"I guarantee it."

"Good. Here's my business card for future contact." He takes an engraved card from his wallet.

"I'll give you mine," I pull one from my notebook, "though contact can be difficult on the river."

"I understand."

I survey this home again, its fine carpets and furniture, lavish drapes … "Don't any other family members want these things?"

"They would take some, but not for the right reasons. Most have busy lives and little interest. Some might sell the books as first editions. I can't allow that."

I shudder. "Of course not."

He lifts both hands. "I'm so pleased this can work. A burden has lifted."

I step to the beautiful shelves one last time and notice light fading through the windows. I check my watch. "Goodness, we still have a tight schedule to keep."

"And a Challenge to complete. We'll talk more next time." He engulfs my hand again.

"We have to eat dinner," Char says, "and we have fresh provisions on board. Can he join us for dinner?"

"Of course."

"Offer accepted." Wade's strong white teeth gleam. "A bachelor never turns down a meal with lovely women."

28

Tuesday, June 30, 1942
Stella, Washington, and west

At dawn, Char clatters down the stairs to check compass settings. "My favorite time of day," she says, taking a deep breath. "I'm ready to pull up anchor and set sail."

I bask in the growing light. "Me, too. Except this beautiful morning makes me feel like writing poetry.

> *The golden disk dimples waves with gold and silver while the*
> *wind carries salt and the songs of singing birds.*

Someday, when I have time, I might seriously try."

"You'd have fun."

I lean forward, eyes straining. "Say, what's splashing upriver? Do you see it? Something's alive and bobbing in the water. Maybe an otter?"

"We have river otters, but not that big. Let me look." Char peers where I point. "I can't see well, but the thing's noisy, too."

"I'll grab binoculars." I squint and adjust the dials to look again and shake my head in disbelief. "I don't believe it. It's Ted on a giant innertube coming this way. Is he crazy? Is this another surprise you know about?"

Char's laugh shows she's a co-conspirator.

"Ahoy, *Books Afloat*!" Ted sings out. "Permission requested to board."

"Permission granted." I collapse in laughter. "Ted Vincent, after the last few days, if you even want to come back, you may, though I wouldn't blame you if you never wanted to see me again."

"I do want to." He swims closer.

"I owe you a huge apology."

I slide my hand along the rail's cool metal as he splashes.

He cups a hand to his ear. "Excuse me. I didn't hear that. Water in my ear. Repeat, please?" He angles his head and pounds that ear. "I thought you apologized." He moves closer with determined strokes, like he's almost learning to swim.

"You heard me. Come up, and I'll explain."

"Yes, ma'am." He splashes closer, lifting one hand in salute, which nearly capsizes him as he ties the innertube to our ladder.

Char laughs so hard her eyes disappear into the laugh lines in her face. As Ted climbs over the rail, he shakes himself like a wet dog, and she hands him a fleecy towel.

"First mate Ted Vincent reporting for duty, late and bedraggled, but present and accounted for."

"Welcome, sailor." I step forward and hug him, wet towel and all. He's better looking, and his eyes twinkle brighter than I remember. He's definitely more handsome than Hollywood's Jimmy Stewart. "I don't know where to start," I confess. "I don't expect you to understand how I acted when I don't myself."

He waves a dismissive hand. "Try me, but you don't need to explain."

"Yes, I do. After how wonderful you've been, I was awful." I choke. "You should hate me."

His eyes hold kindness and something more. "I never will."

"It's just that in that hotel alley, with blood everywhere, I saw my Grandpa crumpled and dead again in the accident. I tried to save him but failed. It was so terrible that I can't forget. And it was my fault."

"You need to get over it, Annie, because it wasn't. But it's okay. We all go nuts sometimes. I did my best to make Mom want to live, but I wasn't enough. She still gave up."

He touches my arm, sending tingles everywhere.

"Ted, you were enough. She was just wounded."

"Maybe." His face is a study of emotions, and he removes his hand.

I place mine on the spot where he warmed me, letting that comfort soak in. "Maybe she was too discouraged to try. I'm sure you and your brother were the brightest stars in her world. I've never heard the whole story."

"I guess not." He finishes drying. "And besides the fact you were in a terrible accident with your grandfather, I haven't heard all of yours. Today might be a good time." He presses his lips together.

They're nice lips. "Soon, but not right now. Do you have dry clothes on board?"

"Yes, I hid some. Plus, I have these." He hoists a small waterproof bag.

"Wait." I eye him suspiciously. "You waved goodbye as we left Longview. You didn't swim the whole way here."

"Nope, afraid not."

"How did you get here?"

"When Char, Wade, and I talked, he said if we were ever nearby and needed a place to stay, to let him know. I hitched a ride on the road last night, and this morning, Wade lent me his truck innertube with this nylon rope tied to shore. If you hadn't let me board, he'd have reeled me in."

"You're kidding. Like a big fish?" I look at him and then at the shore and shake my head.

"Of course, I hoped you'd let me board." He waves his towel toward Wade. "Thanks," he calls over the water.

"Anytime, bud."

I see Wade and wave, too. "I'm embarrassed. What must he think?"

"That a situation went wrong, and I cared enough to get back in your good graces. That's what I told him. If you'll swing *Books Afloat* toward that next point, he said to leave the innertube there."

"Consider it done. Char? You knew about this?"

She shrugs. "Not saying."

"Your face tells me. But you were both right, and I was wrong." I give Ted's cheek a tiny peck. "Thanks for coming back. It means a lot."

He touches where I kissed, face ablaze. "You're sure welcome."

"What now?" Char asks.

I point downstream. "Now that we're back to normal, please steer this section while I update charts. Ted, please check gauges for full steam ahead. We have a Challenge to complete."

He scrambles to the engine room, a huge smile lighting his face.

"Aye, aye, Captain. Full steam ahead."

———

AT THAT MOMENT, happy to be back on board, Ted glimpsed a small cloud cross the sun and cast a shadow across the boat. With his smile still in place, he shivered a moment for no reason at all. Anne and Char stood at the prow, charting their course.

All was right with the world—but Ted wondered for how long.

29

Tuesday, June 30, 1942
Stella, Washington, River Mile 58 to Turnagain Island, River Mile 55

"Take the wheel for a victory mile," Char encourages. "I'll rustle up grub."

Taking the helm, I steer toward the Pacific, the wind whipping my hair as the west wind's salty tang quickens my senses. I steal glances at Ted, hiding my grin, as he quietly improves my job of spooling ropes around cleats. I won't let him see how glad I am he's back. I don't let people emotionally close since Grandpa's death. Not even Ted.

Yet, I connected to Wade—unless that was just gratitude for entrusting me with a wealth of books.

And what about Josh? What's my loyalty to him? My heart says he's alive but wounded and far away, hoping for a normal world and steadfast friends to return to. Or perhaps more than friends? He kissed me at prom when everyone kissed after the last dance. He kissed me again when he left for war, but Ted was there, too, exchanging man hugs as we all cried.

Life flows on, like this river, but brings changes.

Why is life so confusing? Our whole world is changing. There's no going back to the safe way it was. Ted knows me well. He's heard my dreams and was the first to hear about this floating library. New feelings for him stir inside. What if he doesn't return them? I'll stay distant to keep him guessing.

Steep cliffs on both sides of the river are full of birds' nests and musical cries. Old-growth firs and darker cedars stretch between cliffs as the landscape is cut by occasional clear streams, plunging in waterfalls.

"Our oil pressure's good," Ted calls happily, still wearing his wet clothes. "She's in good shape."

He gets my best smile. Faithful Ted—as if much could change in the few hours he was gone. I pushed his friendship to the limit. Why didn't he stay away and give up on me like most men would? Because he's different from most—genuinely nice.

Somewhere, the equally sweet girl he deserves must be waiting. Sometimes, I wonder what she is like. Sometimes, I wish to be her, except I'm stubborn and headstrong—*not* what he needs. Too independent. Too many too manys.

Ted unconsciously whistles another love song after changing into dry clothes. He'd die if he knew I recognize his tune. I nearly hoot as I recall the words, 'I can't give you anything but love, baby …'

He doesn't watch romance movies. Where did he hear this? Somewhere he must have seen *Bringing Up Baby*, and the catchy tune stuck in his head. I'm tempted to sing the words to see his face flame. Instead, I tuck that idea away for future use. He's a true-blue friend who doesn't usually think about girls much. Although when I hugged him this morning, he hugged back tight, and it felt right. I shiver again, recalling his arms around me.

Through thick and thin, from the time I arrived in

Vancouver, Josh, Ted, and I have been friends. It's bad enough having Josh gone, but I drove Ted away. Thank God he didn't stay gone. Now, I can't get his jaunty tune out of my brain. His song makes me crazy. I wring my hands. Some people have green thumbs for plants. Mine usually shrivel and die. I do that to relationships, too—the black kiss of death. I will *not* do that to Ted.

What's wrong with me? Why does Char look at me strangely lately with a knowing smile? I tuck a strand of unruly hair back in place. Someone should write a book on successfully moving from teen years to a stable marriage and family. Could I ever write that book?

Lord, You gave me a job to do. End my daydreams. Don't let me fail and hurt anyone else!

I toss my head to stare at the swirling current. Other than my tumultuous emotions and the musical waves splashing against our boat, everything is quiet. But then, a flock of birds shoots starboard when something startles them. My heart stutters. I search for the cause and see a large, slow-moving log, skimming the surface. Maybe like the one that staved in *Books Afloat*. I slow our engine.

But instead of floating downstream with the current, this log moves upstream in a straight line. I blink to follow its journey. It still moves steadily and at last turns and steers toward a low island. When it's almost past, the object turns ninety degrees and bumps ashore on rippled gray sand below overarching evergreen trees. I slow our throttle and lean across the rail without alerting Char or Ted. What on earth am I seeing?

The log is twenty feet long and two feet wide at both blunt ends. It doesn't show the pointed edges of trees cut by axes. Instead, it looks streamlined. Yet, no log moves upstream against the current. And once ashore, this log doesn't rest on the beach. Its top section opens. A circular piece the size of a city manhole cover is raised by a man's arm and set on land. A bearded head pops into open space, and blue eyes glitter under slash mark eyebrows. Smitty?

Those eyebrows move to and fro like windshield wipers, and the eyes widen. "Annie!"

"Smitty," I gasp. "What are you doing here? And what is that thing?"

"My newest ship." He grins and snaps a salute.

Char races up from the galley. "Have we run aground?" And then she spots her brother-in-law. "Smitty Young, as I live and breathe!" She leaps across open water to reach him.

Ted scrambles up from the engine room as another man moves through lacy evergreen foliage to join Smitty on the beach.

"Johnny Hofer?"

The men stand together. "Not smart enough to outwit 'em, I see," Johnny says.

"They're canny. The jig is up. Let's fill them in." Smitty winks.

My hands flare to my hips. "Johnny? What are you doing here?"

"I said you'd never know where I'd turn up next."

"But I didn't know you meant anytime, anywhere."

Char snatches off her hat. "Smitty, does your doctor know you're here?"

He blows a kiss. "Of course. I'm an obedient sort. But I'm afraid I exaggerated the heart issue because the governor and team said it was more important to continue other activities."

I stand there, elbows angled, unable to say anything.

"Not hardly obedient," Char snorts. "I guess Evie's fine, or you'd tell me. Any news of J.P.?"

"I wish." Smitty's face grows serious. "You're full of questions, and I don't blame you. I'll answer in order." He holds up one finger. "Evie has started college and is doing fine. Two, my doctor approves and is closer than you think. Three," he lifts that finger. "A radio message from J.P. says he's in the Asiatic Pacific but can't say where. He misses you like crazy and plans to win the war and hurry home. He sends *lots* of love."

Smitty draws a heart in the air, which makes Char's face accordion pleat as tears flow. Instead of feisty, she's as gentle as a lamb.

"You should expect surprises, Annie," Johnny calls. "Drop anchor and come ashore."

Smitty grins so wide, his jaw may crack, but right now, I don't care. Anyone who keeps so many secrets from friends deserves some pain.

Ted ties *Books Afloat* close enough to jump ashore without risking her hull. Johnny throws his arms wide and pulls us into hugs.

"Do you live here now?" I ask, releasing him.

"This is our present operations center."

"Does it have a name?"

"Maps call it Tenasillahe Island, Chinook for 'little land.' We call it Turnagain Island since most explorers got this far but turned back before finding the fertile lands upstream. Plus, the narrow channel nearly dividing the island hides our craft well."

"What *is* this thing?" I cross my arms. "Tell us what you're up to."

"Here's the scoop." Johnny rubs the back of his neck. "Smitty and I have been friends a long time." He turns to Smitty and claps his shoulder. "How far back?"

Smitty swipes his jaw. "Almost forever."

"Before the war, we worked projects together and have teamed up for research, now that we're retired. Plus, there's a war to win. Come see our invention." He waves us forward.

I shade my eyes. "A-maz-ing! I've never seen anything like this and wouldn't have spotted you if you hadn't been moving against the current upstream. *Nothing* in nature does that." I fix him with an eagle eye. "What's your purpose?"

"Winning the war and protecting friends like you. With more activity on the river and greater risks, we built this, and it works fine. We'll explain."

Char interrupts. "It's way past time to fill us in. And you should trust me since I'm more sister to you than sister-in-law." Her eyes flash lightning. I'm glad she doesn't look at me that way.

"I don't want to get on the wrong side of you." Smitty grins. "We're volunteers, not enlisted men."

Her brow furrow. "Does Evie know?"

"Only that I do river patrols. She wanted to come along once, but I said no."

"Good. It's bad enough having her dad gone. I don't want her involved in es—, espi— Whatever you call it."

"Espionage. That's why we haven't told her. Or you." Smitty squeezes Char's shoulder. "Don't get your dander up. One of you involved in war at a time is enough. Remember, they say, 'Loose lips sink ships.' We didn't want any of you knowing things an enemy could pry out of you, if trouble came."

"No enemy could pry information out of us." The rock I kick hits Johnny's moccasined foot, and I don't care. "You wouldn't have told us now if I hadn't discovered you!"

"Ow." He clears his throat. "You aimed that rock on purpose."

"Maybe." My lips hold a tight line.

"Don't be mad. We were going to tell you soon. We were ironing out the last kinks when you spotted us. But you're involved now."

"That's right, and I'm mad enough to spit. You should have trusted us. I thought we were in this together."

He steps closer. "It's also our duty to keep you safe for the work you've accepted. If anything happens to you, folks in Vancouver, plus Governor Langlie, will have our hides."

"Who keeps *you* safe?" I spit my words.

Smitty grins. "See, Johnny? I told you she's a spitfire. I'd hate to meet her in a dark alley."

Johnny slaps his knee. "Atta girl. You're ready."

"For what?" I dredge up a smile. "Like my grandma used to say, 'Ugly is as ugly does,' so 'fess up and explain how we can help—or it might go bad for you."

"Step closer then."

We crowd close to see his craft.

When Ted taps its base with his shoe, we hear a metallic ping. "What is this material?" he asks. "Where did you find it? It looks like wood, but it's obviously metal."

"One you don't know about." Johnny slides a glance. "Special metallurgy. Before I became an old geezer, I headed research projects I can't describe."

"I'll bet," Ted says, "except I don't see an old geezer anywhere."

"I like you, Teddy." Johnny taps his chest. "Smitty and I built this sub to spy out who's friend and foe. That also includes protecting *Books Afloat*."

"Obviously, since you keep showing up. Thank you kindly," I say.

"You'll love this part." Smitty pokes me. "I got these plans to build from books, even some in your library." He removes his glasses to polish their lenses on his khaki cotton shirt's sleeve before slipping them back on.

"Show me which books, so I can get smart, too," I say. I pull my camera from my pocket and angle it near the sub until Johnny blocks me by spread-eagling his arms.

"No pictures yet! This is top secret. If you see or hear too much, we have to report." His tone is grim.

"Give us basics." Char stands her ground. "You *owe* us that much."

"I reckon. Johnny did the sub technology. I handled

dimensions and navigation. Annie, remember when you admired the marine history books on my living room shelf?" He leans forward, confiding secrets. "I was amazed how far back men used underwater vessels." He gestures towards *Books Afloat*. "You might have the same books on board describing what I found. Did you know Alexander the Great did underwater travel?"

"You're kidding me." My eyebrows rise.

"Nope. It's true. And Char, you lived in our home. Mom was a great history teacher, but she didn't mention his underwater involvement either."

"I don't think so." Her eyebrows zigzag. "But you and J.P. were history buffs. I wasn't. For the record, I'm a distant cousin they took in. It's a long story I won't tell now." Her voice softens.

"It was fun having you around," Smitty says. "Better after you married J.P., since you're a great cook." He pats his stomach. "Anyway, I knew almost nothing about submarines before the Navy, and they barely discussed it, but Alexander the Great explored river bottoms in a diving chamber three centuries before Christ. The Dutch and Italians had them before 1700, and a British scientist used one under the Thames."

"Don't forget the Americans," pipes Johnny. "Especially Robert Fulton, the steamboat man."

"He was a genius." Ted perks up. "His engine hasn't been improved on much since."

"That's right," Johnny continues. "Did you know Napoleon hired Fulton to build a submarine, but they couldn't finish in time?"

"That would have changed history. Is your driving system like Fulton's?" Ted's fingers flex, as if eager to be involved.

"Close. If Bonaparte had succeeded, he might have won, and then Germany wouldn't be fighting us now. Here, I'll show you."

He lifts the hatch, and Ted peers in.

Char and I elbow close. "Make room for us."

Smitty looks at me. "Tell me this. When you observed this sub going upstream against the current, did you hear engine noise?"

I think, then shake my head. "No, that's the strange part. Just water splashing against the hull."

"We use an alternate power system."

"Undetectable human power." Johnny cackles.

"Undetectable human what?"

"I learned that from history books, too. Bend your back, Johnny. Let's haul it to higher ground and demonstrate." They grip both ends of the craft and slide it higher almost effortlessly. Tangy scents release as they brush evergreen branches in passing.

Johnny sticks fresh pine needles in his mouth and offers handfuls.

"This is a half-size replica of America's first submarine, the *Hunley*," Smitty explains.

"The *Hunley*?" I sputter. "From Confederate Civil War days?"

"You're right. Named for its inventor, it combines electromagnetic batteries with steam. It sank a Union ship in Charleston harbor, got sunk two more times, and recovered twice." He lifts his cap to wipe his brow. "The South lost the war, but the *Hunley* showed what subs could do. Most people don't know it yet, but Japan had midget subs in the Pearl Harbor attack."

"No kidding," Char exclaims. "As small as J.P.'s sub-chaser?"

"Close. And ours uses optional human power."

Ted's eyes gleam. "And electro-magnetic batteries? You're talking my language."

"Explain human-powered." I fan my face. "Oars? Moving rudders?"

"Take a peek." Johnny hikes a pant leg to reveal his well-sculpted calf.

"You're kidding." Char's laugh rings like tumbling water.

"Not bad for an old geezer. I've got hair growing in my ears and more liver spots than Smitty, but pedaling submarines keeps me young." He taps his forehead. "As long as I'm alive and kicking, I want to keep brain cells alive. Now, I'm developing communication for underwater sonar, so enemies can't sneak up."

"Teach me," Ted insists.

"I want to. The government wants us training trustworthy talented young men," Johnny's voice rises with excitement. "And you're a natural."

"The Dutch used submarines before Germany had U-boats. I don't know who helped Japan, but both sides have them now." Smitty's eyes blaze. "Japan's good, but we'll beat them at their own game." He snaps his fingers. "Climb in, take a look. Don't mind the tight fit. See how she works."

Bicycle pedals attached to a wheel welded to piston rods line the bottom of the boat.

"Does that operate the way I think?" I ask.

"Exactly. The piston rods mesh together like scales on a fish," Johnny explains. "Slick as a whistle."

"You power this yourselves?" My eyes widen.

His chest swells. "When we want to."

"May I try?"

"I don't see why not. But it's cramped."

I slide into the narrow space. "This is great. I wish everyone could see how this works."

"Maybe after the war. Go ahead, pedal a while." His face shines. "I have the gears lifted, so you won't actually go anywhere, but you'll get the feel of powering her."

As I push the pedals and hear the gears, rods, and shafts whir, I smile from ear to ear. "No wonder I didn't hear you coming. This is a perfect secret weapon."

Smitty's lips curve. "We call her the *Hunley* after the original inventor, but in our hearts she bears another name." He pushes aside the lacy green ferns hiding the sub's prow. Black letters spell *Never Again*. "To me," his voice rumbles, "this means *Pearl Harbor's Revenge*."

We high five.

"Plus, for Midway and Josh, and all service personnel missing everywhere." I climb out and squint in bright sunlight. "I'm impressed."

"My turn," Ted says, getting in. "What will you do next?" he asks.

"Plenty." Smitty's blue eyes twinkle, and the crow's feet at their edges make him look intriguing—not old.

"I've heard you and J.P. talk inventions for years," Char says, "but didn't dream you'd create this. It just shows that men's experiments can become awesome inventions."

"True. We're sorry we couldn't tell you before," Smitty says. "But now that you're involved, we'll answer questions."

"J.P. would be proud, like I am." She hugs Smitty and looks west. "God bless them all."

"He will." Johnny slaps the sub's side. "This is operational, not perfect. But at least we have more up our sleeves than muscles." He gives a sassy grin and shows a bulging upper arm like Popeye's.

"Now, tell us the truth," I say. "Do you guys believe Japanese subs are near the river?"

They lock eyes.

Smitty expels a sigh. "We're not sure. They may not be in the Columbia now, but after entering once, they'll try again."

"Okay." I square my shoulders. "Then tell us what to look for and what to do if we see them."

Smitty grips my shoulder. "These are serious days, but we're praying." He looks heavenward. "I know Momma is, too." He turns to Char. "I know that's how I survived so many scrapes, including the recent heart scare. God will bring J.P. home. Wait and see. And help us win here."

"I agree." She wipes tears.

I'll pray." Smitty bows his head. "Lord, I love a good scrap. And feel responsible and take control when I shouldn't. From now on, help me hear what You say and do exactly that. I put You in full charge. Amen."

30

Tuesday, June 30, 1942
Turnagain Island, River Mile 55, and west

S mitty's prayer lifted weights from Ted's shoulders. He took a breath that reached his toes for the first time in days. He hadn't helped Mom want to fight to live and didn't have every answer for *Books Afloat*, but God did.

He felt like Gideon asking, 'Who? Me?' when the angel announced, 'The Lord is with thee, mighty man of valor.' When he looked at himself, he felt puny. When he trusted God, he found answers. *God, keep us strong.* And safe. He tuned back into Smitty.

"As I was saying, folks are less scared when they don't know the whole story. We wanted to tell you sooner, but the governor asked us to wait."

Johnny forked his beard with his fingers. "Annie, your sharp eyes are a gift. We don't want you in danger, but being as observant as you are will help keep you safe. We've watched out for you. Ted, you're some kick in the pants paddling up to Annie on that innertube to get back on board." He laughed heartily.

"She knew she was wrong as soon as she kicked you off. She was just too stubborn to say so. Isn't that right, girl?" He poked Anne's arm.

Johnny must be the bravest man in the world.

Anne bristled. "If my face is as fire-engine red as I feel, Johnny Hofer, you're getting a rise out of me. If you think I'm stubborn now, sometimes I'm worse. Ask Ted. Char and I could have managed, couldn't we, Char?"

"If we had to," Char answered. "But three is better. Isn't it, Ted?"

"I like being on board."

Smitty chuckled. "Annie, the best part is seeing you let God help, so you don't *have* to do everything yourself. He's polishing your rough edges—and polishing ours."

She made a strangled sound. "Rough edges? What do you mean?" But her eyes softened.

"I'm not criticizing, just speaking truth. Stubbornness goes with leadership. It helps us carry tasks and not give up. Johnny and I are good examples."

"It sounds nicer if you call it tenacity." Anne's shoulders eased.

"Why split hairs?" Smitty grinned. "It acts the same no matter what it's called."

"How many folks are part of the river surveillance?" Anne asked.

"We're not free to share," Smitty opened his hands. "That would reveal too much."

"The overall plan is secret to protect our people, including you," Johnny added.

"But we're your team. You should fill us in. Do you patrol the whole river?"

"Mostly Kalama to the ocean, where there's the highest risk of Japanese entry," Smitty said. "They've laid low since Fort

Stevens, but we're sure they'll try again. They're also working on new weapons. Johnny, show them that news clipping."

"Sure thing." He reached in a shirt pocket.

"Is it a story Sparks wrote?" Ted asked.

"Nope. Something few are aware of. The government manages to keep secrets when it wants. This is from last week's *Daily Astorian* with no update since, but a sea captain friend in Tillamook confirms it. Here's the header. 'Japan to send fire balloons to burn America.'"

"How awful," Char gasps. "That puts everyone at risk, not just the military."

"Yes, ma'am." Johnny nods. "We don't think the fire balloons are here yet, but we're watching." His eyebrows hike. "In many cases, news isn't shared to avoid panicking the public."

"I can see that," Ted said. "If Sparks hasn't heard about this, he'll be mad he missed the scoop."

"He's savvy and works hard to push his career. He'll probably hear soon."

Anne rubbed her cheek. "It must be hard managing news. How do authorities decide what to tell reporters and what to hold back? We seriously must pray for our leaders."

Ted watched this girl he loved discuss life and death as the river peacefully flowed by.

"You're saying we'd better stay alert at all times." Char propped her chin in her hand.

"That's right. And gather solid evidence—not hearsay or suspicion." Smitty's gaze rested on each one. "We need top-notch surveillance."

"Okay," Anne said. "Give us likely scenarios and how to stop the Japanese."

Ted and Char leaned close like bird dogs on point.

"We're 100 percent committed to stopping them," Ted said. "Or die trying."

31

Tuesday, June 30, and Wednesday, July 1, 1942
Turnagain Island, River Mile 55, and west

Thankful to be back in Anne's graces, Ted knew that could change in a heartbeat.

"We'll reach Cathlamet, River Mile 46, later," Anne said, "and maybe stay tomorrow. After that, Skamokawa at Mile 33.5 is so small, library hours won't take long. We're making good time, getting close to the ocean."

"Barring anything unusual," Ted reminded.

"Or more interesting people." Her lips curved. "We'll hope for the best. Our next stops should go faster, because we're experienced now."

"I'm thankful you and Char think we can complete the Challenge in the days left. So far, Smitty's only given us the name of one volunteer from our river network. We meet him in Cathlamet."

"I'm trying to match his schedule. If we can't, we'll arrange a message drop. I'll radio to confirm tonight's meeting at his boathouse past the village."

299

Ted rolled his shoulders. "It feels good moving forward, even with cloak and dagger stuff."

Anne's eyes brightened. "I love cloak and dagger. Years ago, I asked God to never let me be bored."

"So that's the problem!" Ted rocked on his heels. "Excitement looks good on you, but I'd rather win the Challenge and whisk you home."

"Don't be a spoilsport." She flashed a thumb's down. "After winning, I'll start library trips up and down the river on a regular basis—and other projects."

"Like what? I'm so involved in the Challenge, I haven't looked past it. But don't make plans and leave me out. I'll be there, too."

She kissed the tips of his fingers and brushed them across her cheek. He loved the laughter in her eyes. The literal heat from her body as she stood near curled his toes. He'd never felt this way about anyone. Yet, she scared him, too. He'd like to scoop her up and carry her home—not see her take more risks in wartime. But she'd never let him run the boat and leave her home.

You don't wrap a girl like Anne in cotton batting to protect her—not while there was a war to win, troops to bring home, and a nation to serve. He sent up instant prayers. Anne's courage was partly what he loved about her. Did he really want her to change?

At the helm, Char stood close enough to hear most of what Ted and Anne had said. She looked Ted's way and smiled without comment. They both knew how this discussion would probably end.

Ted lifted a map and pretended to study it to hide the warmth climbing his neck, but he couldn't mask the love in his voice. "Do you ever think about an easier job?"

"Are you kidding?" She stared, disbelieving. "Do you?"

"Sometimes. I'd like you safe."

"Just pray. I believe God wants me here. I thought you were sure, too."

He sighed. "I am. I just don't like the dangers on the river."

"There's danger everywhere, even crossing the street."

"True." After the heat left his face, he lowered his map. "So, tell me about Clatskanie. Do we stop there this time?"

"No, on our way back. Going means entering Wallace Slough on Oregon's side and then the Clatskanie River into town. Once we win the Challenge, we can expand future trips."

"Sounds good." He watched the river surge and splash as it broadened and gained speed from tributaries entering. "What about Cathlamet?"

She checked the *Lower Columbia Boating Guide*. "It was the largest Indian village west of the Cascades when Captain Gray came in 1792. Thirteen years later, Lewis and Clark reported the village had three to four hundred cedar homes."

"I love reading their records and following their route now."

"I didn't know you were that keen on history."

He shot a quizzical look. "Did you forget I chose Lewis and Clark for that junior year history project?"

"Maybe I did." Her eyes snapped into focus. "That's when I was trying to find good things about Oklahoma's Dust Bowl, where I'd come from."

"*Lots* of good things come from Oklahoma, but you're my favorite."

"That's sweet. Do you mean that?"

Her smile made his knees weak. "I *only* say what I mean." His voice deepened. He wished he dared share everything in his heart. He was glad she couldn't hear his heart thudding or see it through his rising shirt fabric.

"Wade said *Skamokawa* means 'smoke on the water' in Chinook," she said, "because there's always fog where the creek enters the river. The early white men called it 'Venice of the Columbia.'"

"Interesting." Venice would be a great place to take a razzamatazz girl on a honeymoon. But not with Italy in war. And not on a mechanic's salary. His neck burned hotter.

"It's chilly this morning." She hugged herself. "I'll make coffee."

He'd love to warm her instead—take her in his arms and taste those lips. After she disappeared into the galley, he whistled a cheerful tune until Char sang the words and winked. Oops—another love song. He should plunge his head in ice water to cool his brain.

Anne brought fresh coffee. "It's not as good as yours, Ted, but I tried."

"It's perfect."

"Char, here's yours."

"This hits the spot. Do you notice the river widening?" Char asked. "A ferry still runs across between Cathlamet and Westport. It takes ten minutes, and it's one of the last ferries in the Pacific Northwest."

"We're about that speed, aren't we?"

"Close," Char pointed. "Look, we're approaching the Julia Hansen Bridge, the third span crossing the Columbia. That high center lets big ships go under without blocking highway traffic. J.P. calls it brilliant engineering and helped cut the red ribbon."

"An important man, your J.P.," Ted replied. "Introduce us when he gets home."

"Oh, I will. I've never known a finer man." Even saying that dampened her eyes. She turned aside like a shy bird tucking its head under a wing.

"You make me believe in lasting romantic love," Ted said.

"As if you didn't, from the great example you see in Bob and Sue."

"Good point." He looked away. "No more news yet of J.P.?"

"Not besides the little bit Smitty told me, and I can't find anyone who knows. I thought my best chance would be Sparks, or his uncle, or Governor Langlie. But nothing." She slipped out of her windbreaker. "Waiting is hardest on those left behind."

"True."

Ted glanced at the high school graduation photo of Josh, Anne, and himself that he carried in his billfold. Anne had one tucked in the front of her log. This way, it seemed like Josh traveled with them.

"It's crazy not hearing news about those missing at Midway either. Why doesn't the military know? It helps to stay busy doing something helpful," he said.

"I'd go crazy otherwise." Char put a hand over her heart. "Just taste that salt air—it's so good I hardly need food." Her hand swept past the forested hillsides. "Those giant ferns show how much rain falls here. And look." She pointed to building clouds. "Our weather might be changing."

Anne put away her *Boating Guide*. "I can't complain. We've had sunshine since the Reynolds' place, so the weather doesn't owe us anything. I think God's been rewarding us for the storm we endured there."

"Still, we'd best prepare. Weather never stays the same long near the coast."

"I've heard." Anne laughed. "You make me think we'd better find stores and buy Sou'westers to help keep us dry."

"That's not a bad idea. Ted, too."

When Char swooped her hat off and approached, he danced away.

"I only wear hats under vehicles changing oil. They might ruin my gorgeous hair." He combed his locks with his fingers, imitating Sparks.

"On open ocean, you would." Char slapped her Sou'wester back on. "Wearing this gets hot and sticky, but you have to admit, we've stayed mostly rain-free."

"We're grateful." He bowed.

The women stood together, checking boat speed, channel depth, and sandbars.

"Soon, the river is a mile wide and broader still at the Columbia's mouth," Char said. "There are treacherous sandbars but fabulous scenery. Just look." She waved a hand.

Anne shielded her eyes. "Gorgeous. Even here, the river's so wide, it's hard to see across. It must be amazing at its mouth."

"Yup. Open ocean but tricky navigating."

She inhales. "Smell that salt brine from the tides. We're closer to my home every day. You're winning the Challenge, Annie. When we're there, I'll make you a Victory cake. Just saying that makes my mouth water. I can't wait for you to taste it."

Anne's smile matched Char's. "Me, too. You convinced me."

Books Afloat's progress stayed trouble-free, much to Ted's relief, with stops in several communities, two farmsteads, and a fishing camp. Anne didn't buy a hat.

The next morning, she crossed more library stops off the calendar as Ted worked nearby inside the library doorway, reinforcing shelves.

"Anne? Can I mention something?" Char asked, manning the helm.

"Sure."

"I had a dream last night that bothered me. Maybe I hollered."

"I thought I heard you." Anne stepped closer. "Do you remember it?"

"Mostly." She tapped a finger against her teeth. "That's my problem. I don't want to."

"What was it?"

She gave a strangled hiccup. "J.P. was on a boat this size in heavy seas. It was too dark to see much, but I heard clanking metal. I saw people, and my blood chilled."

"Why, what did you see?"

"Japanese sailors, like in movie newsreels. There were pilots flying kamikaze planes and men waving rising sun flags." She bit a fingernail. "Next, I was on the boat. It was so real. I even smelled fish and soy sauce."

"That is realistic. I'm sure you're worried about J.P."

"Always, but the dream continued. When seamen boarded, I pretended I was asleep. They tied people up and started destroying the boat." Her voice broke. "My heart pounds even thinking about it." She dabbed her eyes. "Tell me it's nothing, that it wasn't a premonition."

"I don't know. I sure hope not." Anne's voice soothed. "Smitty and Johnny warned us about attacks. Maybe that got you thinking."

"I was so glad to wake up and know it was a dream."

"That reminds us to pray for J.P. and our men. Sometimes I think God nudges us to pray so bad things don't happen."

Char nodded. "That's what I tell Evie."

As Ted moved to work on the doorframe itself, he heard more of the women's discussion.

"I feel dumb, getting scared when I'm a grown woman, but it was terrible."

"I'm sure." Anne took her hand. "No one is strong all the time. I'm finding being an adult doesn't guarantee answers."

She and Char stood at the rail. Fish jumped, and birds flew to nests.

"These critters act like life's normal, but it's not. The dream is hard to shake," Char confessed, "but I feel better telling you."

"I'm glad you did." Anne slipped an arm around her. "You've helped me so many times and taught me we're not meant to carry things alone. They say trouble's divided when it's shared."

"I like that. Thanks." Her smile lingered.

Ted drilled one last screw into the doorframe support.

"Can we tell Ted?" Anne obviously heard him.

Char hesitated. "I'm the oldest. He might think I'm a baby, but I don't care."

"He won't think that. And neither do I. We're a team."

Char took a deep breath. "Yes, let's tell him."

Anne beckoned Ted over, and he lowered his tools. He also wrapped an arm around Char, so she was bookcased between them.

"Thanks for including me," he said. "Working on the door, I heard most of what you said. That sounded terrible, Char."

She leaned against him, her face the color of putty. "What do you think it means? I tried to wake up but couldn't. It was even hard to pray." She massaged her forehead.

"May I pray now?"

"I'd like that."

Ted took her hands. "Lord, You're our hiding place. You heard this conversation. We don't know what tomorrow holds, but we commit our days and loved ones to You."

"Amen," Anne echoed when he finished and blew her nose. "That gives me strength, too."

Char looked up. "Ted, I'm sure it's not easy traveling with two women, and I don't know all your reasons for coming, but thank you. We should call you Saint Theodore." As she sagged against him, he lowered his head to hers.

"It's good," he said. "Being around you is almost like having my mom around again."

"You couldn't say anything nicer." Char sniffed.

"We're all thankful," Anne said.

Being here with Anne and Char released something new in Ted—greater energy than Popeye got eating spinach. He felt like he'd grown an inch taller, and his chest swelled. The next time he passed a mirror, he was sure he'd see he was bigger. *Lord, I don't know if I look different on the outside, but on the inside You're making me Charles Atlas.*

When Anne joined them in a three-way hug, he felt her tremble. He would never allow anything to hurt either of them —even if it cost his life.

A cold prickle passed through him despite the muggy afternoon. Perhaps a premonition like Char's dream that keeping them safe might cost his life.

Thursday, July 2, 1942
Skamokawa, River Mile 30.5 and west

I snug my raincoat tight and peer into thick murk.

"With this heavy rain, radio messages aren't getting through," Ted shouts above the growing storm as he climbs steps from below. "I thought after the first squall passed, frequency would clear, but the second storm's here, and I only have static." He shrugs into his rainslicker and snaps it up to his neck, pulling the hood tight.

"It's the weather system Char spotted yesterday but didn't think it would hit this fast." Thunderbolts roll, and lightning flashes across the sky like a thousand flashbulbs exploding at once.

"Char's hat failed. I guess we should have bought some, too." Ted swipes water from his face.

"She said it was no guarantee—just a deterrent. Besides, this storm might have been worse if she hadn't."

We share a laugh.

"This storm is rough to travel in, but farmers need rain. How can I help?"

"Char's seldom sick, but she's not feeling well. I told her to rest, and we'll manage. My rain gear keeps me mostly dry, but with such poor visibility, I'm cutting speed, so we don't hit anything."

"Smart." He checks gauges. "Wind gusts are twenty knots."

"And rising." Waves rock the boat, and I grip the wheel to keep me upright. "It's hard to see well enough to steer."

"I'm glad folks back home are praying."

"I count on them."

"Should we go to shore to ride out the storm?"

"Does the engine sound strained?"

He listens. "Don't think so, but I'll check."

I set the helm on automatic and test the emergency radio transmitter Smitty gave me. Static garbles even our civil defense frequency. I open my briefcase to activate my final backup device. When its battery switches on, I receive a coded message. Once I apply the cipher, it reads,

Change in plan. Abort today's scheduled drop. Resume original route until intercepted.

I try to make sense of it as Ted returns, saying our engine's fine. He also brings steaming, eye-opening brew.

"You're a lifesaver." I cradle the mug in my hands and take a potent sip. "Just the way I like it, one cream and two sugars." I savor it and drain the rest, placing the mug against my cheek for warmth.

Our eyes meet. "I aim to please."

"You succeed. Come read what just came through in code. This frequency is river network only. It must be from Smitty."

"Bob has it, too."

The wind howls like a banshee. I see Ted's mouth move but can't hear above the storm.

I move to an inch from his face and shout, "Do we proceed downriver and wait for an intercept? Or drop anchor and ride this out?"

His forehead puckers. "Drop anchor. I'll go to the stern to prepare."

And then, above the wind, I hear a screaming engine as a speedboat shoots straight at us from nowhere and cuts speed at the last minute to bounce alongside.

"What on earth?" I stare through pounding rain to see who is so foolhardy.

A swathed figure grabs our boarding ladder and attaches the speedboat's line.

"Surprise!" A familiar voice.

"Sparks?"

"Yes, coming aboard."

"Hello again," calls a figure behind him, and Harlan appears in a hooded raincoat, his face split in a grin.

My heart drops. "You two nearly rammed us and scared me to death. What were you thinking?"

"Almost, but didn't." Sparks vaults onto the deck. He's not wearing wingtips now. "I'm a skilled river man, paying a visit."

Harlan follows. "It's fun surprising you."

I grind my teeth. "You're getting poor results."

"You received our message about the intercept, didn't you?" Sparks steps under the deck overhang and shakes water from his coat.

"How did you know? Who have you talked to?"

"It's proof that we're here, isn't it?"

"Proof of what?" I tremble.

Ted returns, and Char's boots hit the overhead deck as she heads down.

"You're our network contact?" I ask. "What's happening?"

"We're your replacement. The regular man can't make it."

Ted and I lock eyes.

"We had no idea you were in the network," I say. "Why didn't you tell us?"

"We needed to keep things quiet. Can Char steer while we step inside, and I'll explain?"

"If she feels well enough. Char, are you up to it?"

"I'm better than I was."

She doesn't look good, but her face is set as firm as the Rock of Gibraltar. She toggles her rain slicker closed and takes the helm.

Ted steps behind. "I'm coming, too." He sheds his rainslicker outside of the library. "Let's avoid puddles." He, Sparks, Harlan, and I hang our raingear on pegs.

Sparks straddles a ridiculously small library chair. "Our network had a last-minute change. Since Governor Langlie knows I'm committed to the Challenge, he assigned me to reach you. With things on high-alert, plus bad weather, normal radio frequencies aren't working."

"We know." Ted sits, too, his face inscrutable. "Strange, though. Our backup radios have always worked before."

"But there's a new development." Sparks smiles. "Anne, you'll like this surprise."

But his voice holds an edge that makes my heart hammer.

Harlan squirms on a small chair next to Sparks like a toddler needing the bathroom.

Sparks lays a plastic-protected sheet on the table. "These are the new orders. The governor needs you to do something special. Motor to Astoria as soon as weather permits. He'll meet us there for a Fourth of July showstopper to build morale across the whole U.S."

"Wait," Ted says. "Astoria's in Oregon, but Langlie is Governor of Washington. How does that work?"

Sparks' eyes flash. "Don't interrupt. He and Governor Sprague are co-hosting this for both states."

I rub my aching temple. "Tell us what you need."

His eyes burn. "Anne, you're making America proud. Stay on track, and you can reach Ilwaco and finish the Challenge tomorrow or early the Fourth. Don't get me wrong. Ilwaco's a fine place to end your journey. You could lead a good Independence Day celebration there, but Governors Langlie and Sprague want something bigger." He spreads his hands wide. "They want you in Astoria for a Fourth of July that will impact the nation forever."

I tug my hair. "That's quite a change. We had scheduled a two-hour library stop for Astoria plus a fifteen-minute radio interview." I turn my head to try to read the words printed on Sparks' sheet.

But he pulls it far away, so I can't.

"Tell me what they want, and I'll do my best." I lower my voice. "But I need notes."

Ted hands me paper and pen from my library desk. I smile thanks.

"Simply put," Sparks says, "this provides two celebrations and two big news stories, but don't worry, I've got you covered."

"I'm not worried. I'm just trying to understand."

"Trust me. Astoria will be the biggest celebration the West Coast has had this century." He sniffs. "Say, is that coffee? Do you have more?"

"Coming up." Ted hops up and brings the pot, two mugs, and cream and sugar.

Sparks adds both and brings the mug to his lips. "You make good brew, Vincent."

Harlan drinks so greedily, he burns his mouth. "Ouch, scalding, but great. Maybe you should run a coffee shop instead of doing mechanics." He laughs at his joke.

Ted doesn't laugh. "Are you saying you two have been part of the river patrol all along?"

"Not from the beginning." Sparks pats down his springy hair, his green fedora nowhere in sight. "But once the governor saw the value of my work, and that Harlan was heroic on *Books Afloat* twice, he added us both."

Harlan crowed. "I told you I should be here for the finale. You wouldn't listen, but it's going to happen."

"Why didn't the governor tell me?" I ask, not bothering to hide my irritation.

"Network radios aren't working, plus he's busy. He sent us."

"You sent the coded message, Harlan?" Ted's eyes challenge. "Or Sparks?"

"I did." Harlan puffs his chest. "Pastor Bob gave me the code, but we need to give the details in person." Harlan rocks his chair forward, raising its back legs from the floor.

I frown, and he sits back down.

"Pastor Bob let you operate his radio instead of doing it himself?" Ted asks the question in my heart.

"That's right. He was busy, so told me how." Harlan unbuttons his collar. "After Sparks picked me up, we stopped in Cathlamet to get the speedboat and come here. He's really something." He looks at Sparks. Admiration shines in his expression. "A genius at running that boat in bad weather."

"You don't say." Ted gives Sparks an appraising look. "We could have used your help before. What will you do with the speedboat now? Tow it?"

"No. Return it." Sparks drums his fingers on the tabletop.

My brain spins. "Where's your notebook? Aren't you filing a story on this?"

"Tomorrow. We'll take photos when the weather breaks, get quotes from both governors. Plus, what you want to add." He scoots closer. "There's more."

My brain is already past overload. "Okay, Sparks, fill us in."

33

Thursday, July 2, 1942
Skamokawa, Washington

Sparks rattles off plans like a Barnum and Bailey ringmaster. "On the Fourth, after another all-you-can-eat picnic, both governors will host a talent show with winners earning cash prizes and advancing to a national contest."

Ted opens his mouth.

But I'm already saying, "The Reynolds family. Perfect, if we can tell them in time."

Sparks grins. "I knew you'd want them here, so I sent word. They're coming."

"Thank you." He gets my genuine smile.

"You're welcome." He reads the plastic-protected sheet. "After the talent show, top high school bands from Oregon and Washington will compete, and then the Fort Stevens' marksmanship team will show we're in great shape, despite the failed attack."

"Good," Ted says.

"Then, we'll have a flyover of the A-29 Hudson bomber that chased away the Japanese sub."

"That will be a showstopper!" Ted's rain hood had mashed his hair. He combs it with his fingers.

I like his hair.

"But the grand finale will be you sailing into harbor at sunset, lights blazing, to dock at the ferry terminal as crowds cheer, and both Governors praise *Books Afloat* for building morale and setting new records during difficult times."

"Are you kidding?" I clasp my hands, my voice dreamy. "That sounds fabulous."

"You deserve it, and you have almost reached the ocean."

"Don't forget the best part." Harlan's hands jerk to accompany his words. "After you sail in, there will be a terrific pyrotechnic show." He grins like a boy let loose in a fireworks store.

"That's right. It will be the biggest fireworks display the West Coast has seen since this war started."

"Fabulous."

But in the next instant, Ted's eyes question. "Wait a minute. Aren't fireworks restricted by blackout regulations so enemy planes can't locate population centers?"

"Normally, but our leaders are pleased things are going well, so they're making this exception."

"Great—" I catch a glimpse outside through a porthole, "We'll need better weather, though."

"The meteorologist predicts this storm will blow out soon." Sparks glances around the library. "Say, do you have another working radio here? Even a portable? I'd like to hear a weather update."

"I have a small one my dad assembled for me from a kit. Sometimes it works when other frequencies are down, even brings in stations others can't." I walk a few steps to bring the small unit from its cupboard and switch it on. After tuning past squawks and squeals, I find the Cathlamet station that reported weather last night and turn up the dial.

"... cooler than normal temperatures prevail as a late-season storm brings rain squalls and blustering winds that will decrease by evening. Skies will clear by midnight, and moderating temperatures promise a great Independence Day. Have a safe and happy Fourth of July, everyone!"

"And now in local news, police remain mystified by the unexplained death of Evan Dale, owner of Cathlamet Marina, found this morning, apparently drowned in his boathouse, along with the disappearance of one of his boats. Those with information should contact—"

"Give me that." Sparks snatches the radio and hits the *off* button.

"Be gentle. My dad made that." I take it from his hands. "Ted, that man's name sounds familiar. Isn't Evan—?"

"Our contact." Ted studies Sparks and Harlan. "Strange. Did you two see him when you came through?"

"We missed him," Sparks said. "He'd gone home before we arrived but left word which boat we could use. I'll contact Cathlamet police and explain we have the speedboat with his permission. We can give it to the Astoria police."

"We met the owner," Harlan blurts. "Don't you remember, Sparks? You followed him into the boathouse to get the speedboat key."

"No, Harlan, you're mistaken," Sparks growls. "That was his brother, Kevin. Evan went home early. You were farther back and didn't hear clearly."

Harlan rubs his lip. "Hmm. Sorry."

"Here's what we'll do." Sparks' gaze returns to me. "The river is wide here. Once we're across the channel, Astoria's an easy reach. Both governors want to surprise everyone with your arrival, so they've asked us to go to a quiet cove on Oregon's side to wait until sunset and then arrive with lights blazing."

Ted blinks. "If that's what they want, we'll make it happen."

"I have questions. Isn't there any way I can talk to either governor? Or Smitty?"

"No. I wish there were. There's currently no standard radio reception at all. The best I can do is send questions via Morse Code and tell Governor Langlie you're cooperating." His expression softens. "Until then, we should rest for what's ahead. You've had a long haul, and Char's practically staggering."

"It has been grueling." Ted massages his jaw. "And fighting this storm made it harder."

"Speak for yourself." I bat my eyes to send Ted a message he's not getting.

"Anne, be honest. I'm speaking for all of us. You and Char are exhausted."

"That's understandable and nothing to be ashamed of," Sparks says. "Taking a break is essential to doing our best on the Fourth. By crossing to Oregon now and dropping anchor, we'll be in position for these plans to succeed. At anchor there, we should eat and catch a nap." He stands and stretches.

Ted stands, too. "Sorry, Sparks. I can still only offer you the floor in my room."

"That's fine. I'm not tired. I'll figure something out later."

"Dropping anchor and resting will help Char." I rub a kink in my neck. "She hasn't felt well today. Why don't I trade places with her and have her come so you can fill her in yourself?"

"Good idea." Sparks finally grabs a notebook. "Keep *Books Afloat* on this course, and send Char here."

34

Thursday, July 2, 1942
Near Skamokawa, Washington, to Astoria, Oregon, River Mile 14

Ted sped to the engine room for standard checks and hurried back to the library to support Char.

She slipped out of her raingear, hung it on a peg, then sat and listened to Sparks, chin in hand.

"Any questions?" Sparks asked when finished.

"More concerns," she said. "Visibility is so bad that crossing is risky. We could hit a log boom, run down a boat, or get run down."

"Except bad weather means there's little river traffic. You're being asked to do a hard thing, but it's necessary. Governor Langlie brags you're the only one to do this."

She flushed. "I appreciate his confidence. He's a great leader, but not a seaman. My J.P. wouldn't cross in these conditions." She twisted and untwisted her hands. "So, I shouldn't either. I'd like to talk to Smitty."

"I wish you could." Sparks folded his hands around hers. "But all broadcast channels are down."

"Why does it matter whether we rest on this or that side of the river? I'd rather wait."

"I don't blame her," Ted said. "This close to finishing the Challenge, we should use good sense and avoid risks. I have one last radio gadget to try to catch updates. I'll be right back." He hurried downstairs and returned with his small personal network unit. His dimples flashed. "Sometimes, mechanics can make these work when others can't."

Sparks gawked. "Whoa. The boat has two of those?"

"Not officially. This is my personal unit." Ted opened the black case and fiddled with the dials, but even his expertise only brought radio-tube screams and squawks. "Well, that's disappointing." He closed the case.

"No surprise," Sparks said, "when nothing else works."

"I guess not. Is the weather improving at all?" Ted looked beyond the covered area to scan the sky. "Solid murk. I say we wait a few hours for the weather to break."

"Even conditions this bad often improve after several hours," Char said. "I feel a change coming in my bones."

"And when she does," Ted said, "it usually happens."

Sparks shoulders slumped. "I guess I'll have to tell you the real reason we have to cross now."

Ted looked Sparks straight in the eye. "I suggest you do."

Sparks surveyed each face and then the floor. "There's proof of new Japanese activity nearby. At least one sub has entered the Columbia."

"Wha-at?" Ted socked his right hand into his left. "When? Where is it now?"

"Not sure. They're barely past the river's mouth but heading this way."

Char hunched forward, hugging her knees. "Let them try. They'll be sorry."

"We think they'll target the July Fourth activities."

"They won't succeed," Ted huffed out a breath. "I've waited all year for a chance to make a difference."

Sparks flashed a high five. "This is your chance, Vincent."

Char smacked a fist on the table. "This changes everything. I'll do whatever it takes."

"I knew we could count on you." Sparks heaved a sigh of relief. "Let me tell Anne, so we can get underway. We'll man lookout stations. If you see or hear *anything* suspicious, tell me."

"Count on it," Ted said.

All three donned their rain slickers.

From the rail, Ted saw the speedboat tied to *Books Afloat* bobbing below. "Say, what's your plan for the speedboat? Won't it fill with water and be dead weight?"

"I have a plan. Harlan, give me a hand." Sparks hurried down the ladder. "I've got the prow. Climb down and grab the other end. That's right. Now, tip her to slosh out the extra water. That's good."

They finished and returned to deck where Anne, ashen, waited for instruction. Char must have shared more information.

"It's okay, Anne." Ted gave her a squeeze. "This is what we've been waiting for." He moved to the stern and peered into the rain. "No weather change yet." He bowed his head. *Lord, take charge of these coming hours. Give us courage and protection. We commit everything to You.*

The world stayed silent except for the sounds of pouring rain and the river's rush, but Ted also heard the thudding of his own heart.

What am I missing? What is wrong?

HOURS LATER, Char piloted *Books Afloat* across the channel through blinding rain. Ted dropped anchor where Sparks said.

"I never want to do that again." Char sank into a chair with a sigh that emptied her lungs.

"You won't have to," Sparks promised. "You did well in the crisis." He scanned our faces. "You all did. We don't expect Japanese activity until tonight. We suspect the July Fourth celebration is when they'll attack. Two of us will stand guard at all times."

"You have my full support." Ted raised a fist.

"We appreciate that. I also know you're all fairly beat, so Harlan and I will take the first watch while you rest. Once the action starts, we'll fight to the finish."

This Sparks was a new man. One who did put his country's interests before his own. Ted readjusted his brain cells to rethink his opinion of Sparks.

Ted blew a kiss to Anne and went to his bunk. However, he couldn't quiet his mind. The slightest sound could signal the beginning of battle. At last, he slept.

35

Friday, July 3, 1942
Near Skamokawa to Astoria, River Mile 14

I could barely absorb all Sparks had to say. We may have as active a role in defending America as our men at Pearl Harbor or Midway. My nerves vibrate with excitement until exhaustion makes me sleep like the dead.

When my eyes snap open, it's too dim to distinguish the book titles on shelves near my bed. I'm like a diver swimming on the floor of an amethyst sea trying to reach the surface. That's when I hear loud clanking noises that I think woke me and now bring me to my feet. They're more like hammer blows than mechanical sounds. Something is terribly wrong with our engine. As I grab a jacket, a powerful searchlight switches on to make the gray overcast brighter.

I push through the library curtain, but Sparks isn't there. And then my eyes refuse to believe what they see—small men in foreign uniforms board *Books Afloat* from a submarine attached to us with steel ladders. The uniforms display Japan's rising sun. At the rail, Sparks faces me in the same uniform with officer ribbons decorating his chest. He has a holstered revolver and sword at his waist and gives commands in fluent Japanese. He gives me a barracuda smile.

"Sparks? What on earth?"

"Surprise! I'm an officer in Japan's Imperial Navy, and you are prisoners of war." He slaps the bow. "*Books Afloat* is now Japanese property."

My breathing stops as if his hands squeeze my neck. "Noooo!" My stomach lurches as Sparks snaps on handcuffs.

"You didn't guess?"

"I trusted you." I hurl venom. "How could you betray your country?"

"I have reasons. When you hear, you'll understand."

Harlan sprawls in a corner, handcuffed and whimpering. "Sparks said I'd be a hero. He *made* me help. He said you'd be proud. He didn't say it would be like this."

"You helped him, Harlan? You must have known."

"I didn't. Just like you couldn't tell."

He turns from the loathing on my face.

Footsteps echo as two seamen push Ted up from below. He's in ropes, his mouth cut and bleeding, but one seaman has a black eye.

The other waves a Smith and Wesson revolver overhead. "Lookee. Sailorman no can fight now."

"I'll find a way." Ted's eyes hood.

"You're hurt."

I reach out, but the seamen push him past.

"I'm sorry, Anne."

Sparks bows. "How touching that you care. Harlan was right."

Two more sailors haul Char in ropes down from the upper deck. They wave a handgun from her things, too.

"How far will you take this, Sparks?" she snarls.

"Clear to victory." Sparks regards her. "I feel sorry for you.

You're nice. Too bad you helped this bunch. I'd let you go, except your J.P. and his sub-chaser just sank our best sub with all on board. This is your payback."

"Thank God." Her eyes shine. "Here's what I think." She spits.

"Ah, brave and feisty." He slaps her. "Commendable, but pointless. Too bad the world can't hear your story. It's worth writing."

She spots Harlan. "Are you part of this, too?"

"Sparks tricked me." He can't look at her. "It's not my fault."

"Tell the truth." Sparks prods him with his foot. "You're involved past your eyeballs to be a hero to Anne." Sparks nudges him again. "But you're not hero material, are you?"

Harlan curls into a ball. "You said if I found Pastor Bob's code, it would help Anne. You didn't say you'd hurt people."

"You talk too much," Sparks growls. "Now, I have to hurt you."

Harlan cowers smaller, fear twisting his face. "What will you do?"

"Put you in the speedboat where the current's strong but pull the gas line, so it looks like it broke during your getaway, and you got carried to sea. You won't wear ropes, but you'll be unconscious from this untraceable injection." He lifts a hypodermic syringe and approaches. "They'll blame you for Evan's death, too. All the loose ends will be tidied up."

"You killed him?" Harlan's eyes snap wide. "I wasn't involved at all."

"But they'll think you were. So, it doesn't matter."

Face white, Ted strains against his ropes. "Sparks, how can you kill other humans? Harlan is from your part of the country."

"I feel bad about that." Regret softens his voice. "And I do know his grandmother—nice woman. But war is war. He's a fool, and we needed someone gullible."

Ted's eyes slit. "I don't get it. He's young, and you fooled him. You should be ashamed. And why help Japan?"

"Simple. My folks were missionaries there for thirty years. That's where I grew up. The Japanese are good people—family." His eyes mist. "But my folks and I spent sabbaticals in eastern Washington, where we have ties. I met Michiko, a beautiful Japanese girl, here as a foreign exchange student. When we saw war coming, we married secretly. Before I could start her immigration, war broke out."

"Doesn't the government know your ties to Japan?" I ask.

"Sure. But I did most formal education here and downplayed the Japanese connection. Everyone considers me a true-blue American—even my uncle." His voice hardens. "Days after Roosevelt's Executive Order, authorities picked up Michiko for an internment camp. But then, before I could intervene, they shipped her to Japan instead."

His voice cracks. "She and her parents needed food and medicine. So did other friends I've known all my life. I had to help. You'd do the same." His face contorts. "The Japanese people don't want war."

"I'm truly sorry," I say. "It is terribly hard, but some missionary and charity help is still getting through."

"Not enough. And who knows where things will go from here? Our government lies and blurs the facts. My folks spent thirty years teaching that God is love, and that America stands for freedom. They destroyed all that by declaring war."

"But Japan attacked first," Ted says.

"Shut up." Sparks punches Ted's jaw so hard his head snaps back.

"Ted!" I want to reach him but can't.

"He's fine, Anne, don't worry. Besides, no one really knows what happened first. We don't have the whole story. News always gets rewritten."

"I have proof, if you'll listen," Ted pleads.

Sparks thumps Ted's chest. "Don't kid yourself. Each side tells history their way. My friends in Japan are as much family as my blood relatives here. If you met them, you'd agree. So, when the Emperor's men explained how my support could shorten this war and save lives on both sides, I agreed. Michiko, her family, and others received help. It was an easy decision. I'm sure God agrees."

"I'm sure He doesn't." The handcuffs chafe my wrists. I twist and pull to force the lock or slip them off. Nothing gives. "What are your plans for us?"

He gives a tight smile. "You believe in heaven? Good. We'll send you there. Once we blow up *Books Afloat* and other Astoria targets, my sub will carry me home to Michiko. After Japan wins, our world will have peace."

Tears flood Char's cheeks. "Sparks, don't commit treason against your homeland."

"Homeland? Don't you see? I was born here, but I'm part of two nations. Ending the war sooner means fewer die. I am sorry for your deaths, but there's collateral damage in any war." He fingers his sword. "When you agreed to spy, you sealed your fate."

My eyes convey my appeal. "You have a choice, Sparks. Does your uncle know what you're doing?"

"Of course not. Leave him out of this. I've written a letter he'll receive tomorrow, but by then, my actions will have won victory. He'll be proud." He checks his watch. "Enough talk. I'll take care of Harlan and send you three below."

Harlan moans as he's pulled to his feet by ropes. "I helped you. Don't hurt me."

"You know what's coming. Make your peace with God."

"Don't do this!" Ted commands.

Sparks stares. "Really? That's big of you. He caused you trouble, and you're defending him? Is he worth it?"

"He is to me."

I've never been prouder.

"You promised you'd reward me—" Harlan screams as

Sparks plunges the hypodermic into his arm. Immediately, Harlan's eyes roll back until only the whites show. After spasmodic jerks, he slides down motionless.

Sparks cuts Harlan's ropes and tosses them aside, nodding to two sailors. They load Harlan into a canvas sling and lower him into the partially water-filled speedboat, propping him at the tiller as if he's steering. They cut its cable free from *Books Afloat* and wedge their feet against Harlan's craft to give it a forceful shove into the main current. It's on its way in seconds.

"Good riddance," Sparks says, dusting his hands.

"Lord, have mercy," I say.

Char and I fight tears as the speedboat carrying Harlan races downriver.

"God help him," Ted says and bites his cheek.

Gradually, the rain slows, and the winds decrease. We watch until we can't see the speedboat anymore.

"Save your breath," Sparks barks. "It's over for him. You should tell *Books Afloat* goodbye, too. She'll go down with you on board. We will have a Fourth of July celebration in Astoria, but you're it. It will be America's second day of infamy for her evil deeds. You'll reach the ferry terminal like I said, but you'll be the fireworks display."

"Even if you destroy Astoria," I say, "it doesn't mean you'll win the war."

"You're wrong. Those clanking noises? We attached a powerful limpet mine to your hull on a timer with enough explosives to blow sky-high, destroy the ferry terminal, the fuel storage tanks on shore, plus the military installation. Our I-25 sub will reach Washington's ferry facilities on the other side and do the same there.

"With few roads and ferries out of operation, our forces can invade and occupy America's key cities. The U.S. will surrender in days, and this war will end. Just think, Char. Military forces on both sides can return to their homelands."

A laugh rumbles in his chest as a sob catches in Char's.

Ted studies me.

I'm okay, I mouth and tent my fingers.

"Surrender, Sparks," Ted insists. "You'll never get away with this. Stop while you can. We'll explain about your family pressures and recommend leniency. You may avoid the death penalty."

"This cause is worth dying for, but you can't stop us now. It's already begun. You'll go down with your ship in time-honored tradition. Both governors and the nation will sing your praises and read your obituaries."

Ted fights his bonds, but there's no slack. "God will help us. U.S. technology will find your subs and bring you to justice."

"That's where you're wrong, Vincent." Sparks lips curl. "The God I know loves justice and is helping us. We'll submerge until time for your explosion, and then we'll escape. *Books Afloat* is a perfect cover for us since officials do expect you to dock, and no one will guess you carry destruction. Even I couldn't tell you were involved in the river spy network until I traced your radio transmissions."

He turns to me. "Tricky, Annie. I like your spunk. But for your sake, I wish you'd made better choices."

"They're the best I've ever made." I lift my chin.

He starts to slap me but stops. "Never mind. You'll soon pay. Now, you three get below before river traffic picks up." He grabs my arm. "Starting with you, Captain Fancy Pants, who can't even pilot your own boat."

"We got here, though." I resist, but his grip is iron.

"Get down there, or I'll shove."

"Let her go," Ted shouts and thrusts his bound hands toward Sparks' holster to grab his gun.

As Sparks fights for control, the gun fires.

I wait for Sparks to fall, but red blood blossoms across Ted's left shoulder instead.

"Dear God," I cry, "help us."

"Stop, Anne. Two inches lower and it would have been his heart." Sparks shakes his head. "So foolish." He jerks Ted by his ropes and kicks him down the passageway.

Sparks lets me rush downstairs to Ted's side.

"Sweetheart, can you hear me?"

He moans but lies still.

"So, Harlan was right." Sparks holsters his gun and laughs. "You do care for each other."

"Haven't you done enough?"

I kneel by Ted, cradling him in my arms. "You shouldn't have tried, love." He's unconscious, but I speak too softly for Sparks to hear.

Ted's breathing is raspy.

"Please don't die without knowing that I love you."

He's unresponsive, so I stay, continuing to cradle him.

Here, imprisoned in *Books Afloat*, the literal and spiritual darkness matches the night when I was the kid in Grandpa's truck, hearing screaming metal and breaking glass, the impact pushing me to the floor.

Now I am that girl again, repeating the childhood prayers that didn't work then. *Now I lay me down to sleep, I pray the Lord my soul to keep, if I should die before I wake, I pray the Lord my soul to take. God save Grandpa ...*

But God hadn't saved Grandpa. A passerby found him dead in our twisted wreckage, crashed into one of the largest irrigation culverts in Oklahoma. Yet, his hand somehow covered my head, saving me.

I weep now, holding Ted, brushing his hair back from his forehead, tracing his strong jaw. *I failed Grandpa. Don't let me fail someone I love now.*

I can't breathe. "Ted, don't leave me. Please live ..." My sobs join his ragged breathing. "I can't stand it if, if you ..." Tears I've held in for too long suddenly release as I curl again in the fetal position like the hurting little girl I used to be, rocking and moaning, still mouthing prayers.

But at that moment, I hear new words inside. *You were a child then, Anne. It was not your fault. Forgive yourself. Pray this instead. As I lay me down tonight, come, dear Lord, and help me fight, even if our enemies attack, Your mighty power will drive them back.*

My tears stop. Hope stirs. Where did those words come from? *God is here.*

Char has been pushed down the same stairs. I vaguely remember hearing her fall and the clang of the stairway door being locked. Now, she joins me, praying, although her ropes also chafe and burn. In minimum light, with Sparks' red handprint bright on her face, she still radiates courage.

"Remember Esther in the Bible?" she asks. With all help gone, her people were still saved. God will fight for us and win."

I nod. "I don't understand how, but I believe." I try to staunch Ted's bleeding. "How can we stop this."

"We'll find a way." She lifts her restrained hands enough to pull her weathered yellow Sou'wester from her head. "Try this. The lining is soft." Her lips lift. "I'm glad this hat is good for something besides preventing rain."

I pressure it against his wound. "It's helping!"

We both sigh relief.

"What else do we have to help?"

We search the narrow space we're crammed in near the engine room between the galley and Ted's quarters.

"It's hard to see, but there must be more we can use," Char says.

"We'll find something." My voice gains confidence as we struggle. "There's no give to these handcuffs," I fuss.

"Not yet, and my ropes are tight," Char says. "I wish we had Sparks in them."

Our injuries drain us.

Ted still tosses and turns. His forehead burns with fever, but his lips form words, "Limped … Magnus …"

"What did you say, love?" I lean closer. His shoulder is damaged, not his leg. Why is he worried about limping? If we stop the bleeding, this injury shouldn't make him limp.

He rouses more, inching his left hand toward his pocket and repeats, "Limped … Magnus …"

"Magnus?" I ask, trying to understand. "You want us to contact Magnus? I don't know who that is!"

He shakes his head but opens his eyes. The daylight's last gleams fade through the locked door at the head of the stairs. Today is July 3. Summer days are long, but once night falls, Sparks will get underway.

Thin pencil lines of light mark a small square in the hull near Char, and she points. "What's over there?"

"Where?" I hardly see anything.

"Over there. That square outlined with light."

Char scoots on her bottom toward the hull, exploring.

While I hold Ted, praying and whispering love words I doubt he can hear, Char slides her fingers along the narrow light gleams and examines the small square area.

"It's an opening eighteen by eighteen inches. It leads outside since light shines through." She gropes further. "There's a stiff metal latch I can't budge, but it's sharp. If I rub my ropes against it at an angle, it may cut."

I sit up, riveted. "Try for all you're worth!"

Her smile is beautiful. "Believe me. I will."

The ropes cut her wrists, but after sawing back and forth against metal edges, one rope strand snaps. I see crimson blood drops.

But Char lifts her arms in triumph. "Freedom!"

"Thank God." I flash a thumb's up.

Char attacks the latch, working its toggle. She keeps at it until after one mighty heave, it releases and opens, showing the wonderful world beyond *Books Afloat*—the wooded Oregon shore of this powerful river. She gasps fresh air.

"You did it."

"Thank you, Jesus. Show us what's next." She pulls the small door shut in case our captors come and scoots toward me. "What do you think? Can it work for us to escape?"

Hope builds. "I think so. Do you remember me saying Jeb and Janey's son tumbled through the boat's small supply hatch? I'd forgotten and never used it, but that must be it. If it's big enough, it can work." I gesture toward Ted. "But not without him."

"Agreed." She nods.

Ted stirs. "Beautiful," he whispers.

I shed happy tears and lay a finger across his battered lips. "Save your strength."

But he struggles to sit, to speak more clearly, "Limpets, Magnets ..."

Suddenly I understand. "Wait, you're saying. Magnets. The ones in your pocket? And something more. What?"

"Limpet mine on hull," he manages. "Attached magnetically. Magnets in pocket might be strong enough ..."

I remember the magnets he's carried since boyhood that he always fidgets with.

"Char, you're free. Can you get them?"

"I'll try. Not much will stop me." She scoots near, fishes them out, and puts them in his hand.

His fingers close around them, relief brightening his face. "We have a chance."

I have hopeful chills.

"Limpet mines explode on impact," he says. "If my magnets can cancel the clock setting ..." He tries to lift his head. "Must find the timer."

I look around. "I'm not sure where, but we'll find it."

Char listens. "I hear clicking near the engine room. I'll scoot there." She crab walks on her bottom. "Thank God! It's here, set for midnight."

"Good work." My heart soars. "We'll save the ferry system. And there's a chance we can save *Books Afloat* and ourselves."

Ted beams. "Let's hope for all of it."

"Until now, saving *Books Afloat* and winning the Challenge has been my life goal." My voice falters. "Stopping Sparks is vital, but you and Char matter so much more." I barely speak as I bend down and brush his cheek. "Everything is different now."

His eyes shine. "You're different. After we finish this job, I need some serious time with you."

Char's cheeks turn rosy.

Mine are burning. I lean against the cold hull to steady myself. "Ted, can your magnets reset the timer?"

"Yes." He searches my eyes.

And his are beautiful. Their blue-green depths shimmer like living water.

"We can move the time forward to explode *before* we reach the terminal—with the sub attached, so it sinks. Then their threat to the Pacific Northwest ends."

"At least on Oregon's side." His eyes track mine.

"Even if we can't escape, we'll stop them."

Char gasps. "You've given your life for this dream, but—"

"Maybe a bigger dream is defeating our enemy."

"We gain everything if we can." Ted rolls his head along his shoulders. "Whatever it takes."

"They'll kill us anyway. I've had time to think, sitting with you both, wondering if we'd live or die. Destroying *Books Afloat* could save our nation."

"And stop their invasion." Ted's voice strengthens.

"We'll turn the tables on Sparks and our enemies."

The air is electric. Ted and Char stare at me.

"It's terribly risky," Ted says, "but might work. I'd like to save us, too."

"Maybe Char found a way. But either way, we have to blow up *Books Afloat* to stop Japan."

"I like your thinking." He smiles broadly before wincing with pain.

"I'm sorry you're hurt," I say.

"It's a small price."

I turn to Char. "You mentioned the story of Esther. Didn't she destroy her enemies?"

"That's right." She gives two thumbs up.

"Since your hands are loose, can you scoot here and untie me? And then free Annie and tell me what you've found."

"Gladly." She scoots close and gets to work. Her face beams with courage.

Ted grins. "Our chances of outwitting Japan's Navy aren't high, but I love the David defeating Goliath story, too."

"If there's even a 1 percent chance—"

"We'll take it." Ted brushes my hand, and his eyes brighten. "It's dangerous but just might work. Here's how we'll surprise them. And blow up *Books Afloat* with them on board."

I take in the excited face of the man I love. This trip isn't over. Our greatest challenge has just begun.

36

Friday evening, July 3, 1942
Near Astoria, River Mile 14

Burning pain radiated through Ted's shoulder, and blood loss weakened him, but the desire to outsmart their enemies and save Anne and Char energized him. "Lord, you helped David kill Goliath. Help us."

Char's deft fingers worked. "So far, I can't unlock Anne's handcuffs, but I think I'm making progress on your ropes. If that means Sparks is Goliath, he'll still fall."

"Yes!"

As Char labored, Ted studied Anne's handcuffs. If only he had a nail. Or pin.

"You called me Annie," she said. "Is that because I acted like a baby and let you down?"

"No." His hand flexed but couldn't reach her. "You *never* let me down. Haven't you figured out Annie is my love name for you?"

"It is?" She gave her brightest smile. "Then call me Annie all the time."

Char grinned and kept working.

Being bound made Ted feel like when he was a little kid, and Mom and Dad fought. Mom wilted every time. When serious illness came, she had no reserve. He did his best to inspire her but couldn't make her fight to live.

Could he find strength now to save these women he loved? And defeat Sparks and Japan? *What if I'm still the scared boy who isn't enough?*

Now, an answer came inside. *You don't have to be strong. I am strong in you!*

At that instant, Char cut the rope's last strand, and Ted was free. Failure fell away. Confidence flowed like some cosmic tide had reversed, and life flooded in instead of death. "Help me get my belt off."

He unbuckled it, and Char helped him slip it off then around his shoulder. A wince escaped him as she tightened it into a tourniquet.

"Thank You, Lord!" He breathed deep. "Char, I'm weak. I need one more thing."

"Name it."

"Bring the file from my tool bench and a nail if you see one."

"Coming right up." Looking perkier, Char flexed circulation back into her hands. She quickly returned, handing him the file and a nail with a smile. "Did you hear Sparks say J.P.'s sub-chaser sank their biggest sub?"

"Something to celebrate." Ted rasped the file back and forth across Anne's handcuffs. Spirals of silver metal curled away.

"If we can blow up *Books Afloat* with these jokers on board," Char mused, "it would be as good as J.P. sinking that sub. We'd strike another knockout blow against Japan."

"Even if we're on board, but I hope we escape." His hands ached.

Char took over, and the file's soft rasp curled away more

bright metal bits from the handcuff's hasp. The sound of freedom rang in their ears.

"My turn," Ted said. "And now, I'm ready for that nail."

"It's working. They're looser." Finally, the metal band opened. "I'm free," Anne cried and threw her arms around Ted. Trying to avoid his wounded shoulder, she burst into tears.

"Shhhh," Char warned. "We don't want them to hear and check."

"We're almost ready," Ted said. "My tools are weapons. Please bring my hammer, and get Annie the biggest wrench. Char, could you swing the crowbar you'll find there?"

"That suits me fine." She brought the tools and tested the crowbar's heft. "Just right. I'll bet it works like a can opener on enemy heads."

Ted snorted. "Char, you're a violent woman." But the edges of his eyes crinkled.

"It's a perfectly normal response," Char said and hefted the crowbar again.

"Keep the tools hidden. If anyone checks, we need to look tied up."

"Roger. I'll toss the ropes over me again," Char said. "It's so dim, they can't see well down here. Meanwhile, I'll check that hatch more." She pushed the small square opening again. It squeaked in protest but then yielded. "It's small, but I think we can squeeze through. At least, you two can. I'm not sure about me." She poked her middle with a sturdy finger. "I've put on weight, but if I inhale, there's a chance." She glanced down. "Well, half a chance."

"We won't leave without you," Ted promised. "We'll stay and help until you make it." He palmed his magnets, happy to hear them click again. "Most bomb settings are hair-trigger fine. It's possible the timer will blow when I reset this."

"We'll pray it doesn't." Anne's voice held confidence. "We're all three in this together."

"Yes, love." He kissed Anne's cheek. "Once we squeeze through the hatch, the people on watch might hear us splash into the river."

"I doubt it. The current's noisy," Char replied. "And I haven't heard footsteps for a while. I'll pray everyone on board is deaf or distracted."

"Char and I have talked." Anne gazed at Ted. "With your wounded shoulder, she and I want to fireman-carry swim you."

He opened his mouth but closed it.

"I've done it lots," Char said, "so hush."

"Until I think of a better idea?"

She winked and opened the hatch again to peer out. "We're anchored in a slough near shore—not very deep. I see lily pads and vegetation. It smells like skunk cabbage." She wrinkled her nose. "Right now, that may be my favorite smell on earth."

"Gotcha." Ted checked his watch. "It's eight o'clock. The sun sets at 8:30 p.m. They plan to blow the town and us up at midnight, so I need to move things forward." He slid to the engine room. Minutes passed as he tinkered until a small click sounded.

He hardly paused to breathe but felt a steady pulse in his neck. *Dear Lord, I think it's working.*

All three froze as footsteps marched above them, fore and aft. Someone paused and rattled the locked door at the top of their stairway, pulling hard before moving on.

Ted expelled the breath he didn't know he'd held. And worked faster.

37

Friday evening, July 3, 1942
Near Astoria, Oregon, River Mile 14

Ted stilled and listened. First, the noisy rattle of *Books Afloat's* chain as someone winched the anchor. Next, he felt the swing and drift of the boat as she floated free. *Dear God, don't let Sparks come down here to start the engine.* Ted gripped his hammer. All three exhaled when they heard Sparks use the remote auxiliary switch in the wheelhouse instead. The engine caught easily and whined to high revolutions per minute.

Char's head whipped around. "Listen!" Large waves slapped the hull. They're taking us out from shore."

"What's that other sound?" Anne shuddered.

"Sonar submarine echoes," Ted said. "We're still attached to the sub, so we have to hurry. They'll get us in position and detach us. To ensure both craft blow, I have to move up the explosion time for the limpet mine on our hull—" He checked his watch. "To forty minutes from now?"

Anne nodded solemnly. "That sounds good."

He fiddled and adjusted until one final loud click was followed by quieter steady beeps.

"Okay. Forty minutes and counting. He kissed Char's cheek. And Anne's lips.

Anne returned his kiss.

He reluctantly pulled away. "To be continued. It's action time."

All three scooted toward the hatch.

"Kick off your shoes," Ted instructed. "They'll weigh us down. Char, please go first. We'll help you."

"No. We'll fireman-carry you."

He shook his head. "It's not going to happen, but I have a plan."

"If you're sure?"

"I am."

Char kicked off her favorite boots. "After we save Astoria, we'll go shopping." She wedged herself into the hatch but got stuck. She wiggled and wriggled. "Annie, please give me a shove."

"Coming." After two strong pushes, Char was through and hit the water with a splash, covered by the engine's noise.

Ted kissed the tip of Anne's nose.

"Only my nose?" She looked at him questioningly.

"For now. I can't get distracted by the strong effect on me."

"Good to hear." She kissed her fingertips and laid them across his lips.

"I remembered something that will let me swim without you or Char's help."

"Really?"

"Help me slip out of my shirt—I'll show you."

She undid his buttons and eased his wounded shoulder from its sleeve.

He flexed his muscles and stretched a cramp out of his free arm, then smiled wryly. "I saw someone demonstrate survival flotations from clothes. Please tie knots at the end of both sleeves and the neck. Wave it over your head until it fills with air and tie off the shirt's bottom."

She swooped it in circles. "Like this?"

"Yes. It's working. Now I have water wings to float."

"Will the air stay in?"

"I think so. We'll find out." He gave his biggest grin. "But first, one last thing." He looked at her so tenderly he thought she could hear his thoughts without words.

But footsteps sounded overhead.

"Ted, we have to hurry."

"I know. Come close." His Adam's apple worked. "You deserve a better man than me, but no one could love you more. I love you with my whole heart." He cupped her face. "We may die, but if we live, say you'll spend your life with me."

Anne blinked. "You're sure?"

"Very sure." He traced the line of her cheek. "If we live, I'll work hard to prove myself and propose properly, but I have to know now if you'll marry me."

She trembled. "Ted, you don't need to prove a thing. You already have a thousand times over. I'm the one that—"

"No. My timing is off, and I should talk to your dad, but please say you'll marry me."

Her finger traced the dimple in his chin. "Don't you know? I know now I've always loved you. If you want to marry me after how awful I've been, no force on earth could—"

"You're not awful. Just say 'yes.'"

"Yes."

The word barely left her lips before his claimed hers, their hearts beating as one.

"All right," he said. "We have a job to do. Let's go."

They reached the hatch together. In spite of great shoulder pain, he maneuvered and twisted until he worked through the opening and dropped into the Columbia River and stayed afloat. Char guided him to shore.

He beckoned Anne to follow. She skimmed through the opening like a fish flipping from a barrel, but as she fell, she hit the back of her head on one small pipe extending an inch from the hull. She lost control, and after what seemed forever, dropped like a stone beneath the surface and emerged unconscious seconds later as helpless as a rag doll.

"Annie," Ted called, heart pounding. "Annie!" He struggled to reach her and lift her head above the water, tucking his water wings under her as waves drenched them both.

"Lord, save her. *Save Her!*" he cried, not caring if Sparks and the whole Japanese Navy heard him. In time that seemed forever, yet may have only been seconds, his arms cramped as he struggled to hold and protect her. Char was far away but headed their way with long strokes. He fought to raise Anne, although he sank under the water himself.

And then, he felt the smooth exterior of something large rising underneath them. And his heart stopped beating as he felt terror greater than he'd ever known.

The dark metal skin of a surfacing submarine appeared. The craft's cover plate groaned as the hatch opened. Men extended hands to lift Anne from the water. Ted's stomach sickened as he expected to see Japan's rising sun, but instead, he saw friends. And the rescue craft of his dreams.

"Well-played, Ted. We've got her," Smitty said.

Was he seeing things? Smitty and Johnny wedged inside the *Never Again.* After making room for Anne, the duo draped Ted over the prow and held him above the water.

He wanted to laugh and shout. "I can't believe you two. How did you get here in perfect timing? Will she be okay?"

"Her vitals are steady," Smitty said. "She has a nasty goose egg but looks like she wants to rouse. You'll survive, won't you, Annie?"

Her eyes flickered. "Smitty? You're here?"

"Yup."

"If it's a dream, it's a good one." Her head dropped.

Char reached the sub. "Johnny's here, too? As J.P. would say, I'm hornswoggled. How did you two show up again, just when needed?"

"Good seamanship." Smitty grinned. "We've been tracking you the whole way. We'll get Annie ashore so Johnny can check her, and I'll come back for you two. Then we'll camouflage *Never Again* and settle down for our night at the movies."

Johnny cackled. "We wouldn't want to miss that show, but we're fresh out of popcorn. I promise to bring some next time."

"No next time," Ted said with feeling. "You know Sparks attacked us and what he did to Harlan?" He couldn't spit out his words fast enough. "And *Books Afloat* is set to blow at eight forty-five?"

"Yup, we heard all that. Our newest listening device tracks, receives, and transmits when nothing else will. It brought us here."

"Amazing. Another secret weapon?"

"A new, shiny one." Johnny tapped his forehead while Ted's heart gave victory beats.

"Tell me more."

"Later."

When they were safely on land, wrapped in blankets, and screened behind trees, Johnny lit a small hot fire with firestarter material he pulled from his pocket. "I have another hidey-hole nearby, full of supplies. A man can't have too many now, can he?"

"Never in this lifetime." Ted touched Johnny's shoulder as if knighting him. "You never know who might come to visit."

"You're something else, Johnny." Anne beamed at the little man, one hand supporting the back of her head. "Come closer." Her command left no room for refusal.

He approached. "Yes?"

"Another step and bend down. You're wonderful." She kissed both of his cheeks.

He blushed and stammered, "Land o' Goshen!."

"Affection looks good on you, Johnny. Smitty, please come here, too." She stood and hugged them both.

Char came and did the same.

In dry clothes, with his good arm protecting Anne, Ted sighed out great relief. "From now on, instead of Johnny Hofer, I'm calling you Johnny-on-the-Spot. You always show up at the right times, like guardian angels. But how did you do it this time?"

"Like Johnny told you," Smitty said, "we've been watching and listening the whole way. We tap enemy frequencies, too, so that helps."

Ted's eyes widened. "How long before you fill me in?"

"Not long. We're testing another new device that records all conversations. Even yours, Ted." Johnny winked. "You're quite the Romeo these days. And it sounds like Annie's heart is blooming like spring gardens in sunshine."

She flushed to the roots of her hair. "You don't eavesdrop on private conversations, do you? You stop when you can tell it's personal?"

Johnny shrugged. "How's a man to know? Technology is amazing, but we can't be sure what we're hearing. What if *I love you* is code for *start attack now*? In your case, those statements might mean the same thing." He slapped his thigh and rolled with laughter

Anne shook her head while Char hid a smile.

"It was hard not interfering as your situation worsened." Smitty's eyes turned granite instead of their usual sky blue. "Especially when you got heroic, Ted, and they roughed you up. Then we heard shots fired. You took an awful risk."

"Made me lose hair I can't afford." Johnny patted his haystack.

"With what I had at stake," Ted inclined his head toward Anne and Char, "I had to do my best."

"And you did." Smitty bent down. "How's that shoulder?"

Ted tried moving it. "Stiff, but I had to stop Sparks."

Anne nestled her head against Ted's good shoulder.

He lowered his head against hers. "Hope so. We'll know soon."

"We got his taped confession." Smitty tipped a nod. "With enough convicting evidence, even if they survive."

"Which they won't if I did my job right." Ted's jaw firmed. "They shouldn't be on earth much longer—maybe five minutes."

"You're a hero, Ted, plain and simple," Smitty declared. "Who'd guess magnets could stop an invasion by advancing the explosion time. That's one for the record books."

"I hope it works." Ted's cheeks warmed.

Smitty's voice deepened. "You realize that if you hadn't rescued Anne, we couldn't have reached her in time. She was sinking too fast."

Ted gulped. "I've never prayed so hard."

"Also, thanks to you, Sparks can't succeed. Even if he or anyone else escapes, they'll go to federal prison."

"Or be hung or face a firing squad," Johnny added. "That's the current sentence for treason."

"But it's terrible we lost Harlan." Ted shuddered. "If only we could have acted before Sparks killed him."

"Killed him?" Johnny's eyebrows shot up.

Johnny and Smitty looked at each other and grinned.

"You mean before Sparks *tried* to kill him. What makes you think we—"

"You what?" Anne leaned forward and gasped. "We saw him disappear in the speedboat."

"Yes, you did," Smitty spoke evenly. "And there was nothing

he could do to save himself since Sparks drugged him unconscious. But once the speedboat was out of sight, Johnny used our device to call the Coast Guard to rescue Harlan."

"They arrived just in time," Johnny said, his face aglow. "Five minutes more, and he'd have been a goner. He's in the hospital in Astoria telling the authorities everything."

Anne's voice softened. "Will he, will he be …?"

"Face criminal charges? Yes," Smitty answered. "But his biggest offense is stealing Pastor Bob's radio code for someone he believed was in the volunteer network. He had no part in murdering Evan Dale. Sparks acted alone. Harlan will give state and federal evidence since both are involved. Even the theft charge may drop since officials don't want Harlan sharing evidence that could reveal our technology."

"Good point." Ted nodded. "Thank God, you rescued him."

"It was close." Smitty threw another log on the fire. "A fellow wouldn't want a closer glimpse of the pearly gates than Harlan got." He glanced at the river through branches, but the scene remained quiet. "In that way, Harlan has already served a stiff sentence. I think you'll find him changed. And, you know how Pastor Bob loves to help people?"

"Yes." Ann sat up.

"He and Sue are driving here as soon as they arrange gas rations."

"Grandma Foley," Ted said out loud.

Smitty nodded and gave Anne a glance. "They'll ask the court to release Harlan to their supervision. Can you tolerate that?"

"After what he's been through, I think so." She picked up a twig to snap. "It would be hard having him around after what he did, but he almost died. I won't forget his face as Sparks injected the hypodermic and sent him off alone to die."

"Terrible," Char agreed. "I didn't know anyone could be so cold-blooded."

"Sparks believes in his cause, but the ordeal is having a good effect on Harlan," Smitty said. "Bob believes Harlan was misguided but is turning around." He rested a hand on Ted's sleeve. "By the way, Harlan knows you stuck up for him. He's singing your praises."

Ted rubbed his jaw. "That's a switch. We've had differences, but he deserves a chance."

"I'm glad you feel that way." Smitty turned to Anne. "What do you say?"

"Everyone deserves second chances. Even me." She gulped and looked at Ted.

He kissed her forehead. "If probation includes Harlan staying with Bob and Sue plus being accountable to someone outside of their home, he'll be fine."

"Good call. That's Christianity in action." Smitty started to pat Ted's shoulder but stared at his arm in a sling and stopped.

"What time did you reset that timer for?" Johnny asked.

"Forty minutes after we left—which should be about now." Ted checked his watch. And then shook it. "It's waterlogged. Stopped cold. What time is it? We left *Books Afloat* around 8:05. I set the blast for after dark, at 8:45. If my setting works, the mine should blow soon."

Johnny pulled up a sleeve to display his new watch. "My new-fangled glow-in-the-dark waterproof watch—nice to have. I'll give you one as a wedding gift."

He guffawed as Ted gaped.

"You did hear everything, but you know my intentions are honorable."

"Totally, Ted. Right now, my watch reads 8:42 p.m. Greenwich time. Smitty, where's the spyglass? We're ready for action."

"Here." He pointed it west through the tree. "I can't see much of Astoria since lights are off with the blackout. They left some burning at the ferry terminal, so boats don't run aground. So far, Sparks is smart enough to zig and zag to avoid river mines. Otherwise, he'd blow sky high without our help."

"Where do you think he's heading?" Char accepted the spyglass from Smitty.

"He'll dock *Books Afloat* near the terminal," Smitty answered, maybe announce an open house before tomorrow's fireworks, but until he's close, no targets are at risk."

"He shouldn't arrive before the limpet blows. Ted, you deserve this." Char placed the glass in his hands.

"I'm proud of you, Annie," Smitty said. "You poured heart and soul into *Books Afloat*. I know how much she meant to you, and then you had to surrender her to sink the sub."

Ted handed Anne the spyglass.

"Thanks." Anne adjusted the eyepiece. "I'll bet we'll see her blow without the glass. Surrendering and then abandoning *Books Afloat* wasn't a hard choice with so much at stake. In the beginning, it tore my heart out, but when the payoff includes stopping Japan, plus saving Char and Ted, it was no choice at all.

"If anyone had told me even two weeks ago, I'd sabotage *Books Afloat*, I'd have sent them to the state hospital. But everything changed. And I changed. I'm thrilled to give my all— even if there's never a library boat on the river."

"Atta girl." Smitty slid an arm around her. "With that attitude, I'm sure there will be."

Ted shaded his eyes, shoulders slumped. "It's past time. The explosives should blow. I did my best, but it was a rough estimate. I'm not sure of my calculations." His voice deepened. "I hope I didn't miscalcu—"

Shockwaves rocked from horizon to sky and back again as ear-splitting roars sped all directions to the mouth of the Columbia and beyond. A fireball rose from the river to the heavens, turning night to day as a fiery maw consumed *Books Afloat*—and the attached I-25 Japanese sub. At that moment, the world learned that Ted's calculations were perfect.

Flaming debris soared and fell as Anne, Char, Ted, and friends watched until, finally, the bright blaze faded. Fireboat sirens screamed as firemen, police, and Coast Guard boats raced to the scene.

"Good calculations, Ted," Johnny said, his eyes bright with respect. "You deserve a medal for what you did, and I'm telling both governors."

"I did what any ordinary man—"

"No, sir," Smitty interrupted. "You did what only a very brave man would do."

Anne silenced Ted with a kiss. "Sweetheart, listen to our friends. They're better judges of character than us." She dried her tears on her sleeve.

Smitty handed her his handkerchief. "Annie, your sacrifice will be honored, too."

"No, just Ted. Being alive is enough. We'd be dead if it weren't for him." She swiped her eyes again. "I'm sorry for crying. I don't know what's wrong with me, because I'm celebrating inside. I'm thrilled Ted stopped them, and you saved us." And then she boohooed again between smiles.

"It's okay, Annie. You've been through the wringer. You put your heart and soul into *Books Afloat*, and losing it is like the death of a dear friend. Strong feelings don't change in an instant."

"Thanks," she said and blew her nose. "You're right."

Together, the team watched the last remnants of the blaze fall into the river in dying embers and extinguish.

"Astoria's safe, but what about Washington's ferry terminal?" Char asked. "Did Japan succeed there?"

"Nope. As soon as we heard that plan, we stopped them dead," Smitty answered. "Our Navy hit that sub before it entered the river. It fled, and we pursued. First reports say it was too damaged to survive."

"Another score for us, thank God." Char placed a hand over

her heart. "It's sad how many lives are lost, though," she said. "Everyone has some good in them. Even Sparks. He was just terribly confused."

"Very terribly," Smitty agreed. "He also had many chances to change his mind. The worst part is the lives lost, no matter which side they're on."

"Losing *Books Afloat* is nothing compared to what I have." Anne sniffed once more and returned Smitty's hanky. "As much as I love books, the people in my life matter so much more." She took Smitty's hand and Johnny's and squeezed them.

When tears filled Johnny's eyes, he lifted a knotted fist to brush them away. "Consarned eyes leakin' again. I'm too hardboiled for this kind of thing."

"You don't fool us," Ted said. "You're not hardboiled at all."

"Sweet Annie," Smitty said, "we'll do all we can to launch another *Books Afloat*."

"Thank you. If God arranges it, fine. If not, He'll show me what's next, and I'll be fine."

Ted touched her arm.

"Uh, I mean, He'll show *us* what's next."

"That's better. I'm staying in that picture." Ted moved a lock of her hair out of the way and kissed her forehead again.

She clung to him as darkness overtook the scene except for Johnny's small fire on shore that warmed them.

Smitty snapped on a flashlight. "Now that the fireworks are over, let's get you people medical care. Plus, we'll file military reports. I had the Coast Guard boat wait until after the explosion, but they should arrive soon."

Johnny's ears perked up. "Here they come now."

38

Saturday, July 25, 1942,
Astoria, Oregon, River Mile 14

I stand at attention next to Ted as Governors Langlie and Sprague, along with military officers in full regalia, line the Clatsop County Courthouse's stage.

Governor Langlie scans the audience. "Since *Books Afloat's* journey began in Washington, I'm privileged to emcee this ceremony. Governor Sprague will host the reception that follows." He inclines his head in the other man's direction.

"Thank God, we're here celebrating a victory rather than mourning another Pearl Harbor. You know this outcome is largely due to Anne Mettles, who birthed and sacrificed a dream to protect our nation." Applause ripples through the house. "I'm pleased to surprise her today with the return of her parents, who I now invite to center stage. Anne, please join us."

My parents? Here? I gasp and rush into their warm hugs as audience applause explodes again. Soon, my parents follow me back to the mysterious *reserved* seats next to Ted and me.

"We also recognize Captain Charlotte Young for her heroism," the governor says once the furor calms.

Char cranes her neck, obviously hoping J.P. might emerge from the wings to sweep her into his arms. She is *not* wearing her Sou'wester, and her hair is nicely curled.

"Although her courageous naval captain husband cannot be here because he's leading rescue operations near Midway, he sends his undying love and is doing all he can to win this war so everyone can return home soon."

"That's my J.P." Her smile glistens through tears.

"But our main purpose today is to read praiseworthy acts into state and national records, honoring the resourceful courage of a young man who, though gravely wounded, thwarted Japanese sabotage and attack. We appreciate our military everywhere but are equally proud of our valiant heroes serving here at home. Theodore James Vincent, rise and come forward."

Next to me, still favoring his left shoulder, Ted stands. "Pray I don't trip," he breathes.

My heart swells as he reaches the platform without incident.

Governor Langlie slips an arm around him. "Ladies and gentlemen, join me in honoring this incredibly courageous young man."

I stand with the audience amid ear-splitting applause and popping flashbulbs until the governor asks us to take our seats. Governor Langlie is not using notes as he addresses Ted while sweeping vigilant eyes over the crowd to connect with listeners.

Ted's dad and brother sit near the end of the front row, sandwiched between Smitty and Johnny. Behind them, Char, Evie, Jeb, Janey, the Reynolds, and many river folks are crowded in. My heart fills. Though it's only been a short time since this journey began, I can hardly remember not knowing these precious people.

The Governor commands the room. "I couldn't be prouder

of Ted Vincent than if he were my own son." He leans forward and singles out Ted's dad. "Mr. Vincent, congratulations on raising a fine young man."

Ted's dad's face transforms. His mouth works, but no words come. Next to him, his younger son operates a camera.

"Therefore, in this Clatsop County Courthouse on today's date, by the power invested in me by our United States Congress, I award our nation's highest civilian honor, the Congressional Gold Medal. Although our global contest continues, we are sure of final victory when young men of this caliber risk their lives for our nation. Theodore James Vincent, we gratefully honor you."

I choke with pride as Ted bends enough for the governor to slip the wide blue ribbon over his head and around his neck. The gold medallion flashes golden beams.

"Ladies and gentlemen, few civilians have received this award. By its conferral, our grateful nation acknowledges bravery and heroism far beyond the call of duty. Please rise and thank its newest recipient, our own Pacific Northwest native son, Theodore James Vincent."

I shoot out of my seat with those around me to cheer, whistle, and stamp our feet.

The Governor waits until the throng calms. "Ted, we invite you to say a few words."

God, help Ted say what's in his heart. Ted waits for us to be seated. As he surveys the crowd, his eyes find mine.

"First of all, thank you, Governor Langlie, for this great honor. I thank God for sparing our lives and helping us strike a strong blow against Japan." He turns to his father. "Thank you, Dad, for your lifelong example as I've grown to manhood."

His dad's shoulders heave. He makes a curious noise between a sniff and snort and elbows Ted's brother to sit up straighter.

Ted faces our row and snaps off a smart salute. "Captains

Horatio Hornblower Young, Charlotte Young, and John Frederick Hofer, thank you for your friendship and support, which also far exceeds the call to duty."

Smitty and Johnny beam. Char turns the color of fresh beets.

When Ted's eyes return to mine, love lights his face. I return his gaze without shame.

"I especially honor Anne Elizabeth Mettles for her courage and determination in the face of terrible odds. In one thousand ways, this medal should truly be hers."

I shake my head, signaling him to stop, but he doesn't.

"As we took the Governor's Challenge to fulfill our mission and defeat the enemy, Anne and I became more than friends. I hoped Congress would award this medal to her, but since they conferred it upon me, I can remedy the situation. On *Books Afloat*, when neither of us knew if we would live or die, Anne and I had serious talks. Backstage tonight, I had a chance to ask her father an important question."

I turn to my father and then my mother. They stare straight ahead, their faces revealing nothing.

"I am delighted to have their blessing in this matter nearest my heart. Governor, may I have Anne come to the stage?"

"Of course. Anne, please come."

The Governor takes my elbow as I climb the steps and guides me to Ted.

Ted takes my right hand. "Anne, I appreciate the gratitude our nation has conferred for actions you also shared. But there is one additional supremely important question I must ask."

He drops to one knee, and my heart stops.

"I have your parents' blessing to share this medal in the way that makes me the most-blessed man on earth. Anne Elisabeth Mettles, will you please do me the honor of marrying me?"

There is no sound as a thousand people hold their breath.

And then, with tears and trembling, I hear myself say, "Ted Vincent, nothing on earth would please me more."

Ted stands and sweeps me into his arms. He needs no coaching for what follows. He gives a lingering kiss that makes the audience hold its breath again. My heart is singing its way to the stars. If Ted beams any brighter, I'll need sunglasses.

"Thank you, Anne. And Governor Langlie. I am the happiest man in America."

Governor Langlie clears his throat and rests a hand on our shoulders. "Ladies and gentlemen, we don't have a date set yet, but it is my hope that we may be looking forward to a joint-state wedding celebration."

I want time to consider that.

The governor continues, "It thrills me that our nation is in the hands of such young people. With that kind of leadership, we'll win this war and see the United States reach undreamed of greatness."

Roars of approval fill the place.

"There is one further development Governor Sprague and I wish to announce. After the effort these young people displayed while answering the Governor's Challenge, they convinced us we need a floating library on the river. What do you think?"

"Yes!"

"Wonderful"

Shouts ring out on all sides and grow in volume. It seems every hand rises and waves.

"Governor Sprague and I think so, too. There's also been quite a wonderful response from grateful citizens."

The audience roars again.

"Funds have poured in from all sides despite hard times. Both states have found ways to match individual donations." He gazes at us with a heartwarming smile. "If Anne and Ted are willing, we'd like to put a *Books Afloat II* on the Columbia with enough books to reach even more people on the river."

I can't help it. I cry unashamedly as Ted holds me close. His eyes shine with moisture, too, as Smitty, Johnny, Char, and all of our friends and family in the front rows go crazy with joy.

It takes a while for the audience to settle down.

Governor Langlie beams. "We'll soon transition from this wonderful ceremony to the reception Governor Sprague will host."

He catches Oregon's Governor's eye, then stands and points to the double doors leading to the reception. "Thank you, Governor Sprague. We invite you all to stay and celebrate with us." He turns and looks in the wings, looking reassured when he finds the person he's looking for.

"In closing, I've asked Ted and Anne's good friend, pastor Bob Vengeance, to lead this assembly in prayer. Although his and his wife, Sue's, Navy seaman son, Josh, is still missing in action near Midway, they're people who know that God brings victory and holds all things in His capable hands."

Hair neatly combed and face shining above a blue serge suit with his shirt collar and necktie a bit tight around his neck, Bob strides to center stage with the confidence of a man knowing that life's happiness and successes lie in God. He stands behind Ted and me, pulling us close.

"Ted and Anne, congratulations. Ted has delighted me by asking me to perform your wedding when a date is set."

Ted wears a goofy grin. "It won't be long, Pastor."

I give Ted a squeeze, my heart bursting with joy.

"So, by the power invested in me as a minister of the Gospel, I end this gathering with the wonderful priestly benediction prayer. 'The LORD bless thee and keep thee: The LORD make his face shine upon thee and be gracious unto thee: The LORD lift up his countenance upon thee and give thee and our great nation peace.' God bless us all."

He pulls us close again as Ted and I say in unison, "And God bless America."

ABOUT DELORES TOPLIFF

From Washington State, Delores married a Canadian, so enjoys U.S. and Canadian citizenships. She teaches online for the University of Northwestern-St. Paul, Minnesota, near her two doctor sons and families. She brags on five amazing grandchildren and is something she didn't think she'd be—a snowbird, dividing her year between Minnesota and Northeastern Mississippi.

She started composing rhyming stories in the third grade. Her classmates' approval encouraged her writing. Two of her award-winning children's books are rhymed adventures.

Delores has visited Israel eight times and has written a

travelogue for people wishing to arrange their own trips there. She is also writing a contemporary novel based in Israel.

Books Afloat is based on true WWII events, when a Japanese submarine did enter the Columbia River. Watch for *Strong Currents*, Book 2 of the Columbia River Undercurrents series, scheduled to release in January 2022.

Her time-slip novel, *Wilderness Wife*, available in September 2021, addresses, "Can a centuries old love story that changed North American history cross the years to inspire others that true love is worth fighting for?" It contrasts Marguerite McLoughlin, an abandoned native real-life frontier Canada heroine who preserves her family in ways that inspire a 21st Century young woman.

Travel is Delores's favorite means of learning, including visiting the many exchange students who have lived in her home through the years and became family. She is a seasoned world traveler taking mission trips to Mexico, South America, Europe, and Asia. In non-COVID-19 times, she guides small groups to Israel and is finalizing her travel guide with tips for safe, economical, fun journeys there for all ages—even grandmas.

Besides writing, her hobbies include photography, archaeology, and jewelry making, even using porcupine quills gently gleaned from living animals. She loves connecting with readers and speaking to book clubs and writing groups.

Find her blogs and more including her many stories in inspirational compilation books on delorestopliff.com. Like and follow her on Facebook at Delores Topliff Books.

MORE HISTORICAL ROMANCE FROM SCRIVENINGS PRESS

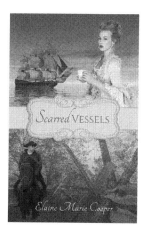

Scarred Vessels

by Elaine Marie Cooper

In a time when America battles for freedom, a man and
woman seek to fight the injustice of slavery while
discovering love in the midst of tragedy.

In 1778 Rhode Island, the American Revolution rallies the Patriots to
fight for freedom. But the slavery of black men and women from
Africa, bartered for rum, is a travesty that many in America cannot
ignore. The seeds of abolition are planted even as the laws allowing
slavery in the north still exist.

Lydia Saunders, the daughter of a slave ship owner, grew up with the
horror of slavery. It became more of a nightmare when, at a young age,
she is confronted with the truth about her father's occupation.
Burdened with the guilt of her family's sin, she struggles to make a
difference in whatever way she can. When she loses her husband in the

battle for freedom from England, she makes a difficult decision that will change her life forever.

Sergeant Micah Hughes is too dedicated to serving the fledgling country of America to consider falling in love. When he carries the tragic news to Lydia Saunders about her husband's death, he is appalled by his attraction to the young widow. Micah wrestles with his feelings for Lydia while he tries to focus on helping the cause of freedom. He trains a group of former slaves to become capable soldiers on the battlefield.

Tensions both on the battlefield and on the home front bring hardship and turmoil that threaten to endanger them all. When Lydia and Micah are faced with saving the life of a black infant in danger, can they survive this turning point in their lives?

A groundbreaking book, honest and inspiring, showcasing black soldiers in the American Revolution. *Scarred Vessels* is peopled with flesh and blood characters and true events that not only inspire and entertain but educate. Well done!

~ Laura Frantz, Christy Award-winning author

of *An Uncommon Woman*

Under This Same Sky

by Cynthia Roemer

She thought she'd lost everything ~

Instead she found what she needed most.

Illinois prairie - 1854

When a deadly tornado destroys Becky Hollister's farm, she must leave the only home she's ever known, and the man she's begun to love to accompany her injured father to St. Louis. Catapulted into a world of unknowns, Becky finds solace in corresponding with the handsome pastor back home. But when word comes that he is all but engaged to someone else, she must call upon her faith to decipher her future.

Matthew Brody didn't intend on falling for Becky, but the unexpected relationship, along with the Lord's gentle nudging, incite him to give up his circuit riding and seek full-time ministry in the town of Miller Creek, with the hope of one day making Becky his bride. But when his old sweetheart comes to town, intent on winning him back—with the entire town pulling for her—Matthew must choose between doing what's expected and what his heart tells him is right.

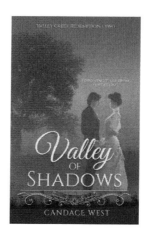

Valley of Shadows

by Candace West

Valley Creek Redemption Book Two

A shattered heart.

A wounded spirit.

A community in crisis.

Lorena Steen gave up on love years ago. She forgave her long-time estranged husband, but when circumstances bring her to the Ozark town of Valley Creek, she discovers forgiving is far from forgetting.

Haunted by his past acts of betrayal, Earl Steen struggles to grow his reclaimed faith and reinstate himself as an upstanding member of Valley Creek. He soon learns that while God's grace is amazing, that of the small-town gossips is not.

When disaster strikes, the only logical solution is for Earl and Lorena to combine their musical talents in an effort to save the community. But even if they're willing to work together, are they able to? Or will the shadows that descend upon Valley Creek reduce it to a ghost town?

Safe Refuge

Newport of the West—Book One

by Pamela S. Meyers

In two days, wealthy Chicagoan, Anna Hartwell, will wed a man she loathes. She would refuse this arranged marriage to Lyman Millard, but the Bible clearly says she is to honor her parents, and Anna would do most anything to please her father–even leaving her teaching job at a mission school and marrying a man she doesn't love.

The Great Chicago Fire erupts, and Anna and her family escape with only the clothes on their backs and the wedding postponed. Father moves the family to Lake Geneva, Wisconsin, where Anna reconnects with Rory Quinn, a handsome immigrant who worked at the mission school. Realizing she is in love with Rory, Anna prepares to break the marriage arrangement with Lyman until she learns a dark family secret that changes her life forever.

Scrivenings
PRESS
Quench your thirst for story.
www.ScriveningsPress.com

Stay up-to-date on your favorite books and authors with our free e-newsletters.

ScriveningsPress.com

Made in the USA
Monee, IL
29 June 2024

60542443R00205